Through her marriage to Reggie Kray, Roberta Kray has a unique and authentic insight into London's East End. Roberta met Reggie in early 1996 and they married the following year; they were together until Reggie's death in 2000. Roberta is the author of many previous bestsellers including *No Mercy*, *Dangerous Promises*, *Exposed* and *Survivor*.

ROBERTA KRAY

DECEIVED

sphere

SPHERE

First published in Great Britain in 2018 by Sphere

1 3 5 7 9 10 8 6 4 2

A CIP catalogue record for this book
is available from the British Library.

ISBN 978-0-7515-6963-6

Typeset in Garamond by M Rules
Printed and bound in Great Britain by
Clays Ltd, Elcograf S.p.A.

Papers used by Sphere are from well-managed forests
and other responsible sources.

MIX
Paper from
responsible sources
FSC® C104740
www.fsc.org

Sphere
An imprint of
Little, Brown Book Group
Carmelite House
50 Victoria Embankment
London EC4Y 0DZ

An Hachette UK Company
www.hachette.co.uk

www.littlebrown.co.uk

Prologue

1937

She lifted the long mink coat from the bag on the floor and held it up in front of her before slipping it around her shoulders. As she stared at her reflection in the mirror, she imagined she looked like one of those rich Mayfair ladies, the sort who took afternoon tea at the Ritz and treated the waiters with polite disdain. She turned to the left and the right, viewing the effect. Yes, if she kept her mouth shut, she could easily pass for a woman of substance.

She stroked the soft mink, wishing she could keep it, but fancy furs didn't pay the bills or put food on the table. Anyway, the coats were too hot to hold onto. As soon as Hull found out they were missing, he'd do his nut. To thieve off a thief was a risky business at the best of times, but when that thief was Lennie Hull, you were just asking for trouble. Ivor didn't care – said the cheating bastard owed him – but that wouldn't count for much when his legs were being broken.

She flinched at the thought of it.

Still, they'd be away soon, out of here and out of London. She glanced down towards the five bags full of ermine, sable and mink. They'd bring in a pretty penny once they found the right buyer. Her gaze lifted to the clock on the mantelpiece. Half an hour, Ivor had said, and it was way past that. How long did it take to buy petrol?

'Come on, come on,' she muttered.

Nerves were starting to get the better of her. She lifted a hand to her mouth and chewed on her nails. The seconds ticked by slowly. The sky was darkening, the low clouds full of rain. That song, 'Stormy Weather', crept into her head. 'Don't know why there's no sun up in the sky . . .' she crooned. She lit a cigarette and paced from one side of the room to the other. Had something gone wrong? No, she just had the jitters.

It would be fine once Ivor got back. She had never known a man like him before: smart and witty and fearless. Just the thought of him took her breath away. She'd grown up surrounded by villains, most of them with big ideas and cotton wool between their ears, but he was a world apart. He had a talent, a skill that none of them possessed. There wasn't a lock he couldn't open in England – maybe the whole world – or a safe either. All of which meant he'd never be out of work. It was the kind of work, however, that came with risks. The East End was full of copper's snouts, lowlifes who'd grass you up for the price of a pint. And who wanted to spend years in the slammer with nothing to look forward to but more of the same? It was a mug's game and he knew it.

Ivor had no respect for the law, for authority, but he wasn't a fool. 'The system always wins out in the end,' he said. If it wasn't a bent copper planting evidence, it was some loose-mouthed idiot bragging about a job in the boozer. He was forever looking over his shoulder, forever waiting for the knock on the door. And even though he'd grown up in Kellston, he didn't really fit in. He wasn't one of the boys. He was different, and people round here didn't like different.

'It's time to make a move, love,' he'd said. 'Time for pastures new.' And she hadn't disagreed with him. She'd be glad to see the back of this place, although she'd miss her friends. Still, it would be an adventure. And who cared where they lived so long as they were together? The cash from the furs would give them a fresh start, a chance to get established.

She stubbed out her ciggie and went back to the window. She wondered what it would be like up north. She had never been further than Epping in her life.

Her gaze strayed to the clock again – ten to ten. They'd intended to leave at the crack of dawn, but that plan had gone for a Burton when Ivor had climbed into the Humber and discovered some tea leaf had emptied the petrol tank in the middle of the night. With the local garage closed until nine, they'd had no choice but to sit it out until opening time. Of course he could have gone and done some siphoning of his own, but that was always risky. Getting nicked was the last thing he needed.

She peered out of the window again. Where was he? It was then that she saw the motor, a dark saloon, turn the corner and start crawling down the road as though the driver was counting off the numbers on the houses. Her whole body froze. For a moment she stood rooted to the spot. She knew who it was and why they were coming. The name rose to her lips and hung there in an agony of disbelief.

Lennie Hull.

How had he found out? The furs weren't due to be moved from the warehouse until tomorrow. And how had he guessed that Ivor had nicked them? But none of that was important now. Jesus, they were for it! She had to scarper, and fast. They'd be here in a minute, and one flimsy front door wasn't going to hold them for long.

Finally the adrenalin kicked in. Shrugging off the mink, she legged it to the kitchen, pulled back the bolts and threw open the door. She rushed through the back yard and along the narrow weed-filled alley that ran behind the terrace. Should she duck into one of the neighbours' yards and hide in the lavvy? No, it was too risky. Hull and his goons would search every square inch until they found her.

She ploughed on until the alley eventually turned and rejoined the road further up. Here she stopped, knowing that the moment she stepped out they would be able to see her. She could wait until they forced their way into the house, but what if they decided to come round the back instead? She'd either have to make a run for it or double back, and if she did the latter, she'd be trapped with nowhere to go. No, her only option was to walk out as if nothing was wrong, to act as though she was just an innocent woman on her way somewhere. She took a deep breath. *Hold your nerve, girl.*

She saw the motor out of the corner of her eye as she turned left, but didn't stare. It was parked in front of the house, the occupants in the process of getting out. Four of them, maybe five: big fellers, suited and booted. They were about twenty yards away, far enough perhaps for them not to recognise her. She set off in the opposite direction, spine straight, head up, heels click-clacking on the pavement. Not too fast, not too slow. *Don't look back.*

She might have got away with it if she'd taken her own advice. Past the first lamp post, and then the second, trying to stay calm even though her head was exploding, but she just couldn't resist that quick glance over her shoulder. Big mistake. Hull and the others were at the front door, giving it a hammer, but the driver was leaning against the saloon with his arms folded across his chest and his gaze focused right on her.

Blind panic engulfed her as their eyes met. She made a split-second decision, and it was a bad one. Reason went out of the window. Before her instincts could engage with her brain, she took off. Almost immediately she stumbled and knew she'd have to ditch the heels. Quickly she kicked off her shoes and started to run again.

From behind she heard a shout: 'Oi!' And then the sound of the saloon doors banging shut.

She was dead. She knew it. She ran as fast as her legs would carry her, her stockinged feet slapping against the cold pavement. But it wasn't fast enough. She could hear the motor getting closer. Her face was twisted, wet with tears, as she hurtled forward, intent on only one thing – if she could just reach the cemetery, she might be able to give them the slip, to hunker down and hide among the tombstones.

She had to get off the main road before they caught up with her. Out here she was a sitting duck. Which way now? She knew Kellston like the back of her hand, but her mental map was being ripped apart by fear. There was a network of alleyways criss-crossing the district, but if she chose the wrong one, she could finish up in a dead end, trapped like an animal. Was it the next right? She thought it was. She prayed it was. Anyway, she had no choice. She dived across the road and sprinted into the gloom.

She heard the squeal of brakes as the motor pulled up. This time she didn't look back, and kept on running. Her heart was pounding, the breath bursting from her lungs. The alley twisted and turned, the high brick walls looming over her. On the ground there was hard soil and sharp stones that dug into the soles of her feet, but she didn't slow down. On and on until she finally found what she was looking for.

The gate was ancient and rusty, hanging off a single hinge. She pushed it just far enough for her to squeeze through, and then launched herself into the undergrowth. There had been a path here once but now it was overgrown, a mass of brambles and stinging nettles. As she stumbled through them, thrashing her arms, she could hear the heavy thud of footsteps back in the alley.

She was exhausted, but terror spurred her on. Here, in the older part of the cemetery, she should be able to find somewhere to hide. Eventually she emerged into clearer territory, full of long grass and weeds but easier to negotiate. She flew past weathered graves, granite towers and grey stone angels until she reached a dark place overhung by trees. A row of mausoleums, like an avenue of small abandoned houses, lay ahead. She got as far as the fifth before her legs gave way and she slumped to the ground.

Even as her backside hit the earth, she heard the male voices travelling through the air. Sick panic rose into her throat. Crawling on her hands and knees, she dragged herself round to the back of the tomb, curled up and tried to make her body as small as possible. It was then that the pain made contact with her brain. Her stockings were torn and her legs, arms and feet were covered in scratches and bright red welts from where she'd been stung.

She whimpered and quickly clamped her hand across her mouth. If they heard her, she was done for. She held her panting breath, pressed her cheek against the cool brick and listened. Now the voices were coming from different directions as the men spread out searching for her. How many? Two, three? She reckoned Hull and at least one of the others would have stayed behind to retrieve the furs – and wait for Ivor.

Ivor, Ivor. She repeated his name in her head like a mantra. When he got home, he'd be walking straight into an ambush. There wouldn't even be the saloon parked outside as a warning. Perhaps they'd grabbed him already. She shivered, and her heart thudded in her chest. Hull would make an example of Ivor, of them both.

She closed her eyes and prayed. *Please God, keep him safe. Please God, don't let them find me.*

It was starting to rain. The water pattered against the leaves and made a pocking sound as it dripped off the roof of the tomb. She stayed tightly curled, rigid with fear. Her teeth began to chatter. She clamped her jaw shut, scared the noise would betray her. Footsteps drew nearer. She heard the boots, heavy on the earth, and the sound of snapping twigs. The smell of cigarette smoke floated in the air.

This is it, she thought. This is the end.

The steps advanced, closer and closer, until her pursuer was only a few yards away. And then he stopped. There was a long silence as though he was trying to decide what to do next. Or maybe he was just listening. She held her breath. All that separated them was the square brick tomb. If he decided to check round the back, it would all be over.

She pressed herself closer to the wall, wishing she could pass right through it into the darkness on the other side. The dead felt no fear, no horror. All she wanted was to be safe again. Time passed as slowly as it had in the house. Then there had been anticipation; now there was only dread.

The man remained where he was for what felt like an eternity. Then, like a miracle, he began to walk away. She heard his steps receding, growing fainter, but she stayed completely still. Maybe he was just toying with her, playing a game. Maybe it was a trap so she would show herself. She wasn't going to fall for that one. No mistakes. No sudden stupid movements. Patience.

And so she waited . . . and waited. The cold and damp crept into her bones. She thought about which exit to head for. There were three in all, including the old gate she had used. Best to stay clear of that. So, one of the others. But where could she go from there? Not back to the house, that was for sure; there'd be a welcome committee installed in the living room.

With no money, and no shoes on her feet, she needed somewhere close by and someone she could trust. Her friend Amy

7

was her best bet. She had a flat on the high street, above the baker's. Yes, that was the place to go. Which meant she had to circle round the cemetery to the main entrance, but not until she was certain the coast was clear.

Carefully she stretched out one leg, and then the other. How long had she been here? Over an hour, she thought. Her joints were stiff and aching. She concentrated hard, listening for any unwanted sounds. There were none. No voices. No footsteps. Surely they must have given up by now.

If it had been warmer and dryer, she would have stayed where she was for even longer. But the cold was starting to get to her. She was shivering and soaked through. Much more of this and she'd end up with pneumonia. She hauled herself upright and tiptoed round the side of the tomb to peek along the narrow path. Empty. But she couldn't see far. Someone could be hiding in the trees.

She had to make a move at some point, but fear made her legs leaden. Her intention was to sneak through the darker parts of the cemetery, keeping off the main thoroughfares, until she reached the perimeter wall. From there she could edge round to the main gate. She thought this over. All things considered, it wasn't much of a plan, but it was all she'd got.

Her heart was in her mouth as she set off. Her feet, cut and sore, made every step a painful one. She tried to stay in the shelter of the trees and bushes, keeping her eyes peeled for Hull's men. Her ears strained to hear the slightest sound. She moved slowly, taking care where she trod. She sniffed the air, paused and went on. As she passed between the old graves, her gaze skimmed over the names of the dead, the young and the old, the husbands and wives, the mums and dads.

Ivor was in her thoughts. There was still a chance he'd got away. Maybe he'd realised something was wrong as he approached the house. All she could do was hope. He'd have to make himself scarce, lie low until the heat was off. But he'd come back for her. She was sure of it.

The wall was within spitting distance when it happened. She heard the tiniest of noises behind her, no more than a shifting in the air. As she whirled around, her worst nightmare became reality. A man was rising up from behind a pink granite tombstone, his face scarred and brutish, his mouth stretched into a devil's grin. He had a shooter in his hand and it was pointed straight at her.

'You took yer time, doll. I was starting to think you were never coming. Been freezing my bollocks off here.'

She backed away from him, but only as far as the wall. A thin whimpering sound escaped from her lips. It was too late for regrets, but they still tumbled through her head: if only she'd stayed where she was, if only that petrol hadn't been nicked, if only Ivor had stayed well away from those bloody furs . . .

'What's the matter, darlin'?' he mocked. 'Cat got your tongue?'

With nothing left to lose, she raised her chin and stared him defiantly in the eyes. 'Go on, then. If you're going to shoot me, you may as well get it over and done with.'

'I ain't gonna shoot you,' he said. 'Not here, at least. Wouldn't want to disturb these poor souls, now would we?' He glanced round at the graves and sniggered at his own joke. 'Nah, you and me are going to take a little walk, all nice and calm like. You'll go first and I'll be right behind.' He gestured with the gun. 'Get going, then. Towards the gate. And don't do anything stupid. We pass anyone, you keep yer gob shut, right?'

She nodded.

'So what are you waiting for?'

She walked slowly, unsteadily, her legs like jelly. Her guts were churning, bile rising into her throat. 'Where are we going?'

'Where do you think?'

'To see Hull,' she said, her voice quivering with fear.

'*Mr* Hull to you, darlin'. And he ain't best pleased with you and your feller. I can tell you that for nothing.'

She could have pleaded with him to let her go, begged and grovelled, but she knew it was pointless. She plodded on, one painful step after another. If she'd had the strength, she would have made a run for it – a bullet in the back was better than the long, lingering punishment Hull would have in store for her. She bowed her head but didn't bother to pray. She was beyond hope or faith. God had abandoned her. She was on her own.

1

1949

Judith Jonson had officially been a widow for five years. 'Missing in action' was what the telegram had said, but she hadn't immediately given up hope. Missing wasn't dead. Missing wasn't a body blown into a thousand pieces or a man lying on his back with a bullet through his heart. A chance still remained that Dan had been taken prisoner or become separated from his regiment. A chance still remained that he was out there somewhere.

She had clung onto this dream for too long, refusing to accept – even when the war was over – that her husband was never coming home. It had been too stark a fact to face, too devastating a blow. Although her head had told her one thing, her heart had said another. Deep down she'd continued to believe he was still alive; she had felt it in her bones, in her soul. To accept that he was dead was to give up on him, to give up on *them*.

Judith was still coming to terms with her loss, trying to deal with the sharp edges of a grief she should have confronted long ago. Sometimes it took her unawares, creeping up when she was at work, on the bus, or simply washing the dishes. The emotions she felt were strong, even violent. They tore through her, rocking her body and taking her breath away. She would have to close her eyes for a few seconds until the worst of the pain was over.

Dan was gone. She had to get used to the idea. Her grief was hardly unique; there was barely a person she knew who hadn't lost someone close – a husband or boyfriend, a brother, father, son or uncle. They all carried the same burden, the same aching sense of loss. But life went on, and somehow a way had to be found to deal with it.

Judith's way was to keep busy. During the day she worked for a firm of solicitors called Gillespie & Tate – typing, filing and answering the phone – and at night she filled the hours before bed with anything that kept her occupied. She sewed, read, wrote letters or tended her vegetable patch at the local allotment. What she dreaded most were the weekends. Free time was her enemy, providing the kind of space bad thoughts could creep into.

This Saturday, however, wouldn't be a problem. As the bus travelled through the town of Westport, she gazed out of the window at the rows of shops – all closed for the evening now – and wondered what she could wear for Charlotte's wedding. Clothes rationing was over, but she wasn't sure about buying something new. Money was tight and she had to be careful. Although she had savings in the bank, she was reluctant to dip into them; most of the money had been deposited by Dan, cash put aside to start his own business, and it didn't feel right using it. What if he came back and . . . Judith's hands curled into two tight fists. She knew she had to stop thinking like that. There wasn't going to be a miracle, not after all these years.

Don't think about Dan.

She glanced at the clock on the town hall – a quarter to six – and wondered if Charlotte was happy. George Rigby was a small, rotund, rather pompous man, a civil servant who had a tendency to lecture. On the plus side, he had his own hair and teeth, and a nice semi-detached house overlooking the park. Judith smiled. As it happened, she didn't suspect Charlotte of anything more cynical than 'settling', a current trend among her single friends as they approached the age of thirty.

She understood why they were doing it. Time was running out if they wanted children, a family, a more respected position in society. She would have done the same, perhaps, if she'd had irrefutable proof of Dan's death: settled for someone who was kind and decent, even if they were a little dull. It wasn't easy being alone. She frowned and gave a tiny shake of her head. No, it might not be easy, but it would be even harder to live with a man she didn't love.

The bus was gradually emptying, and she noticed that a copy of the *Daily Mirror* had been left behind on one of the seats. Judith leaned across the aisle and retrieved it. Something to distract her for the rest of the journey. The paper was full of news about John Haigh, who'd been hanged for murder at Wandsworth prison yesterday. She wondered what it was that had turned him into a monster. He had killed six people, maybe more, and then disposed of their bodies in acid. All for money. She shuddered at the horror of it.

Quickly she flicked through the pages, looking for something less gruesome to read. While her eyes scanned the print, her thoughts turned again to Charlotte's wedding. It would be a simple affair, a short service at the register office followed by a reception at the Astor Hotel.

George was a widower and didn't want too much fuss. It didn't seem to matter what Charlotte wanted.

Judith hoped she wouldn't be seated beside a possible 'prospect' at the hotel. Having secured her own future, Charlotte was forever trying to fix up her unattached friends with suitable partners. She pulled a face. Invariably these men bored her to tears, making her jaw ache from trying not to yawn. There had to be a spark, didn't there, something to make the pulse race and the heart flip? Or maybe that was hopelessly romantic. Maybe that kind of love only showed up once in a lifetime.

Don't think about Dan.

But it was too late. Eleven years had slipped away and she was sitting at her desk in the reception area of Gillespie & Tate. The front door opened. She looked up from her typewriter to see a tall man in his mid twenties, over six feet, with a narrow, angular face and hair so blond it was almost white.

'Good morning. How can I help?'

'I'm looking for a good solicitor.'

'Then you've come to the right place. Mr Gillespie or Mr Tate?'

He shrugged. 'Who would you recommend?'

'They're both excellent.'

A slow smile crept onto his lips. 'I'm sure they are, but which one would *you* prefer to do business with?'

Although she was only eighteen, Judith knew better than to be drawn into publicly favouring one of her bosses over the other. 'Let me check the appointment book and see when we can fit you in.'

'Dan Jonson. That's Jonson without an h. Tomorrow morning would be good.'

'Ten thirty with Mr Gillespie?'

'Ten thirty sounds fine.' He nodded, thanked her, turned to go and then turned back.

'Tell me, er . . . sorry, I don't know your name.'

'Judith.'

'Tell me, Judith, what's this town like?'

'Like?'

'Is it a good place to live?'

'I suppose so.'

He rocked back on his heels a little, inclined his head and

frowned. 'If you don't mind me saying, that's not the best recommendation I've ever heard.'

Judith gazed up at him, studying his face more closely. His eyes were grey, the colour of flint, but not hard. His voice – she thought the accent was southern – betrayed more than a hint of amusement. Was he laughing at her? A flush rose into her cheeks. 'I've never lived anywhere else, so I've nothing to compare it to.'

'All right, let me put it another way. Why do *you* stay in Westport?'

Now it was Judith's turn to frown. No one had ever asked her this question before. 'Why wouldn't I? I've got friends here, and a job.'

'And family?'

She shook her head. Her parents had passed when she was young, and the aunt who had raised her had died of cancer a couple of years ago. 'No, no family.'

'Me neither. Not always easy, is it?' Before she had a chance to reply, he walked over to the window, nudged aside the net curtain and gazed out along Earl Street. 'Seems like a busy town.'

'In the summer,' she said. 'That's when the visitors come. It's quieter in winter.'

'London's always busy.'

'Is that where you're from?'

'For my sins.' He was quiet for a moment and then said, 'You can get tired of a place. It can wear you down.' He glanced over his shoulder and smiled. 'Or maybe a place can get tired of you. Who knows?'

'I've never been to London. What's it like?'

He put his hands in his pockets and shrugged again. 'Like anywhere else, only bigger: crowded, noisy, full of people trying to keep their heads above water. It's good and it's bad if you know what I mean.'

Judith wasn't sure she did, but she nodded anyway. Normally

her conversations with clients didn't extend much beyond the weather. They were simple, uncomplicated exchanges where nothing more was expected of her than a general agreement as to the dampness of the air or the bitterness of the wind. 'So what brings you to Westport?'

A shadow flickered across his face. 'Nothing in particular. I just fancied a change, somewhere different.'

'A fresh start,' she said, wondering if he was running away from something – or someone. A love affair, perhaps, that had gone wrong. Not that she knew much about love. Her experience was limited to a schoolgirl crush on the curate, a few slow dances at Trinity Hall and four dates with David Beckles, after which she'd been unceremoniously dumped. The latter still rankled, not because she'd been especially keen – no one could be as fond of that boy as himself – but because she'd wasted precious time on him.

'Yes, a fresh start. That's exactly what I'm looking for.' He moved away from the window and came to stand beside her desk. 'But what I really need is someone to show me round. How about it? At the weekend, perhaps, if you're not too busy. What do you say?'

Judith was taken by surprise at the request. Or was it a proposition? She hesitated, unsure of his motives. A part of her wanted to say yes – she was interested in this man, intrigued by him – but she didn't want to come across as the type of girl who could be picked up at the drop of a hat.

'Don't make your mind up now,' he continued, seeing her hesitation. 'Have a think and let me know tomorrow. I'd be grateful, though, for the tour and the company.'

Judith watched him leave, her heart beating a little faster than usual. She was attracted to him, although she wasn't entirely sure why. He was older than her, and more striking than handsome with his height and that shock of pale fair hair. But there was something about Dan Jonson that piqued her interest. *For my sins*, he had said. She shouldn't make too much of it. It was just a turn of phrase, words people used, and yet she sensed a deeper meaning. There was an air of mystery about him, something she couldn't quite put her finger on. It disturbed and excited her at the same time.

That evening, she decided to take him up on the invitation. Where was the harm? It would be broad daylight and they'd be in a public place. Nothing bad could happen. She worried he would find the town dull after the bright lights of London and started to plan an itinerary – the promenade, pier, lido, botanic gardens – wondering what might appeal to him most. How could she even begin to guess? She knew barely anything about him.

Judith dressed with extra care the following morning, choosing one of her better dresses and taking time to curl her shoulder-length red hair with the curling irons. She applied a small amount of make-up, some rouge and a lick of lipstick, and thought the effect was relatively pleasing. She went to work with a spring in her step and settled at her desk with a heady sense of anticipation. Dan Jonson would arrive at ten thirty, maybe even a bit before, and ask if she had made a decision. She would agree to meet him, although not with *too* much enthusiasm. She didn't want to look overly keen.

It was Mr Tate who scuppered her plans. Emerging from his office at ten past ten, he placed a large brown envelope on her desk.

'Could you walk these over to Porter's, please? They need to be signed, so you'll have to wait.'

'What, right now?'

'If it isn't too much trouble,' he said drily.

Judith shook her head. 'No, not at all. I didn't mean . . . I just wondered if I could do it later. There's a client booked in for half past ten. If I go now, there'll be no one on reception.'

'Oh, I'm sure we'll manage.'

With no other choice, Judith picked up the envelope and rose to her feet. She knew, even as she put on her coat, that she probably wasn't going to make it back in time. It was a fifteen-minute walk to Porter's, and there'd also be the waiting around while the papers were read and eventually signed. It would be well after eleven before she got back, and by then Dan Jonson would have been and gone.

As she left the office, she glanced up and down Earl Street, hoping to catch sight of that shock of blond hair, but there was no sign of him. What would he think when he arrived and found her absent? That she was deliberately avoiding him, perhaps. She wished that she'd said yes when he'd first asked instead of hesitating like that. The arrangement could have been in place by now, the weekend something to look forward to.

Judith walked at a brisk pace. There was a chance, albeit a slim one, that Dan Jonson's business might take longer than the allotted half-hour slot. She had no idea what he wanted to see Mr Gillespie about, and wondered what line of work he was in. Something interesting, she guessed, unable to imagine him in a mundane kind of job.

It was a glorious day, the sun shining brightly. She cut down to the promenade and hurried through the summer crowd, dodging left and right, barely glancing at the beach or the rippling sea. Normally she would have stopped for a while, taken a few minutes to drink in the scene, but not today. She was on a mission: the sooner she got there, the sooner she could get back.

She smelled the factory before she saw it, a sickly-sweet aroma floating in the air. Porter's made confectionery: brightly coloured sticks of rock, lollipops, humbugs and sherbet lemons. She veered off the promenade and strode quickly up Conway Road. By the time she reached the door, she was hot and flustered, her cheeks red from rushing, her dress sticking to her back.

The receptionist was a middle-aged woman with a superior expression. She looked Judith up and down, simultaneously pursing her lips as if she didn't approve of what she saw.

'Yes?'

'I've got some papers,' Judith explained, slightly out of breath. 'From Mr Tate for Mr Porter.'

The woman held out her hand. 'You'd better give them to me, then.'

'They need signing.'

'I'll let him know.'

Judith watched the receptionist casually place the envelope on her desk. Sensing a lack of urgency in her manner, she said, 'They're important. I need to take them back with me.'

'Mr Porter's in a meeting.'

'How long is he going to be?'

The woman didn't answer directly. Instead she flapped a hand in the general direction of an old leather sofa. 'You can wait over there.'

Judith gave a frustrated sigh, but with no other choice, she went and sat down. She felt hot and sweaty and frustrated. There was a clock on the wall, the big red second hand racing round its face. It was almost ten thirty. If he was prompt for his appointments, Dan Jonson would be at the office by now. Impatiently she tapped a foot on the carpet. Why had Mr Tate chosen today of all days to send her halfway across town? And why did Mr Porter have to be in a meeting? The fates were conspiring against her.

With nothing else to do, she stared at the walls, at the bright posters: sweets, sweets and more sweets, a swirling mass of candy colours. There was a distant hum of machinery. She could have ended up working here – the factory was one of the

19

major employers in Westport – if her aunt hadn't insisted on her learning to type. Office work was cleaner and better paid, and the hours were shorter too. She liked her job but she missed the camaraderie of other girls, the chatter and the gossip.

It was a quarter to twelve before the papers were eventually signed and returned to her. Judith didn't bother rushing back. It was too late now. She sauntered along the promenade thinking about lost opportunities and what might have been. It was only as she was walking down Earl Street that her spirits lifted again. Maybe he had left a note for her, or would phone later on. Maybe he had made another appointment. Maybe he would drop into the office later today or tomorrow. If he was genuinely interested, he'd find a way.

There was no note when she checked her desk at Gillespie & Tate. He had made no further appointment either. Her other hope – that he would find a way to contact her – remained with her for the afternoon and the following day and the day after that. Gradually it began to fade. By the end of the month, she had almost, if not completely, forgotten about him.

It would be three more years before she saw Dan Jonson again.

2

Judith was so absorbed in the past that she almost missed her stop. The bus was halfway along Trafalgar Road before she realised where she was, gave a start and quickly got up. As she descended onto the pavement, she realised she was still holding the copy of the *Daily Mirror*. Oh well, she would take it home and put it in the bin.

The evening was still warm and she savoured the feel of the fading sun on her arms. The air smelled of dust and salt and cut grass. A few seagulls wheeled overhead before circling back to the beach. She sauntered along the road, glancing into windows as she passed, snatching glimpses of other people's lives. The houses were large Victorian constructions, imposing red-brick buildings with front and back gardens. Once they had been the homes of the wealthy middle classes – some still were – but most had been converted into smaller dwellings.

Number 25, where Judith had lived since getting married, was one of the latter, the three storeys of the house each divided into two flats. She paused at the gate and looked up at the first floor, a tiny hopeful part of her still expecting to see Dan at the window. But of course he wasn't there. She walked up the path and unlocked the front door.

After checking through the pile of mail in the shared hallway – nothing for her – she headed up the stairs. The green carpet was worn down the middle, almost threadbare, and the banister was shiny from use. Inside the flat, she took off her coat, hung it up on a peg and went through to the living room, where she placed her handbag and the newspaper on the table and opened the window to let in some air.

For a while, she stood gazing down on the street, watching other people wend their way home from work. It had been on an evening like this, the sun still shining, that she'd bumped into Dan again. Except, of course, that it hadn't been exactly like this. Certainly not quiet and peaceful. The country had been at war and the streets full of men in uniform. She would have walked straight past – he was in a crowd, a sea of khaki, outside the Red Lion – if he hadn't called out her name. She'd turned and seen him smiling, moving towards her. What had she felt? Surprise, naturally, but something else too, an emotion she had not quite been able to grasp.

'It's good to see you again. How are you?' His hand touching her elbow as if it had been a few weeks rather than three years. 'Come and have a drink. Will you? Say you will.'

And so she had. And that had been the start, or the second start. They had sat and talked as though they had been friends for ever. No, more than friends. She had felt a connection to him, something deep and intense, a feeling she might have called love if the notion hadn't been so ridiculous. He was a stranger, and yet he wasn't.

She had only got a vague explanation as to why he hadn't followed up on his suggestion of a tour – something about having taken a job in Leeds – and she hadn't pressed him. To have done so might have made her look too eager, too interested. She had brushed it aside as if it was of no consequence. She had learned, however, that he'd been working as a locksmith in Liverpool before the war broke out. And that he had big ambitions. He was going to open his own business when the time was right.

'Security,' he'd said. 'That's what people are going to want after this war is over: safe houses, safe businesses, good-quality protection. I can give them that. You have to think big, Judith. Life's too short to waste.'

She had liked hearing him talk, and she had liked the silences too, the way they could be quiet together without it feeling awkward. They had fallen in love quickly and passionately. Nothing had mattered to her but him; he'd been the centre of her universe, day and night, the axis around which everything else revolved. Dan, having sustained a shoulder injury, had been on leave until he'd recovered enough to return to his regiment. Knowing that time was in short supply, he had acquired a special licence and they married within a month of meeting again. A whirlwind romance, everyone had called it, but she felt like she'd known him all her life. He'd been strong and tender, thoughtful and kind. Even in remembrance, she felt the intimacy of his kisses.

Judith folded her arms across her chest. It was the war, she thought, that had made everyone crazy, heightening their emotions so they lived every day as though it might be their last. But she had no regrets. They might have married in haste, but there had been no repentance.

She moved away from the window, walked into the kitchen and put the kettle on the hob. While the water was boiling, she went to the pantry, retrieved the dish with the remains of last night's rabbit stew, lifted it to her nose, sniffed and shrugged. Not too bad. It was hard to keep food fresh in the warm weather, but she reckoned it was safe enough to eat. With so much rationing still in place, it didn't pay to be fussy.

23

Back in the kitchen, she lit another gas ring and set the stew on to simmer. She made a pot of tea and then peeled some potatoes, putting aside the skins to take down to the allotment. As she looked around for something to wrap them in, she remembered the newspaper she'd picked up and went to get it.

Placing the *Daily Mirror* on the counter, she opened the paper in the middle, dropped the peelings onto it and folded the centre pages round them to make a small, neat parcel. She was about to throw out the rest of the paper when her gaze alighted on a photograph she hadn't noticed on the bus: the aftermath of a dramatic robbery, of a car crashed into the plate-glass door of a jewellery store in the West End of London. A smash and grab. Two policemen were standing at the entrance to the shop, and beyond them a crowd had gathered on the street.

At first her gaze was concentrated on the car, but it gradually widened to include everything else too. It was then that her heart skipped a beat. Standing on the corner, in the centre of the crowd, was a tall, blond man. He had his face partly turned away, but she'd have known him anywhere. Her eyes widened. She gasped. It couldn't be. It *was*.

By now, her pulse had started to race. She snatched up the paper, peered closer and then held it at arm's length, trying to get his features into focus. Her hands were shaking. She felt dizzy and disoriented, as though the earth was spinning beneath her. It wasn't possible, and yet . . . Judith went hot and cold. She stared and stared, wondering if she was going mad, if her eyes were playing tricks on her. But she knew the way he stood, recognised that slight slouch of his shoulders, the lines of his body. And even though his face wasn't clear, she was sure it was *his* face.

'Dan,' she murmured.

Her knees buckled and she staggered sideways, let go of the paper and grabbed the edge of the counter to prevent herself

24

from falling. Time seemed to stop, to become suspended in that single moment. It couldn't be him. He was gone, dead, killed at Anzio. But her eyes, her instincts, her heart told her something different. The man in the crowd was Dan. It *was* him.

She heard her breathing, shallow and fast, like a sound that was coming from someone else. Her mouth was dry. Euphoria exploded in her, splintering her grief, causing hope to ricochet like shrapnel round her body. He was alive. He was in London. He'd been standing on a street corner only a couple of days ago. Which street exactly? She suddenly had to know. Snatching up the paper, she quickly read down the article. New Bond Street. Yes, the name was familiar to her. A posh part, she thought, the kind of place rich people shopped. But there was nothing to stop anyone from walking down it, from pausing to stare at a spectacle. Her eyes flew back to the photograph again.

She willed the background to come into focus, for it to reveal its secrets. She stared and stared until her eyes hurt. She turned her head away and rubbed her face. As she glanced out of the window, she noticed her neighbour, Annie, coming up the drive. Without a second thought, she rushed out of the kitchen, through the living room and out onto the landing.

Annie climbed slowly up the stairs, humming a tune. She was a curvy, dark-haired woman in her late thirties and nearly always cheerful despite the disappointments in her life. She looked up, saw Judith, smiled and then frowned. 'You all right, love? You're white as a sheet. Look like you saw a ghost.'

'That's the thing. I just ... I don't know ... I think ... ' Judith, struggling to find the words she was searching for, shook her head, trying to clear her thoughts. 'I've got to show you something.'

Annie reached the landing, drawing level with her. 'Show me what?'

'It's in the flat.'

'It's not a mouse, is it? I can't stand mice.'

Judith tugged on the sleeve of her jacket. 'No, it's not a mouse.' She quickly pulled her into the flat and through to the kitchen. 'There,' she said, indicating the newspaper lying on the counter. 'The picture! Look at the picture at the top of the page!'

Annie looked at the photograph and laughed. 'Cheeky bastards.'

Judith leaned over her shoulder. 'The crowd on the corner. Do you see?' She waited, but no cries of astonishment escaped from Annie's lips. 'There,' she prompted, pointing a finger. 'Look at him. Look at that man.'

'What about him?'

'It's Dan!'

Annie gave a startled jump. 'What?'

'It is,' Judith said insistently. 'You knew him. Can't you see? The way he's standing? He always did that – leaning a bit to one side. And his height. And his hair. Everything is so ... *him.*'

Annie scrunched up her eyes and peered again at the photo. She waited a moment before saying diplomatically, 'Well, I'm not saying it's not, love, but you can't really see his face properly. It's all a bit blurry, isn't it?'

'I know, but ...'

'How can you be sure?'

'I *am* sure. I'm positive.' But doubt was creeping into Judith's mind. Was she only seeing what she wanted to see? Now that Annie had failed to recognise him, her conviction was starting to fade. 'I mean, he's so like Dan, don't you think? Everything about him. As soon as I saw the picture, I thought ...' Her voice broke and tears sprang to her eyes. 'It *has* to be.'

Annie turned and patted her on the arm. 'What we need is a brew and a sit-down. I've got to get these shoes off; my feet are bleedin' killing me. Yes, a nice cup of tea and then we can work out what you're going to do next.'

26

'You believe me?'

'Why shouldn't I? You were married to him, love. I should think you'd know your own husband when you see him.'

Relief flooded through Judith. She could have hugged Annie. 'There's tea in the pot. I've just made it.'

The two women sat side by side on the sofa, a light, flowery scent wafting in the air. Annie worked at Gillows, a big department store in the centre of town, where she served on the perfume counter and helped herself to as many free samples as possible. Judith watched as she kicked off her high heels, stretched out her legs and wriggled her toes.

'You don't think I'm crazy, then?'

'No more than the rest of us. But just be cautious, right? Don't get your hopes up too much. You can't be sure of anything at the moment. What you need is a clearer photo, or a different one. Whoever took that snap probably took others too. You should ring the *Mirror*, see if you can track down the photographer.'

Judith picked up her cup and put it down again. She glanced over at the clock. 'That's a good idea. Is it too late now, do you think? I could go to the phone box and . . . No, I'll wait until the morning. It probably is too late now.'

'Yes, wait until the morning. You should sleep on it first.'

'Sleep on it?' Judith repeated, wondering if Annie had just been humouring her. 'Why would I need to do that? In case I come to my senses, you mean? God, you do think I'm crazy, don't you?'

'I don't. I swear. All I mean is that it won't do any harm to try and get things straight in your head before you go any further. You've had a shock, a big one. You need some time to take it in. A few hours isn't going to make much difference after five years. And look, it doesn't matter a damn what I think – or anyone else come to that – you've got to do what's right for you. If I thought I saw Joey in a photo, I'd be just the same. You have to follow it up, don't you, or you'll always be wondering what if?'

Judith, whose thoughts were still in a spin, gave a nod. 'Sorry, I didn't mean to snap.' She remembered Joey, a big solid Yank with a broad smile. If he hadn't died on the beaches at Normandy, Annie would have been living in New Hampshire now, a wife and maybe even a mother. The war had taken all that away from her. She was still blowsy and loud and determinedly cheerful, but there was something brittle there too, as though she'd been broken and the pieces carelessly stuck back together.

'Oh, don't worry about that. You know me, love – water off a duck's back.' Annie sipped her tea, glancing at Judith over the rim of the cup. She was quiet for a moment. She opened her mouth as if about to say something more, and then closed it again.

'What?'

'It doesn't matter.'

'I know what you're thinking,' Judith said. 'If it is Dan in the photo, then why is he in London and not here? Why didn't he come home?'

Annie gave a shrug. 'The war did strange things to people. You hear all kinds of stories: men not remembering who they are or where they live. Or just not being able to cope with what they went through. It changed them, love. You have to be prepared for that.'

Despite the warmth of the evening, Judith shivered. 'What if he decided the marriage was a mistake, *I* was a mistake? Maybe that's why he didn't come back.'

'Come off it. He loved the bones of you. Anyone could see that. You two were made for each other.'

That was what Judith had thought too. Now she was starting

to wonder. Maybe there were things she hadn't known about him, hadn't understood. These worries cast a shadow over her earlier joy. Fear stirred in her guts. What if Dan was alive but had chosen to live the rest of his life without her? It was a question she could barely contemplate, so she pushed it away, driving it from her mind.

3

Judith yawned as the bus made its way through town. She had slept fitfully and the remnants of her dreams – all strange, all disturbing – lingered in her head. Twice she had got up in the middle of the night and gone to look at the picture in the paper. She had wanted to see it again as she had the first time, to have that flash of recognition, to feel that certainty, but no amount of staring could bring the moment back.

This morning she planned to get off a stop early, close to the railway station. There she could be sure of finding a free phone box. She had a purse full of change, a scrap of paper and a pen. It would have been more convenient to ring the *Daily Mirror* from the office, but first she'd have had to ask permission, and that in turn would have involved explaining her reasons. Of course, she could have just rung without telling anyone, but she didn't want to chance it. Mr Tate was a stickler for the rules – no private calls from work – and he went through the phone bill with a fine-tooth comb. Judith valued her job too much to take unnecessary risks.

She didn't like Mr Tate and suspected the feeling was mutual.

He was a haughty, self-opinionated man who reminded her a little of Charlotte's George. What was it with small men? They were like those tiny yappy dogs, always overcompensating for their lack of size by biting at your ankles. Mr Gillespie, on the other hand, was polite and respectful and invariably kind. He had taken her on when she was only eighteen, giving her an opportunity, a chance to prove herself, when other employers were looking for someone more experienced.

Judith gazed out of the window, studying the people on their way to work. What were they thinking about? What they were going to cook for their tea tonight, perhaps, or what kind of Friday they would have, or what they were going to do at the weekend. Her own thoughts felt surreal in comparison: a random picture in a newspaper, a husband who had risen from the dead.

Thinking of the weekend reminded her that Charlotte's wedding was tomorrow. Normally, when there was trouble, Charlotte would be the first person she turned to, but this was hardly the time to be announcing that Dan might still be alive. No, she wasn't going to spoil the big day by shifting the spotlight on to herself. She would explain later, after the honeymoon, when they could sit down together and have a proper chat.

A part of her was relieved by this justification for keeping silent. She knew that Charlotte would be kind but sensible, gently pointing out that the chances of the man in the photograph being Dan were slim, being careful not to encourage any false hope. Hope always brought with it the possibility of crushing disappointment.

The bus drew to a halt outside the station and Judith joined the shuffling queue to get off. Once she'd escaped the crush, she walked quickly, weaving between the commuters on their way to Liverpool and Manchester. She found the row of phones, chose the one at the end, piled up her coins on the shelf, lifted the receiver and dialled the number for the operator.

'The *Daily Mirror*, please,' she said, 'in London.'

'Which department do you require?'

'Er . . . I don't know. I'm not sure. Photographic?'

'I'll put you through to the main switchboard.'

When the call was answered, Judith dropped her coins into the slot. 'Oh, hello. Good morning. I'm ringing about a photograph you had in the paper yesterday. It's on page ten – the one of the car in the jewellery shop door. I was wondering—'

The man sounded interested. 'Do you have information about the robbery?'

'No, no, nothing like that. Only I thought . . . I think I recognise someone in the background, a man in the crowd. I was hoping there might be other pictures, you know, ones that are a bit clearer.'

'I see,' the man said, his voice becoming flat. 'Well, I can't help you with that. You'll have to talk to Bob.'

'Bob?'

'Bob Hamilton. He's the one who took the photo.'

'Is Mr Hamilton there?'

'No, he's not in the office much. Out and about, isn't he?'

'So how can I get in touch?'

'Try later, I suppose. Or you could leave your number and I'll pass it on.'

Judith weighed up the two options and came down in favour of the second. She could be trying all day and still not get hold of him. She gave her name and the number of Gillespie & Tate, crossing her fingers that neither of those two gentlemen would be in the vicinity if and when she got a call back. The receiving of private calls was a lesser crime – no cost to the firm except in time – but was still frowned upon.

She put down the phone, gathered up her remaining change

and left the station. It was disappointing that the photographer hadn't been there, but at least she'd set the wheels in motion. Although early for work, she didn't loiter. She wanted to make sure she was behind her desk in case Mr Hamilton tried to ring her.

Three hours later, Judith was still waiting. Every time the phone rang, she jumped, wondering if this time it would be Bob Hamilton. Every time, she was disappointed. Her nerves were frayed, her concentration shot. It all meant so much, too much. One decent photograph, one clear image, and she would know for sure. The day dragged on. She typed and filed and made cups of tea for the clients. On two occasions Mr Tate took pleasure in pointing out mistakes she had made and whole contracts had to be retyped. Lunch came and went. She stayed at her post. It was after four o'clock before she finally got the call she'd been longing for.

She thanked Bob Hamilton for ringing and quickly explained the situation. The only thing she didn't mention was that she thought the tall, blond man might be her husband. Instead she referred to him as a cousin she'd lost touch with during the war. She didn't want to come across as some crazy lady he might be tempted to hang up on, but in the event it didn't make any difference.

'Sorry, that's the only shot I took with the crowd in it. The others are all close-ups of the car.'

The news came as a blow and Judith felt her hopes deflate. 'Oh,' she murmured. 'That's a shame.'

'Well, I hope you find him.'

'Thank you.'

Bob Hamilton hesitated and then said, 'I don't know if this is of any help – it probably isn't – but I do know one of the fellers, the one to your cousin's left, wearing a raincoat and hat. His name's Tombs – T-O-M-B-S, Alfred Tombs.'

Judith scribbled down the name. She tried to visualise the photo in her head but couldn't recall the man with the hat. She'd been too preoccupied with Dan. 'Does it look like they might be together?'

Hamilton gave a snort. 'Let me ask you a question. Is your cousin the law-abiding sort?'

'Yes, of course.'

'Then no. Not a chance.'

'So this Tombs, he's what, some kind of criminal?'

'He's that all right. Look, I've got to go. I've got the guv'nor yelling in my ear.'

'All right, and thanks for ...' But the line had already gone dead.

Judith put down the phone and pondered on what she'd learned. She wished she had the picture with her so she could see how closely the two men were standing together, but it was probably irrelevant. More likely they had just stopped independently of each other to gawp at a spectacle. But what if ... What if what? She could think of no reason at all why Dan would be in the company of a criminal. But then she could think of no reason why he would be in London either.

Mr Gillespie came out of his office and stood beside her desk. 'Is everything all right, Judith?'

'I'm sorry about the mistakes in Mr Tate's documents,' she said quickly, fearing a reprimand. 'I do apologise. It won't happen again, I promise.'

'We all make mistakes. Try not to worry about it. But you're looking tired, my dear. Perhaps you should take some time off. Don't you usually go on holiday in August?'

She nodded. 'Yes, usually.' Under normal circumstances she would book her holiday for the same dates as Charlotte and they would go up to the Lakes or the Dales and spend the week walking. Those days were gone, however. From now on, Charlotte would be holidaying with George.

'Why don't you take next week off? Have a rest. Mr Tate won't be here, so . . .' He stopped and frowned. 'But maybe it's too short notice for you.'

Judith was about to agree that it was, but then had a change of heart. 'Would you be able to manage?'

'Oh yes, Mrs Gillespie can come in and help.'

This wasn't exactly reassuring news – Mr Gillespie's wife had a random method of filing which meant that documents could end up anywhere and usually did – but she decided it was a price worth paying. 'All right, then. Thank you. I'll do that.'

As her boss returned to his office, she began tidying her desk. A plan had occurred to her, an idea that filled her with excitement and trepidation. Why not go to London? If Dan was still alive, there was only one way to find him, and it wasn't by sitting here in Westport.

4

'You're going to London?' Annie said, her eyes widening.

'Shh, no need to tell the whole world.' Judith raised a finger to her lips and glanced around. They were in the foyer of the town hall, waiting for Charlotte to arrive. George was already in attendance, smartly suited with a carnation in his lapel, standing to one side with a couple she presumed were his brother and his wife. 'Yes, Monday morning. I've bought my ticket. I'm all ready to go.'

'Where are you going to stay?'

Judith gave a light shrug of her shoulders. 'I'll find somewhere. There must be lots of places. A bed and breakfast probably, a cheap one.'

'But where are you even going to start? Looking for him, I mean. London's not like Westport; you're not going to bump into him on some street corner.'

'I know that. I'm going to try Kellston first.'

'And where's that when it's at home?'

'The East End. It's where he grew up.'

'That's a rough part,' Annie said. 'I've heard about it. You'd better be careful. You could get robbed or attacked or—'

'Of course I'm going to be careful, for heaven's sake. What else would I be?'

Annie raised her eyebrows. 'All right, keep your hair on. I'm only saying.'

'You were the one who claimed you'd do the same in my position.'

'I didn't say I'd waltz off to London on my own, did I?'

'What else am I supposed to do? I'm not going to find him by staying here. I've got to know if it's him, Annie.'

She must have raised her voice, because George looked over and frowned. Judith nodded and smiled and made a small, unnecessary adjustment to the angle of her hat. 'Sorry,' she murmured to Annie. 'I know you're concerned, but I'll be fine. You won't tell Charlotte, will you? Promise me.'

'She won't be happy.'

'All the more reason to keep quiet about it. I will talk to her, just not yet. She'll only worry.'

'*I'm* worried.'

Judith patted her arm. 'Yes, but it's not your wedding day, so you'll have to grin and bear it.'

As if on cue, Charlotte walked in. She had swept up her long fair hair and was wearing a pretty pink suit and matching low-heeled shoes. They fussed around her, kissed her cheek and told her how lovely she looked. There was a brief whirl of activity as the guests gathered together, and five minutes later they were all inside the wedding room listening to the registrar.

Judith gazed at Charlotte, hoping she was happy. She *looked* happy. Maybe George had more about him than Judith imagined. Maybe he had hidden depths. Well hidden, it would appear, but perhaps she shouldn't be too quick to judge. She should make more of an effort to get to know him better. After all, Charlotte was intelligent and kind and unlikely to attach herself to someone who was entirely without merit.

Judith's gaze drifted, along with her thoughts. The last time she'd been here, in this very room, she'd been marrying Dan. Memories flooded back. What had she felt on that day? Love and lust, trust and boundless hope. It had been a new beginning, the start of a new life. And yes, it had all been tinged by the shadow of war, but she'd truly believed he would come back to her. *Till death do us part.* But what if it wasn't death that had parted them? Doubt fluttered at the edges of her thoughts.

She had studied the picture in the paper again, examining the villain called Tombs and trying to work out if the two men were actually together. It was impossible to tell. She gave a small shake of her head, trying to free her mind of the worries that were gathering there. On Monday she would be on a train, heading for London. It was the right thing to do. She was sure of it. She'd go mad otherwise. If she did nothing, the possibility that he was still alive would always be there, dogging her, haunting her, filling every waking moment.

The vows were exchanged, the partnership sealed, and the groom kissed the bride. There was a ripple of applause from the guests. They stood and gathered round the couple, offering their congratulations and wishing them well. There was more kissing, along with handshakes and affectionate slaps on the back. Judith embraced Charlotte. 'Be happy,' she said.

The hotel was only twenty yards away, and so they walked along the road in twos and threes. A lively wind was blowing off the Irish Sea, and the women held on to their hats. Annie linked her arm through Judith's and leaned in to say softly, 'I never thought I'd be envious of anyone marrying George Rigby.'

Judith grinned at her. 'And I never thought I'd hear those words come out of your mouth.'

'Oh, you know what I mean. I miss having someone around, someone to talk to. I hate coming home to an empty flat every night.'

Judith nodded. She understood. Although she had not lived with Dan for any prolonged period of time, she always felt his absence. The flat had a curious stillness about it, an emptiness that couldn't be filled. She squeezed Annie's arm. 'Maybe we can fix you up with one of George's pals.'

'None of that lot would be interested in me.'

'Why ever not?'

'I'm not their type, love. Too common, aren't I? They wouldn't marry a shop girl.'

It was true, Judith thought, that Westport was rife with snobbery, with a them-and-us attitude dividing the middle and lower classes. Annie was never short of dates – blokes like George often took her dancing, for meals or for drinks at the pub – but it never developed into anything serious. The men came and went. She was good company, always up for a laugh, a sing-song and probably a lot more, but they didn't see her as marriage material. 'You're too good for them,' she said. 'That's the problem.'

'That must be it. Or maybe I'm too bad.'

Judith laughed. 'You'll find someone. I know you will.'

The Astor was an old-fashioned sort of place, past its best but still respectable. Once it had been *the* hotel to stay in, the resort's crowning glory, but those days had long gone. Now dusty chandeliers hung from the high ceiling of the dining room, the wallpaper was fading, and the red plush chairs showed signs of wear, the gilt peeling from their backs, the cushioned seats a little frayed around the edges.

The top table consisted of Charlotte, George and their respective parents. The rest of the room had been divided into tables of four, each with a centrepiece of three white lilies. Judith and

39

Annie had been seated with two men they'd never met before: Charles Rigby, a cousin of George's, and Martin Davenport, one of George's work colleagues. Annie seemed pleased enough with the arrangement – Martin was a debonair greying gentleman in his early fifties, suave and confident – and she didn't waste any time in engaging him in conversation. Charles, however, was a different kettle of fish.

Judith, who had already guessed that Charlotte had picked him as a prospective suitor, felt her heart sink. She wasn't in the market for a new husband, and even if she had been, Charles would not have made the shortlist. He had a somewhat superior air – a family trait, perhaps – and kept glancing at his watch as though he had somewhere more important to be. It was only when he mentioned that he worked as a barrister in London that her ears pricked up.

'Really? How interesting. Whereabouts?'

'Lincoln's Inn, of course.'

'Ah,' she said, feeling that she had made a faux pas even by asking. 'Yes, Lincoln's Inn.'

'Do you know London?'

'Not really, although I do have a friend who lives in Kellston.'

At the mention of the district, Charles's face twisted a little, like he'd just popped a slice of lemon in his mouth. 'The East End.'

'Are you familiar with it? What's it like?'

'Flat,' he said shortly.

'Flat?'

Martin leaned across the table. 'What he means, my dear, is that it was badly bombed during the war. Mr Hitler made an almighty mess of the place.'

'It's a shame he didn't finish the job,' Charles said. 'It's a sewer, a breeding ground for criminals. Half the rabble of London come from there.'

'You should be grateful,' Martin said drily. 'Aren't that rabble

40

bread and butter for you lot? If it wasn't for their misdemeanours, you wouldn't get all those delightful court fees.'

Charles gave a thin smile.

'Bit rough, then, is it?' Annie enquired. 'Not the sort of place you'd want to go for your holidays?'

Judith scowled at her. She would have kicked her under the table if she wasn't afraid of catching Martin's leg by mistake.

'Not the sort of place you'd want to go at any time,' Charles said.

The food arrived – cutlets, potatoes and green beans – and the subject was dropped. A few brief speeches and a toast to the bride and groom followed the meal, and then the hotel band struck up. Martin and Annie took to the dance floor, but Charles didn't ask Judith if she'd care to join them. She was both grateful and insulted. His manners, it seemed, left a lot to be desired.

With Annie out of the way, she took the opportunity to interrogate him further. 'Is the East End really that bad?'

Charles took a sip of his champagne and smacked his lips. 'Worse,' he pronounced, almost gleefully.

'Worse?'

'It's the filthy underbelly of London, swarming with thieves and murderers and every other kind of lowlife. All the detritus of the city gathered in one place. Yes, it really is *that* bad.'

None of this filled Judith with confidence. 'Is it to do with the poverty, do you think? I've heard it's quite a poor area.'

'Poverty is no excuse for breaking the law. *Thou shalt not kill. Thou shalt not steal.* How much clearer can the rules be? These people have no morals whatsoever.'

Judith felt her hackles rise at his sanctimonious response. Dan had been one of 'these people', raised in the East End, but he'd been decent and honest. It was hardly fair to tar everyone with the same brush. 'That can't be true,' she said. 'There are good people everywhere.'

41

Charles snorted. 'You think I'm exaggerating? Believe me, I'm not. Criminals breed criminals. It's a fact. It's in their blood; they just can't help themselves.'

Judith might have argued the point – surely circumstances and environment were factors too? – but she wanted to pick his brains about something else before Annie got back. 'I suppose you must meet quite a lot of criminals in your line of work.'

'It's hard to avoid them.'

'Have you ever come across a man called Alfred Tombs?'

'Tombs? Of course! There's not a prosecutor in London who hasn't come across him at one time or another.'

'Is he from the East End?'

'Why on earth do you want to know about a man like that?'

'Oh,' she said, trying to sound casual, 'I read something about him in the paper. I'm just curious.'

'Yes, he's from the East End, and a prime example of what I've been talking about. Robbery, extortion, gambling – he's up to his neck in it. Fashions himself as the boss of the underworld, although it's doubtful anyone is actually in charge of that rabble. They're a law unto themselves.'

'So why don't the police arrest him?'

'They have, on numerous occasions, but making the charges stick is more of a problem. He's slippery as an eel, that one. Which isn't to say he's *never* been convicted. No, he's done his fair share of time, but he's learning from his mistakes. Older and wiser, isn't that what they say? These days he keeps his head down and pretends to be a respectable businessman.'

While Judith thought about all this, she kept one eye on Charles and the other on the dance floor. She didn't see how Dan could possibly have a connection to Alfred Tombs, but it was the only lead she had at the moment, so she might as well make the most of it. 'What kind of businessman?'

'Pubs, clubs, imports and exports – you name a pie and he's got his finger in it.'

'In the East End?'

'Heavens, no, not *just* the East End. Mayfair, Soho, anywhere there's money to be made. Men like Tombs spread their nets wide.'

Judith nodded. She had a plan forming in her head. If the worst came to the worst and she could find no trace of Dan in Kellston, she could always try and track down Tombs. The prospect didn't fill her with joy, but at least it was an option. 'So he can't be a difficult man to find – for the police, I mean.'

'Finding him is one thing, convicting him quite another. He's got an alibi for every crime. Still, one day he'll make a mistake and then we'll have him.'

Judith could see the anticipation shining in his eyes. Although usually on the side of law and order – how else could society operate? – she was uncomfortable at being on any side that had Charles Rigby on it. 'I'm sure you will.'

He frowned, perhaps hearing something less than admiring in her tone, and looked at his watch again.

'Do you need to be somewhere?' she asked, irked by his rudeness.

'I have to get back to London today. Important business.' He pushed back his chair and stood up. 'Excuse me, I need to find a phone.'

Annie came back to the table and sat down. 'Where's Prince Charming?'

'Phone call.'

'God, he's such a bore. What were you talking about?'

'Nothing much.'

Annie gave her a look. 'Nothing much about what?'

Judith hadn't told her about Alfred Tombs and didn't intend to. She knew how Annie would react. 'His job, mainly. He likes to talk about himself. In fact, I think it's his favourite subject. Where's Martin gone?'

'He's getting some drinks from the bar. He's all right, you know, quite a laugh.'

The two of them lapsed into silence, each preoccupied by their own thoughts. The beat of the music filled the room, along with the gentle tap and slide of soles on the dance floor. The smell of lilies drifted in the air. Judith gazed over at Charlotte. It was the beginning of a new life for her friend, a fresh start, a new journey. Soon Judith too would be going on a journey. This time on Monday she'd be in London. The idea both frightened and excited her. Her hand shook as she lifted her glass to her lips and sipped the last few drops of champagne.

What was going to happen next? She trembled, nervous as a new bride.

5

DS Saul Hannah's eyebrows would lift whenever anyone talked about the war being over. *That* war, perhaps, the one in Europe, but another was still raging on the streets of London. Criminals had grabbed the opportunity of a decimated police force to wreak havoc on the capital with a relentless campaign of robbery, fraud, kidnapping and illegal gambling. The police had been fighting a losing battle until the formation of the Special Duties Squad in 1946.

Saul had been chosen for the squad because he was a dedicated cop, and he was dedicated because he had nothing else in his life. Having lost his wife and daughter in the Blitz, all he had left was his work. He clung onto this like a drowning man, working day and night, channelling all his energy into anything that stopped him from thinking too much about the things he couldn't bear to think about.

The department had quickly become known as the Ghost Squad, due to the fact that it barely existed in an official capacity. This was because its methods were unconventional. It was the job of its members to gather information – by any means they cared to use – and to pass it on to the relevant department, usually the Flying Squad or CID, who would make any subsequent arrests.

Saul was good at what he did. Different cops had different ways of extracting information from their snouts, some using fear, others a more gentle approach. He favoured the latter, the carrot rather than the stick. It was too exhausting to play the hard man all the time, to be the bastard, to bully and threaten, and anyway, it wasn't in his nature. His informants responded better to a quid pro quo approach – I'll scratch your back and you scratch mine. This usually involved a letter to the court requesting leniency when a snout was caught red-handed, or letting them off with a caution if the information offered might hook a bigger fish.

People had their own reasons for informing. It could be as simple as wanting to avoid a prison sentence, the reward money (loss adjusters would pay a ten per cent reward for information leading to the return of stolen property), revenge, turf wars, or even, as in the case of the woman he was waiting for, an opportunity to get rid of an abusive husband.

Saul scratched the base of his neck where the sun was shining on it. He was sitting on a low wall in what remained of someone's front room. Once there had been two rows of houses on this land, an entire street, but now there was only rubble and weeds. The place was deserted, desolate. He could feel the dust in the back of his throat as he breathed in.

When it came to snouts, patience was required, especially in the case of women like Maud Bishop. It wasn't always easy for her to escape the family home. Sometimes, when things were bad, she didn't turn up at all. Fear and loathing ruled her life. Michael Bishop was the worst kind of man, violent and unpredictable, an armed robber with an appetite for sadism. He wasn't fussy who he knocked about: security guards, cops, prostitutes and, of course, his own wife. The only time Maud had any respite was when he was locked up.

Saul lit a cigarette and gazed out across the wasteland. He would stay for half an hour before he gave it up as a bad job. She might come and she might not. He wasn't going to stress. Nothing was predictable in this line of work; you just had to roll with it, to grab the opportunities when they came along.

It was another twenty minutes before she put in an appearance. He heard her before he saw her – the quick footsteps, the crunch of glass beneath her shoes – and stood up. He watched her walk towards him, her shoulders hunched, her expression furtive. She was a skinny, gaunt-faced woman who looked about forty but was probably ten years younger.

'Maud,' he said, and nodded. He didn't ask how she was, as the answer was obvious.

She was sporting an ugly black eye. The lid was swollen and the damaged flesh around it was the colour of ripe plums. He felt sorry for her in a vague, unfocused kind of way. He didn't do strong emotions any more; he had cut himself off from other people's suffering, barely able to cope with his own.

'I can't stay long,' she said, looking left and right before glancing over her shoulder. Her head swivelled back and she stared at him again, her face full of fear. 'He'll bloody kill me if he finds out about this.'

Saul reckoned he'd probably end up killing her anyway. 'He won't find out, not from me, at least.'

She worried at her lower lip for a moment as though she might be about to change her mind, but her options were limited. It wasn't the first occasion she'd grassed on her old man; last time, he'd got nine months for burglary. A thin sigh escaped from her mouth. 'I don't know much, not yet, but it's something big, I'm sure of it. Hull's been round the house. I heard the two of 'em talking in the kitchen.'

Saul nodded. Pat Hull ran a firm over in Hoxton, a gang of thieves who specialised in breaking and entering, and hijacking lorries. He'd taken over from his older brother Lennie, who'd been shot through the head in '44. Lennie hadn't, of course, been fighting for his country, but feathering his nest at home. He'd been dispatched by a person or persons unknown in the back streets of Kellston.

'I reckon it's to do with some tom,' Maud said.

'Jewellery?'

'Watches and the like.'

'You know when and where?'

She shook her head. 'Not yet. I'll find out, though. Switzerland – that's where it's coming from. I heard them say.'

Saul's first thought was Heathrow. An expensive consignment of watches was more likely to come in by air than road. 'Soon, you reckon?'

'Not that soon. I mean, not tomorrow or nothin'. He gets all quiet when it's coming up, won't say more than he has to. Starts picking at his food and ... I dunno. A fortnight, a few weeks, maybe?'

'Shooters?' he asked. 'Are they going to be carrying?'

She grimaced. 'What do you think?' Her gaze flew around the wasteland again. 'I've got to go. I've got to get back.'

Saul took a fiver out of his wallet. 'Here,' he said, pressing the note into her palm. 'Let me know when you've got anything more.'

'Ta.' Maud slipped the money into the pocket of her shabby brown dress, then turned and quickly walked away.

Saul stayed where he was, giving her time to get clear. There was no one else in sight, but he never took unnecessary risks. Informing was a dangerous business for both the giver and receiver. He had no regard for his own personal safety but was always protective of his snouts. For them, being labelled as a grass would have major repercussions.

He lit another cigarette and thought over what Maud had told him. If this job was as big as she reckoned, it would be a major coup catching Hull in the act, and a chance to send him and Bishop down for a good long stretch. Unfortunately, Saul himself wouldn't be in on the arrests if and when they happened. Part of his job was to keep a low profile and to make sure nothing could connect him to his snout.

Information was the lifeblood of the force, especially in this time of ongoing austerity. With so many items in short supply – food, whisky, tobacco, nylons, furs – the villains were having a field day. The black market was still flourishing, with eager customers queuing up for anything the racketeers could lay their hands on. The fraudsters were being kept busy too, forging petrol and ration coupons, not to mention fake identity papers for any deserter who wanted a fresh start.

Saul curled his lip. This war, the battle against crime, would never be over. All they could do was to try and contain it. And if that meant playing dirty, so be it. The police had always paid for information that came their way, but the Ghost Squad went out actively to look for it. Saul's list of informants was a long one. He never wrote down their names, but kept them in his head. It was all about trust. Some snouts were easier to manage than others. There were a few, the sly ones, who informed in order to divert attention from their own dodgy dealings, but Saul hadn't been born yesterday; he was always one step ahead, always in control of the situation and never controlled by it.

He dropped the butt of his cigarette, ground it down with his heel and yawned. He'd been up half the night doing the rounds of the pubs and clubs in Soho looking for a small-time villain called Monaghan. There was a rumour the feller had crossed Alf Tombs and taken a beating for it. There was nothing Saul liked more than a criminal bearing a grudge; they had a tendency to let their mouths run away with them. Sadly, the bloke hadn't shown his face. Either he'd been at home licking his wounds or he'd decided to stay away from his regular haunts. Still, he'd surface eventually, maybe tonight or tomorrow, and when he did, Saul would be there with a round of drinks and a sympathetic ear.

Tombs was at the top of every London cop's 'Most Wanted' list. The man was responsible for half the crime in the capital. He'd started young, robbing shops and houses, and through the years had progressed to more ambitious and lucrative jobs. Post offices were a speciality. Recently there had been a spate of smash-and-grabs at high-end jewellers in the West End. They had Tombs written all over them. The police could pull him in, question him, search his gaff – and they frequently did – but without any evidence, they were powerless to act.

Saul began to walk through the wasteland, heading for Mansfield Road. This end of Kellston, flattened by bombs, had an eerie feel to it. On the ground there were everyday items mixed in with the rubble: a teaspoon, broken cups and saucers, the handle of a saucepan. He closed his mind to the people who had died here. If he let one ghost in, the rest might try to follow, and there wasn't room in his head for all that sorrow.

He ran his tongue along dry lips. He craved a drink, but the pubs weren't open yet. Course, there were always places to go if you needed a snifter, illegal joints hidden away in back-street basements, but he didn't fancy any of those dingy rooms with their dubious clientele. Not today. Not when the sun was shining. Anyway, he didn't want to take the chance. All too often the black dog was lurking in those gloomy dens, ready to attach itself to his side, to pull him into darkness.

Once he reached the road, Saul strolled down to the high street and went into Connolly's. The café, a gathering place for the locals, was moderately busy without being crowded. He chose a table towards the back and sat down. He saw Elsa ferrying plates and mugs of tea across the room, and she saw him too. Neither acknowledged the other.

It was another few minutes before she came over. 'What can I get you?'

'Tea,' he said. 'Ta.'

'You want something to eat?'

'What's on?'

'Faggots,' she said. 'That's the special. Or there's cottage pie, liver, baked potatoes.'

Saul thought about it. He had an empty feeling inside him, but wasn't sure if it was hunger. He looked into her eyes; they were blank, as though she'd never met him before. 'What do you recommend?'

'Cottage pie,' she said.

'I'll have that.'

Elsa nodded, scribbled down the order in her notebook, turned away, went back to the counter, tore out the page and put it through a spike. Then she moved on to the next customer.

While he waited for his food, Saul watched her criss-crossing the room, sliding between tables, clearing the used plates onto trays and wiping down the surfaces. Elsa couldn't be described as beautiful, but she moved with effortless grace, like a dancer on a stage. Her face was sharp and angular, with high cheekbones and dark hooded eyes. How long since they first met? It must be getting on for two years now.

To look at her, you'd never guess she was doing anything other than her job. But she was all eyes and ears, watching and listening, taking in every scrap of information. She knew all the villains in the area, who their mates were, who they were married to and who they were screwing on the side. She knew when a job was in the offing, and who was working with whom. Sometimes she knew where the stolen goods were stashed. No one took any notice of a waitress; she was invisible, like a ghost sliding by.

Saul saw her, though. He saw her naked, had sex with her – he would never call it making love – but still knew as little about her as when their paths had first crossed. He didn't mind this; preferred it, in fact. They weren't in *that* kind of a relationship. If pressed, he'd be hard pushed to put an actual name to it. Convenient, perhaps? He had no deep feelings for her. He didn't even like her that much. She was moody and secretive, distant and sarcastic, the very opposite of everything he found attractive in a woman.

Once, he had asked her why she did it, why she chose to inform.

'For the dough, of course,' she'd replied scornfully. 'What else?'

He suspected that wasn't the whole story. There was more to it, some other motivation, but he wasn't interested in finding out what. That was her business, not his. Saul never paid her for sex – he would have viewed such an exchange as demeaning – but with money changing hands for the information she gave him, usually before or after they'd screwed, he supposed, to an outsider, that the line might be somewhat blurred as to what he was actually paying for.

Elsa brought the food and placed the plate, cutlery and mug of tea in front of him. As she leaned forward, he caught a faint whiff of vanilla.

'Tonight,' she said softly. 'Nine o'clock?'

He nodded. 'Yes.'

Then she was gone, without another word. He kept his gaze on the table, resisting the urge to follow her with his eyes. He picked up the mug and drank. The tea had a dusty taste, as though the leaves had been dried out and reused. He wondered what she had for him. Something good, he hoped, something that would help him nail another lowlife. There were some, he was sure, who wouldn't approve of his methods, but he didn't give a damn. So far as he was concerned, the end always justified the means.

6

Judith gazed out of the window as the train rattled through the outskirts of London. Rows of houses stood back to back, their yards full of washing flapping in the wind. It was a sunless morning, with thin grey clouds racing across the sky. The carriage was full, the passengers squashed together, but she was barely aware of her fellow travellers. In her head, she was going over a plan of action for when she arrived at Euston.

Kellston would be her starting point. Once she found her way there, she would book into a B&B and then start knocking on doors. She glanced down at the open book in her lap. On Saturday, after Charlotte's wedding reception, she had gone to the bookshop and asked if they had any road maps of London. Mr Buchan had scratched his chin, said there wasn't much call for that kind of thing but that he might have something in the second-hand section. He had disappeared into the basement and come back five minutes later with a dog-eared copy of the *A–Z Atlas of London and Suburbs*.

Judith remembered Dan telling her that he'd grown up on Mansfield Road. Back then, when they were courting, she had wanted to know everything about him: where he'd lived, what school he'd gone to, what he'd been like as a child. He'd laughed at her endless questions, but that hadn't stopped her. She had stored up all the information, every precious detail, in her memory. Now she was glad of it.

She traced the route with her finger: left out of Kellston station, right up the high street and then right again into Mansfield Road. It seemed straightforward enough. She could only hope that one of the residents not only remembered Dan but knew where he was now. Communities like these were close, weren't they? If he had come back, someone would be aware of it.

Judith's plan B was to visit the local library, where hopefully they would have a list of all the locksmiths in the district. Dan could be working for one of them. If she drew a blank, she would have to extend the search to the West End, where the *Daily Mirror* picture had been taken.

Both of these plans seemed to her eminently sensible. She had brought along with her the only photograph she had of Dan, taken on their wedding day. Although she had the *Mirror* picture with her too, it wouldn't be much use for identification purposes. It could, however, be essential if she wanted to track down Alfred Tombs. She hoped it wouldn't come to that. Charles Rigby had painted a fearsome portrait of the man: Tombs was clearly a criminal of the worst kind, and not the sort of person she would ever want to approach. She would do it, though, if she had to. There was no point in her coming to London if she wasn't going to explore every possible avenue. What was the worst that could happen? Her stomach shifted uneasily. No, she wasn't going to think about it. She would cross that scary bridge only if and when she had to.

The train finally pulled into Euston, and Judith retrieved her case from the overhead shelf. She got off, walked along the platform, showed her ticket to the man at the barrier and passed on through to the crowded station concourse. Following the signs, she descended to the Tube by escalator, feeling a certain sense of wonder that she was actually in London. This was the capital, the place where everywhere happened, a far cry from the small-town comings and goings of Westport. Recalling Annie's warnings, she held on tightly to her handbag. Imagine being robbed as soon as she got here! She glanced over her shoulder. No one was paying her any attention.

She queued up to buy a ticket for the Tube before making a careful study of the Underground map. The route didn't seem too complicated: four stops along the Northern Line to Moorgate before a change to the Metropolitan and District Line and one more stop to Liverpool Street. From there, she would have to take an ordinary train to Kellston.

The platform was busy, but she found a bench with a space at the end and perched on the edge. It felt strange, unnatural, to be down in the bowels of the earth. Her eyes scanned the people around her before moving on to the sooty curved walls of the tunnel with its bright advertisements for shampoo and raincoats and gin. Immediately ahead was a poster for a play: *Death of a Salesman*. She found the title disturbing and quickly glanced away.

She felt the train before she saw it, a slight but distinct shifting of the air. There was a rumble like distant thunder before it rolled in. She stood up, waited for the doors to open, joined the crush to get on, stepped into the carriage and sat down in the first available free seat. As the train moved off, she hoped she was on the correct one and going in the right direction.

It was a relief when the train arrived at King's Cross a few minutes later. She'd had visions of having to jump off, of trying again, of spending half the day going round and round in circles. Now that she knew she hadn't made a mistake, she was able to relax. She wondered if Dan ever used the Tube. Her gaze slid across her fellow passengers as she looked for his face, his eyes and mouth, the shock of fair hair. The odds might be slim – he was just one man in a city of millions – but she believed in fate.

By the time she'd negotiated her way to Liverpool Street, Judith was glad to be back on the surface of the earth again. Although she appreciated how efficient the Tube was, a quick and easy method of getting around London, the narrow tunnels made her feel claustrophobic. Some of the smells weren't too pleasant either. There wasn't much ventilation, and the body odour of her fellow travellers lingered in the stuffy air.

The journey to Kellston was a slow one, with stops at numerous places she'd never heard of. The view from the window was none too inspiring: cranes, building sites, ramshackle warehouses and endless rows of squat terraces, their walls blackened by steam from the trains. The only green she saw was along the side of the tracks, straggly weeds poking through the nooks and crannies.

The scene didn't improve as the train approached Kellston, becoming if anything even more grey and dismal. But she refused to be downhearted. It didn't matter what the place looked like so long as Dan was somewhere in it. The thought that she might see him soon made her heart leap in her chest. Whatever had happened to make him stay away, whatever had gone wrong, she would find a way to make it right.

Judith hurried off the train, eager to begin the search. She climbed the stairs and exited the station. Her first job was to find somewhere to stay. Although she'd packed sparingly, she didn't want to be carting her suitcase around. Her luck was in. Directly opposite was a row of B&Bs, nearly all of them with a sign saying 'Vacancies' in their front window.

She crossed the road, wondering which one to choose. Well, she wasn't going to waste much time on the decision; she only had a week and didn't intend to squander a minute of it. A week to find Dan. Was that possible in a city this size? Before her confidence could ebb away, she strode purposefully up the short path of an establishment called Sycamore House and rang the bell.

The door was answered by a man in his fifties wearing fawn trousers, a stained white shirt and braces. There was an unlit cigarette dangling out of the corner of his mouth. He gave a nod, glanced down at her case and back up at her again.

'After a room, are you?'

Judith hesitated, worried that she'd made the wrong choice. What if the room was as grubby as the man standing in front of her? But it was too late to backtrack now. 'A single,' she said. 'Just for a few nights.' She could always move on, find somewhere else if it was truly dreadful. 'How much would that be?'

'Seven bob,' he said.

'A night?'

One of his eyebrows arched up. 'That's good value, love. You won't find anything cheaper round 'ere.'

Judith had no idea if this was true or not. She'd have paid less for a hotel room in Westport, but London was an expensive place. Should she shop around, try somewhere else? No, she had more important things to do. 'All right.'

'You'd better come in, then.'

She followed him into the hall.

'Front or back?' he asked. 'It's quieter at the back. You don't get the noise from the street.'

She was about to agree that this would be better when it occurred to her that there might be advantages to being at the front. She could look out of the window and see everyone who went in and out of the station, everyone who walked past the house. 'I'd prefer the front, if that's all right.'

'You sure?' he asked doubtfully.

'Yes, I'm sure.'

He gave a shrug, opened the drawer of a small table, took out a key and gave it to her. 'Second floor, first on your left. Bathroom's at the end of the landing.'

'Thank you.'

'Breakfast is between six thirty and eight.'

Judith climbed the stairs quickly. She found the room, unlocked the door, stepped inside and looked around. Her heart sank. It was small and dingy, with an odd, musty smell. The carpet was worn, almost threadbare, and there were cobwebs in the corners of the ceiling. She laid her case on the narrow bed and went over to the window. From here there was an excellent view of the street at least, but she didn't linger. It was time to start looking for Dan.

7

Judith was halfway up the high street when she noticed the library on the other side of the road. She stopped and stared at the building, dithering for a moment, undecided. In the end, figuring she might as well do it now as later, she crossed over and went inside.

The rooms were large and cool and hushed. There were several people sitting at tables, a few more perusing the books on the shelves. She went to the counter, where a severe-looking woman was working through a pile of novels, opening them and slipping tickets into the inside pouches. 'Sorry to disturb you, but I don't suppose you have a list of local locksmiths, by any chance?'

The librarian glanced up. 'There's one just past the station. Taylor's, they're called. Beside the café. You can't miss it.'

'Thank you. Are there any others in the area?'

The woman looked at her more closely, wondering perhaps why anyone would need more than one locksmith. 'Others?'

'Yes, I, er ... I want a few quotes. You know, to get the best price.'

The woman seemed to sense that she was lying. Her tone

became even chillier as she gestured towards the rear of the library. 'You could try the telephone directories. They're in the reference section.'

'Thanks,' Judith said. 'I'll do that.' She could feel the older woman's gaze on her as she walked away. Why hadn't she told the truth? Because the truth sounded plain crazy: *My husband was presumed dead but there's a chance he could be working as a locksmith in Kellston.* She didn't need to see any pitying looks – time enough for that when she went knocking on doors. For now, she simply wanted to gather whatever information she could.

There were a couple of directories covering the East End. She took them to a table, sat down and got out her notepad and pen. Within a quarter of an hour she had a list of over twenty locksmiths, one other in Kellston, up at the top end of the high street, the rest in places like Shoreditch, Bethnal Green, Hoxton, Whitechapel, Poplar and Stepney. And that, she suspected, was just the tip of the iceberg. There could be lots more businesses that were in adjoining areas or weren't even listed.

She sighed as the enormity of her task began to sink in. And what if she was looking in the wrong place entirely? The *Mirror* picture had been taken in the West End, not the East. Maybe that was where she should be focusing her attention. As she pondered on this, she tapped her pen against the pad. An elderly man sitting at the far end of the table scowled at her and cleared his throat disapprovingly.

Judith stopped tapping, put away the pen and pad, stood up, placed the directories back on the shelf and hurried out of the library. She had to get on with her search before she lost heart. As she strode up the high street, she tried to prepare herself for what lay ahead. Door-to-door enquiries: wasn't that what the police called it? She checked her bag to make sure the photograph was still there. She'd placed it in an envelope with cardboard on either side so it wouldn't get creased. Maybe she should have shown the picture to the librarian – but Dan had never been a great reader. She doubted he'd ever crossed the threshold of a library in his life.

The street seemed to go on for ever, long and straight, with shops on either side. It was shabby but busy, a hustling, bustling place full of people. Buses roared past, spewing out their exhaust fumes. She passed a butcher, a tobacconist, a pawn shop and a café called Connolly's. Peering in through the window of the latter, she saw a list of the day's specials chalked on a blackboard. The prices didn't seem too steep. Maybe she would eat there later.

As she continued northwards, the shops petered out and the street became much quieter. It was only when she reached the end that she realised why. Her heart sank as she surveyed the bleak landscape in front of her. Where Mansfield Road should have been, there was only ruin and desolation. Most of the area had been flattened, destroyed by bombs, and all that remained was a few walls and a heap of rubble.

She stared at the destruction with horror and disappointment. What now? Her shoulders slumped as the reality sank in. Nothing was left of Dan's childhood home or the homes of his neighbours. Her plan, like the street, had been blown into a million pieces. Tears of frustration sprang into her eyes. This had been her best hope, and now it was gone.

For a while, she couldn't move; her feet were rooted to the spot. She wondered how many people had died here, their lives wiped out, their futures ripped away from them. It was too terrible to take in. There was an eerie feel to the place, a sense of ghosts – resentful ghosts – lurking in the rubble. She felt their gaze on her, their bitter indignation. The hairs on the back of her neck stood on end.

She shook her head. She was just being fanciful. The dead

couldn't harm you. It was the living you had to watch out for. At least that was what Aunt Laura had always said. But the feeling she was not alone persisted. Instinctively she took a step back. There was nothing here to harm her, and yet she still felt threatened.

The nearest houses were a fair way off. She started walking again, trying to jolly herself into a more positive frame of mind. All right, it was a setback, but she couldn't give up at the first hurdle. There might still be people living in the vicinity who remembered Dan. She skirted round the wasteland, knowing that at some time in the past he must have walked here too. It was strange to think of it. Had he come back from the war and stood where she had stood? How awful it must have been to see everything destroyed. But then maybe he had seen far worse things, things she couldn't even begin to imagine.

Eventually she arrived at a tangle of streets, the first of which was Talbot Road. She took a few deep breaths, trying to steady her nerves. Anxiety tugged at her guts. The long terrace stretched ahead of her, and behind every front door was a stranger she would have to talk to. 'You can do it,' she murmured. 'You *have* to do it.'

Quickly she took the photograph from her handbag, marched up to the first house and rapped on the door.

Her knock was answered by a girl in her late teens with a baby in her arms. 'Yes?'

Judith smiled at her. 'I'm really sorry to bother you, but I'm looking for this man.' She held up the photograph. 'His name's Dan Jonson. I don't suppose you know him, do you?'

The girl glanced at the photo and shook her head. 'Nah.'

'His family lived in Mansfield Road.'

But this snippet of information didn't jog the girl's memory. She shook her head again. 'Nah, I ain't never seen him before.'

'Do you know anyone round here who might be able to help?'

The girl gave a shrug. The baby began to cry, a soft whimpering sound that gradually grew in pitch and volume. 'Sorry,' she said, retreating back inside and closing the door.

Judith wasn't too disheartened. The girl was probably too young to remember the Jonsons anyway. She moved on to the next house. An older woman came to the door and gave her a hard look.

'What do you want?'

Judith held out the photo. 'I'm really sorry to bother you, but I'm looking for this man. His name's Dan Jonson and he used to live round here, on—'

'No, love,' the woman interrupted. 'I don't know him. I've never seen him before.'

'Are you sure, only—'

She shut the door in Judith's face.

Judith moved on to the third house, and the fourth, and the fifth. By the time she'd completed the street, she was no better off than when she'd started. Some of the residents were friendlier than others, but it was the same story again and again: nobody recognised Dan, and nobody had heard of the Jonsons.

She shifted her search on to Henry Road but had no joy there either. A tiny glimmer of hope came when she was almost at the end of Boxley Street. An elderly woman, her face as wrinkled as a prune, peered down at the photo.

'What did you say his name was?'

'Dan, Dan Jonson. Do you recognise him?'

'He looks a bit like . . .'

Judith waited, but no further information was forthcoming. 'Who does he look like?' she prompted, grasping at the only straw she'd had to date.

Another woman came to the door. 'What's going on, Mum?'

'This young lady's looking for someone. She's got a photograph.'

The daughter frowned at Judith, and then at the picture. 'He's not here, that's for sure. We don't know him.'

'Your mother thought she might.'

'Yes, well, her memory's not what it was. She gets confused. Don't you, Mum?'

The old woman sighed and shook her head. 'It's my eyes, you see. They're not as good as they used to be. I thought ... but no, it's not him, not him at all.'

Judith would have pressed her further – who was this man who looked like Dan? – if it hadn't been for the daughter staring daggers at her. Clearly she'd outstayed her welcome. 'All right. Thanks for your time.'

The daughter pulled her mother inside and closed the door.

The sound of doors shutting was becoming familiar to Judith. She made a mental note of the address: 18 Boxley Street. Maybe it would be worth coming back if she could catch the old woman when the daughter wasn't around. It was probably something and nothing, but it was the nearest she'd got to a lead all morning.

She continued to trudge the surrounding streets for the next two hours, up and down, up and down, always getting the same answers to the same questions. How was it possible that Dan had grown up in this area and yet nobody recognised him? It didn't make any sense. The only conclusion she could draw was that she'd been lied to, either by the locals – but why would they? – or by Dan himself. Maybe this wasn't where he'd lived after all. Maybe everything he'd told her had been pure fiction.

She dwelled on this as she retraced her steps. She didn't want to believe it, but she couldn't dismiss it. After all, this was a man who was supposed to be dead. What bigger lie could there be? If he was capable of allowing her to believe that, he was capable of anything. And yet she didn't want to think badly of him. It was too soon to be imagining the worst. She was just tired and frustrated, disappointed by her lack of progress.

Her next port of call was the locksmith at the top end of the high street. She went inside and approached the counter, behind which a man was working on a machine that sounded like a dentist's drill. He finished what he was doing, turned to her and nodded.

'How can I help?'

This time Judith tried a different tack. Instead of immediately producing the photograph, she smiled brightly and said, 'Hello. I'm looking for Dan Jonson. He does work here, doesn't he?'

'There's no Dan Jonson here, I'm afraid. Only me. Sure you've got the right place?'

'I could have sworn he said the high street.'

'You could try Taylor's down by the station.'

'Yes, I'll do that. Thank you. I suppose you know most of the other locksmiths in the East End?'

'Some,' he said.

She took out the photograph and put it on the counter. 'This is Dan. Have you come across him at all, seen him around?'

The man looked at the wedding picture and suddenly smirked as if a penny had dropped. His gaze slid to her face and then down to her stomach, as if he expected to see a tell-tale bump. 'Done a runner, has he?'

Judith felt her cheeks redden. 'Not exactly. It's complicated.'

He carried on grinning at her. 'Sorry, I don't know the geezer. Like I said, you should try Taylor's.'

Judith left the shop with her face still blazing but with something new to think about. Maybe all the other people she'd shown the photograph to had jumped to the same conclusion. But so what if they had? Unless they'd been trying to cover for Dan, to put her off the scent. No, that was just ridiculous. Why would they protect him like that? Most of the people she'd talked to had been women. Wouldn't they be more inclined to take *her* side? But then again, she was a stranger, someone they'd never met before. Perhaps their loyalty would always lie with the local boy, whatever he might have done.

With her mind full of conflicting notions, she headed for Taylor's. On her way, she thought some more about the picture. If she folded it in two, then only Dan would be visible. She could use the same story she'd told the *Daily Mirror* photographer: that she was looking for her cousin. Perhaps then people would be more willing to help.

She went over to the doorway of a boarded-up shop, stopped and reached into her bag. It broke her heart to have to fold the photograph – she'd never get the crease out again – but she had to do it. There wasn't time to get a copy made. Anyway, if it meant she stood a better chance of finding Dan, it was worth the sacrifice. She gritted her teeth and quickly made the fold before she could change her mind.

She set off again, walking briskly towards the station. The sky had lightened and a thin glimmer of sunshine was breaking through the clouds. A good omen, perhaps. The last couple of hours hadn't exactly been fruitful. Things could only get better, right? She clung on to this hope as she headed for locksmith number two.

Taylor's was bigger and busier than the other shop. There was a short queue and she had to wait while keys were being cut. There were two men working, both small and round, with the same sandy-coloured hair and similar features. Definitely father and son. It was another five minutes before she finally made it to the counter. She painted on a smile and said to the older man, 'Hello. I'm looking for Dan Jonson. I don't suppose he works here, does he?'

'Who?'

'Dan Jonson,' she repeated. 'He's my cousin. We lost touch during the war and I'm trying to track him down. He's a locksmith. He used to live round here.' As she reached into her bag for the photograph, the man glanced over his shoulder.

66

'Jimmy, you ever heard of a bloke called Dan Jonson?'

The younger man stopped what he was doing. 'Can't say I have.'

'A locksmith, by all accounts. Wasn't there a Dan working over at Bailey's? Tall bloke.'

Judith's heart skipped a beat. 'Yes, he's tall.'

'No,' Jimmy said, 'there's no Dan there. You're thinking of Don Edwards, and he's long gone.'

'Am I? Yes, you could be right.'

Judith put the photograph on the counter. 'This is Dan.'

The older man gazed at it and shook his head. 'Can't say he looks familiar. Jimmy, come and take a gander at this.'

Judith watched Jimmy's reaction, and what she saw set her pulse racing. His eyes flicked from the picture to Judith and back to the picture. Indecision hovered on his face. There was a long pause – too long – before he too shook his head. 'No, I don't know him.'

He was lying. She was sure of it. 'You do. You recognise him, don't you?'

Jimmy grew defensive. 'I just said, didn't I? I've never seen him before in my life.'

'Look, I'm not here to cause any trouble, I swear. If you could just tell me where to find him and—'

'I can't tell you what I don't know, lady. I've never set eyes on the geezer.'

'Please,' she urged, 'if you know anything, anything at all. I really need some help here.'

But Jimmy remained unmoved by the plea. 'If I could, I would. Now I'm sorry but I have to get back to work.'

Judith turned to the older man in the vain hope that he would provide some support, but all he did was push the photograph back towards her.

'Sorry, love.'

Frustration made her want to storm round the counter, grab hold of Jimmy and shake the truth out of him. What was wrong with the man? She could sense, however, that no amount of persuasion – violent or otherwise – was going to make him change his mind. Not right now, at least. He had taken a position and was going to stick to it.

A new customer came into the shop and Judith was obliged to pick up the photograph and step aside. She hesitated, but knew there was no point in staying. This was a battle she wasn't going to win today. 'Thank you,' she said stiffly before walking out.

Back on the street, she took a moment to absorb what had just happened. If she was right – and she was certain she was – Jimmy had recognised Dan, but only from the picture. The name itself hadn't meant anything to him. When he'd been asked about Dan Jonson, he hadn't batted an eyelid. It was only when he'd come over to the counter that his whole demeanour had changed. She sucked in a breath as the full implication of this sank in: Dan *was* alive but he was using a different name. Or maybe Dan Jonson hadn't been his real name in the first place. That would explain a lot. Why no one remembered the Jonson family, for instance. Although there could be a more disturbing reason why nobody would talk.

She felt a chill run through her as she thought of Alfred Tombs. Could Dan be involved in something bad? No, she couldn't believe that of him. There had to be another explanation. But what? She remembered what Annie had said about men losing their memories, but even if that had happened, it didn't account for Jimmy's reaction.

Although she had intended to use one of the station payphones and call round all the locksmiths in the surrounding areas, she couldn't see the point now. Her only other option was to visit each one personally, showing the photograph without mentioning a name. She worried that it would be a waste of time, that no one would tell her anything even if they did recognise him, but with little else to go on, there was nothing to lose.

She went over to the bus stop and checked out the information on the board. She found there was a bus going to Shoreditch and decided that would be as good a place as any to continue the search. With the help of the *A–Z* she'd be able to find her way round. While she waited in the queue, she stared fiercely at Taylor's. She had to figure out what to say next time she approached Jimmy. She couldn't let it go. His lie was the one chink of light in what to date had been a pretty dismal day.

8

Judith didn't know how far she'd walked, how many miles she had covered, but her legs and feet were aching. And for what? Of all the locksmiths she had visited after Taylor's, none had identified Dan. The only thing her tour had produced was a nagging hunger – she hadn't eaten since breakfast – and a sense of alienation. There was something about the East End that disconcerted her. She was an outsider here, someone who didn't belong, and the knowledge made her uncomfortable.

It was getting on for four o'clock as she traipsed back up Kellston High Street towards the café. Maybe some food would revive her. She had spent all day talking to people who had nothing to tell, and the effort had been exhausting. What she needed now was a chair to sit down on and something to fill her stomach.

Connolly's was quiet, with only a few tables taken. She chose a seat by the window and looked over at the board where the day's specials were listed. Her budget was tight and she couldn't afford to spend too much on meals. Her gaze slid down the list as she looked for the cheapest option.

A thin, dark-haired waitress came over with a notepad. 'What can I get you?'

'Tea, please. And I'll have a baked potato.'

The girl scribbled it down. 'Anything else?'

Judith decided she might as well ask. She took the photo of Dan out of her bag and held it up. 'I'm looking for this man. I don't suppose you've seen him in here? Or anywhere else, come to that.'

The girl stared at the picture for a while, then shook her head. 'Sorry, I haven't. But I've not worked here long, so . . . ' She gave a shrug. 'Sorry.'

Judith nodded, unsurprised. She'd already got used to disappointment. 'Thanks anyway.'

She put the photograph away, settled back and gazed out of the window. Jimmy was still her only decent lead, but she'd have to tread carefully there. There was no point in approaching him again until she had a plan as to how she was going to do it. While she racked her brains, she watched the people going by, and the buses and cars. London was such a busy place. She'd thought Westport got crowded in summer, but it was nothing compared to here. Everyone seemed to be constantly on the move.

Her tea arrived and she drank it gratefully. She was parched. Glancing at her watch, she wondered if it was worth going to the West End and having a wander round for a couple of hours. But just the idea of it made her feel tired. No, she'd get an early night and start off fresh tomorrow. If she was going to check out the locksmiths around New Bond Street, she'd have to find a library close by and make another list. There were still plenty of businesses to visit in the East End too; she'd barely covered a quarter of them.

When her food arrived, she tried not to wolf it down. Never had a baked potato tasted so good. There was margarine on it

71

rather than butter, but even that didn't detract from its tastiness. When she'd finished, she put her knife and fork down and sat back with a sigh. Somehow things always seemed better when you had a full belly. She mustn't get downhearted. Her search had only just begun and there were bound to be setbacks.

The waitress came over and put another cup of tea in front of her with a smile. 'On the house, love. You look like you need it.'

'Oh, thank you.'

The girl pulled out a chair and sat down opposite her. 'I'm Elsa, by the way.'

'Judith.'

'So, Judith, who is he, this feller you're trying to find? That's if you don't mind me asking.'

Judith didn't mind. The waitress was the first person she'd met who'd actually shown any interest. 'My husband, Dan.'

'Ah, disappeared, has he?'

'It's a long story.'

'That's all right, I'm on a break. What makes you think he's in Kellston?'

'I don't know that he is. I only came here because it's where he grew up. I thought someone might remember him.' Judith hesitated, wondering how much she should tell, but there didn't seem any good reason for holding back. She quickly ran through it all, from the telegram telling her that Dan was missing to the photograph she'd seen last week in the *Daily Mirror*.

Elsa raised her eyebrows. 'So you think he's still alive?'

'I suppose it sounds crazy, but I've never really believed he was dead. And I know you'll think that's only wishful thinking or denial or whatever you want to call it, but it's how I feel. Sometimes you just know things. It's hard to explain.'

'Have you got the *Mirror* photo?'

Judith nodded, took it out of her bag and placed it on the

table. 'Here,' she said, pointing. 'This is Dan. He's got his face turned away, but I'm sure it's him.'

Elsa studied the photograph. She peered and frowned. 'Mm, it's not much to go on.'

'It's enough,' Judith said sharply. She could read the scepticism on the girl's face. 'I don't expect you to understand. Why would you?'

'I didn't mean it that way,' Elsa said. 'Honest, I didn't. All I meant was that London's not the easiest place to find someone – especially if they don't want to be found.'

'Sorry,' Judith said, regretting that she'd snapped. 'I'm just tired. I think I must have walked across half of east London today.'

'And not a sniff?'

'Well, there was a sniff as it happens.' Judith recounted what had taken place at Taylor's.

'So, you see, I'm pretty sure Jimmy recognised Dan from the photograph, but not from the name.'

'Which makes it tricky.'

'But at least I know he's out there somewhere, that I'm not just chasing after rainbows. If I could only get Jimmy to talk . . .'

Elsa glanced around the café, then leaned forward and lowered her voice. 'Oh, they won't tell you anything, not the people round here. You could show them a picture of the bleedin' King and they'd swear they'd never set eyes on him before. They close ranks if you're not one of them. Even if they do know where your old man is, they'll keep their mouths shut.'

'But why? I don't understand.'

'To protect him, love. And themselves. They'll figure if he wanted you to know where he was, he'd tell you himself. They won't put themselves on the line in case it comes back to haunt them.'

'So what can I do?'

Elsa gave a shrug.

Judith gestured towards the *Mirror* picture, still lying between them on the table. 'Do you know this man?' she asked, pointing to Tombs.

'No, I don't think so.'

'His name's Alfred Tombs. I think he's ... I don't know, a criminal of some sort.'

'Oh, he's that all right.'

'You've heard of him?'

'Everyone's heard of him. I mean, everyone round here. He runs the manor, doesn't he? And half the West End too.' Elsa looked more closely at the photograph. 'I think you're right. I've only seen him a couple of times, but ... yes, that could be him.'

'It's hard to tell whether they're together or not. Do you know where Tombs lives, or where I could find him?'

Elsa grimaced. 'You don't want to do that.'

'I don't see what choice I've got. In less than a week I'll have to go home. If I could ask Tombs directly, then—'

'Then he could tip Dan off that you're looking for him. And then what? He might just disappear again. Anyway, you need to stay away from the likes of Tombs. He's a gangster, love. He's dangerous.'

'I don't care what he is,' Judith said with more bravado than she felt. 'Apart from Jimmy, he's the only lead I've got. I could spend the next four days searching high and low, visiting every locksmith in London, and still come up with nothing.'

Elsa put her elbows on the table. 'Actually, I've just had a thought. There's a feller who knows a lot of people round here, from the priests to the villains and just about everyone in between. I could try and set up a meet if you like. I can't promise he'll be able to help, but he might.'

'Who is he, this man?'

'He's called Saul.'

Judith waited, but Elsa didn't elaborate. 'Saul?'

'That's all I know. It's up to you. Do you want me to ring him?'

'Yes, of course.'

'I won't be able to do it until later. Tell you what, come back tomorrow evening, about seven. Sit at one of the tables at the back, a corner one if it's free. It won't be busy at that time. If he hasn't turned up by half seven, you'll know he's not coming.'

It all seemed very cloak-and-dagger, but Judith was prepared to try anything. 'Will you be here?'

'No, I don't work Tuesdays.'

'What does he look like, this Saul?'

Elsa inclined her head and frowned. She stared into the middle distance while she thought about it. 'Ordinary,' she said. 'Average height, average build. Brown hair. Don't worry, he'll find you.'

'Will he want anything? I mean, will be expect to be paid?'

'No, he won't ask for any money.' A couple of customers came into the café. Elsa sighed, glanced at the clock on the wall, pushed back her chair and rose to her feet. 'I'd better get on. Good luck with everything. I hope you track him down.'

'Thanks. Thanks for all your help.'

'One last thing. Promise me you won't go near Tombs before you've talked to Saul. You don't want to get mixed up with the likes of him if you don't have to.'

'I won't,' Judith said. 'I promise.'

Elsa nodded and walked off.

Judith put the photographs back in her bag. She gazed out of the window while she finished her tea. It had been a stroke of luck, she thought, coming into Connolly's. The bill had come with the food, and she put the payment on the plate along with a generous tip for Elsa, then left the café. As she headed down the high street, her mood lightened considerably – it was amazing what some food, a bit of help and a friendly face could do – but her feet were still killing her. Her plan for the evening was to

75

go back to Sycamore House and study her *A–Z* before having an early night.

She was almost at the B&B when she saw Jimmy Taylor come out of the locksmith's and cross the road. As he got closer to her, she hesitated. She'd intended to think it over, how exactly she'd make her next approach, but deciding it was fate, she stepped right in front of him, blocking his path.

'Hello again.'

It took a moment before recognition dawned, and then his face fell. He tried to sidestep, to manoeuvre round her, but Judith wasn't having any of it. She moved too. The two of them did a little dance on the pavement, to the right, to the left, before he put his hands on his hips and glared at her.

'What do you want, lady? I don't know nothing. I've already told you.'

Judith smiled. 'Look, I know that you know who Dan is – and probably where he is too. So unless you want me to keep on coming to the shop, to keep on asking every single day until you're sick of the sight of me, why don't you just pass on a message? Tell him Judith's here. Tell him I'm staying at Sycamore House.' She made a brief gesture towards the B&B. 'Tell him I'm not going home until I've talked to him. All right?'

'I can't pass on a message to someone I don't know.'

'I'm sure you'll find a way.'

'I'm telling you, I don't—'

'Judith,' she repeated firmly, interrupting him. 'You can remember that, can't you?' And then before he could make any more protestations, she turned on her heel and flounced off. She wasn't used to confrontations, however mild, and her heart was beating fast. Had she done the right thing? She resisted the urge to glance over her shoulder. Jimmy's eyes were still on her – she was sure of it – but whether he was going to do as she asked remained to be seen.

9

Alf Tombs had assumed his listening pose: elbow on the arm of the chair, chin on his hand, head tilted slightly to the right. Renee was giving him the needle. The subject was a familiar one – he'd heard it a thousand times before – but he was letting her have her say. Maybe if she got it off her chest, he might eventually get some peace and quiet.

'You could give it all up. Why not? There's enough in the bank. You don't have to keep on with the jobs. We could start a little business, something legit, a caff or a pub perhaps. I'm a grafter, Alf. I'd make it work. We could do it together. Then I wouldn't need to be worrying about you day and night.'

'I'll think about it.'

Renee huffed out a breath. 'You always say that. You're fifty-two. You can't keep doing this for ever.'

Alf nodded as though she had a point, even though she didn't. A bloke like him couldn't just retire from his profession. There were people who depended on him: the men he worked with, the wives and kids of men inside, the fellers who had fallen on hard times and the endless list of relatives who expected his help even if they didn't deserve it. He was no Robin Hood; he simply understood that loyalty had a price. You had to keep people sweet if you wanted them to keep their mouths shut.

'We could make a real go of it,' she said. 'Our own little business, and no worries about a knock on the door in the middle of the night.'

What Renee didn't grasp was that the nice little business wouldn't last five minutes. Most of their customers would be crooked and too many would be after a free meal or a free pint or a free bloody anything. They'd be tapping him right, left and centre until all the profits had disappeared into thin air. No, it just wouldn't work. And anyway, he had a few years left in him yet. He wasn't ready to hang up his boots, no matter what Renee wanted.

A man got used to a certain lifestyle, and although he'd never been flash, he liked the good things in life: well-made suits and shirts and shoes, a decent haircut, wholesome food, a comfortable place to live and the occasional holiday. The Kellston flat wasn't fancy but it was big enough for the two of them, nicely furnished, with a bit of garden out back. He could have afforded something much grander, but he knew better than to flaunt his wealth. The filth picked up on that kind of thing. Of course, they knew he was at it, that he was always earning from one job or another, but it had been a good few years since they'd caught him in the act.

Renee sipped her tea and gazed wistfully at him. 'We could go to Kent, out in the country somewhere. Or a town if you'd prefer it.'

'Wouldn't you miss the Smoke?'

'I wouldn't miss you going AWOL for days at a time.'

'You know what it's like.'

'What it's like, love, is lonely. It's bad enough when you're banged up, but even when you're out, you're hardly home.'

Alf couldn't deny this. He often spent whole days on a job, and then there was business to sort out after: the shifting and sale of the gear, the distribution of the money, a few drinks with the lads. He was also running several spielers now, gambling joints where the games went on all night. It was easy money, with minimum risk. Occasionally the clubs would be raided and shut down by the law, but all they had to do was change location. Within a week a new club would open and it would be business as usual. Old Bill were always playing catch-up, always on the back foot.

'There's a few things in the pipeline, but after that—'

'After that, there'll be a few more things. I know what you're like. Why not knock it on the head? There's no risk in a caff and you won't have to be looking over your shoulder twenty-four hours a day.'

But what Alf liked was variety in his work. He couldn't imagine doing the same thing day in, day out. He'd die of boredom. No, he wasn't cut out for it. He'd had a good war, made and spent a fortune, but even now there were still plenty of opportunities out there. Supply and demand, that was what it was all about. With so many shortages, he had customers virtually queuing round the block for whisky and nylons and furs.

'Maybe in the new year,' he said. 'We'll see how it goes.'

'The new year,' she echoed. 'What's going to be different then?'

Alf didn't bother to answer. He couldn't fault Renee as a wife – she'd stuck by him through thick and thin – but the woman didn't understand that what he did was what he was. Crime was a way of life to him, had been since he was a boy. And he'd worked hard to get where he was today, using his brains as well as his muscle. Now that he was at the top of the tree, he wasn't going to climb down just because Renee was shaking the branches. There'd come a time when he was too old for the business, when he could no longer command the respect he needed, but that time wasn't here yet.

He shifted his hand and examined the bruises on his knuckles. Monaghan had got what he deserved. He'd chivved him too, run the blade right down his cheek so everyone would know that Alf Tombs had sorted it. Monaghan had stolen from him, taken the cash that was supposed to be delivered to Ruby Beech – her old man was doing a five-stretch for robbery – and put it in his own pocket. The thieving bastard had been taught a lesson, one he'd remember every morning when he looked in the mirror. If you let one lowlife take a liberty, the rest wouldn't be far behind.

There was a knock on the door and he got up to answer it.

'I thought you were staying in this evening,' Renee said.

'I am. I promised, didn't I?'

She gave him a look as if to say that his promises didn't count for much.

Alf opened the door to find Jimmy Taylor standing on the front step. 'What can I do for you, son?'

'Sorry to disturb you, Mr Tombs, but I reckoned I should let you know. There's been a piece asking after Doyle. She's been in the shop with a photo. And not just our place neither; she's been all over from what I've heard.'

'And?' Alf asked, wondering why he was being bothered by this.

'I don't know where to find him and . . . Well, I reckon she's out to cause trouble. Said I should pass a message on that she ain't going home until she's talked to him. Judith, that's her name. She's staying at Sycamore House on Station Road. Thing is, Mr Tombs, she claims she's his cousin, but she calls him Dan, so . . .' He shrugged. 'She can't be, can she? I reckoned he ought to know.'

Had it had been to do with any of the other boys, Alf would

80

have laughed it off – it wasn't the first or the last time a bloke had lied to a woman about his identity – but because it was Doyle, he thought twice. Maybe he should follow it up. It was probably something and nothing, just some dewy-eyed tart with a broken heart, but if she started poking her nose into Doyle's business, she'd be poking it into his too. And he didn't need that right now, not with a couple of big jobs in the offing.

He reached into his back pocket, took out his wallet and offered Jimmy a note. 'Here, have this for your trouble.'

'Ah, no, Mr Tombs, I'm not after . . . I don't want any money. I just wanted to let you know.'

'All right, son, ta. I appreciate it.' When the lad continued to stand there, Alf asked, 'Was there something else?'

Jimmy shook his head. 'I'll be off, then.'

Alf nodded, went back inside and put on his hat. He poked his head into the living room. 'I've got to go out. I'll only be an hour.'

'I'll expect you when I see you.'

'An hour,' he repeated. 'I've some business but it won't take long.'

Renee didn't ask what sort of business. She never did. She just raised her eyes to the ceiling.

Outside, the air was still and heavy, as though a summer storm was on its way. He got into the car and adjusted the rear-view mirror, keeping his eyes peeled for the law. From time to time they liked to follow him around, trying to keep tabs on where he was going and who he was meeting. The problem was that they weren't very good at it. He could always spot a tail, and feel it too, like a sixth sense prickling the back of his neck. It was good sport losing them and never took long. He knew Kellston up and down and back to front: every twisting street, every alleyway, every short cut that had ever existed.

This evening, however, he was on his own. A few spots of rain dotted the windscreen as he pulled out. He lit a fag and pondered on Doyle. Woman trouble. Well, he wasn't alone there. Renee would already be totting up her resentments, preparing a bill for when he got home. He didn't mind staying in with her once in a while, not if it kept her happy, but sometimes he wondered if it was worth the bother. Maybe the relationship had run its course. They had always wanted different things, and always would.

Alf trusted Doyle, insofar as he trusted anyone. The bloke wasn't the sort to shoot his mouth off about what he'd done or what he was planning to do; he kept his head down and stayed away from trouble. But he was difficult to read. You never really knew what he was thinking. People talked about honour amongst thieves, but it was all rubbish. When push came to shove, it was every man for himself.

Greyness had fallen, a premature dusk, and there was that feeling of everything holding its breath. Alf heard a distant rumble of thunder. He sucked on his fag and threw the butt out of the window. The heavens opened as he approached Old Street, the clouds releasing long, driving rods of rain that battered the road in front of him. He drove on to City Road, took a right and wound round to Ironmonger Row, past the baths, pulling in by a small terraced house.

He waited for a while, hoping the rain would ease, but when it showed no sign of abating, he ran from the car up the path and into the shelter of a small porch. He brushed the rain off his shoulders, raised his hand and gave a couple of knocks on the blue door. It was answered by Doyle, clearly surprised to see him.

'Alf. What brings you here? Is there a problem?'

Alf peered past him into the hall and kept his voice low. 'Are you on your own?'

As if in response, a female voice drifted from the back of the house. 'Who is it, Ivor? Is it for me?'

Doyle glanced over his shoulder. 'No, it's not for you.' He moved forward into the porch, pulling the door to behind him. 'I'd invite you in, but you know how it is.'

'It's all right. I understand.'

'Is there trouble?'

'There might be – for you. There's a woman in Kellston claiming to be your cousin. She's been doing the rounds of the local locksmiths trying to track you down.'

Doyle frowned. 'It must be a mistake. I haven't got any cousins.'

'That's what I thought, but from all accounts she won't take no for an answer. Reckons she's going nowhere until you talk to her. Says her name's Judith.'

At the mention of the name, Doyle recoiled as if he'd been hit, his body colliding with the door frame. 'Judith? What? It can't be. She can't be . . . '

Alf didn't think he'd ever seen a face turn so grey. 'Easy does it,' he said, stretching out a hand to steady the man. 'Christ, you look like you just saw a ghost.'

10

Saul Hannah lay back on the bed with his hands behind his head. He watched through half-closed eyes as Elsa moved around the room picking up her clothes from where she'd dropped them on the floor. She had a feline quality, something almost feral, like a wild cat quietly patrolling its territory. He had no idea what went on in her mind. Even when they were having sex, when he was inside her, when he was looking straight into her face, there was no real connection between them. They were like strangers who met and fucked and went their separate ways. Except they kept on doing it.

Outside, the rain was thrashing against the window, making the glass shudder and shake. His breathing was starting to settle now, his heart rate slowing, his thoughts regathering into short, straight, practical lines. He stretched out his legs and wriggled his toes. He felt the sweat cooling on his skin. Her smell was still on him, the scent of perfume and that other distinctive female odour. He sniffed, leaned over to grab his jacket and took out a pack of cigarettes.

'Are you making a brew?' he asked.

Elsa slipped into a robe, covering her nakedness. 'Does it look like it?'

'I wouldn't mind one – if it's not too much bother.'

She pulled a face, sighed and left the room. A short while after, he heard the hiss of the gas ring and the clatter of the kettle. He lit a fag and smoked it while he got dressed. Then he went through to join her.

The living room of Elsa's basement flat was small but tidy, with everything arranged to make the most of the limited space. It was stylish, he supposed, in an inexpensive sort of way. Not exactly to his taste, but then his taste was purely functional. There was no separate kitchen, just a corner reserved for a few cupboards and the gas rings. Two easy chairs were covered in a matching stripy fabric, and he chose the one furthest from the window. On the wall directly ahead was a large framed print of three women gathered at the base of a tree. Gauguin, he guessed, but wasn't sure. He wasn't big on art. The clothes were bright, the tree cobalt blue. He shifted his gaze again. To his right was a folding table, and on it was a half-full bottle of whisky and a vase containing a bunch of white roses.

'So what's new?' he asked.

Elsa had her back to him as she filled the teapot with hot water. 'One of the Rossini brothers – the younger one, the one with the limp – he's been flogging petrol coupons. He was at it in the caff, bold as brass. All fakes, of course. They must be. That lot are too lazy to do any actual robbing.'

Saul nodded. There would be no end to the forgeries until the austerity measures were lifted. God alone knew how many printing presses were churning out fake coupons, some of them better than others, but all of them instantly snapped up by drivers desperate to keep their cars on the road.

'You seen anything of Roy Monaghan?'

Elsa glanced over her shoulder. 'No, not for a few days. Have you tried the Black Lion?'

'Yes, and the Fox, and every other pub, bar and dive he usually hangs out in.'

'Is it true about him and Alf Tombs?'

'What have you heard?'

Elsa gave the pot a stir and put the teaspoon in the sink. 'Same as everyone else, I expect. They're saying he took some money, that Alf gave him a hiding. He's a lowlife, that Monaghan. He'd nick the last crust of bread from his grandma.'

Saul stared at the bottle of whisky, feeling that familiar thirst rising in his throat. She must have seen him looking, because she asked, 'You want a shot?' The answer to that was yes, but he resisted the temptation. He had a late meeting at Scotland Yard in an hour and it wouldn't do to turn up stinking of Scotch. 'I'll stick with the tea, thanks.'

Elsa came over with two mugs, handed one to him and sat down in the other chair. 'I had a girl come into the caff this afternoon. She's searching for her old man, thinks he might be in Kellston somewhere. I've arranged for you to see her tomorrow in Connolly's, seven o'clock if that's all right.'

Saul frowned. 'Since when did I become the missing persons department? I don't do absent husbands.'

'Hear me out first. Believe me, this girl's got a story. Her name's Judith and her husband was reported missing during the war. Nothing unusual about that, but then she opens a newspaper last week and who should she see in a photo but her darling Dan standing in the middle of New Bond Street.'

'Fascinating,' he said drily. 'I still don't see why this should concern me.'

'Will you listen? I haven't finished yet. It's who he was standing with that's interesting.' She left a short, dramatic pause. 'None other than Alf Tombs!'

Saul's ears pricked up. 'Are you sure?'

'Of course I'm sure. Now I didn't recognise this Dan bloke myself, but Jimmy Taylor did – you know, the locksmith on Station Road – 'cept he pretended he didn't. She's been showing that photo all over Kellston but no one's given her the time of day. She reckons Dan's using a different name, as Jimmy only reacted when he looked at the picture.'

'Why Kellston?'

'This is where he grew up, apparently.'

'And what does this Dan look like?'

'He's in his late thirties, fair hair, very blond. You can see the photo for yourself if you turn up tomorrow. Anyway, I thought the Tombs angle might grab you.' Elsa leaned back, crossed her legs and sipped her tea. 'How I figure it, for what it's worth, is that this Dan got a little overenthusiastic during the war. He met Judith, had the hots for her, and decided the only way he was going to get into her pants was to marry her. Anyhow, he has his fun, rejoins his regiment and then gets cold feet about the whole thing. When he has the good fortune to be missing in action, he sees a way out. He comes back to London, changes his name and starts a new life – perhaps even gets married again. With Judith believing she's a widow, he doesn't have to worry about her showing up on his doorstep. At least that's what he thinks. Then a press photographer snaps him in a street, she sees the picture and it's game over.'

Saul rolled the idea around in his head. As theories went, it wasn't such a bad one, but there was a flaw. 'It's impossible to take on a new identity in a place where people know you. Why come back here at all? Why not go somewhere new, somewhere no one's going to recognise you or ask tricky questions?'

'Mm,' Elsa said, 'you've got a point. Maybe it was the other way round. Maybe he was already married and came back to his original wife and kids. You're the detective, you figure it out.

87

The one sure thing is that the bloke isn't going to be happy about Judith being on the scene, especially if there's a bigamy charge looming on the horizon. And even if there isn't, I shouldn't think he'll relish the thought of seeing her again. If you can make it all go away, make *her* go away, it could give you some leverage.'

What she meant by leverage, Saul surmised, was information on Alf Tombs. And he couldn't deny that the idea was appealing; every good cop wanted that villain off the street. It would be a major achievement to get him behind bars again. In his head, he was already going through all the men he knew of who worked with Tombs and who would match the description. He already had one in mind, but first he'd have to check that photograph.

Elsa put down her mug and rose to her feet. 'I'm going to get dressed.' As she walked across the room, she added, 'That Judith won't give up in a hurry. She's even talking about approaching Tombs direct, so if you don't want her to do that, I'd make sure you meet her at the caff tomorrow.'

Saul nodded. 'I'll be there.'

'She's a redhead, pretty. I told her to sit at the back.'

'I'll find her.'

'I'm sure you will.'

Saul waited until the bedroom door had closed before standing up and taking out his wallet. He removed a couple of notes, laid them on the table beside the bottle of whisky and left without saying goodbye.

11

At breakfast Judith devoured her bacon and eggs and as much toast as she could manage, determined to get her seven bob's worth. With food rationing still in place, she wondered where the B&B got its supplies from, but thought it best not to enquire too closely. Even in Westport there was a black market operating for basic goods, and in London you could probably get anything you wanted – so long as you had the money. She was as guilty as the next person when it came to buying illicit goods; the war, she suspected, had made cheats of them all.

Mrs Jolly, wife to the man who had booked her in, served breakfast in the dining room at the front of the house. There was only one big table and so everyone had to sit together. Judith had been relieved to discover that her three fellow guests, all middle-aged males, had almost finished their meal by the time she arrived, and so she was spared the awkwardness of having to make small talk while she ate.

The house was only a few yards from the road, and she could see and feel the red double-decker buses as they rumbled past. The traffic had woken her early in the morning, the noise lifting her out of a long, dreamless sleep. There had been the heavy tread of footsteps too, like a small army marching by. Voices had risen up to her window, early morning greetings and brief snippets of conversations.

As she gazed out through the net curtains, Judith wondered why the place was called Sycamore House. The only tree in sight was a spindly elm, and even that was ten feet away. She might have asked Mrs Jolly about it if the woman's demeanour had matched her name, but the landlady's face had a sour, dejected expression, as though life was in the process of wearing her down: she traipsed back and forth from the kitchen, clearing plates and cups and teapots, her sighs echoing around the dining room. Anyway, Judith wasn't really interested in how the B&B had acquired its name. She was just looking for a distraction, something to think about other than her search for Dan.

As soon as she'd finished breakfast, she left the house, glancing up at the low cloud-filled sky and scooting across the road just as the first drops of rain began to fall. Yesterday's storm had briefly cleared the atmosphere, but now the air was growing heavy and oppressive again. She put up her umbrella and joined the queue. Fortunately, she didn't have to wait long for a bus. As it travelled towards the West End, she kept her face close to the window, her eyes scanning every face they passed.

The roads grew increasingly busy as the journey continued, with cars and buses and taxis all jostling for position. There was a downpour that obscured her view for a while, the rain battering hard against the glass. As more passengers joined the bus, it began to smell of perspiration and wet coats. Her thoughts turned away from her surroundings and towards the mysterious Saul. Would he be able to help? If Elsa was right about nobody in the East End talking to strangers, he could be her once chance to crack that wall of silence. She wished she didn't have so long to wait. Seven o'clock seemed like a hundred lifetimes away.

Judith got off the bus at Oxford Circus and joined the throng. Crowds of people were rushing in and out of the Tube as if their lives depended on it. Everything seemed to move quickly in London, everyone in a mad dash to get somewhere. Following suit, she walked briskly, heeding Annie's warnings about thieves and keeping one hand tightly on her bag. She knew exactly where she was going – last night's study of the *A–Z* had been time well spent – and soon found New Bond Street leading off to the left.

It didn't take long to grasp why this part of Mayfair was a target for crime. The stores were the most expensive she'd ever come across, the goods all top of the range: clothes, art, antiques and jewellery. She discovered the shop in the photograph about thirty yards down the road. The door had been repaired and there was no indication now of the damage that had been caused by the thieves. She shifted to the side of the pavement, took the *Mirror* picture out of her bag, examined it and then walked a little further along until she was in the exact spot where Dan had been standing. It made her tremble to think that less than a week ago he had been right here, his feet on this bit of pavement, his living, breathing body occupying this single piece of space.

The minutes passed and still she didn't move. This spot was her connection to him and she didn't want to relinquish it. Her gaze shifted from the jeweller's and travelled up and down the street. Where had he been coming from when he'd stumbled upon the scene, and where had he been going? Maybe if she carried on standing here all day and night for a week or a month, he would eventually pass this way again.

Knowing that such a vigil was hardly practical, she set off again as another heavy shower set in. She put up her umbrella and for the next hour walked up and down the street, sidestepping the puddles and watching the people. She peered into shop windows, each one an Aladdin's cave of gold and diamonds, silks and furs, pondering on who could actually afford to shop here. Well, the rich, she supposed, the lucky few who didn't have to think twice about spending a fortune on a coat or a necklace.

Eventually, when it was obvious that Dan wasn't going to miraculously appear, she made her way back to Oxford Street. She came across a newsagent, went in, bought a paper and asked where the nearest locksmith was.

'There's one in Coventry Street,' the woman said. 'Piccadilly. Do you know the way? It's just past the Lyons' Corner House.'

Judith nodded. 'Thanks. I'll find it.' As she left the shop, she wondered if it was obvious she was a stranger to the city. She'd been trying her best to blend in, but perhaps her best wasn't good enough. Everything about her – her accent, her clothes – marked her out as being different.

She retraced her steps along New Bond Street, into Old Bond Street and then on to Piccadilly. If she had thought Oxford Street was hectic, it was nothing compared to Piccadilly Circus. The place was jam-packed, a heaving mass of humanity, a mix of rich and poor, black and white, thin and fat and everything in between. She heard male American accents as she passed through the crowd: GIs, perhaps, who had never returned home. There was a constant rush of traffic, a roar of engines and a beeping of horns. The buildings were covered in bright advertisements for Bovril, chewing gum and Guinness.

As she stopped to get her bearings, she had a sudden feeling of panic. How easy it would be to just disappear in a city this size, to slip between the cracks in the pavement and never be seen again. No one, not a soul, knew exactly where she was at this moment. She quickly glanced left and right, up and down, as though an unforeseen danger might be hurtling towards her.

Before she could become completely overwhelmed, she hurried on. *Pull yourself together, Judith.* She was a grown-up, almost thirty, and more than capable of taking care of herself.

Finding the Lyons' Corner House wasn't difficult. It was a large, imposing building, the restaurant spread over a number of floors. For some reason, the sight of it made her feel better, perhaps because there was a Lyons' in Liverpool too. It seemed a safe and familiar place, somewhere she could seek sanctuary if the need arose. Maybe later she would get a cup of tea there and something to eat.

The locksmith was a few yards into Coventry Street. She didn't hold out much hope as she marched into the shop, the photograph of Dan already clasped in her hand. There were no customers there, only a man behind the counter who was old and wizened, with a pair of glasses perched on the end of his nose.

'Hello,' Judith said, smiling brightly. 'Sorry to bother you, but I'm looking for my cousin. He's a locksmith, you see, and ... well, we lost touch during the war.' She passed the picture over without mentioning a name. 'I don't suppose you recognise him? I was hoping he might be working round here.'

'Now, let me see.' The old man moved his glasses up his nose and took a close look. Then he moved the photo away from him and studied it from a distance. 'Not round here, love,' he said. 'Sorry. I know all the local lads.'

Judith, who hadn't been expecting anything else, nodded and held out her hand for the photograph. 'Thanks anyway. Sorry to bother you.'

But the man wasn't finished yet. Frowning slightly, he continued to stare at the picture. 'I'll tell you what, though, he does remind me of someone. It's been a long time since I've seen him, mind. He looks a bit like Ron Doyle's boy. Now what was he called? It's just on the tip of my tongue.' His frown grew deeper and then suddenly cleared. 'I've got it! *Ivor*, Ivor Doyle! Is this him?'

Judith had a split second to make a decision. In that moment, with nothing to lose, she decided to run with it. 'Yes, Ivor, that's right. The family used to live in Kellston.'

'Kellston, was it? Could have been. I was thinking Shoreditch, but it was a long time ago.' He tapped his forehead. 'The memory's not what it used to be. You get to my age, you're lucky if you can remember where you live yourself.'

She smiled, trying to keep her voice light. 'I can't find a trace. I've asked around, but I can't find anyone who knew them.'

'Well, Ron and his missus are long gone, ain't they? The shop closed down in . . . well, it must be getting on for twenty years.' He gave the photograph back to her. 'Ivor's cousin, eh? Fancy that.'

'On my mother's side,' she lied. 'I'm in London for a few days, so I thought I'd try and track him down. It's a shame to lose touch, isn't it?' Even while she was speaking, Judith was furiously trying to think of what else she could ask that might lead to definitive proof that Dan and Ivor were one and the same person. 'So, when was the last time you saw Ivor?'

'Ah, hard to say. Probably not since Ron's funeral.'

As she could hardly ask when Ron had died – as 'family', this was a fact she should already be aware of – she could only take a guess that it was around the same time the shop had closed. 'Poor Ivor,' she said. 'It was hard for him. He wasn't very old then, was he?'

'That's right. He was just a lad.'

She wondered what constituted a 'lad' in the man's eyes – it could be any age from five to thirty-five. She tried a different tack. 'Ivor used to have a friend called Dan Jonson. I'm sure he was a locksmith too. I don't suppose that name rings any bells with you?'

He shook his head. 'No, can't say it does. I used to know a Dan Berryman – or was it Barryman? Covent Garden, that was his patch back in the day. But we're talking the early thirties and he was getting on then, so that's not much use to you. Sorry, love.'

'You can't think of anyone else who might be able to help?'

'I can't, love, not off the top of my head. But be sure to say hello if you find him. Tell him Harry Cole was asking after him.'

'Yes, I will.' Judith was still trying to think of any other avenue she could pursue when a couple of workmen walked in. She picked up the photograph and put it in her bag. 'Thanks anyway.'

'You take care now.'

Back on the street, Judith didn't know what to think. Could she trust Harry's memory? He was getting on, and a likeness wasn't a positive identification. She didn't want to believe that Dan was actually Ivor Doyle – it would mean he was someone else, someone she had never really known – but she couldn't dismiss the possibility. And if Harry was right, she was a few steps closer to finding her husband. That had to be a good thing, didn't it? Suddenly, she wasn't so sure. For the first time since her search had begun, she was starting to have doubts. What if the man she had married turned out to be a total stranger to her – a liar, a deceiver, a cheat? She paled, her stomach twisting. The thought of such a betrayal was enough to take her breath away.

12

By seven o'clock, Judith was a bundle of nerves. She'd arrived ten minutes early for her appointment with Saul and, as instructed, had chosen a table at the rear of the café. Her eyes rose again and again to the clock on the wall, to the second hand sweeping slowly round the face. Although she had made a number of telephone calls to various locksmiths during the afternoon, this time asking if Ivor Doyle worked there, she had been met with the same answer over and over again. No one had heard of him. Or so they said. She didn't know who or what to believe any more.

Connolly's was quiet, but the noise in her head more than made up for it. While she sipped her tea, she was inwardly debating the chances of Ivor and Dan being one and the same. *Ivor Doyle.* She rolled the name, like a heavy stone, from one part of her mind to another. No, she couldn't trust old Harry, not after so many years had passed. But what if he was right? She was sure that Jimmy Taylor, the Kellston locksmith, had recognised Dan's photo. It was only the name that had been wrong.

She racked her brains, trying to remember the conversations

96

she'd had with Dan. If only she'd asked him what his parents' Christian names had been. But it wasn't the sort of question that had ever occurred to her. What she did know was that his mother had passed when he was a child, his father when he was seventeen. Except ... was any of that true? If Dan wasn't his real name, then maybe nothing else was either.

The minutes went by, and at twenty past seven, she was convinced the meeting wasn't going to happen. It was at that very moment that the door to the café opened and a man walked in. He was in his early forties, slim, brown-haired, ordinary-looking. She stared. Was it him? He matched the description, vague as it was, that Elsa had given her. She watched him brush the summer rain from the shoulders of his overcoat before he casually scanned the room. Their eyes met and he strolled over to her table.

'You must be Judith,' he said as he pulled out a chair and sat down opposite her. 'Sorry I'm late. Something came up.'

'It's all right.'

'Let me get you another drink. Tea, is it?' Before she could reply, he'd beckoned over the waitress. 'A couple of teas, please, love.' He turned his attention back to Judith. 'So, you're looking for your husband. Elsa's explained the situation. Do you have the photograph with you?'

Judith hesitated. Although there was nothing overtly disturbing about Saul, she had a sudden feeling of unease. In truth, she didn't know this man from Adam, and seeing as most people had gone out of their way *not* to talk to her, she questioned his motives. 'Look, I don't mean to be rude, but who are you exactly?'

'What did Elsa tell you?'

'Only your name, and that you know a lot of people.'

'That just about sums it up.'

Judith frowned. 'But it doesn't explain why you're here, why you're offering to help.'

'Does it matter?'

'Yes,' she said. 'I think it does.'

Saul leaned forward, put his elbows on the table and lowered his voice. 'If you want the truth, I'm a police officer.'

Judith shrank back, startled. 'What? No, I don't understand. I never asked for . . . I don't want the police involved. This is nothing to do with—'

'It's all right,' he said softly. 'This isn't anything official. It's off the record, a favour if you like. Elsa asked me to help. She felt sorry for you.'

'I don't want to get him into trouble. That's not why I came to London. I just . . . I just want to find him, to talk to him.'

'I get that. You don't have to worry. There's only one condition attached to my help, and that's that you don't tell anyone, anyone at all, about this meeting or about Elsa. She's put herself on the line for you. If anyone found out . . . well, the people round here don't like cops much. There could be repercussions for her, unpleasant ones.'

Judith stared at him. She didn't want to be involved with the police, either on or off the record, but what choice did she have? If she was going to uncover the truth about Dan, she had to grab any leads that came her way. 'I won't tell anyone, I promise. You have my word.'

The waitress came with the teas and they both fell silent.

After she'd gone, Saul said, 'Would you like to show me the photograph?'

Judith drew it out of her bag and laid it on the table in front of him. 'This is Dan, although I don't think he's calling himself that now.' She watched his face for any sign of recognition, but there was none. 'Do you know him?'

Saul gave a light shrug of his shoulders. 'I'm not sure.'

This wasn't the answer she'd been hoping for. 'What do you mean?' she responded sharply. 'Either you do or you don't.'

He looked up from the photograph, his eyebrows arching. 'Do you have any idea how many men of his age live in London? He looks familiar, but I can't say a hundred per cent. I'll have to check it out, have a search through the records back at the office.'

'Why would you have a record of him there?'

'Why do you think?'

'He isn't a criminal.'

Saul's expression bordered on the smug. 'But he does hang out with that great pillar of the community, Alfred Tombs?'

Judith wasn't liking Saul much. 'I've no idea if he "hangs out" with him or not. Just because they're standing together doesn't mean they know each other.'

'But you're worried they might.'

Judith didn't answer.

'Do you have the newspaper picture with you?'

She dug into her bag again and pulled it out. 'Here,' she said.

Saul nodded. 'Yes, that's Tombs all right.'

'And that's Dan,' she said, placing a finger on the man to his right. 'They could have just stopped at the same time, couldn't they? There's a small crowd. It doesn't have to mean anything.'

Saul glanced between the two pictures. 'You did well recognising him from this. I don't think I would have done.'

'You weren't married to him.'

'And you're absolutely sure it's the same person?'

'Yes,' she said, putting as much conviction into her voice as she could muster. This wasn't the time for doubts or hesitations. 'I'm sure.'

'Tell me about what's happened. Elsa's given me an outline, but I'd like to hear it from you.'

Judith hurried through the story. She stuck to the facts, omitting any unnecessary detail, everything from her first meeting with Dan to when she saw the picture in the *Mirror*. After she'd finished, she took a quick breath and added, 'Does the name Ivor Doyle mean anything to you?'

'Where does that come from?'

'I've been doing the rounds of the locksmiths, showing them the photo. One of them, a chap in the West End, came up with it. He seemed to think he recognised him. So, have you heard the name before?'

'Ivor Doyle,' Saul repeated. The space between his eyes creased into two deep lines. 'There's a few Doyles around the East End. I'll check it out.'

Judith felt a growing sense of disappointment. For a man who was supposed to know so many people, he wasn't coming up with much. Perhaps Elsa had exaggerated the extent of his social circles. 'Thank you.'

He drank some tea and put the mug down. 'That's if you're certain you want me to go ahead.'

'Why wouldn't I?'

'Because you might not like what I find out.'

Judith smiled grimly. 'Nothing could be worse than not knowing. I can't spend the rest of my life wondering why he didn't come home. I need the truth, however much it might hurt.'

'It's easy to say, but you might feel differently when you're actually faced with it.'

'I won't shoot the messenger, if that's what you're worried about.'

'I'd rather you didn't.'

'And I won't fall to pieces or do anything stupid. I'll deal with it, whatever it is. At least I'll know. They say ignorance is bliss, but it isn't. There's nothing worse than being in the dark.'

Saul nodded. 'If he's in London, I can find him. But you'll have to be patient. It may take a little time.'

'How much time?'

'I'll know more in a day or two. Why don't we meet back here on Thursday? Seven o'clock again. Would that suit you?'

'Thursday?'

'Is that a problem?'

'No, except . . . well, it could be. I'm only in London until the weekend, you see. It doesn't give me much time.'

Saul drummed out a beat on the table with his fingertips. His mouth twisted a little, perhaps in irritation. 'I can't perform miracles.'

'No, of course not.'

There was a short silence.

He expelled a light breath, glanced at the photographs and back at Judith. 'All right. I'll see what I can do. Meet me here tomorrow at seven.'

'Thank you.'

He drained his mug, stood up and left. Judith put the photographs back in her bag. She continued to sit for a while, wondering if she was any further along than when she'd arrived. It still bothered her that Saul was a police officer. She'd been raised to respect the law and those who upheld it, but she found him rather sinister. If Dan was in some kind of trouble, mixed up with this Tombs man, would Saul really turn a blind eye? She sighed. It was too late to do anything about it. The wheels were already in motion.

By the time she left the café, the rain had stopped. Night was falling and the grey pavement glistened in the twilight. She walked slowly, deep in thought, hoping she would get some answers before she had to go home on Saturday. If she could, she would stay an extra day, but travelling was tricky on a Sunday.

It was when she was approaching the junction with Station Road, her mind beginning to focus on her surroundings again, that she was struck by the disturbing notion that she was being watched. It was a weird sixth-sense thing, a tingling on the back of her neck, an inexplicable knowledge that somebody's gaze was on her. Quickly she glanced over her shoulder, but her view was blocked by a group of girls who were walking four abreast, their arms linked together. As she tried to peer round them, she thought she saw a figure scurry down an alleyway. Or was it just her imagination? She hurried on towards the B&B, eager to get behind closed doors.

13

Jimmy Taylor slunk along the alley, relieved that he'd got away with it. He wasn't sure why he'd been following her. Just for the hell of it, he supposed. And because he wanted to get his own back. He hadn't liked the way she'd talked to him yesterday, as if he was some kind of liar. And yes, all right, so he *had* been lying, but that wasn't the point. She had no right to speak to him like that. The stupid tart didn't even know Ivor Doyle's real name.

Jimmy hadn't lied to protect Ivor – he barely knew the bloke – but in order to ingratiate himself with Alfred Tombs. Mr Tombs was number one round here. If you wanted to get on, he was the one to work for. There were plenty of villains in the East End, but none of them were as smart or as successful. Trouble was, people were queuing to get in on the act and Jimmy was at the back of the line. It didn't help that he was an outsider. The locals didn't trust strangers, and you didn't stop being a stranger in a hurry.

It was three years now since Jimmy's father had decided to up sticks, leave the sleepy south coast town he'd been born in and bring his family to live in London. There were prospects in the capital, that was what he'd said. The streets might not be paved with gold, but there were plenty of new buildings needed after the Blitz, and new buildings needed doors, and doors needed locks.

Jimmy had ambitions too, but they weren't the same as his dad's. The locksmith business involved long hours, with small rewards. Yes, there was a living to be made, but it was a basic one. Big money, that was what he was after. The girls round here – the good-looking ones, at least – didn't look twice unless you could flash the cash. His meagre salary wasn't going to impress anyone.

What he had to do was prove to Mr Tombs that he could be trusted, and that he could be useful to him. He'd made a start, but now he had to build on it. At nineteen, he had his whole life ahead of him, and he didn't intend to waste it cutting keys for gossipy old ladies. London was full of opportunities, there for the taking, and he wasn't going to stand by and watch them slip through his fingers.

He pushed his hands into his pockets and kept on walking until he reached another alley that wound round onto Station Road. Maybe the redhead – Judith, that was her name – could be the solution to his problems. As yet, he didn't know exactly how or why, but her connection to Doyle was interesting. He'd been locking up the shop, intending to go for a pint, when he'd seen her leave the B&B with a worried expression on her face. It had been an impulse to follow and see what she was up to.

When she'd gone into Connolly's, he'd been tempted to go inside too, but hadn't dared. The caff was quiet and she might have noticed him. Instead, he'd crossed the road and sheltered in the doorway of the butcher's. By the time twenty minutes had passed, he'd been starting to feel like a fool. The woman was only having a brew. It was then, just as he was about to leave, that the bloke had arrived.

Jimmy didn't know who he was, but she'd talked to him for fifteen minutes or so. And he was pretty certain she'd shown him the photograph. He'd been too far away to see clearly, but she'd definitely taken something out of her bag and passed it across the table. So what was going on? Something that spelled trouble for Doyle, that was for sure. Maybe the bloke was one of those private detectives who made a living from rooting around in other people's dirty laundry. Not a cop, he thought. He didn't look like a cop, and anyway, Jimmy knew most of the local constabulary by sight. Some of them even drank in the Fox.

He might have followed the man, tried to find out who he was, if it hadn't been pissing down with rain. Instead he'd waited to see what Judith would do next. In the event, it hadn't been that fascinating. Ten minutes later, after the rain had stopped, she'd come out and headed back along the high street. He'd kept his distance, letting a group of girls get between them. It was a good thing he'd been careful, or she would have clocked him when she glanced over her shoulder.

By the time he made it back onto Station Road, there was no sign of her. She must have gone into Sycamore House. As he drew level with the B&B, he resisted the urge to look up at the windows and instead crossed the road and went into the Fox. After his unplanned spying mission, he was in need of a drink.

At the bar, while he was waiting to be served, Jimmy's gaze roamed over the barmaid's curves. She was a blonde in her early twenties with a narrow waist and a good pair of tits. He didn't stand a chance, but a man could dream.

'Pint of mild, please, love.'

'Coming up.'

'You're new, aren't you? I've not seen you here before.'

'That's right.'

'How are you finding it, then?'

She gave a dry smile. 'Oh, it's easy, hon. I just took a right turn out of the station and here it was.'

Jimmy stared blankly back at her.

'It's a joke,' she said. 'Never mind.'

Jimmy didn't like it when people laughed at him. Was she? He wasn't sure. His eyes narrowed into slits while he tried to figure it out. He couldn't always tell with girls; they had a language of their own, a way of saying one thing when they really meant another. He pursed his lips. She wouldn't mock if he was working for Alf Tombs. She'd show him some bloody respect.

The blonde pulled his pint, placed the glass on the counter and held out her hand for the money. 'That's a bob, ta.'

Jimmy paid, tried to think of something smart to say, came up with nothing and took his drink over to an empty table. It wasn't empty for long. No sooner had he parked his backside on a chair than Sean Kelly sauntered through from the back of the pub and sat down beside him.

'I see you've met the lovely Marcie, then,' he said, smirking. 'What do you reckon?'

Jimmy, who was still wrestling with his feelings of inadequacy, gave a shrug. 'She's not all that.'

'You gone blind or what?'

'I've seen better is all I'm saying.'

'Since when did you get so fussy?' Sean leered at the barmaid across the room. 'Christ, I wouldn't kick her out of bed.'

Jimmy had never even managed to get a girl into bed, never mind kick one out. It filled him with dismay that he was still a virgin, a humiliating state of affairs he worked hard to keep under wraps. He'd considered paying for it, going to one of the tarts on the Albert Road, but was too afraid of catching something. Be just his luck to fall for a dose and have to visit the doctor, where there was bound to be some nosy neighbour sitting in the waiting room, some vile old bitch who wouldn't be slow to mention his presence there to his mother. Gossip spread as quickly as the clap round here.

While Sean prattled on – sex and football were his only two topics of conversation – Jimmy's gaze flicked back to the barmaid. She was chatting to a dark-haired spiv, flashing her teeth and giving him the glad eye. Resentment smouldered inside him. He was sick of being overlooked, ignored, of never being given a second look. It was time for a change. He scratched the top of his thigh, then his balls, and thought about the redhead. She had come here to cause trouble, but two could play at that game. If he could find a way to get rid of her, Ivor Doyle would be happy – and if Doyle was happy, then Alfred Tombs would be too. He'd heard the two men were tight, like father and son. But how to go about solving the problem of the mouthy bitch? While he slurped his pint, he pondered on it.

14

Saul Hannah was sitting in a Soho dive called Starlight. There was nothing starry about it, or anything light come to that. It was a gloomy basement with about as much good cheer as a charnel house. Midnight had come and gone and there were only six other customers, all of them down-at-heel losers with nowhere better to go. He fitted in nicely.

He was on his second whisky, still reeling from the news he'd been presented with at Scotland Yard: the Special Duty Squad was to be disbanded in a month. The reason given – that the crime wave had been contained and therefore the squad was no longer needed – was clearly disingenuous. Why fix something that wasn't broken? It was a bad move, the worst, but no one was interested in his opinion. He had his own theories about what was behind the decision, most of which revolved around political infighting and petty power struggles. There were rumours that Division weren't happy about so many leads going to the Flying Squad, and stories too that the top brass found the running of informants (and the amount they were paid) distasteful.

Saul curled his lip. What *was* distasteful was villains getting away with murder, quite literally in some cases. Crime in London might be down, thanks to himself and his colleagues, but it was still rife. A move like this could easily reverse all their good work. Of course, he'd still have his snouts when he was assigned to West End Central in October, but he wouldn't have the same amount of time to go chasing after them.

He drained his glass, caught the barman's eye, and ordered another. With only a month left on the squad, he intended to make the most of it and that meant concentrating his efforts on Tombs. If he could purge London of that man's nefarious activities, then decent people would sleep more easily in their beds. It was for this reason – and because his throat was as dry as sawdust – that he was sitting in this godforsaken dump waiting for Roy Monaghan to finish emptying his bladder and come back to join him.

It was a few more minutes before Monaghan emerged from the gents', shambled across the room and, with some minor difficulty, climbed onto the bar stool. He was a slight, dishevelled man in his mid fifties with a narrow, bony face and a receding hairline. What defined his appearance, however, was the angry wound that ran from the top of his left ear, along his cheek to the corner of his mouth.

'I ain't no tea leaf, Mr Hannah,' he grumbled, picking up his glass. 'Alf got it all wrong. A loan, that's all it were. I had a bit of a shortfall, see, a few debts that needed paying. She'd have got her money before the week was out.'

'You been playing the tables again?' Saul was aware that Monaghan was a hopeless gambler, the sort who chased his losses and never knew when to quit.

Monaghan shrugged. 'I had a run of bad luck. You know how it is.'

Saul studied his face. 'That's going to leave a nasty scar.'

'Tell me something I don't know. I tried to explain, for all the good it did. Once Alf's got an idea in his head . . . He wouldn't listen to reason, wouldn't give me a chance. And look what the bastard's gone and done now.' His hand fluttered up to his face, his fingertips gingerly touching the edges of the wound. He winced. 'It ain't right, is it? It ain't bloody right!'

'Not much thanks for all those years of loyal service,' Saul said, stirring the pot. 'A liberty, that's what it is. He shouldn't be allowed to get away with it.'

Monaghan's eyes grew wary. 'I ain't going to the law if that's what you're getting at.'

'It never crossed my mind, but maybe I could pick your brains about something – or rather, some*one*.'

'Who's that, then?'

'Let me get you another drink. A double, is it?' Saul called the barman over. 'Another whisky for my friend here. Make it a large one.'

Monaghan, placated, took a few quick sips before putting the glass down on the bar. 'What's on your mind?'

'Ivor Doyle. What can you tell me about him?'

'Doyle?'

'Yes.'

'Tall geezer, fair hair.'

'I know what he looks like. What's the deal with him and Tombs?'

Monaghan grinned. 'He's the man with the magic fingers, ain't he? They say he can open any lock in the country. Don't know if it's true, mind, but that's the story. Lives over near Old Street but keeps himself to himself. He and Alf go way back.'

Saul had recognised Doyle when Judith Jonson had shown him the photograph, but he hadn't let on. He had a file full of villains who had worked with Tombs, complete with mug-shots – a veritable rogues' gallery. Information on Doyle was slim: over the past year he had been pulled in for questioning about various robberies, but nothing had stuck. His only conviction had been for breaking and entering when he was fifteen years of age. Since then, his sheet had been clean. The man was clearly as slippery as his boss.

Saul had more questions to ask. Anything that would eventually help him to nail Tombs would be useful.

'Was he around during the war?'

Monaghan shook his head. 'He disappeared a year or so before. Can't remember when, exactly. There was some trouble and he scarpered.'

'What sort of trouble?'

'He and Hull had a falling-out.'

'Would that be Pat Hull or the late lamented Lennie?'

'Lennie,' Monaghan said.

'A falling-out over what?'

'Whatever thieves usually fall out over. I don't know the details. Doyle cleared off and I didn't see him again until . . . ' Monaghan frowned while he thought about it. 'Let me see, it must have been just before the end of the war. It was after Lennie went to meet his maker, that's for sure.'

'Any connection?'

Monaghan's mouth slid into a sly smile. 'Your guess is as good as mine. Maybe he felt it was safe to come back once Lennie wasn't around.'

'Or maybe he was the one who eliminated the problem.'

'I really couldn't say, Mr Hannah.'

More like he *wouldn't* say, Saul thought. Doyle had probably got fake identity papers before he left London – there were plenty of forgers who'd be willing, for a price, to provide the necessary documentation – and started afresh up north. While he was there, he'd met Judith, and later married her.

'Does the name Dan Jonson mean anything to you?'

'No.'

'Does Ivor Doyle have a wife?'

'What's that got to do with anything?'

'I'm just curious.' Saul had discovered nothing in the files about Doyle's marital status, but then there wasn't much full stop. He was a man who appeared to have stayed under the radar for most of his criminal career. 'Has he?'

'How would I know? Like I said, he keeps himself to himself.' He turned the now empty glass around in his fingers and slid his tongue over his lips. 'Although now I come to think of it, there could be a girl. A blonde. What's her name?' He glanced down at the glass and then over at Saul. 'It might come back to me.'

Saul nodded at the barman and got another round. 'Tell me about the blonde.'

15

Maud Bishop stood at the top of the stairs, straining her ears as she tried to listen in to the conversation taking place in the kitchen. It was a small house and the kitchen door was ajar, but the two men were speaking quietly. The night air was cool and she shivered in the darkness. If Mick caught her earwigging, he'd add a few more bruises to the ones she'd already got. She gently rubbed her arm where the flesh was sore and discoloured from her elbow to her shoulder. It was worth the risk, though. It was worth anything to see the bastard banged up.

She was gathering information in bits and pieces, a word here, a word there, and trying to put them together like a jigsaw: September, shooters, someone called Temple. From what they were saying, it sounded like the latter was the inside man. There was always an inside man on big jobs like this, usually a security guard happy to take a beating for a share of the profits.

Although Maud had been raised in the kind of family that viewed grassing as the eighth deadly sin, she had no qualms about what she was doing. It wasn't just for her, but for her kids too. At seven years old, Stanley was already starting to copy his dad, lashing out and name-calling, getting into fights. Before long he'd be out of control and then there would be no going back. He'd end up in Borstal, then jail, and that would be the story of his life. The only way to stop it was to get away from here, to get away from Mick, and the only way to do both those things was to make sure she had money when he went down for a long stretch.

Harsh laughter floated up the stairs. 'I reckon the fuckin' bastard's still trying to work it out.' Pat Hull was talking about Tombs and the New Bond Street job. Someone had tipped Pat off about a plan to do a smash-and-grab at the Mayfair jeweller's, and so he and Mick had got in there first. 'He'll be steaming, all that tom he's missed out on.'

Maud knew Mick must have made a bundle from the robbery, but none of it had come her way. It didn't matter that the rent was overdue or the kids needed new shoes. He would spend it all on tarts and booze and gambling, lose a fortune on the tables and then take it out on her. She rubbed her arm again, feeding her resentment. She could have told Saul about Mick's involvement, but without any evidence – the goods would have been moved on by now – it wouldn't have achieved much. Anyway, she was keeping her powder dry, saving it for the big one. When Mick went down, it had to be for a very long time. If this job was as major as it sounded, there would be good rewards at the end of it. The law would arrest Mick in the act, and the insurers – under instructions from Saul – would give her the money she deserved.

With four kids to feed and clothe, life was a constant struggle for Maud. Not that *he* cared. On more than one occasion she'd had to steal from his wallet, grabbing a note or two while he was out cold from the booze. Sometimes she got away with it and sometimes she didn't. She had spent the entire war hoping that a bomb would drop on his head, but Hitler hadn't been obliging.

If it wasn't for the kids, she'd have put a knife through Mick's heart years ago. But who would take care of the little ones when the courts placed a noose round her neck?

The only thing that kept her going was the knowledge that it would soon be over. She could put up with whatever he did to her because the end was in sight. Once he was safely behind bars, and once she'd got the money, she'd pack up, take the kids and leave. She'd tell the neighbours they were going to stay with her sister in Hounslow, but her plan was to head for Scotland. There were factories there, places she could get work, and most importantly of all, it was as far away from *him* as she could get.

Pat Hull laughed again, and slapped his palm against the table. The noise made her flinch and she instinctively took a step back. There was a clink of glasses, the sound of a match being struck. She hated Pat almost as much as she hated Mick. He was just like his brother – vicious scum. He didn't know who'd killed Lennie, but she did. She smiled into the darkness. It was a secret she'd take to her grave.

16

Judith was at a loss as to what to do next. She woke to blue skies and sunshine on Wednesday morning, got dressed and went downstairs for breakfast, then returned to her room. With a whole day to kill before her next meeting with Saul, she had no clear idea as to how she was going to fill the time. Should she carry on with the locksmiths, maybe try Hoxton or Whitechapel, or go back to the West End? She had little confidence that either of these choices would yield useful results, but doing something was better than doing nothing.

She perched on the edge of the bed while she weighed up the options. Perhaps she should try and track down Alfred Tombs instead. But Elsa's warning echoed in her head. No, she would leave that as a last resort. If all else failed, she would start on it tomorrow. There would be a couple of days left, time enough, surely, to find someone as notorious as him.

She stood up, put on her jacket and went back downstairs. As she left the house, she remembered the feeling she'd had the night before, the sense that she was being followed. Her gaze nervously scanned the street, flicking left and right, but nothing struck her as odd and no one seemed to be paying her any attention. In the broad light of day, her suspicions felt frail and insubstantial, a product of her imagination and the shadows of dusk.

While she was waiting at the bus stop, she glanced along the road and noticed the Fox. The public houses were somewhere she hadn't tried yet. If Dan was living round here, he must be drinking in one of them. The idea of going into a pub alone made her uncomfortable; it was something she would never do at home. If only she had some company, Charlotte or Annie, but she was utterly alone.

The first bus that came along was going to Tottenham Court Road. Having still not made a firm decision as to what she planned to do, she yielded to fate, climbed on board and took a seat near the front. As they travelled towards the West End, she tried to get her thoughts in order. The whole Ivor Doyle business continued to bug her. What if it was a complete red herring? What if this Doyle man just had a look of Dan about him? She could end up wasting days attempting to chase down some random bloke who had nothing at all to do with her. Except he *was* a locksmith, and parts of the old man's story tallied with what she knew about Dan. A sick feeling swirled around in her guts. If they were the same person, it meant that Dan had deserted her.

She briefly closed her eyes, trying to blink away this unwelcome and painful conclusion. But she wasn't tempted, not even for a moment, to abandon the search. She would see it through to the bitter end, no matter what the outcome.

By midday, she had covered a couple of miles, circling round to Piccadilly and criss-crossing the West End in an aimless kind of fashion. She wasn't really sure what she was looking for. The chances of bumping into Dan were probably about three million to one, but the knowledge that he'd been in the area a week ago spurred her on. Eventually she found herself back in New Bond Street, staring again at the jewellery store. She felt pulled to the spot as though it had a magnetic force she couldn't resist.

She was sure of one thing at least: Dan couldn't have had anything to do with the robbery. Although she had no idea when the *Mirror* photograph had been taken – fifteen minutes, an hour, two hours after the event? – you didn't stand around gawping in the street if you'd just committed a crime. She sighed. It was hard to believe she could even be thinking this way. The Dan she'd known had been decent, law-abiding, a man with principles. But decent men came home to their wives after the war. So why had he been here, standing beside one of the most notorious villains in London? She had no answer to the question.

She stared intently at the jeweller's, taking in all the details like a thief casing a joint. When she'd exhausted every square inch of the building, she began to walk up and down the street, retracing her steps from yesterday. She felt there had to be a lead somewhere, a clue as to Dan's whereabouts. But why should there be? Just because he had passed this way once didn't mean he would do it again. But it didn't mean he wouldn't either. She clung to this slender straw as her gaze raked the crowd, her eyes searching for that familiar face.

She was on her third lap, going up one side of the street and down the other, when the man approached. He was in his late thirties, broader-shouldered but only slightly taller than her, with pale brown hair cropped close to his skull.

'Hey, Red,' he said in a broad American accent. 'You okay? You're looking kind of lost.'

'No,' she said, startled by this unsolicited approach. 'I'm not. Lost, that is. I'm just . . . just waiting for someone.'

'Lucky someone,' he drawled, grinning widely. 'You want to get a coffee?'

She wondered what part of 'waiting for someone' he didn't understand. 'No thank you.'

'Oh well, you don't ask, you don't get. There's a swell little coffee bar just around the corner. You sure you're okay? You look kind of blue, if you don't mind me saying. Rainy skies and all that.' He glanced up at what was in fact a clear blue sky, and shrugged. 'I guess you're not from round here.'

'No.' Judith was already edging away. She didn't want to be rude, but nor did she want to continue this exchange. 'Sorry, but I really have to go.'

'I'm not from these parts either, in case you hadn't guessed. This guy you're waiting for, is he a Yank?'

Judith hadn't told him it was a man, but she shook her head anyway. 'No. Look, I'm sorry, but—'

'Yeah, you've got to go, right? I get the message. But I'll tell you something for nothing, hon. He's not worth it. Any guy who keeps a broad like you waiting must need his head examining.'

Despite herself, Judith smiled. It was nice to be appreciated by someone, even if that someone was a chancer with a silver tongue. 'Goodbye, then.'

'See you around, hon. You ever change your mind, you can usually find me at Carlo's. It's in Beak Street. Pete's the name, Pete Stanhope.'

Judith nodded. 'Goodbye, Pete.' As she walked off, she wondered if she should have shown him the photograph of Dan. If he made a habit of hanging around the area, he might have noticed him. She dithered – on the one hand, she didn't want to encourage the man, but on the other, he might have some useful information – and by the time she turned to look for him again, he'd gone. She peered through the crowds of people, but he'd already drifted away.

As she turned the corner on to Conduit Street, Judith stopped to examine her face in a shop window, wondering if she looked as 'blue' as he'd claimed. Well, she had plenty to be sad about. She inclined her head and frowned. She didn't think she looked any different from usual, but that wasn't necessarily a good thing. Perhaps whatever was etched on her features – despair, sorrow, melancholy – had been there for so many years that she no longer noticed it. She made a feeble attempt at a smile, and her lips trembled.

Quickly she moved on, striding down to Regent Street. What next? Suddenly she felt afraid. She wanted to get away from the noisy, hectic West End. The crowds were pressing in on her. She hated the dirt and the clamour and the constant traffic. The air smelled of exhaust fumes. She didn't understand why anyone would choose to live in London; it was big and grasping, like a monster wanting to suck the oxygen from your lungs and squeeze you dry.

As she reached the next corner, she noticed a bus, stopped at the lights, that was heading in the direction of Kellston, and ran to catch up with it. Grabbing the rail, she managed to swing herself onto the platform just as it was moving off. She swayed with the rhythm of the vehicle, found an empty seat near the front and sat down, slightly breathless, by the window. The conductor took her money and gave her a ticket.

Judith leaned her cheek against the glass, grateful for the coolness. She was hot and bothered, and had no idea of what she was going to do next. She felt safer, though, now that she was off the streets. The faint sense of panic began to subside, but it was not replaced by anything more comfortable. How was she ever going to find Dan if she carried on like this? She had to be strong, single-minded, determined, but these were all things she currently seemed to lack.

Staring out at the buildings, she could see that many of them, even after four years, still showed damage from the war. There was blasted brick and boarded-up windows. A cage of scaffolding covered many of the exteriors. There were gaps in the rows, places where theatres or shops or restaurants had once stood. It would take a long time to put everything right, if that was even possible. Some damage was irreparable.

The door to a hairdressing salon opened and a middle-aged woman with short iron-grey hair stepped out. There was something about her – the stiff back, the stern expression – that reminded Judith of her Aunt Laura. Judith had been orphaned at the age of six when both her parents had succumbed to a virulent strain of influenza. Her father's older sister, a confirmed spinster without a maternal bone in her body, had taken her in, put a roof over her head and tried to make the best of an arrangement that suited neither aunt nor niece.

Judith had only vague, wispy memories of her parents: the floral scent of her mother's perfume, the rough tweed of her father's jacket. She often wondered what kind of person she might have been had they survived. Someone different, or just the same? Growing up had been a challenging and often lonely experience. Aunt Laura, who had no experience of children or any idea of how to relate to them, had treated her as an adult and communicated with her accordingly. This had made for a somewhat eccentric form of child-rearing, but Judith didn't feel any resentment. Somehow they had muddled through. Although she had missed out on parental love and affection, she had at least learned the skills of self-reliance.

One of her aunt's most favoured pieces of advice had been 'Never depend on a man, my dear, not to look after you, not for anything.' To this day Judith still didn't know if her insistence on the matter was down to personal experience, an independent spirit or general prejudice against the male sex. Still, the instruction had been a useful one.

For all her aunt's shortcomings as a surrogate mother, Judith was still grateful. Had it not been for her intervention, she would probably have grown up in a children's home. She was aware that sacrifices had been made and future hopes thwarted in order that she could be fed and clothed and provided with a place to live.

Even as she thought about Aunt Laura, she sat up straighter. What she needed now was backbone. She had left Westport full of determination, and this wasn't the time to let the situation get the better of her. Dan was out there somewhere and she was going to find him. London might be a scary place, full of strangers and people who didn't want to talk – or, just as bad, a man she didn't know who *did* want to talk – but *none of it* was going to get the better of her. Although she had never wanted to discover that her husband had left her high and dry, she felt more alive than she had in a long time.

Within half an hour, they were back in Kellston. Judith got off the bus at the station and began walking up the high street towards Connolly's. She would have some lunch while she figured out what to do next. When she was within a few feet of the café, she suddenly remembered the old lady at Boxley Street. Perhaps it was worth trying there again. There had been something in the woman's face, a flicker of recognition, and if the daughter was out, Judith might be able to press for more information. It wasn't much to go on, but slim leads were better than none.

She walked past Connolly's, slowing to glance in through the window. Was Elsa there? She couldn't spot her. Apart from the Yank – and his intentions had been dubious – the waitress was the only person who had shown any real interest, listening to her story without judging. In this hard, fast city, it wasn't easy to find kindness. Hopefully Elsa would be around later.

The sun was still out and a light breeze caught her hair. She looked over the road towards a small park, an oblong expanse of green that afforded the only colour in an otherwise grey and dreary landscape. There were trees and bushes, a few benches, and a path that led through the middle to a row of houses at the far end. Maybe, if it was still warm, she would sit there for a while when she came back. No sooner had this thought crossed her mind than she heard footsteps behind her.

'Judith!'

She stopped dead in her tracks, stunned. Her pulse started racing and the hairs on the back of her neck stood on end. She would have known that voice anywhere. As she spun round, the shock was already registering on her face.

17

Judith had imagined the scene a thousand times: the locking of
eyes, the mutual intake of breath, the nanosecond of stillness
before they fell into each other's arms. But this wasn't like that.
The man who stood before her was Dan, and yet he wasn't. She
was gazing at a stranger. He was thinner, his face gaunt, almost
haggard, the cheekbones sharp as razors. But it was the way he
was looking at her that made her blood run cold. His expression
was blank, indifferent, as though he barely knew her.

'What are you doing here?'

Judith flinched at his tone. She stared at him, still trying to
fully absorb his presence. Her legs had turned to jelly and her
heart was beating so fast she could feel its manic thump against
her ribs. At first, she couldn't answer – her mouth was dry,
clogged with words that wouldn't come out – and she struggled
to catch her breath. How was this real? He was here, in front of
her, but nothing was as it should be. Eventually she found her
voice. 'Shouldn't I be asking you that?'

His lips showed the flicker of a smile. 'How did you know?'

'I'm your wife, for God's sake. I've always known.' She paused.

'I mean, I knew you weren't dead. I was sure of it. I didn't know you were in London until last week, when ...' Suddenly, the effort of explaining felt like too much. 'It doesn't matter.'

'I'm sorry.'

'Sorry?' she echoed with incredulity. Anger was building inside her, tears pricking at her eyes. 'Is that all you've got to say?'

'What more can I say? I never wanted to hurt you.'

'What's happened to you? I don't understand. How can you ... You're just standing there as if ...' She could hear her voice quavering, breaking, while her dreams fell apart. 'How could you have done this to me?'

'You should go home.'

The hardness in his voice made her wince. 'I'm not going anywhere until you explain, until you tell me why. You owe me that much, don't you?'

His gaze slid away as if he couldn't bear to look at her. He hesitated, then gestured towards Connolly's. 'Shall we go to the caff?'

Judith shook her head. She couldn't bear the thought of being enclosed by four walls, or of people overhearing their conversation. Most things were out of her control, but this she had a choice about. 'Over there,' she said, pointing towards the green.

As they crossed the road, she stumbled and he took hold of her elbow to steady her. The protective gesture, at odds with his coldness, filled her with confusion. She glanced at his face, but it showed nothing. Once she could have read him like a book, but now his emotions, if he had any, were locked up tight.

They walked along the path until they came to a wooden bench, where they sat down with a space between them. She could feel the sun on her skin but its warmth didn't penetrate. Inside, a chill was creeping through her bones. She waited for him to speak, desperate to hear what he had to say but dreading it too. The seconds ticked by and he still didn't open his mouth.

'Dan?' she prompted.

He took a breath, exhaled a sigh. 'I don't know where to start.'

'How about with your name. Is it Dan Jonson or Ivor Doyle?'

He gave a thin, brittle laugh. 'You've been busy.'

'So, which is it?'

'Doyle,' he said. 'It's Ivor Doyle.'

Judith's heart sank. Although it didn't come as any great surprise, she'd been hoping that at least the name she'd known him by would be real. 'When did you change it?'

'I got in some trouble back in the day – I won't bore you with the details – and decided to get out of London, head up north and make a fresh start: new name, new place, new life.'

New wife, she could have added, but she kept quiet, her eyes on his face. He was gazing straight ahead, his brow furrowed, his hands clamped on his knees. Looking at what? Just the past, perhaps.

'I bought some fake ID papers to make sure I couldn't be tracked down. Then the war came along and … Well, that changed everything. I got injured at Anzio, shipped back over here and spent a few months in hospital. I was—'

'Were you badly hurt?'

'I survived, as you can see. But I suppose I was in a bad way for a while. My ID tags had got lost, so they didn't know who I was, and by the time I was well enough to tell them, I'd decided not to. I'd had it with the bloody war. As soon as I could walk again, I legged it out of there and came to London.'

'Why didn't you come back to Westport? I was there. I was waiting.'

'For a dead man. Dan Jonson was gone for ever.'

'I was waiting for *you*,' she said. 'Whatever goddam name you were using.'

'For a deserter,' he snapped back. 'Was that the kind of man you wanted for a husband?'

'You did your share. You're not a coward. You went out and fought, and that's a damn sight more than some people did. I wouldn't have judged you.'

He gave a shrug as though her judgement was neither here nor there. 'You'd have got the telegram by then.'

'You could have written. You could have let me know you were alive.'

'And then what? I couldn't come back to Westport.'

'I would have come to London.'

'And done what? Turned your back on your home and your friends? Lived a lie for the rest of your life? Because that's what it would have meant. Dan Jonson had ceased to exist. I was Ivor Doyle again.'

Judith leaned forward and rubbed her face with her hands. 'You could have given me the choice.'

Ivor's voice softened. 'I know what you're like, Judith – you're loyal and kind. You'd have come to me out of some misplaced sense of duty, and spent the rest of your days regretting it.'

Out of love, she wanted to scream at him.

And then, as if he'd read her mind, he said, 'The man you loved doesn't exist any more. Don't you see? I tried to be that man, *was* that man for a while, but now ...' He lifted and dropped his shoulders again. 'You wouldn't like Ivor Doyle much. He isn't honest. He isn't good or decent. He looks after number one and he doesn't give a damn about anybody else.'

'I don't believe you,' she said.

He took a pack of Camels from his jacket pocket, flipped open the lid, pulled out a cigarette and put it in his mouth. His hand shook a little as he struck a match. 'Believe what you like.'

Judith gazed out across the stretch of green, willing this to be a nightmare she would soon wake up from. She watched an elderly woman walking her dog, the mutt stopping to sniff at the base of every tree, and wondered at how other people's lives were going on as normal while hers was being ripped apart. The sun's rays slid through branches, striping the grass with midday shadow. She breathed in slowly. Smoke from his cigarette floated in thin wisps through the air.

'How did you find out I was in London?' he asked.

She opened her bag, took out the *Mirror* picture and handed it to him. 'You should be careful about which street corners you stand on.'

He studied the picture, gave a hollow laugh. 'Most people wouldn't have recognised me from this.'

'No, but I'm not most people, am I? I'm your . . . ' The word 'wife' died on her lips as the reality struck her with force. 'Oh God, we're not even married, are we? Not legally. We can't be. Dan Jonson is just a figment of your imagination. It was . . . it was all a sham.'

'Not a sham. It wasn't that.' He pulled on the cigarette, blew out smoke. He gave her a fleeting sideways glance. 'I meant it, everything – at the time.'

'At the time,' she murmured, the words piercing deep into her heart. 'Well, that's comforting.'

He flinched at the bitterness in her voice. 'You're better off without me.'

'It would have helped if you'd figured that out before we got together.'

He opened his mouth, thought better of it and closed it again.

Her hands twisted in her lap. After a while she asked, 'What kind of trouble?'

'What?'

'When you left London, you said you were in trouble.'

'Does it matter?'

'It might.'

He dropped the cigarette butt on the ground. His gaze lingered on it for a few seconds, watching it smoulder. 'Someone robbed me – a man called Lennie Hull – and so I helped myself to what he owed. He wasn't happy about it. In fact, safe to say he'd have probably broken my legs if he'd been able to find me. It didn't seem the smartest move to hang around in London.'

'But you still came back,' she said.

'That's because Lennie's not a problem any more. While I was away, someone did me a favour and blew his brains out. I say a little prayer of thanks every night.'

Judith watched him closely while he talked. She sensed he was deliberately trying to shock her, to speak in a fashion that would prove he wasn't the person she thought he was. But she already knew that. He'd pretended to be dead, hadn't he? Nothing could be as callous as that brutal fact. As she studied his profile, she noticed the network of scars running along his right temple and over his ear. From the war, she presumed, and felt a stab of pity even though she didn't want to. She looked down at the newspaper cutting he was still holding.

'Are you working for Alfred Tombs?'

His gaze dropped to the photograph. 'Who have you been talking to?'

'Everyone. At least it feels like that.' She didn't mention that most of them hadn't been talking back. 'Are you? Are you working for that man?'

'I know him. I don't work for anyone but myself.'

'I suppose his sort are always in need of a good locksmith.'

He didn't respond to the comment. Instead, he handed back the photograph and asked, 'What are you going to do?'

'Do?'

'About us. You could go to the law and report me. I wouldn't blame you. After all, I did lie to you, deceive you. I treated you badly so I presume you'd like some justice.'

Judith wondered what would constitute justice after what he'd done to her. 'Make it all public, you mean? Let everyone know how stupid and gullible I am? Perhaps they'll write a nice little piece about us in the paper: "Westport girl duped into marriage by East End villain". That'll give the neighbours something to gossip about.'

'It's up to you.'

'What would be the point in me going to the police? You'll just do another of your disappearing acts.'

He shook his head. 'I'm not going anywhere.'

Judith didn't believe him, and she certainly didn't trust him. At this moment, she wasn't sure what she wanted to do. Shock had thrown her into turmoil. She knew what she wanted to say – that he'd misjudged her, betrayed her, almost destroyed her – but pride held her back. She wouldn't give him the satisfaction. 'I don't know yet. I haven't decided. I need ... I need to think about it.'

'I understand.'

She glared at him. She couldn't bear his calmness, his lack of feeling. As if there was no passion in him at all. And suddenly she snapped. 'Do you? Only I don't think you understand anything. Do you have any idea what the last five years has been like for me? Getting that telegram and ... ' She gulped down the lump that was lodged in her throat. 'But I didn't give up, despite what everyone said. I wouldn't accept it. I carried on believing in you, in *us*. And now ... now I can see that you don't even care. Maybe you never did. Was that it? I was just someone to amuse yourself with until you went back to your real life.'

'No,' he said. 'No, it was never like that.'

'So what was it like?'

But he wouldn't be drawn. 'If you don't want to go to the law, then go home. Go back to Westport and forget you ever saw me. Get on with your life.'

'You think it's that easy?'

'You've got two choices,' he said bluntly. 'It's up to you.'

Judith could feel what little self-possession she retained gradually slipping away. She was on the edge, staring over a precipice, afraid she was about to plunge into nothingness. Like those dreams she sometimes had when she was falling, falling, falling … She was losing control. She wanted to lash out, to claw and bite and batter, to hurt him as badly as he'd hurt her. Quickly, before she did something she'd regret, she stood up and walked a little way along the path. He didn't follow her.

She stood taking long, deep breaths until the red mist had lifted. Only then did she turn around and walk back to the bench. There was still something she had to ask. Despite the desire to cling onto her pride, she couldn't stop herself. 'Is there someone else? Another wife? A girlfriend?'

He hesitated, but then shook his head.

She didn't like that hesitation. Folding her arms across her chest, she gazed down at him and narrowed her eyes. 'Well, I don't suppose you'd tell me if there was.' For the first time, she noticed his clothes, a smart suit, white shirt and tie. Expensive. Her old summer dress, if not exactly shabby, felt inferior in comparison. Why on earth was she thinking about clothes? What did shirts and shoes and jackets matter when all her hopes and dreams had just been smashed to pieces? She blurted out her next question before she could properly think about it.

'Are you happy?'

He seemed surprised by the question, baffled even. It took him a while to come up with an answer. 'About as happy as I deserve to be.'

She snorted. 'I don't think you have any conscience at all. How can you? I bet I've barely crossed your mind in the last few years. Just some girl you used to know, safely consigned to history. A mistake you made, but one you didn't need to worry about. If it hadn't been for that picture, you'd have got clean away with it.'

He stood up then and faced her. There was something in his cold grey eyes that alarmed her, and instinctively she took a step back. 'Maybe you should look at it in a different way,' he said. 'You know the truth now. You can let go. You're free of me.'

Judith couldn't see how she'd ever be free of him. He'd haunt her for the rest of her life. How would she ever trust anyone again? 'It isn't that simple.'

'It's as simple as you want it to be. Go back to Westport and leave the past where it belongs.'

She felt a perverse desire to do the very opposite of what he suggested. 'You can't tell me where to go. I might stay in London for a while. Yes, why not? I could do with a change.'

'There's nothing for you here.'

'That's not your judgement to make. I'll decide what I'm going to do.'

His eyes bored into hers, hard and intense. But then, after a few long seconds, he simply shrugged. 'Do what you like. It doesn't make any difference to me.'

'I will. I'll do exactly what I want.'

'Fine. I have to go.'

She hissed out a breath. 'Oh, I'm sorry. Have you got some-where more important to be?'

'Take care of yourself, Judith.'

He moved around her and started heading up the path towards the high street.

Judith called after him. She still had things to say, so much to say. 'Don't walk away from me!'

But that was exactly what he did.

18

Judith's jaw was clenched as tightly as her fists. She might have run after him if her legs had been strong enough to carry her, but she was on the point of collapse. The awfulness of what had just happened was gradually sinking in. As Dan – Ivor – disappeared out of sight, the horror spread like poison through her body and she began to shake uncontrollably. Staggering back to the bench, she dropped down and put her head in her hands.

Anger and hate, grief and despair filled her mind. All that waiting, all those years of hope, and for what? The man she had loved had been an illusion. Dan Jonson was nothing but a name on a piece of paper. She was not convinced that he had ever loved her back. He had discarded her as easily, as carelessly as litter.

'Ivor Doyle,' she muttered, the name like acid on her tongue.

Tears ran down her cheeks. She found a handkerchief in her bag and dabbed at her eyes. So what next? She could go to the police and report him. There was temptation in the prospect of revenge, of seeing him punished, but that would also mean enduring her own very public humiliation. She would be the subject of gossip, of pity and scorn. For the rest of her life she would be the woman who'd been duped by a sweet-talking con man.

She rocked back and forth, understanding nothing and everything, overwhelmed by his betrayal. A part of her wished she had never seen that photograph, never come to London, but time couldn't be turned back. She'd been a fool in every way. She had given her heart to a liar and a cheat. She had sacrificed some of the best years of her life, convinced that one day he would come back to her.

Gradually, her body stilled. He should be made to pay, she thought, but she didn't know how. It wasn't fair that he just carried on doing whatever he wanted to do, after she had been devastated. She had always been taught that no bad deed went unpunished, but God seemed to have overlooked Ivor Doyle's sins. Perhaps she should take matters into her own hands. She dwelled on this for a while, finding some satisfaction in the notion. The idea of ruining him, of wrecking his life in the same way he'd wrecked hers, brought her temporary consolation. But then another thought entered her head: wouldn't that make her just as bad as him? Well, she didn't care. She hardened her heart, yearning for revenge.

Time passed. Ten minutes, fifteen, she wasn't sure how long. The sun continued to shine, its rays streaming through the trees and dappling the ground around her feet. She frowned. Even the weather seemed to be mocking her, its brightness and warmth in stark contrast to the darkness of her soul.

She jumped up from the bench, suddenly wanting only one thing – to get as far away from *him* and from London as she could. She'd had enough. For now, all she desired was to be back in Westport, to be in familiar surroundings while she licked her wounds and tried to work out what to do next.

She traipsed back along the high street, seeing nothing. While she walked, she replayed her conversation with Dan – with *Ivor* – over and over in her head. She hadn't even asked him how he'd known she was here. The Taylor boy, probably. Her message must have got through after all. It would have been a shock when he'd got the news. She had risen from the past like a buried secret, a ghost from his previous life. He could have gone into hiding, of course, but instead he had chosen to confront her. She wouldn't give him credit for that. It wasn't out of any sense of decency, she was sure; more likely a wish to dispose of the problem as quickly as he could.

Judith picked up the pace as she turned the corner into Station Road. It wouldn't take her long to pack, and then she could catch a bus to Euston. With luck, she'd be home by early evening. She would have to miss her appointment with Saul, but there was no point to it now. He wouldn't be able to tell her anything she didn't already know.

She walked up the path to Sycamore House, opened the unlocked door and stepped into the hall. It was then that she saw it – her suitcase sitting at the bottom of the stairs. She stared at it, bemused, unable to fathom how it had made its way down here from her room. She was still trying to figure it out when Mrs Jolly appeared from the back with a look on her face that would have scared the devil himself.

'You're back, then,' the woman said, stating the obvious.

'Yes, but why is my case—'

Mrs Jolly folded her arms across her chest and glared at Judith. 'We don't want your sort here, dearie. This is a respectable household. So if you'd just take your things and go . . .'

'What?'

'You 'eard me. Let's not make it difficult, eh? You and me both know what you're up to. It's Albert Road you should be staying, not here.'

Judith didn't have a clue what she was going on about. 'I don't understand. Why are you—'

'Oh, you understand well enough. I've heard all about you and what you're up to. I wasn't born yesterday. You might pull the wool over some folk's eyes, but not Mrs Jolly's.'

'Is this about Dan?' she asked.

'I don't know no names, and I don't want to. That's your business, not mine. Now, if you don't mind, I'd like you to leave.'

Judith did mind. Although she'd been planning on going anyway, she hadn't anticipated being thrown out on her ear. Her head, already in turmoil by her meeting with Dan, was starting to spin. With no idea of what rule she'd broken, she had no way of defending herself. It was hardly a crime to go looking for your husband, so why, if that was the reason, was she being punished for it? She could feel her face burning as indignation rose inside her. 'I've paid until Saturday. I'm not going until I get my money back.'

Mrs Jolly pursed her lips as if all her bad opinions of Judith had just been confirmed. She unfolded her arms, put a hand into her apron pocket and reluctantly took out a few shillings. 'Here,' she said. 'And don't show your face round here again. You're not welcome in this street.'

Judith slipped the money into her bag, picked up her case and walked out. The return of the money didn't provide much consolation, but small victories were better than none. She felt humiliated, angry and tearful, at a loss as to what she was supposed to have done. Loathing swept over her, not just for Mrs Jolly but for all Londoners. With only a few exceptions, she'd been made to feel as welcome as a fox in a henhouse.

Although she'd intended to get the bus from outside the station, Judith changed her mind as she left Sycamore House. She had visions of Mrs Jolly and all the neighbours lurking behind net curtains watching her every move. Instead she headed for the high street, where there was another bus stop halfway along. She walked quickly, eager to get around the corner and escape any prying eyes. Someone had been whispering in the landlady's ear and it didn't take a genius to work out who. Dan was clearly determined to get rid of her one way or another.

What had he said? She had no idea, but whatever it was had been enough to throw her into disgrace. It made her mad and sad and desperate to get away from this horrible place and everyone in it. As she passed the café, she thought about the meeting with Saul scheduled for this evening. Well, there was nothing she could do about that now. Except, of course, there was. She could see Elsa through the window, carrying a tray towards a table at the back. She could let her know, get her to call him. It would only take a minute to nip inside. She dithered, glancing along the street to see if the bus was coming. It wasn't. In truth, she didn't want to talk to anyone, but common courtesy nagged at her conscience. It was hardly fair to leave Saul in the lurch when she could avoid it.

She pushed open the door and went inside. She hovered near the entrance, trying to catch Elsa's attention. Eventually the waitress noticed her and came over. She took one look at Judith's face, glanced down at the suitcase and asked, 'What's happened?'

'I'm going home. Today. Now. Could you let Saul know? I won't be here this evening.'

'What's happened?' Elsa repeated. 'You're white as a sheet. You look like you saw a ghost.'

'Something like that. Anyway, would you let him—'

'You need to sit down,' Elsa said, steering her towards an empty table. She pulled out a chair and gently pushed Judith into it. 'Here, before you fall down. When was the last time you had something to eat?'

'Breakfast, but I'm not hungry.'

'You need food inside you,' Elsa insisted. 'Wait here and I'll bring you a bowl of stew.'

'I can't. I've got a train to catch.'

'There are plenty more trains. You can catch a later one. I can't let you leave like this. Look, I'm off shift in twenty minutes. Have some food and then we can talk.'

Before any further objections could be made, Elsa took off towards the counter. Judith could have got up again, walked out, but she didn't have the energy or the will. The day's events had drained her dry. She moved her case out of the way, sat back and let the sounds of the café float over her, the clatter of plates and the general chatter. There was something soothing about doing nothing, about letting someone else take control.

A few minutes later, Elsa brought the stew, patted her on the shoulder and left again. Judith ate slowly, barely tasting anything. From the café she could see the green, but not the bench where she and Dan had been talking. *Ivor*, she reminded herself yet again. It was hard to believe that less than half an hour ago she'd been sitting right beside him. Where was he now? She hadn't even got an address. He had disappeared as suddenly as he'd arrived, melting into the street, going back to where he belonged. For him, it was over, but for her, too many questions remained unanswered. What he had given her wasn't enough. She felt cheated and bereft, abandoned in some strange kind of limbo.

Judith was hardly aware of time passing. She finished her stew and watched the world go by outside the window. Then Elsa was standing beside her with a light summer coat over her arm.

'Come on,' she said. 'Let's get out of here.'

Judith pulled out her purse to pay for the food, but Elsa waved away the offer. 'It's sorted. Don't worry about it.'

'But—'

Elsa picked up the case. 'Honestly, it's fine. We'll go to my flat and have a brew. It's not far from here.'

Judith rose to her feet and followed the girl. Why not? There was no particular urgency about her journey home, other than a desire to get out of London. And she could do with someone to talk to. Everything had been so awful, so shocking, she could barely think straight.

'I take it you've found him,' Elsa said as they crossed the road.

'Yes.'

'Not good news, then?'

'You could say that.'

'I'm sorry.'

Elsa cut across the corner of the green. As they joined the main path and passed the bench, Judith noticed the cigarette butt lying on the ground. It seemed suitably symbolic of her marriage: something that had been temporarily enjoyed, sucked dry and then thrown away. She gave Elsa a brief summary of her dreadful meeting with Ivor Doyle. Ordinarily she would not have confided so freely, but as the girl already knew half the story, she didn't see the harm in telling her the rest.

'What a bastard,' Elsa said. 'You can't let him get away with it. It's not right, what he's done to you.'

'And how am I supposed to do that? I don't want to get the police involved.'

'Why not? They should put him in jail where he belongs.'

'But that's not going to change anything.'

'It's not to do with changing things. It's making him pay for what he did.'

'Revenge,' Judith said softly.

'There's nothing wrong with revenge. An eye for an eye. That's fair enough, isn't it? It's what he deserves. It's the *least* he deserves.'

139

'You're right,' Judith said, 'but I still don't want to send him to prison.' Despite everything he'd put her through, she didn't want to be responsible for having him locked up. 'I don't want him to get away with it either, though.'

Elsa gave her a quick sideways glance. 'You don't have to, love, not if you don't want to. There's more than one way to skin a cat.'

19

While Elsa was making the tea, Judith told her about being thrown out of the B&B.

'I don't even know what I'm supposed to have done. I went back and my case was packed, and Mrs Jolly was looking at me like I was something she'd found on the bottom of her shoe.'

'What did she say, exactly?'

'I don't know, something about it being a respectable household and that my sort wasn't welcome. Oh, and she mentioned a place called Albert Road, said that's where I should be staying, not at hers.'

Elsa barked out a laugh. 'That was below the belt.'

'What do you mean?'

'It's the local red-light district, love. She's suggesting you're a whore.'

Judith's mouth fell open in shock. 'What? How could she think—'

'That so-called husband of yours must have had a word with her. God, he really is a piece of work.' Elsa passed over a cup of tea. 'Sorry, I've got no sugar.'

But sugar was the last thing on Judith's mind. 'I can't believe he'd do something like that.'

Elsa's eyebrows flew up. 'You're talking about a man who pretended he was dead. What are a few more lies on top of that? He clearly wants you out of Kellston – and fast.'

Judith stared down at the carpet. Not content with ruining her life, Ivor Doyle was now trashing her reputation too. Her face burned with anger and dismay. 'So now everyone thinks I'm a . . . a prostitute.'

'Not anyone that matters. Who cares what that old cow thinks?'

Judith couldn't be quite as blasé about it. '*I* care.'

'So don't let him get away with it. He thinks he can walk all over you, do what he likes, say what he likes. You have to start fighting back. Don't let him push you around like this. You don't *have* to leave London. You can do exactly what you want.'

Except that leaving London was exactly what Judith wanted. She had to get away from the nightmare, to put some distance between her and the man she had once loved so much. She wanted to be somewhere she felt safe. 'I know. I just need . . . some time, I suppose. I'm not saying I won't come back, just that I have to figure things out first.'

'What's there to figure? Don't be a victim. You're better than that.'

Judith, who was still coming to terms with the fact that she *was* a victim, albeit of Ivor Doyle's duplicity rather than the war, gave a thin smile. 'What did you mean earlier about there being more than one way to skin a cat?'

'He wants you to go. Well, why should you dance to his tune? You should stay here and make things awkward for him. I doubt he's told you the whole truth, far from it. You deserve that, at the very least.'

Judith couldn't argue with her, but it wasn't that easy. 'I've got a job. I have to be back on Monday.'

'Take some time off. What do you do, anyway?'

'I'm a legal secretary.'

'London isn't short of solicitors. You could easily get work here if you wanted it.'

Judith didn't want it, but as she opened her mouth to say as much, she was distracted by the sound of footsteps descending to the basement, followed by a couple of sharp raps on the door. Elsa stood up.

'I'll get rid of them, whoever they are.'

Judith heard a quick murmured conversation before Elsa returned with the policeman, Saul, in tow. She jumped to her feet, startled. 'What are you doing here?'

'Sorry,' Elsa said. 'I rang him from the caff to let him know you wouldn't be able to make it this evening, but I didn't ask him to come to the flat.'

'She didn't,' Saul said. 'I swear. But she mentioned you were coming here for a brew and so I thought you might like to know what I've found out before you leave.'

Judith picked up her case, preparing to go. 'I think I already know as much as I want to, thank you.' This wasn't strictly true, but she was worried about Saul being involved. Although she'd been prepared to accept his help when the search for Dan had seemed hopeless, the situation was different now.

'You may as well hear him out,' Elsa said. 'Where's the harm?'

The harm, Judith thought, was that he was a policeman and it was his job to uphold the law. She wondered how many laws Ivor Doyle had broken. Probably too many to count. But she didn't want to be a part of any convictions that might be coming his way. The idea of having to stand up in a courtroom and give evidence, of being a public spectacle, was enough to make her stomach turn over.

'Five minutes,' Saul said. 'And what I said yesterday still stands. This isn't in any official capacity.'

Judith hesitated, but curiosity finally got the better of her. 'All right then.'

Saul took the chair where Elsa had been sitting, and Judith sat back down too. Elsa moved across the room and leaned against the small kitchen counter with her arms folded across her chest.

'I take it you've seen him,' the policeman said.

Judith nodded.

'That can't have been easy.'

Unwilling to share her emotional upheavals with this man, she gave a light shrug. 'I know that his real name is Ivor Doyle, if that's what you've come to tell me.'

'It was one of the things. And that he's a known associate of Alf Tombs. But I'm sure you've gathered that already. No convictions in the past five years, although he's been pulled in for questioning a few times. A bit of a mystery man, our Mr Doyle – keeps himself to himself. Still, I suppose that's not surprising bearing in mind his history with you.'

'Is that all you've got?' Elsa said scornfully. 'It was hardly worth the journey.'

Saul threw her a dirty look.

Judith sensed the tension between them, a definite hostility that seemed odd bearing in mind that they were supposed to be friends. '*Is* there anything else?'

Saul left a long, deliberate pause before he answered. 'Only the girl,' he said eventually.

Judith stiffened. 'What girl?'

'Her name's Nell McAllister. He lives with her. Apparently, they go way back.' He paused again, his gaze briefly darting away before returning to meet hers. 'Well before . . . '

'Before me, you mean.'

'Yes. From what I've heard.'

The news didn't come as any great surprise to Judith, but it was still a blow. Her hands gripped the arms of the chair. 'Are they married?'

'Not as far as I know.'

'What *do* you know about her?'

'I believe she used to be a singer; no one famous, just in the nightclubs. She's about the same age as you, a little older perhaps, slim, blonde.'

'You see?' Elsa said. 'While you were grieving, the bastard was rolling in the hay with his old girlfriend. That's the kind of man he is.'

Judith didn't need Elsa to spell it out for her. It was unlikely, she thought, that Nell even knew of her existence. And Ivor Doyle would want to keep it that way. No wonder he was so eager to get rid of his 'wife'; her appearance on the scene wouldn't do much for domestic harmony. She rose with as much dignity as she could muster. 'Do you have an address for him?'

Saul opened his wallet, took out a scrap of paper and handed it to her. 'Ironmonger Row. It's near Old Street.'

'Thank you.'

'Are you going there?' Elsa asked.

Judith slipped the address into her pocket, picked up her suitcase and started walking towards the door. 'I'm going home.'

'But you're coming back?'

'Oh yes,' Judith said. 'I'm definitely coming back.'

20

Alf Tombs liked Mayfair better than anywhere else in London. This was where the money was, where the pavements were lined with gold – and with jewels, furs, arts and antiques too. It was a veritable Aladdin's cave just waiting to be plundered. Being here on the streets was usually enough to lift his spirits, but today his mood was less than joyous. He was still seething from losing out on the New Bond Street job. All those hours spent staking out the place, only to have Pat Hull step in the day before and steal the tom from under his nose.

'Someone must have been talking,' Ivor Doyle said.

Alf nodded. Coincidences happened, but he didn't believe this was one of them. Hull had been prodding and poking at him for the past twelve months, trying to provoke a reaction. 'Maybe Monaghan got wind of it. I wouldn't trust that bastard as far as I could throw him.'

'Well, he's sorted now. What are you going to do about Hull?'

'Give him a taste of his own medicine.'

'What are you thinking?'

They were crossing the landscaped gardens of Hanover

Square, heading for Conduit Street. Alf sighed into the warm evening air. He had always thought it a waste of time and energy when villains went to war with each other, but sometimes it couldn't be avoided. Hull was making him look like a fool and it had to be stopped. 'I've heard a whisper about an airport job he's got planned. Swiss watches, top of the range. Should be worth a bundle.'

'When?'

'September the fifth. There's a flight in from Zurich in the late afternoon. The tom's going to be stored in a warehouse overnight before it gets delivered in the morning. Hull's probably planning the raid for the early hours, three or four o'clock.'

'It doesn't give us much time to get organised.'

'Enough,' Alf said. 'Let's face it, if Hull can plan a job like this, a monkey can. I don't know all the ins and outs yet, but I reckon if we play it right, we can slip right in there before him. All we need is some more information, and we've got a few weeks to get it. That firm's as leaky as a bleedin' sieve. Mick Bishop can't keep his mouth shut when he's had a few bevvies.'

'I take it they've got an inside man?'

'Security guard by the name of Temple. Gerry Temple. I've checked him out – he's got no form. An amateur. He'll break as soon as the law get their hands on him, realise he's looking at a long stretch and sing like a canary. And that's the sweet thing about it, see? He'll put the finger on Hull and his men. So long as we get our timings right, and keep our faces covered, Temple won't be any the wiser as to who's turning over the warehouse.'

The more Alf thought about it, the more he was liking the idea. It would be one in the eye for Hull, and a good earner too. Double the satisfaction. He glanced at Doyle, who looked distracted.

'You don't think it's got legs?'

Doyle shrugged. 'I'm up for it if you are.'

'What's on your mind?'

'Nothing.'

'Does nothing mean a redhead who likes to call herself your cousin?'

Doyle turned his face away and glanced up at the grand houses overlooking the square. 'She's gone. She won't be coming back.'

'You sure about that?'

'I'm sure. She's a small-town girl. London's not for her.'

Alf still hadn't got to the bottom of the Judith Jonson business. Doyle hadn't told him much, only that she was some broad he'd met on his travels. But there was more to it, much more. Even a blind man could see that. No one turned that shade of grey just because an old flame had shown up on his patch. The redhead had put the wind up him, no doubt about it; she'd come bearing trouble, and trouble, like a bad smell, had the habit of lingering. He didn't give a damn about Doyle's love life, but he needed him to be on his game if they were going to take on Pat Hull.

'I hope you're right. You ain't been yourself since she put in an appearance.'

'I've sorted it. We won't be seeing her again.'

Alf dropped the subject, but he wasn't convinced. In his experience, women usually did the very opposite of what you wanted them to do.

21

Although Saul Hannah had only lived in London since the war, he already knew the streets of Soho like the back of his hand. If someone had put a blindfold on him, he could still have hazarded a guess as what part he was in purely by the smells and sounds: the aromatic food shops of Wardour Street; the fruit and flowers of Rupert Street; the hum of machinery in the sweatshops of Poland Street; the cooking smells of the restaurants on Greek Street; the sounds of Dean Street where musicians of every ilk rehearsed for their shows.

He knew every dive, every club and pub, every theatre and restaurant. He knew the pimps and prostitutes, the pickpockets, the hoisters, the bookmakers and the spivs. Quietly he moved amongst the population, watching and listening, harvesting information and sowing seeds of doubt. The underbelly of London with its filth and degradation, its lies and treachery, had become the place he felt most at home.

Tonight, however, he was preoccupied by other things. The faces drifted past him largely unseen. He was thinking about the Ghost Squad coming to an end, and he was thinking about

Judith Jonson. It was her eyes that were haunting him, those green-grey eyes full of hurt. When he'd told her about Nell McAllister, it was as though he'd stabbed her through the heart. He wasn't proud of himself, but it was better she knew the truth. Ivor Doyle had moved on and left her behind. She was old news. Was she going to let it drop? He didn't reckon so. When she said she was coming back, he believed her.

A woman scorned could cause a heap of trouble, and trouble was what Saul revelled in. The whole Doyle business was a can of worms, and who knew what might slither out once it was opened. She was going to shake things up, and that could only be good. But it was risky too – for her at least. Doyle wouldn't be happy, and neither would Tombs. The latter relied on his locksmith and wouldn't want to lose him. If Doyle was under threat of being arrested, Judith could find herself in serious danger.

Saul went into a pub and bought a whisky, then sat down at the bar and lit a cigarette. During this process, he surreptitiously scanned the room, but couldn't see any familiar faces. That was good. He'd arranged to meet with Bernie Squires, a colleague from the Flying Squad, in fifteen minutes. While he waited, he smoke and drank and thought some more about Judith Jonson.

She'd declined his offer of a lift to the station until he'd pointed out that the car would take half the time of the bus, and that he was going in that direction anyway. He hadn't been, but what the hell. He'd wanted an opportunity to get to know her better away from the watchful eyes of Elsa.

Judith hadn't said much for the first five minutes, staring glumly through the windscreen. Still coming to terms, or trying to, with the utter duplicity of her 'husband'. Hearing about Nell had knocked her for six, even though she must have guessed that Doyle would hardly be living as a monk. Still, it was one thing suspecting it and quite another to hear the brutal truth.

'Are you married?' she'd asked eventually, turning to look at Saul.

'Widowed.'

'Oh, I'm sorry.'

'Portsmouth,' he'd explained, 'in the Blitz.'

'That's terrible. You must miss her.'

Saul never usually talked about his wife, never even mentioned her, but he'd sensed he'd have to bare at least a little of his soul if he wanted to win her confidence. 'Every day. I was in North Africa when it happened, fighting the good fight. It didn't seem right still being alive when she wasn't. It tears you apart, doesn't it? Like there's just nothing, no one, to carry on for. When I came back after the war, I couldn't face going home – well, I didn't have a home to go to – so I came to London instead. I've been working here ever since.'

She had left a respectful pause before saying, 'Sometimes the hardest thing is just carrying on.'

'I can't believe what he did to you. It was beyond cruel.'

She'd turned away again, said nothing.

'Just promise me something, all right? Promise you won't do anything rash.'

'Like blowing out his brains, do you mean?'

'You wouldn't be the first. What I mean is doing anything that will result in your life being ruined any more than it already has been. He's done enough damage. Don't let him do any more.'

He had dropped her off at Euston and watched her walk into the station, her head bowed, her red hair resting on her shoulders. The best thing, for her at least, would be to never come back, to stay in Westport and find a new future for herself. But he knew that wasn't going to happen. She hadn't finished with Ivor Doyle yet, not by a long chalk.

He ordered another drink and sipped it slowly. He still wasn't sure how any of this would pan out. It could be weeks, months even, before she returned. He had given her a phone number, told her she could ring any time and leave a message. She had stared at the piece of paper for a while before thrusting it carelessly into her pocket. He didn't expect her to call. She didn't trust him, and she was right not to.

It was after seven when Bernie Squires turned up and slid onto an adjacent stool, bringing with him the smell of Brylcreem and a faint whiff of cigars. He was a slender, dapper man in his late forties, a sergeant with the Flying Squad and probably the nearest thing to a friend Saul had on the force.

'Drowning your sorrows?' Bernie asked. 'I heard about the Ghosts being disbanded.'

'Bad news travels fast.'

'And it is bad news, the bloody worst. What are they thinking? With you lot out and about, we've virtually halved the crime rate in the past few years.'

'And that, apparently, is one of the reasons we're no longer required.' Saul smiled wryly. 'What can I say? A victim of our own success.'

'They're morons.'

Saul bought Bernie a pint of bitter, and they moved away from the bar to an empty table where they wouldn't be overheard. The two men bad-mouthed the top brass for a while, venting their frustrations. Once this subject had been exhausted, Saul moved on to the Hull job.

'Any progress on the Heathrow heist?'

'We've got a date: Monday the fifth of September. There's a consignment of watches flying in from Zurich. Seems like your snout knows what they're talking about.'

'I think he's reliable.' Saul was always careful to protect the identity of his informers, even to the likes of Bernie. That way there couldn't be any mistakes, any accidental slip-ups that might lead back to the source. And he always referred to them as 'he' whether they were male or female. 'We should get a better idea of the time nearer the date.'

'It'll probably be the early hours of the morning, if Hull sticks to his usual MO. And let's face it, the bloke's not renowned for his imagination. Or his subtlety. They'll be in there, waving shooters about like it's the bloody Wild West.'

'And that will be the end of Pat Hull's career.'

'Let's hope so. When it comes to charm, he's in the same league as the dearly departed Lennie.'

'I never had the pleasure. What's your take on who killed him?'

Bernie laughed. 'There's a list as long as my arm. He wasn't what you'd call Mr Popular.'

'Would you put Ivor Doyle on that list?'

'There was bad blood between them, that's for sure. But then there was bad blood between Lennie and half the East End. Whether Doyle was actually in London at the time is debatable. He certainly turned up shortly after.'

Saul nodded. 'Yes, that's what I heard.' He found himself thinking about Judith Jonson again. She was already aware that the man she'd loved was a liar and a cheat, but what if he was a murderer too?

22

There were delays on the railway and Judith didn't reach West-port until after eight o'clock. She had spent the journey in a daze, gazing out of the window at a landscape that was nothing more than a blur to her. Now, as the bus travelled through town, night was falling. She was relieved to be home, away from the madness of London and back in familiar surroundings. So much had happened in one day, she was barely able to digest it.

By the time the bus reached Trafalgar Road, she was ready to drop. She was worn out, exhausted, as though the very life had been wrung out of her. There was a tightness in her chest that refused to go away, a squeezing-out of all hope and happiness. She had left Westport full of expectation and had returned with her dreams shattered.

She walked slowly along the road, weighed down by despair. Her suitcase, although barely half full, dragged on her arm. It was an effort just to put one foot in front of the other. Glancing up at the house as she stepped through the gate, she noticed a light on in Annie's front room. Right now, she didn't want to talk – the mere thought of any kind of conversation filled her with dismay – and so she entered the property with all the furtiveness of a burglar.

She climbed the stairs with the same level of care and stood on the landing for a moment, holding her breath while she slid the key softly into the lock, opening and closing the door as quietly as she could. Once inside, she paused for a moment and then hurried through to the kitchen, where she dropped the case, switched on the boiler for a bath and put the kettle on the hob.

While she was waiting for the water to boil, she wandered into the living room, her eyes taking in all the details of her home. It was then that it struck her: she couldn't carry on living here. The flat was too full of memories, too full of *him*. This was the home they had chosen together, and he seemed to lurk in every part of it – *that* was the place he'd always sat, *that* was the spot where he'd often stood – like a mocking ghost that wouldn't leave her alone, a constant reminder of everything she'd lost.

Yes, she would find somewhere new, a fresh space, a home untainted by his presence. Although she'd miss having Annie just across the landing, it was for the best. She didn't have to move far away; there were plenty of affordable flats in the area. As soon as she got back from London, she'd give notice to the landlord and start looking.

She winced even as she thought about returning to the city. Could she really go through with it? But she had no choice. It was either that or let him get away with his betrayal. She had no firm plan as to what she would do when she saw Ivor Doyle again, but the thought of doing nothing was out of the question. She had to fight back. She had to find a way to shake up his life the way he had shaken up hers.

Taking the slip of paper out of her pocket, she gazed down at it. Saul's handwriting was thin and spidery, but the phone number was legible. What was it she wanted? Recompense, she supposed, for everything Ivor had put her through. But no, that wasn't really the word. Revenge was what she was actually after.

Judith had a restless night's sleep despite her exhaustion. She tossed and turned until the first light of dawn slid through the window. As her eyes flickered open, the first thought she had was of payback. It slithered into her mind like something cruel and venomous. She had always considered herself a decent person, honest and open-hearted, but now her head was filled with the prospect of vengeance.

She got out of bed, padded into the bathroom and stared at her reflection in the mirror. If she had expected to see a change, nothing was instantly obvious. Her face, apart from some shadows under her eyes, seemed unaltered. But there had been a shift inside her, something seismic. She was no longer the same person.

'Judith Jonson,' she said aloud.

But that wasn't who she was. Jonson was a fake name, a name that had been assumed. She wondered if he'd picked it himself or had had no choice in the matter. And how had he felt when he'd spoken his marriage vows using an identity that wasn't even his? Nothing, she imagined. The man was beyond guilt, beyond conscience.

A wave of disgust flowed over her. How had she been so blind, so stupid? She had never suspected, not even for a second, that he wasn't exactly who he'd said he was. Quickly she turned away from the mirror. There was no point to all this endless introspection. She had things to do, people to see.

This morning she would have to go into work and try to persuade Mr Gillespie to let her have more time off. How exactly she was going to achieve this was still unknown to her. She couldn't tell the truth, but she didn't want to lie. Perhaps she could find a middle ground, say that she was feeling unwell – she was, after all, sick to her stomach – and hope he would be sympathetic.

She washed and dressed, but couldn't face breakfast, which was probably fortunate as there was little in the larder and the shops weren't open yet. A cup of tea with powdered milk was the best she could manage. She drank it standing by the window. The door to Annie's flat banged shut at half seven, and she appeared on the front path thirty seconds later. Judith watched her walk down the street towards the bus stop. She was unsure as to how much she would eventually tell her, but that decision could wait. Annie wouldn't be home again until after six.

It was still too early to head into town, so she started sorting out the flat instead. She pulled out her aunt's old trunk from the back of the pantry, with the intention of filling it with her possessions. That wouldn't take long. She owned very little other than clothes and shoes, some jewellery, a few books, and a lamp she had bought at Westport market. The flat had come fully furnished and so she didn't have to worry about chairs and tables or the bed.

It was only when she opened the wardrobe that she stopped short. On the far right were all the clothes *he* had left behind: a suit, three shirts, a pair of trousers and a couple of ties. She had never had the heart to get rid of them. In fact, she had grown so used to them being there that most days she barely noticed their presence.

Her first impulse was to grab a pair of scissors, to vent her fury and frustration by shredding the lot. The thought was an appealing one and she let it simmer for a while before eventually changing her mind. It wasn't worth the effort. *He* wasn't worth the effort. She had more important things to do with her time. Instead, she roughly pulled the garments off the hangers and dropped them into the trunk.

She then divided her own clothes into what she would take to London with her and what she would leave behind. With no clear idea of how long she'd be in the city – two weeks, three? – she erred on the side of caution and packed more than she would probably need. Recalling the expensively tailored suit Ivor Doyle had been wearing, she chose the smarter items she owned to put in the suitcase. She refused to feel shabby in his presence; it was a matter of pride.

When all the packing was done, she cleaned the flat from top to bottom, dusting, scrubbing the kitchen and bathroom floors, running the vacuum over the carpets and polishing the windows. By the time she had finished, it was after ten o'clock. She looked around, pleased with the result. Then she sat down and wrote a letter of notice to the landlord, enclosing a cheque for the rent.

Judith took a deep breath as she arrived at the offices of Gillespie & Tate. Was she ready? Not exactly. But it had to be done. Unpaid leave was what she was going to request; a few weeks to recover from some vague under-the-weather malady. And if he said no? Well, she'd cross that bridge when she came to it. But when she stepped into the reception area, she got a surprise. Sitting behind her desk wasn't the plump Mrs Gillespie, but an attractive blonde in her mid twenties. The girl, dressed in a stylish pink suit, looked her up and down with an expression that could only be described as disdain.

'Can I help you?' she asked.

'I'm Judith.'

The girl's brows arched as if she didn't have a clue who Judith was. 'I'm sorry, do you have an appointment?'

Judith noticed that her replacement – obviously some sort of temp – had completely rearranged her desk. She felt a spurt of irritation at having her territory invaded, and struggled to maintain a smile. 'Judith Jonson,' she explained. 'I usually sit where you are now.'

'Oh.'

She heard more than surprise in that single syllable. There was something else, a kind of judgement, though possibly she was being oversensitive. It didn't help that she'd decided to forgo any make-up today in the hope of looking frail and pale enough to elicit some sympathy from her employer. Now, as she stared at her usurper's heart-shaped face and flawless skin, she was regretting that decision. 'I'd like a word with Mr Gillespie. Is he free at the moment?'

'Mr Gillespie isn't here.'

'Do you know when he'll be back?'

'If you could just wait here a moment.' The girl rose from her desk, smoothed down her skirt and crossed the reception area to knock on Mr Tate's door. She went inside, coming back out a minute later. 'You can go in now.'

Judith had no desire to talk to Mr Tate, but the choice had been taken out of her hands. 'Thank you,' she said stiffly.

'Ah, Judith,' he said as she entered the office. 'We didn't expect to see you until Monday. I take it you haven't heard about Mr Gillespie?'

She felt a jolt of alarm. 'What's happened? Has something happened to him?'

'I'm afraid he fell ill at the weekend, a mild heart attack. Please don't worry, though, he's quite all right. He'll be out of hospital and back home soon.'

'How awful. Poor Mr Gillespie.'

'Indeed. I'm sure we all wish him a speedy recovery.' He fiddled with some papers on his desk, glanced down and then up again. 'However, he was thinking of retiring at the end of this year, and with recent events . . . well, he's decided to bring things forward.'

'He won't be coming back?'

'No.'

Judith felt her heart sink. Mr Gillespie had always been her ally, her protector, and she couldn't imagine working here without him.

'There are going to be changes,' Mr Tate continued, 'but nothing for you to worry about. I'll be taking on a couple of junior partners and so there'll be plenty of work to go around. I see you've already met Natasha. She'll be staying on as my personal secretary and ... erm ... ' He paused to clear his throat. 'And as receptionist. That way you'll be free to spend more time helping the new partners settle in.'

The penny dropped. She was going to be sidelined, made to type all the boring stuff and probably shoved into that poky rear office, where she'd spend her days in splendid isolation. 'You're taking me off reception?'

'Oh, it's no reflection on you, Judith. You've done an excellent job, but I think you'll be better deployed in a new position.'

Judith, who felt like she'd had too many changes foisted on her over the past few days, smiled but shook her head. The words sprang out of her mouth before she had time to consider them properly. 'Actually, I've been thinking recently: maybe it's time for me to move on. I've enjoyed working here, but ... things are changing, aren't they? Perhaps we all need a fresh start.'

Mr Tate stroked his moustache while he considered this unexpected – but definitely welcome – turn of events. He didn't try and talk her out of it. 'Well, if that's what you'd prefer ... '

'I think it's for the best.'

He nodded. 'Very well, then. Although I'd just like to say that we've appreciated all your hard work through the years. You'll be missed.'

She didn't detect much sincerity in his voice, but thanked him regardless. Then she added reluctantly, 'I suppose you'll want me to work out my notice?'

'Oh, I don't think that will be necessary. It's only me here at the moment, so I'm sure Natasha can manage.'

Judith was relieved. It meant she didn't have to delay her plans to return to London. Although she'd have preferred to have a reference from Mr Gillespie, that was hardly feasible at the moment. 'Could you post a reference to me?' she asked. 'Would that be all right?'

'Of course.'

'Thank you.'

They politely wished each other the best, and Judith left the room. Natasha stopped her typing to look up at her. The girl wore a smug expression, as if she thought she'd got one over on Judith by stealing her position.

'Is everything all right?' she asked.

'Couldn't be better,' Judith said, smiling brightly.

'I'll see you on Monday, then.'

Judith didn't bother to put her straight. She felt the girl's snooty gaze follow her out through the door. It was only when she was back on Earl Street, walking away, that the full force of what she'd done struck her. She had just made herself voluntarily jobless. And soon she'd be homeless too. Was she mad? Perhaps she was, but she felt a glorious sense of liberation. This was swiftly followed by a wave of panic. She stopped and breathed in the salty sea air. One thing was for certain: there was no going back.

23

Elsa slid into the booth, her eyes gleaming. 'You came.'

'Clearly,' he said, glancing at his watch as if to press home the point that his time was precious. 'What do you want?'

She looked around the pub, making sure no one was close enough to hear, and leaned forward a little. 'To make a deal, of course.'

'And what kind of deal would that be?'

'The sort where I give you what you want and you give me what I want.'

'Don't play games, love. I'm not in the mood. If you've got something to say, just spit it out.'

'All right,' she said. 'Cast your mind back to the twelfth of October 1944, a rainy night in Kellston. It's a Thursday, not too late, about ten o'clock. Lennie Hull has been in the Fox and now he's winding through the back streets – not too steady on his feet, he's had a skinful – heading for home. A girl approaches him. She's blonde, wearing a cream raincoat. Maybe she's drunk too, or maybe there's something else wrong with her. Anyway, she gets right in his face, yelling at him, giving him what for.'

Elsa paused and looked at the man sitting across from her. 'Any of this starting to ring bells?'

'I've no idea what you're talking about.'

'Let's not go down that road. It's stupid and pointless. I was there, you see. I saw everything.'

The man shrugged, still trying to play dumb. But his cocky demeanour had turned more wary now. He was watching her closely, narrow-eyed, and the corners of his mouth had tightened.

'You're whistling in the wind, love. If you were there, why didn't you go to the law?'

Elsa flapped her hand dismissively. 'Why would I? So far as I'm concerned, Lennie Hull got what he deserved. He was a filthy, vicious bastard and I hope he rots in hell. No, I don't give a damn about that. I did the decent thing back then and kept my mouth shut.'

'So what happened next in this fairy tale of yours?'

'She pulls out a gun, doesn't she, starts waving it around. But we both know what Lennie was like. He didn't believe she was going to shoot him, not for a minute. So he's standing there laughing at her, taunting her, telling her to pull the bloody trigger. Thinks she won't dare, thinks she hasn't got the nerve. And, well, we both know what happened next.' Elsa smiled slyly. 'She must have gone into shock – who wouldn't with Lennie Hull's brains all over them? – because she just stood there looking down at him. Then she took off like a bat out of hell.'

He didn't say anything for a while, just gave her the stare.

She stared right back.

Eventually he made a decision. 'Go to the law,' he said. 'Tell them what you like. I don't care. Where's the evidence?'

'Ah,' she said, 'that's the thing. She dropped the gun, didn't she? Panicking, I suppose. She just left it there in the gutter for anyone to find. Seemed a shame, so I picked it up and took it home. You don't have to worry; I've got it somewhere safe. And you can have it – for a price.'

'I don't like blackmailers.'

Elsa screwed up her face. 'That's a nasty word. We're not talking blackmail here, just a friendly deal. I got to thinking recently that it was quite a favour I did, keeping quiet about everything. No trouble for anyone. But these are hard times and I reckon I'm owed. A favour for a favour, right? I'm not being greedy. A couple of grand, that's all I'm asking.'

'In your dreams.'

'Oh, I think it's a fair price. I mean, it's not just the law you have to worry about; there's Pat Hull too. I'm sure he'd be interested in finding out who topped his brother.'

'You think I care about Pat Hull?'

'Nice try, but we both know the bloke's a psychopath. He's an eye-for-an-eye type, wouldn't you say? It could get kind of messy. Look, why don't you think about it and get back to me? Sleep on it, perhaps. You know where to find me.'

Elsa left the pub feeling pleased with herself. She was one step nearer to a nice little windfall. It was always tricky doing this kind of business, but she reckoned she'd held her own. In a few days' time, she was sure she'd have her money.

24

Judith hadn't liked lying to Annie, but telling her the truth had seemed an even more daunting prospect. She didn't want to have to explain something she hadn't yet come to terms with herself. Since finding out that Dan was still alive, she had barely even cried. It was easier to keep a stiff upper lip in the company of strangers, but she was scared of breaking down, of falling apart, if she tried to explain everything to her friend.

In the end she had simply told her that nothing had come of the visit to London, but that it had been tiring and upsetting and she'd decided to take more time off work to go and stay with a former work colleague who lived in Ripon.

'Just for a week or two until I get back on my feet again.'

Annie had been fully supportive of this plan, but less impressed by the decision to give up the flat. 'But why? Why move out?'

'Because I'll always be reminded of him if I stay. It's too full of memories. No, it's time to move on, get somewhere new. I'm sure I can find a flat close by.'

'What about Charlotte? She'll be home at the weekend. What am I going to tell her?'

'You don't need to tell her anything. I've written a letter. It'll be there by the time she gets back.'

'Have you told her about London?'

Judith had pulled a face. 'Not exactly.'

'Or in plain language, no.'

'What's the point? It's over and done with. I just want to put it behind me.'

Annie had understood that Charlotte would fuss and worry, and had perhaps been quietly pleased to be in charge of a secret. 'All right. I won't say a word, I promise.'

'Thank you.'

Judith had experienced a moment of doubt during this conversation. Maybe she had made too many hasty decisions, knee-jerk responses she hadn't thought through. But it was too late for regrets now. She was already on the train, heading for London. It had been her intention to wait, to gather some strength before returning to the city, but somehow that plan had fallen by the wayside. With the practicalities taken care of – notice given on the flat, her job resignation, and Annie agreeing to hold on to the trunk in case the tenancy ran out before she got back – all that was left was to face her demons.

She sighed into the emptiness of the train compartment. Yes, Ivor Doyle was certainly a demon, something dark and dangerous and damaging. But she wasn't going to back down and let him walk all over her. Her hands balled into two tight fists. Did he think he'd seen the back of her, successfully packed her off never to bother him again? Well, he had another think coming. She would be like one of those Furies in Greek mythology, an avenger of wrongdoing, an angry spirit of justice and vengeance.

Judith was feeling more frazzled than furious by the time she finally made it to Kellston. There had been a long delay on the run-in to Euston. A body on the line. The thought of it had made her queasy.

'A jumper, probably,' one of the men in the compartment had said, with a kind of weariness that suggested it wasn't that uncommon an occurrence.

She wondered what level of desperation it took to do such a thing. Or maybe it was simply a sense of emptiness: nothing to get up for in the morning, nothing to keep on going for. She feared that bleakness, sensed that it hovered on the horizon, waiting for her when her anger was spent. She tried to shake the thought from her mind, but it lingered there like a quiet dread.

It was mid afternoon, just after three o'clock, when she walked out of the train station, glanced warily across the road towards Sycamore House and then headed up the high street. The afternoon was cool and cloudy, for which she was grateful. Her suitcase was heavy, and she frequently shifted it from one hand to the other. She needed a place to stay, preferably somewhere clean and inexpensive, and was hoping that Elsa could point her in the right direction.

Elsa was the main reason she'd decided to base herself in Kellston again, that and the fact that it was relatively cheap. It was a disappointment, therefore, to see no sign of her as she stepped into the café. An older lady, grey-haired, was waiting on tables. Judith took a seat by the window. She ordered a cup of tea when the woman came over, and asked, 'Is Elsa not working?'

'She'll be back in tomorrow.'

Judith thought that was just her luck, to have walked halfway up the high street only to find that Elsa wasn't here. With no other choice, she turned to the woman for help instead. 'I don't suppose you know of any B and Bs round here?'

'Oh, you'll be wanting Station Road,' came the reply. 'There's plenty there. A whole row of them.'

If Mrs Jolly had done her worst, Judith knew she wouldn't be welcome in any of those establishments. 'I was looking for somewhere quieter, really. Off the main road, perhaps?'

The waitress thought about it. 'Well now, I suppose you could try Silverstone Road. I think there's a couple down there.'

'Is that far away?'

'Straight down the road, on past the station and it's second on your left.'

Judith, although distinctly underwhelmed at the prospect of having to lug her case all the way back down the high street, smiled and nodded. 'Thank you. I'll try there.'

While she sipped her tea, she wondered how far Mrs Jolly's gossip might have travelled. It made her nervous to imagine knocking on a door only to be turned away as soon as she gave her name because her reputation had preceded her. No, that was just ridiculous. It wasn't as if she was on the list of London's Most Wanted. But however much she reasoned with herself, the worry continued to gnaw at her.

By the time Judith left Connolly's, it had started to rain, a thin mizzle that didn't look like much but which seeped under her collar and made her feel cold and shivery. She stopped to put up her umbrella, and glanced over at the green. Elsa didn't live that far away. Would it be rude to drop by uninvited? She decided to risk it.

Walking as quickly as she could with the case weighing her down, she crossed the road and cut across the grass, averting her eyes from the wooden bench. A few minutes later, she was in Barley Road. She went to the house on the corner, descended the rickety metal staircase and knocked on the door. There was every chance, she thought, that Elsa wouldn't be here. The girl was probably out and about, shopping or meeting friends. She prepared herself for disappointment.

It was a pleasant surprise, therefore, when she heard movement from inside, shortly followed by the sound of a bolt drawing back. Elsa smiled widely when she saw her.

'Hello, I didn't expect to see you back so soon.'

'Unfinished business,' Judith said. 'Look, I'm sorry to call by unannounced, only—'

'Oh, don't worry about that. Get out of the rain. Come in, come in.'

Judith shook her brolly before following her inside. 'I'm looking for a B and B, but I can't go back to Station Road. I was wondering if you knew anywhere decent round here.'

'I'll make a brew and have a think. Or would you rather have something stronger? I've got whisky if you'd like one.'

Judith turned down both offers. She was having enough trouble keeping her emotions in check without adding alcohol to the mix. 'No thanks, really, I'm fine. I just had a cup of tea in the café.'

'Well, sit down and make yourself comfortable. Sorry the place is a bit of a mess. I've been doing some packing. I'm moving out in a couple of weeks.'

'You're going?' It was a blow for Judith. Elsa was the closest thing to a friend she had here, and now she was about to lose her. 'I didn't realise. Are you leaving London, or just here?'

'London. I'm sick of it, to be honest.'

Her words evoked a memory in Judith's mind: Dan standing by the window in the offices of Gillespie & Tate. *You can get tired of a place. It can wear you down.* She felt the dull thump of her heart. If only he'd chosen a different firm of solicitors. If only she'd never met him in the first place. 'Where are you going?'

'I haven't decided yet. Abroad, I think. Somewhere warm. Morocco, maybe. I've heard it's wild over there.' Elsa must have seen a change in Judith's expression, because she quickly added,

'But not right now. I'll probably be here for as long as you are, so anything I can do to help . . . '

'I haven't really got a plan.'

'Well, you haven't come back just to put the cat among the pigeons.'

'That Nell needs to know what he's really like, what he did to me. I'm not going to let him get away with it.'

'Good for you. He deserves it. Give him a taste of his own medicine. I take it you're going to see him soon?'

'Tomorrow, I think. I don't suppose he'll be best pleased.'

'Do you want me to come with you?'

Judith shook her head. 'Thanks, but this is something I have to deal with on my own.'

'Moral support, then. Everyone needs that.'

Judith nodded. 'First I have to find somewhere to stay. The waitress in Connolly's suggested Silverstone Road. What do you think? Should I give it a try?'

'Yes, there's a couple down there, but . . . You know, I don't think you should be on your own right now. Why don't you stay here for a while? I've got a spare room. Well, it's more of a cupboard really, but there's a bed in there. It's got to be better than some overpriced bed and breakfast with a witch of a landlady watching your every move.'

'But you've things to do. I don't want to be in the way.'

'You won't be, I promise. To be honest, I'd be glad of the company. It gets kind of lonely being on my own all the time. Anyway, we should stick together, us girls, take care of each other. What do you say?'

Judith couldn't think of a reason to say no, and so she didn't.

25

Alf Tombs was leaning against the bar in the Fox. It was only six o'clock, but already the place was heaving. It was Friday, payday for the workers, and people were out to enjoy themselves. The pub was lively and attracted a varied clientele. You could find yourself rubbing shoulders with anyone from the neighbourhood butcher to the local MP. There was healthy representation from the criminal classes – thieves, fences, the occasional armed robber – and there were cops from Cowan Road police station too. Even the odd tart slipped in for a quick gin when business was slack.

He was studying his own reflection in the mirror that ran along the rear of the bar, thinking he wasn't wearing too badly all things considered, when a familiar face appeared beside him.

'Evening, Mr Tombs. Can I buy you a drink?'

It seemed to Alf that every time he turned around recently, Jimmy Taylor was there. The kid was like one of those stray dogs – eyes pleading, tail wagging – that attached itself to you and refused to let go. 'I'm all right, son. But thanks for asking.'

Jimmy continued to hover by his shoulder. 'It's just . . . '

Alf waited, but the kid didn't finish. 'Just?'

'It's about the girl, the redhead, you know the one who was looking for Ivor Doyle.'

'What about her?'

'Only she's back. I saw her, clear as day, walking out of the station this afternoon with a suitcase. I just thought you might want to know. Well, you and Mr Doyle.'

Alf, although he was interested, pretended that he wasn't. He glanced around the pub in a casual fashion before his eyes came back to rest on Jimmy. 'I suppose she's staying at Sycamore House again?'

Jimmy shook his head. 'Nah, she didn't book in there. I mean, she wouldn't, would she, not after . . . ' He paused, somehow managing to look both smug and shifty at the same time. 'The thing is, Mr Tombs, I had a quiet word with the landlady; told her Judith Jonson wasn't what you'd call the respectable sort. Did I do right? Seemed to me she was out to cause trouble, and no one wants that.'

Alf raised his eyebrows. 'I wouldn't like to be in your shoes when she finds out.'

'Well, she ain't going to find out.' But suddenly Jimmy didn't sound too confident. 'Is she?'

'You'd better hope not. In my experience, women don't take kindly to being called whores. They tend to get a touch upset about it.'

Jimmy shrugged, saying with bravado, 'She should have thought on, then, shouldn't she? She's the one who started all this.'

Alf didn't quite get his line of reasoning, but then reasoning probably didn't figure that highly in the kid's thought process. 'Do you know where she's staying now?'

'She went up the high street. I haven't seen her since.'

'All right, I'll take care of things from now on.'

Despite the dismissal, Jimmy didn't move away. He wiped a hand down the side of his trouser leg. 'Er, Mr Tombs, I hope you don't mind me asking, but if you've ever got any jobs going . . . I'm a hard worker, loyal. I'll never let you down.'

Alf tried to keep a straight face. It seemed like every kid in London wanted to be a gangster these days. 'Sure, son, I'll let you know.'

The exchange was terminated by the arrival of Ivor Doyle. Jimmy nodded and went back to his mates at the rear of the pub.

'Who was that?' Doyle asked.

'Name's Jimmy Taylor. I told you about him. He's the one who tipped me the wink about your lady friend turning up out of the blue.'

'What did he want?'

Alf grinned. 'He's after a job. Did I tell you he's a locksmith? You'd better watch out. I reckon he's looking to step into your shoes.'

Doyle made a mock grimace. 'I'll try not to lose too much sleep over it.'

'Oh, and there was something else too. It appears your lady friend is back in Kellston.'

Doyle flinched and stared at him hard. 'What? Judith? No, she can't be.'

'Young Jimmy saw her come out of the station this afternoon, suitcase and all. I thought you'd got it sorted.'

'I did. I have. He must be wrong.'

Alf shook his head. 'I don't think so.'

Doyle raked his fingers through his hair. 'Shit.'

'Maybe you weren't quite as persuasive as you thought. Anyway, least you know now. If she turns up on your doorstep—'

'She doesn't know where I live.'

'Are you sure of that? Look, if she's making a nuisance of

herself, I can help you out. Maybe have a word, huh? Make it clear she's not welcome in Kellston.'

'No, I'll deal with it myself.'

Alf could have said he hadn't made much of a job of that to date, but he resisted the temptation. 'The offer's open if you need it.'

'Do you know where she is now?'

Alf shook his head. 'Not at Sycamore House. Jimmy saw her turn onto the high street, but that was it.' He decided not to mention what the kid had said to the landlady, unsure as to how Doyle would take it. Ivor Doyle was the sort who didn't like other people interfering in his business, whatever their intentions. 'She can't be far away.'

Doyle's face had grown tight and angry. Two bright stripes of red appeared along the sharp angles of his cheekbones. 'What the hell is she playing at?'

'The same game all women play when they feel hard done by. It's called getting their own back. You want a pint?'

Doyle shook his head. 'Things to do. Have you got my wedge?'

Alf glanced around before producing an envelope. It was in Doyle's hand in a fraction of a second, and in his pocket moments after. The money was a share of the proceeds from a haul of spirits they'd liberated from a warehouse a week ago. 'Don't go getting into trouble,' he said. 'She ain't worth it, mate, none of them are.' What he really meant was that he didn't want Doyle getting into a row and ending up in a cell at Cowan Road. 'You've got Nell to think about.'

'It's Nell I *am* thinking about. She doesn't need this any more than I do.'

Alf thanked his lucky stars that he had a wife like Renee. She might not be perfect, far from it, but at least she wasn't crazy. Nell McAllister had a screw loose and everyone knew it. The girl wasn't all there – Lennie Hull had seen to that – and it wouldn't take much to tip her over the edge again.

Doyle left, and Alf returned to his pint. He had the feeling the redhead was about to stir up a hornets' nest. He looked over at Jimmy Taylor, frowned and wondered if he could find some use for him after all.

26

Judith waited until she heard Elsa leave for work – she was on the early shift today – before getting up and using the bathroom. She didn't want to get in the way or do anything that might make the other girl regret having asked her to stay. The spare bedroom was tiny, more like a cell than anything else, but it sufficed. She'd slept pretty well, all things considered, and although she wasn't exactly prepared for what lay ahead, it was a help that she didn't feel exhausted.

For breakfast she cut a thin slice off the coarse brown loaf and smeared it with butter and jam. She ate standing up in the kitchen area in the corner of the living room. The flat was small but stylish. Elsa had made the best of the available space. She studied the Gauguin print on the wall, drawn to its colours and sense of vibrancy. Her aunt, although keen on art, had disapproved of Gauguin, not so much for his paintings as for what she described as his 'depraved lifestyle'. He had, after his marriage fell apart, gone to Tahiti and taken a thirteen-year-old wife.

Judith nibbled on the bread. She wondered if, fundamentally,

176

all men were the same – selfish and predatory and driven by lust. She had been naive when she married Dan Jonson, innocent and inexperienced. He'd exploited her weakness and betrayed her trust. That was what she had to keep in mind whenever her resolve wavered.

Elsa's opinion of the male sex wasn't that high either. They'd had a long conversation last night, and although Elsa hadn't been specific, she'd made her feelings clear: wherever men were involved, you had to watch your back. Judith had asked about Saul.

'Saul Hannah's all right. You can trust him. Well, so far as you can trust any bloke. But he won't go back on his word, if that's what you're worried about.'

'I don't really understand him. I mean, he knows Ivor Doyle's broken the law, in more ways than one, but he's prepared to ignore it. I didn't think the police did that kind of thing.'

Elsa had laughed. 'They play by their own rules, love, just like the villains. He's not interested in Doyle. London's full of deserters, thousands of them. The prisons would be bursting if they rounded them all up. And marrying you under a false name – well, I doubt he's bothered about that either. He's got bigger fish to fry.'

'Like Alfred Tombs?'

'Exactly. It's the bosses the law are trying to bring down, the men at the top. They're the ones with the nous and the contacts. You topple them off their perch and the rest soon come tumbling after.'

Judith thought about this as she finished her breakfast, wondering about Saul's motives in offering to help her. Not that it mattered any more. Now that she'd found who she'd been looking for, there was no reason for her to ever see Saul Hannah again. He had a streak of sadness in him that she recognised, his past coloured by tragedy and loss. Which wasn't to say that she liked him. There was something cold about the man; something odd and distant.

She went back to her room, where she dressed carefully, choosing one of her best summer frocks. She applied make-up and brushed her hair until it shone. She told herself that none of this was for *his* benefit; just so she didn't feel at a disadvantage. It was protection against his judgement. It was armour.

Judith got off the bus at Old Street roundabout and took a moment to get her bearings. Once she'd worked out where City Road was, she was fine. She'd mapped out the route on the *A–Z* and knew which way to go. As she wound through the streets, she hoped that Ivor Doyle would be in. It was ten thirty, and as he didn't have what could be called a regular job, she was counting on him being at home. And if he wasn't? Maybe it would be Nell who answered the door. And then she'd have to make a decision as to whether she told her the truth. She could justify this course of action by claiming the girl had a right to know, but she was aware that this was disingenuous. There was only one thing that could follow such a revelation, and that was devastation.

Judith didn't want to dwell too much on this. None of it was her fault so why should she feel guilty? It was Doyle who'd created an evil mess. If there was fallout, it was all down to him. But what if there were kids? The thought hadn't even entered her mind before. Now that it had, she felt a sickness in the pit of her stomach.

She slowed her pace when she reached Ironmonger Row. The first building she noticed was a large red-brick construction, the public baths. There were people going in and out, and as she passed the doors, a warm, steamy smell floated into her face. Further on, to the right, was a row of small two-up, two-down houses. She checked the numbers and then crossed the road.

When she reached number 24, she stopped by the gate. What she was about to do was final, irreversible. She stared at the house with its neat little porch and gleaming windows. In another life, at another time, this could have been the home she'd shared with Dan. She took a deep breath. Before such reflections could get under her skin, she marched up to the door and knocked.

It was Ivor Doyle who answered. He seemed more angry than surprised when he saw her standing in front of him. 'What the hell are you doing here?'

'We need to talk,' she said.

'I've said all I've got to say.'

'Well, it's not all about you. Aren't you going to invite me in?'

As if to bar her path, he stepped over the threshold and half closed the door behind him. 'Go away, Judith. Go home. Why are you making this so bloody difficult?'

'Difficult?' she echoed with incredulity. 'Is that what you call it? Well, I've been home, thought about it all and now I'm back. You can't order me around. I'm not leaving again until I get a proper explanation from you.'

'You've already had it.'

'No, all I've had is half a story. It's not good enough. You owe me more than that.'

He shook his head. 'I've got nothing more to say.'

'I'm not going anywhere.'

'You do what you like. I'm going back inside now.'

Seeing him start to retreat, Judith quickly blurted out the threat. 'Then I'll talk to Nell instead. Don't you think she deserves to know the truth?'

That stopped him in his tracks. His reply was low but fierce. 'Don't you dare bring Nell into this.'

'But she's already in it. Does she know you're actually married to someone else? Well, I say married, but I don't suppose it's actually legal in the eyes of the law. Let me put it another way: does she know you went through a wedding ceremony with someone else?'

Ivor Doyle's face was white. He glared at her and there was venom in the look. 'Would you really do that to a sick woman?'

'What do you mean, sick?'

'Just that. She's ill, very ill. This is the last thing she needs.'

Judith, caught on the back foot, wasn't sure whether to believe him or not. 'How do I know you're telling the truth?'

'You don't,' he said.

'What's wrong with her?'

His gaze slid away. 'It's complicated.'

'And what's that supposed to mean?'

'It means I don't want to discuss it standing out here on the street.'

Judith suspected this was all a tall tale, just something to deflect her. When it came to telling the truth, he simply couldn't do it. His whole life, every part of it, was a tissue of lies. 'So let me come in and we can discuss it in private.'

'No,' he said sharply, glancing over his shoulder as if to make sure they weren't being overheard. He gestured along the road. 'Look, there's a café just up there. Keep on going and you'll come to a square. It's on the left. I'll meet you there in five minutes.'

Before she even had time to reply, he went back inside and closed the door. She stood for a moment, unsure as to what to do next, and then turned around and began to walk. It was probable, she thought, that she was wasting her time. In reality, there was nothing Ivor Doyle could say to make things better, and yet she couldn't let it go. She needed answers, explanations, even if those things hurt her. She needed some kind of closure.

She found the café without any trouble. It was quiet, in that lull between breakfast and lunch, but a few of the front tables by the window were occupied. She went to the back, away from other customers, and ordered a pot of tea for two. While she waited, she nervously played with the wedding ring on her left hand. Why was she still wearing it? She hadn't wanted to remove it in Westport in case Annie noticed, but there was no reason to keep it on in London. She twisted the ring, moved it up and down her finger, but couldn't quite bring herself to take that final step.

It was closer to ten minutes than five before he finally showed up. She watched as he strode through the café, his jacket slung carelessly over his shoulder. He was wearing dark trousers and a white shirt with the sleeves rolled up to his elbows. He saw her, nodded and slid into the chair opposite hers.

'There's tea,' she said, gesturing towards the pot, 'if you want it.'

He gave a small, impatient shake of his head. 'Why have you come back to London, Judith? What's the point of all this?'

'The point is I need answers. I've already told you that.'

'I've given you answers. Just accept them and move on.'

She ignored the instruction. 'Tell me about Nell.'

'You have to leave her alone. What I did . . . well, none of it's her fault. Don't make her pay for my mistakes.'

Judith flinched. 'Is that what I was, a mistake?'

'I didn't mean that. You were never . . . ' He stopped, as though he feared saying too much. 'It's complicated, like I said.' He sighed, glanced around the café and looked back at her. 'Nell isn't what you'd call stable. She has problems, mental problems. She had some sort of a breakdown and . . . ' He shrugged. 'It's tough for her, just dealing with everyday stuff. I don't want her involved in this.'

'But she is involved whether you like it or not.'

'Only if you make it that way. I didn't leave you for her if that's what you're thinking. We didn't meet up until a long time after.'

'Meet up *again*,' she said. 'She was an old girlfriend, wasn't she?'

'Who have you been talking to?'

Judith didn't answer him directly. 'I'm just curious, that's all. You can't be surprised by that.'

'What I'm surprised about is that you're here. Why are you wasting your time like this?'

'It's my time to waste. I can do what I want with it. And you haven't answered my question.'

'All right, yes, she was. We used to go out. We were a couple. We split up, I left London and that was that. Happy now?'

'I'm not sure if that's the word I'd use, exactly.'

'What do you want from me? I can't change the past, what I did. It's done with. I understand you want to punish me, so just get it over with. Go to the cops and have me arrested.'

'Maybe I don't want to put you in prison.'

'So what do you want?'

'Some answers, for God's sake. It's what I keep telling you. I used to know you, Dan but . . . ' She stopped and shook her head. '*Ivor*. I can't get used to calling you that.'

'You don't need to get used to it,' he said, with unnecessary cruelty.

'Thank you for reminding me.' She glared at him for a moment. 'The thing is, you know I wouldn't have judged you for what happened in the war. I'd have listened. I'd have understood. But you never gave me that opportunity; you just gave up on us.'

Her words seemed to touch him. His voice softened, and there was a sadness in his eyes she hadn't seen before. 'You think you could have coped with it, but you couldn't. There was only one way for me to make a living after I deserted – and it wasn't on the right side of the law. You wouldn't have wanted that kind of life.'

'But Nell does?'

'Nell grew up around villains; she knows the score.'

'So that's how you make a living, is it? Stealing from other people.'

'That's about the sum of it.'

Judith found it almost impossible to associate this man with the one she had fallen in love with. It was as though an impostor had stolen Dan's face and voice and mannerisms, a stranger she had nothing in common with. Or maybe Dan had only been an actor, playing a part for a while – the loving, dutiful husband – before moving on to the next drama.

'How did you get my address?' he asked.

She shrugged, not prepared to tell him about Saul Hannah. 'It wasn't that hard. You can find out anything if you really want to.'

He picked up a teaspoon and played with it, tapping the bowl against the white tablecloth. 'Are you going to tell Nell?'

That was something else she wasn't prepared to divulge. First, she'd check out his story and see if the girl really was ill. There was every chance that Doyle was playing her. 'Who knows?'

'Don't play games, Judith. They always end badly.'

'Are you threatening me?'

He gave a thin smile. 'I'd never do that. Just a friendly warning. I wouldn't want to see you get hurt.'

'It's a bit late for that.'

'You don't know what you're messing with. Go home. Haven't you got a job to get back to?'

'As it happens, I haven't. I don't work for Gillespie and Tate any more. But there are plenty of lawyers in London. I'm sure I'll find something soon.'

Anger flashed in Ivor Doyle's eyes. 'You can't stay here.'

'You can't stop me. It's a free country, apparently.'

'Do you want money? Is that it? Tell me how much.'

Judith gave an empty laugh. The offer made her hate him even more. 'You're a joke. Do you really think you can pay me off? How much is an illegal wife worth these days?'

'I've told you everything you want to know. What more do you want?'

'You haven't told me half of it.'

He sighed, threw the spoon onto the tablecloth and folded his arms across his chest. 'We've been over this. I left the hospital, came back to London, looked up Alf Tombs and asked him for work. Later, I bumped into Nell and we got together. There, that's it. I could pad it out, but what's the point?'

'The devil's in the detail,' she said.

'What do you want me to say?'

Judith wanted to hear some hint of regret, of remorse, but there wasn't any. 'I had the right to know you were still alive.'

'Of course you did, but I took the coward's way out. I'm a miserable bastard, a waste of space. What do you want me to do about it now? Say I'm sorry? All right, I'm sorry.'

Judith curled her lip. It was the kind of hollow apology that meant nothing.

'Where are you staying?' he asked.

'Why?'

'What's the big mystery? You know where I am; why shouldn't I know where you are?'

Judith inferred some menace from the question. She kept her answer vague. 'With a friend.'

'I didn't know you had any friends in London.'

'Why would you?'

He unfolded his arms, took a pack of cigarettes from his jacket pocket and lit one. 'You're not at a B and B, then?'

'Well, I could hardly go back to Sycamore House, could I? Not after what you did. I mean, I know you wanted to get rid of me, but that was just plain nasty.'

He gazed at her blankly. 'You've lost me. I don't have a clue what you're talking about.'

'Why is it that every time you open your mouth, I feel like a lie comes out?'

'Maybe you're getting paranoid in your old age.'

'Or maybe I'm just getting smarter.'

He took a drag on the cigarette, exhaled and peered at her through the smoke. 'I don't think a smart person would stay in London.'

'What you think or don't think is meaningless to me.'

'You start stirring things up and—'

'And what?'

'Believe me, I'm just trying to protect you.'

'It's a bit late for that.'

He rolled his eyes. 'Better late than never, huh? I'm not stringing you a line. You don't understand this world, not the one I exist in. It's different to yours. If you're not careful, it'll eat you up and swallow you alive.'

Judith knew it wasn't her he was trying to protect, but Nell. 'I'll take my chances.'

'You shouldn't.'

She watched him smoke, watched his mouth, listened to him trying to persuade her to leave. The more he tried, the more determined she became to stay put. So long as she was getting under his skin, she was happy. It was a small victory, but better than nothing.

'So, this friend of yours. Are they in Kellston?'

Judith didn't reply.

He smoked some more of his cigarette. 'Think how much happier you'd be if you could just let go.'

'I believe what you mean is how much happier *you'd* be.'

'You've got cynical, Judith. You never used to be like that.'

'I wonder why that is?'

He left a short silence. 'So where do we go from here?'

It was a reasonable question, but not one Judith knew the answer to.

27

The skin on Maud Bishop's hands was red and cracked from the lunchtime washing-up; pots, pans, plates, cups and cutlery had all passed through the sink she was leaning over. Still, it was a job, so she wasn't complaining. It put food in the babies' mouths and kept the bailiffs at bay. Course, she had to pay for someone to take care of the kids while she was at work, but there was still a small profit at the end of it. She'd have preferred to be waiting on tables – the waitresses got to keep their tips – but with her face in the state it was in, she'd only have put the customers off their food.

She was counting down the days now until Mick and Pat Hull went out on the Heathrow job. But she wasn't counting her chickens. Things could go wrong and frequently did. The heist could get cancelled if something didn't smell right or someone fell sick or the plane didn't bring in the goods it was supposed to. She ran through all these possibilities in her head as if the procedure of listing them could somehow prevent them from happening.

'Please, God,' she murmured, 'make it a goer.'

Elsa came into the kitchen and dumped another tray by the sink. 'You talking to yourself, Maud?'

'No law against it last time I looked.'

'You got something on your mind?'

'Nothing for you to be bothered about.'

Elsa laughed. 'Mind my own business, in other words.' But she didn't take her own advice and continued, 'Your Mick giving you grief again?'

'When doesn't he?'

'You shouldn't have to put up with it. If I was you, I'd get the hell out of Kellston: pack your stuff, pick up your kids and run for the hills. That bastard's never going to change.'

Maud stared at her wide-eyed, wondering if she knew or had somehow guessed about her plans. 'What?'

'You can't just sit around waiting for him to go down again. It might never happen. Although it probably will. He's not what you'd call a genius, is he? But in the meantime, you're stuck with him. You deserve better, love. You know you do.' Elsa paused and then said, 'What's the matter? You look white as a sheet.'

Maud fiddled with a greasy strand of hair that had come loose. 'Nothin',' she said quickly. 'It's just hot in here. Don't you think? Or maybe it's just me. I've been a bit under the weather lately.'

'Christ, you're not up the duff again, are you?'

And now Maud had something else to worry about. She was due any day but didn't have the usual symptoms, the bloating and the tender breasts. She shook her head, hoping that she wasn't pregnant. She sent up the same desperate prayer every month – God must be sick and tired of it by now – but she couldn't cope with another kid. Four was enough, more than enough. 'I don't know. I don't think so.'

'Only there's things you can do if you are. You don't have to have another one.'

Maud knew what she meant, a back-street abortion, but they didn't come cheap. They were risky, too. Theresa Buchan had bled to death after some woman had ripped her baby out of her. 'And where would I find that kind of money?'

'I could help you out,' Elsa said.

'Since when did you have money to throw around?'

'It wouldn't exactly be throwing it around, would it? I've got a bit coming my way in a week or two. A legacy from an aunt who died. It's not what you'd call a fortune, but I could spare a few quid to help you out.'

'You've never mentioned an aunt.'

'I hardly ever saw her. She lived on the Isle of Man. Just let me know, right? And the sooner the better. You don't want to wait until it's too late.'

Maud was never sure what to make of Elsa. She could be sharp-tongued and sarcastic one minute, sweet as pie the next. Truth was, Maud didn't really trust her. The woman had what her mother would have called 'side'.

Elsa moved closer and said softly, 'You ever think about that Lennie business?'

Maud stiffened. 'What are you talking about that for?' she hissed. 'It was years ago.'

'Because it's not the kind of thing you forget in a hurry. Doesn't it worry you that Nell might say something?'

'Why would she?'

Elsa shrugged. 'Why do crazy people do anything? She's not right in the head. She might spill her guts, confess to one of those doctors she sees. You haven't told anyone, have you?'

'Who would I tell? My Mick? He'd bloody kill me.' Maud glanced over her shoulder, making sure they were still alone. 'What's going on? Have you heard something?'

Elsa shook her head. 'No. I'd have said if I had.'

'So there's nothing to worry about, is there?' Maud dried

her shaking hands on a cloth, wondering what was going on. 'I mean, you got rid of the gun, so . . . You did get rid of it, didn't you, Elsa?'

'Course I did. I told you. It's been sitting at the bottom of the Thames for five years. Even if it was dredged up, there'd be nothing to connect it to Lennie's murder.'

'So that's that. And if Nell was going to tell, she'd have done it by now.'

'You're probably right. So long as we both keep quiet, it'll be fine.'

Maud heard a hint of accusation in her tone and snapped straight back, 'You think you need to tell me that? I ain't said a word, never have and never will. You reckon I'm the sort to go shooting my mouth off? Well, I ain't and that's the beginning and end of it.'

'All right, keep your hair on. I'm not saying you would. But if anyone comes in, starts asking questions, make sure you let me know.'

'Why would anyone be doing that after all this time?'

'I don't suppose they will.' Elsa scratched the back of her neck. 'I don't know. I've just got a bad feeling. I dare say it's nothing, just one of those weird things. You know how you get the jitters sometimes? They kind of creep up on you. It's been on my mind, that's all. I keep going over it.'

Maud had never seen Elsa get the jitters over anything. Even during the Blitz, after a bomb had dropped two hundred yards down the road, she'd still been cool as a cucumber. It made her wonder what the girl was up to. 'You sure you ain't heard nothin'?'

'I haven't, I swear. Don't worry.' Elsa picked up a pile of clean trays. 'Look, I'd better get back to work before John starts creating.'

Maud watched her go, her eyes full of suspicion. They shared a secret and she wished they didn't. Even after five years it still made her feel nervous and unsettled. Elsa was a law unto herself and God alone knew what went on in that head of hers. One thing was certain, though: if Pat Hull got wind of what they'd done, they'd both be dead meat.

28

Jimmy Taylor had a new, self-important swagger. He was one of the chosen and he was going places. Well, perhaps not very far at the moment – he was only walking the streets of Kellston, knocking on doors – but it still felt like a mighty step up. Alf Tombs had asked him to find the redhead, Judith Jonson, and he didn't intend to let the gang boss down. In his eyes it was a privilege to have been asked to do it – and a foot in the door when it came to joining the firm.

He had, however, spent hours going from one B&B to another with no success. She had to be somewhere close by. He had seen her turn the corner into the high street. Trouble was, there were a lot of B&Bs in the district and finding the one she was staying in was proving harder than expected.

Every time he knocked, smiled and asked if Judith Jonson was booked in, he got the same reply.

'Sorry, there's no one by that name staying here.'

He was starting to wonder if she was using a different name. After Mrs Jolly had chucked her out, she could have been worried that other landladies would do the same. That would make her a bugger to find. And what if she'd caught a bus and gone somewhere else: Shoreditch or Hoxton, maybe? Christ, he could spend the rest of his life looking and never get a sniff of her. But no, he felt in his guts that she was still in Kellston.

It occurred to him to try the caff. That was where she'd been on the evening he'd followed her. He crossed the road, went inside and sat down at a table. A dark-haired girl came over to serve him. He'd seen her around but didn't know what she was called.

'Get us a brew, love,' he said. 'And, er, I'm looking for a friend of mine, a redhead, name of Judith Jonson. Don't suppose you've seen her, have you? She comes in here from time to time.'

'Lots of people do,' the waitress said.

'She's not been in Kellston long. She's from up north. Red hair, yeah? Ring any bells?'

'Why are you looking for her?'

'Like I said, she's a friend.'

'You should know where to find her, then.'

Jimmy didn't care for the way she was talking to him, all sarcastic like she thought he was a joke. 'Have you seen her or not?'

'No.'

He didn't believe her. 'You sure about that? Red hair. About the same age as you.'

'It gets busy in here. One face is much the same as another. Sorry.'

Jimmy watched her walk back to the counter with his order. The bitch was lying, he was certain of it. But knowing that didn't help him any. There were times when he hated bloody women, the way they talked down to him, the way they looked straight through him as though he wasn't even there. The waitress needed a good slap, something to teach her a lesson. That way she'd think twice about lying to him again.

While he waited for his brew, he took pleasure in the thought. All he wanted was a bit of respect. It wasn't too much to ask.

Instead what he got was smart talk and sneering. He wondered what it would be like to throttle a woman, to watch the breath slowly leak out of her. Good, he reckoned. It was what most of them deserved. That Judith Jonson was a prize cow too. Maybe Alf had something unpleasant in store for her. Shit, he hoped so.

The caff was starting to empty now that lunch was over. The man behind the counter spoke to the waitress, calling her Elsa, and he heard her reply, 'I'm off in fifteen minutes, John. Can't you get Maud to do it?'

This gave Jimmy an idea. He could follow her, find out where she lived and perhaps use a more persuasive method to get her to talk. A few threats would probably do the trick, nothing too heavy, just a hint that the man he was working for didn't like being messed about. She wouldn't be so cocky then, that was for sure.

He quickly drank his tea, left the money on the table and headed back outside. With no clue as to what direction Elsa might take, he dithered for a while before crossing the road to the green and parking his backside on a bench, from where there was a clear view of the door to the caff. He was going to be late back to work, but he didn't care. Some things were more important than cutting keys.

While Jimmy waited, he replayed the moment Alf Tombs had approached him in the Fox, his chest puffing up at the memory of it. Right in front of his mates, the gang boss had taken him to one side and said casually, 'Do us a favour, son, and let me know if you find out where that Judith's staying.'

Jimmy had played it cool and not asked any questions. 'Sure, Mr Tombs, I'll do that.'

He still didn't know exactly why Alf wanted to know, but guessed it had something to do with Ivor Doyle. Anyway, he was determined to find the woman before anyone else did. It would make him look good and show that he could get results.

Twenty minutes passed before Elsa finally emerged from the caff. He prayed she was going straight home and not shopping or anything – and he hoped that home wasn't too far away. What would he do if she got on a bus? He could end up halfway across London. In the event, she crossed the road from exactly the same spot he had and started heading towards the green. For a second he thought she'd spotted him and quickly bent down, pretending to tie his shoelaces.

She passed close enough for him to see her slim ankles as she went by, but she didn't stop or say anything. He didn't think she'd clocked him. He waited a short while before raising his head again. She was now almost halfway across the green and going in the direction of Barley Road. He stood up and started to follow, keeping a safe distance in case she suddenly turned around.

Jimmy liked the thrill of tailing her. It gave him a feeling of power, of control. It changed the balance of things. She had no idea, he thought, that he had her in his sights. He walked at a leisurely pace as though he was taking an afternoon stroll, careful not to stare but always keeping her in view. People often knew when they were being watched, some weird sixth sense that prickled the back of their necks. He knew this because it wasn't the first time he'd followed a woman.

When Elsa reached the end of the green, she turned right along Barley Road and went to the house on the corner, where she disappeared down a flight of steps to the basement flat. Jimmy proceeded with caution in case she came back up again and bumped straight into him. After a few minutes, when he reckoned it was safe, he sauntered over to the house and casually glanced down the steps. She'd gone inside. The tiny patch of courtyard was empty apart from a battered bin and a pot of red geraniums.

Suddenly Jimmy got cold feet about what he intended to do.

What if she called the law and accused him of threatening her? He already had a caution after that misunderstanding with the blonde tart last year. And he couldn't explain about Judith Jonson to the cops, not without involving Alf Tombs, and that was out of the question. No, he had to use his brains for once, hold fire and think it through.

While he pondered on the possible consequences, his gaze took in the lock on the door. A Yale, easy to manipulate. On a good day he could get inside in thirty seconds flat. But that didn't help him when it came to tracking down the Jonson girl. Reluctantly, he turned away and set off back the way he'd come. Perhaps it would be smarter to keep an eye on the caff; odds were that she'd turn up there at some point. But he couldn't resist a glance over his shoulder. He wasn't finished with Elsa, but she could wait. Now that he knew where she lived, he could visit whenever he wanted.

29

Soho on a Saturday night was a revelation to Judith – the crowds, the pimps and prostitutes, the rhythmic sound of jazz floating out of windows. The sounds and smells were alien to her, new. It seemed to be a place without boundaries, beyond the reach of law and order, and she found herself both repulsed and fascinated by it.

'I hope you didn't mind meeting me here,' Saul said. 'There was someone I had to see and I wasn't sure how long it would take.'

Judith, who was simply relieved that he'd got here on time – standing around on street corners probably wasn't advisable in Soho – quickly shook her head. 'Of course not. It was good of you to agree, especially at such short notice.'

'Let's go for a drink. There's a place I know, not too far away. You might find it interesting.'

'More interesting than here?'

Saul grinned. 'In a different kind of way.'

They set off, weaving through the crowds. The day had been hot and the evening retained the sun's warmth. A sense of expectation hung in the air, along with the smells of tobacco, perfume and another sweet scent that might have been marijuana. Men lurking in doorways called to each other. Girls with red mouths and wriggling hips made short forays up and down the street, searching for potential customers.

Judith tried not to stare, not to act like a small-town girl gazing straight into the eyes of sin. Nonchalance was what was called for, although she wasn't quite sure if she was pulling it off. Saul Hannah appeared indifferent to the sights around him, neither shocked nor curious. He possessed a quiet confidence she found reassuring.

'So, you met with Doyle again,' he said.

'This morning. That's why I wanted to see you. He told me Nell was ill, but it's hard to know what to believe. Do you know if it's true?'

'She's had problems, that's for sure. I've asked around. Rumour has it she spent time at Silver's a few years back.'

Judith looked at him blankly. 'Silver's?'

'Sorry. Silverstone Hospital, near Kellston station. It's actually an asylum, a dismal, godforsaken place, the sort of institution that gives Bedlam a bad name.'

'He wasn't lying, then.'

'You sound disappointed.'

'No, just surprised. He's lied about so much, I half expected this to be a tall story too.'

They crossed over Oxford Street, turned right and went up Rathbone Place. Judith was still thinking about Nell McAllister, wondering what had happened to make the girl's life disintegrate in such a fashion. Maybe the answer was simple: Ivor Doyle had happened.

'I suppose that makes things tricky,' Saul said.

'I wouldn't want to do anything to ... I don't know ... tip her over the edge again.'

'Perhaps that's what he's counting on.'

Judith shot him a glance. 'Perhaps it is.'

'It's a difficult situation.'

They were quiet for a while, and then Judith asked, 'Where are we going?'

'The Montevideo club. It shouldn't be too busy at this time of night. It'll be an experience.'

'Why's that?'

'Because it's owned by Alf Tombs.'

Judith stopped dead and stared at him. 'What?'

'Don't worry, Doyle won't be there. He doesn't frequent any of Alf's establishments. I just thought you might like to put a face to the name.'

'I'm not sure I do,' she said.

'It's up to you. We don't have to. But he doesn't know who you are, does he? He won't recognise you if that's what you're worried about.'

Judith considered it. Perhaps she was a little curious. She'd never seen a gang boss before, and wondered what the man Ivor Doyle worked for – or with – was actually like. 'All right, just for a quick drink. Is it far away?'

Saul pointed up the road. 'Charlotte Street.'

'Charlotte Street,' she repeated, frowning. Immediately she thought of her friend, but it reminded her of something else too. 'Why does that sound familiar?'

'There was a murder there a couple of years ago: a bloke on a motorbike who tried to stop some armed robbers. Antiquis was his name. It was all over the papers. He was shot in the head and died in hospital.'

'I remember that.' Judith could also remember the shock she'd felt, that someone trying to do the right thing had paid such a high price. 'He had a wife and children, didn't he?'

'That's right. Six kids left without a dad. And for what? The whole robbery was bodged; they got away with nothing. There was no need to shoot him, but that's what it's like now. With these people, life doesn't have any value.'

'How do you stand it, doing your job? You must see awful things.'

'It's just a different kind of war. You get on with it. Most times it's not enough, but you do what you can.'

Judith thought she had misjudged Saul Hannah, mistaking reticence for something more sinister. She suspected he was probably a good person at heart, although she still wasn't sure if she actually liked him. Still, liking or not liking was irrelevant. She wanted more information on Nell, on Ivor Doyle, and he was the one who could provide it.

The Montevideo was tucked away on the corner where Charlotte Street met Goodge Street. It was an unprepossessing building, the stone walls pitted by bomb damage and stained grey by fumes. The only indication that it was a club was a gold-coloured oblong sign with black lettering placed three quarters of the way up the door.

'It's nicer inside,' he said.

As it happened, he was right. With its large seating area, plush blue velvet chairs and discreet lighting, the room was pleasant and comfortable. They chose a small table off to the side and sat down. The place wasn't busy yet, but there were enough customers for it not to feel empty. Soft jazz came out of speakers, and there was a steady buzz of conversation.

Looking around at the other women, Judith was glad she'd chosen something decent to wear. This morning, straight after seeing Ivor Doyle, she'd gone to a West End store and bought an elegant pale green linen dress with money from the savings account. She had done it to spite him as much as anything else, to fritter away some of the cash he'd accumulated. Why should she give it back to him? It was all he'd left behind after dumping her.

'What would you like to drink?' Saul asked. 'They do some decent cocktails here.'

Judith didn't have an extensive knowledge of cocktails, but she didn't want to appear totally unsophisticated. 'That would be nice,' she said. 'Why don't you choose?'

Saul got the attention of one of the girls who was serving and ordered a couple of sidecars. After she'd gone, he said, 'I didn't expect to see you back so soon. How long are you staying for?'

'For however long it takes. Although if you ask me what "it" is, I'm not sure I even know. I thought it was telling Nell what Ivor Doyle was really doing while he was away from London, but somehow that doesn't seem quite so appealing now. If I expose him, then I'll hurt her too.'

'That's the trouble with having a conscience. He probably didn't think twice about what he did.'

'No,' she agreed. 'I doubt he did.'

The drinks arrived and Saul raised his glass. 'Here's to … what do you think?'

Judith considered it. 'To better ideas?'

'Why not?' he said, clinking his glass against hers. 'Here's to better ideas all round.'

She took a sip of the sidecar. It was smooth and warming and delicious. She tasted brandy and felt it slide down her throat like liquid velvet. 'Mm, that's good.'

'Yes, you can't fault the cocktails. So, where are you staying at the moment?'

'Elsa's,' she said.

He seemed surprised. 'Really?'

'Just until I get somewhere sorted. She's been very kind to me. It makes such a difference having someone on your side.'

Saul's lips shifted into a wry smile. 'Yes, Elsa always likes to be there for people.'

Judith thought she heard a hint of irony in the words,

although she could have been mistaken. She looked at him, but his face gave nothing away. 'I suppose you'll miss her when she's gone.'

'Gone where?'

'Oh, hasn't she mentioned it?' This made Judith feel awkward. She'd presumed, with the two of them being friends, that Elsa would have shared her plans with him. 'Well, I don't think anything is absolutely decided. She just said that she might be going abroad.'

Saul gave a short laugh. 'Elsa's always talking about getting out of London. I'd take it with a pinch of salt. Where would she get the money to clear off like that?'

Judith shrugged and quickly changed the subject. 'Is Alfred Tombs here?' she asked, looking round for any likely candidates.

'Not yet. He'll turn up, though. He always does on a Saturday night.'

Judith sipped some more of her cocktail. 'Do you know anything else about Nell?'

'I heard she used to sing here, but that was before my time. Quite a looker, by all accounts, at least until Lennie Hull got his hands on her.'

'What do you mean?'

'There was trouble between him and Doyle – thieves falling out, you know how it is. Doyle got away, cleared off, and so Lennie took his revenge on Nell instead. Cut up her face pretty badly, broke one of her legs and generally made a mess of her. He was a vicious sod, that Lennie Hull.'

Judith winced at the thought of it. 'Did she go to the police?'

'No. I suspect she couldn't have, not without implicating Doyle in whatever crime the two men fell out over in the first place.'

'Why would she protect him when he'd just gone off and left her?'

'You'd have to ask her that.'

Judith reckoned she already knew the answer. Doyle was good at making women trust him, fall in love with him, believe in him. Nell must have forgiven the lying bastard, but *she* wasn't going to. Her expression hardened as she thought of everything he'd done to her. 'I suppose you think I'm a fool for marrying him in the first place.'

'Of course not. You weren't to know what he was really like, and the war wasn't a time for thinking about the future.' He played with the stem of his glass, twisting it in his fingers. 'You should be careful, though.'

'Careful?'

'Ivor Doyle isn't going to appreciate you being in London.'

'I don't care what he appreciates. In fact, I'm glad if it bothers him. He's going to wonder what I'm going to do next, and if that gives him a few sleepless nights, then it's worth it. Does that sound vengeful? I suppose it does. I suppose it *is*. But at the moment, until I figure out what to do next, it's better than nothing.'

'When I said careful, I meant ...' He hesitated, as if in two minds whether to go on. 'Look, I don't know anything for sure, but Ivor Doyle reappeared on the scene shortly after Lennie Hull's murder. Now that could have just been coincidence, or that news travels fast and he heard it was safe to come back, or ...'

He left the final 'or' hanging in the air for Judith to complete herself. It landed in her mind with a shuddering thump. 'You don't think ...? What, that *he* might have done it? No, he couldn't. I mean, I know he's done some awful things, but he's not a murderer.'

'Are you certain of that?'

Judith, of course, wasn't certain of it at all. Everything she thought she'd known about her husband had recently disintegrated, until all that was left was a ragged tissue of lies. But was he capable of murder? Once she could have put her hand on her heart and said no, but things had changed. 'There must have been others who'd have been more than happy to see the back of Hull.'

'You're right, but let's just say if I had a shortlist I'd put Doyle on it. He had the motive – what Lennie did to Nell – and he could well have had the opportunity. That doesn't make him guilty, only a possible suspect. It's why you need to be careful; to watch your back, just in case.'

Judith felt a shiver run through her. If Ivor Doyle had killed Lennie out of revenge, then how far was he prepared to go to protect Nell now? The question hung in her mind, heavy and monstrous. If he suspected she was about to reveal his past, to hurt Nell with her revelations, then maybe he wouldn't think twice about shutting her up – permanently.

'I don't mean to scare you,' Saul said. 'Maybe he is innocent, but you can't take anything for granted.'

'No,' she murmured. 'I understand. You think I should keep my distance.'

'That's up to you.'

Judith didn't know if she was capable of staying away from him. Despite the risk, there was still too much unfinished business, too much anger and resentment. It seethed inside her, hot and turbulent, like a storm slowly gathering force. How could she forget about him, go home and start again? It wasn't possible. She had to stand up and be counted, whatever the consequences.

'And there's someone else I'd put on the list,' Saul said, making a slight gesture to the right with his hand. 'Mr Tombs has entered the room.'

Judith looked over at the man. She wasn't sure what she'd expected, but it wasn't this. There was nothing that screamed gangster in his appearance or demeanour. Alfred Tombs was in his fifties, smartly dressed, with an interesting rather than hand-some face, greying hair and dark eyes. She followed his progress as he went from one of the central tables to another, smiling, laughing, shaking hands. He seemed pleasant and genial, a far cry from the image she'd had in her head. 'He just looks . . . I don't know, ordinary, normal.'

'And yet he's as far from that as you could imagine.'

Judith tried not to stare. She switched her gaze back to Saul. 'Why would you put him on the list?'

'Why not? Lennie Hull was the type to cause offence. He had a big mouth and a small brain. Maybe he overstepped the mark once too often.'

Judith found herself hoping that Tombs *was* the guilty party. But that element of doubt remained. Maybe, this morning, she had been talking to a killer. Her body stiffened with fear. The very thought made her blood turn to ice.

30

It was still early, only a few minutes past nine, when the taxi dropped Judith off in Barley Road. Saul had hailed the cab on Charlotte Street, opened the door for her and given the driver the fare in advance. She had protested – she could easily get the bus home – but he'd swept the suggestion aside.

'For my sake. This way, I'll be sure you get back safely. Take care of yourself, all right?'

She had spent the journey staring out of the window and seeing nothing. The streets of London had passed by in a blur, her mind too preoccupied by Ivor Doyle to take in anything else. Two strong cocktails hadn't helped matters. She hadn't eaten since lunch and the alcohol had gone straight to her head. She felt anger, confusion and resentment, shot through with an unattractive streak of self-pity. *Why me?* an inner voice whispered over and over again.

Although there was a lamp on in the flat, the curtains were closed and there wasn't much light. Judith tentatively made her way down the steps, holding on tightly to the rail. It was only when she reached the bottom and was about to start rummaging in her bag for the key that she realised the front door was ajar. She gently pushed it open. 'Hello? Elsa?'

There was no response.

At first, she wasn't worried – maybe Elsa had nipped round to a neighbour to borrow some tea or sugar – but as she walked into the tiny hallway, she knew that something was wrong. There was an odd stillness in the air, like the aftermath of a storm. It didn't feel right, didn't feel normal. She stood there for a few seconds trying to make sense of the change, to process it, to understand it. And then, when that failed, she advanced into the living room.

She gasped at the scene she was confronted with. The flat had been ransacked, turned upside down, with everything strewn across the floor. The cupboards had been emptied, their contents swept out, the crockery smashed. The chairs, lying on their backs, had been ripped open and their insides disgorged. Nothing had been left untouched or undisturbed. It was all chaos and destruction.

She walked through the debris in a state of shock, the soles of her shoes crunching on broken glass. The Gauguin print had been ripped from its frame and torn. The bottle of whisky lay shattered, its contents having long since seeped into the carpet. A smell of alcohol permeated the air. How could anyone do such a thing? It wasn't as if Elsa had much to steal. So far as Judith knew, there was nothing of real value in the place, but someone had clearly thought otherwise.

Elsa's bedroom was in a similar state of disarray, one curtain off the rail, the mattress dragged off the bed, the drawer of the bedside table pulled out and thrown across the room. Her clothes and shoes lay in a tangled heap on the floor. Judith took one look and withdrew.

She had a pretty good idea of what she was going to find when she went to her own bedroom – more of the same. Although she hadn't brought much with her from Westport, the idea of some filthy burglar's hands rifling through her possessions filled her with disgust. She took a breath, went over to the half-open door and gave it a push with the tips of her fingers.

If she had thought she was prepared, she was mistaken. *Nothing* could have prepared her for the horror that was revealed. Elsa was lying on the floor with one arm thrown back. Her dark hair was streaked with crimson. There was a gaping wound in her skull, and blood had pooled around her head and neck. Her eyes were open but glassy, unseeing. There was no doubt that she was dead, murdered, and beyond any help.

Judith's hand rose swiftly to her mouth, stifling a scream. She backed away, shaking, her legs barely able to carry her. Her heart was thrashing in her chest. It couldn't be real. It couldn't be happening. She staggered out of the flat and stumbled up the steps. For a moment she leaned against the railings, thinking she was going to be sick. A dry retching came from her throat.

Frantically she looked up and down the street. It was empty. She turned instead to the ground-floor flat, where a strip of light escaped from between drawn curtains. Lurching to the door, she hammered on it hard.

'Help me! Please, I need some help!'

The following fifteen minutes were odd, disjointed, dream-like. Somehow she managed to tell the man and his wife about Elsa. The middle-aged woman drew her inside, sat her down, put the kettle on and dispatched her husband to investigate.

'Billy, you go and take a look, but don't touch nothin'. Then call the law, or better still, go down to Cowan Road and fetch them yourself.'

Judith drank the hot, sweet tea, her hands clamped around the cup. It was impossible to get what she had seen out of her head, and yet she still couldn't believe that Elsa was actually dead. She felt mired in one of those nightmares you couldn't wake up from. Voices rose and fell around her. People spoke, but their words didn't register. They seemed to come from far away, alien, a foreign language she couldn't understand.

It was only when the police arrived that reality sank in. She gave a stumbling account of what had happened, of how the door had been open, how she had found the flat in disarray and how she had found Elsa. That was when the tears began to flow, and the faster she wiped them away, the faster they came. 'Why would anyone do that to her?'

But there was, as yet, no answer to that question.

They asked if she knew if anything was missing, but she had no idea. They asked about family, if there was someone they should contact, but she didn't know that either. A boyfriend? No, she didn't think so. She gulped as she spoke, her voice hoarse, almost strangulated. She couldn't concentrate on what they were saying. All she could think about was Elsa lying dead in the flat below.

With Judith struggling to provide even the most basic of information, Billy and his wife stepped in to fill in the details on how long Elsa had lived there, where she worked and what she was like.

'She was a nice girl, the poor soul,' the wife said. 'Never no trouble. She kept herself to herself. I can't think of no one who'd wish her harm.'

'A burglary, then, was it?' Billy asked the police sergeant. 'Looking for money, I suppose. They turned that flat over good and proper.'

'You went inside, Mr Phillips?'

'Only to check she was ... you know, to make sure. I was careful.' Billy gave a quick glance towards his wife. 'I didn't touch nothin', I swear.'

Mrs Phillips narrowed her eyes at the sergeant. 'Don't you

be trying to pin this on him. He's been right here with me all evening. He didn't have no choice but to go in, did he? What if the girl had still been alive? What if—'

'No one's trying to pin anything on your husband, Mrs Phillips. I'm just trying to establish the facts.'

'I'll tell you what the facts are, mister: none of us are safe in our beds these days and you ain't doing nothin' about it. Those hoodlums are everywhere. They should be locked up, the whole bleedin' lot of 'em.'

The sergeant brushed aside the rant and turned again to Judith. 'When was the last time you saw Elsa alive?'

Judith tried to keep her voice steady. 'This afternoon, but only briefly. It was about . . . I'm not sure . . . about a quarter to four, I think. I only came back to get changed and then I went out again.'

'And how did she seem?'

'What do you mean?'

'Was she worried about anything?'

'No. No, why would she be? She was fine.'

'I saw her come back from work at half two,' Mrs Phillips said.

The sergeant nodded. 'You didn't see her go out again?'

'No, but that doesn't mean she didn't. I ain't looking out of the window all day and night. She could easily have gone and come back again without my seeing.'

The questions went on for a while longer. Judith could hear the activity outside: the footsteps, the voices, the sound of cars arriving, of doors shutting. Wheels were being set in motion, a murder investigation beginning. Dead. Elsa was dead. A part of her felt numb, another part frantic. Why Elsa? Why her flat? Why had she been the unlucky one in this city of millions?

Eventually the sergeant closed his notebook. 'We'll probably need to speak to you again, Mrs Jonson. Do you have some-where you can stay tonight?'

Judith hadn't even thought about it. She stared blankly back at him.

'A relative, perhaps, or a friend?'

Judith shook her head. 'I've not been in London long. I'll go to a B and B. Do you know when I'll be able to collect my things?'

'Not tonight, I'm afraid – they'll be sealing off the area – but I'm sure it will all be returned to you in the morning. If you come with me, I'll find someone to give you a lift.'

'Thank you,' Judith said, relieved that she wouldn't have to walk the streets in the dark. She stood up and thanked Mr and Mrs Phillips too. 'You've been very kind.'

'We've only done what anyone would.' Mrs Phillips patted her arm. 'We've got to stick together in times of trouble. I'm sure we could find a space for you here if you need somewhere to stay for the night.'

'No, really, I'll be all right. But thank you. I don't know what I'd have done if you hadn't . . . ' But a lump had lodged in Judith's throat and she couldn't get any more words out.

'You take care, love, and you know where we are if you need us.'

A small crowd had gathered outside, alerted by all the activity. As Judith followed the sergeant, she thought she caught sight of the locksmith, Jimmy Taylor, but she couldn't be sure. It was dark, and the faces in front of her swam and merged. She was passed over to a young constable, who escorted her to a squad car and opened the door.

'Where would you like to go?'

Where Judith would have liked to go was home, away from London, away from this nightmare, but clearly that wasn't an option at the moment. 'I think there are some B and Bs on Silverstone Road, aren't there? One of those will do. It doesn't matter which.'

'I'll take you to Mrs Gillan's. She's a good sort.'

Judith got into the car, sat back and gazed out through the windscreen. She felt sick and dazed, unable to shake the image of Elsa from her head. If only she hadn't gone out to meet Saul. If only she'd been here. Elsa must have opened the door to her killer, or come back while the burglary was in progress and surprised him. Either way, she would have stood up to the man, challenged him, fought him to the bitter end. That was the sort of girl she had been.

Judith stared into the darkness. She thought about Elsa's plans for the future – all over now, all finished. Somewhere out there was a man who had snuffed out her life in an instant. The police would find him, wouldn't they? They had to. Her hands curled in her lap, two tight white fists. Her mouth trembled as she said a silent prayer for Elsa's soul. She would never forget her – and she wouldn't rest until her killer was brought to justice.

31

Saul Hannah heard about Elsa in the early hours of Sunday morning. He was drinking at a dive in Shoreditch, one ear to the ground, when a reporter called Henry Lake came in and started talking about the murder of a waitress in Kellston. Even before Lake revealed her name, he knew who the victim was. He had that chill down his spine, the gut feeling that something bad was coming.

A call to Scotland Yard confirmed the information. Saul went home, had a bath, poured himself a Scotch and lay on the bed while he tried to figure out what to do next. Oddly, he was not that shocked. Although maybe it wasn't that odd. The war and his job had inured him to the horrors of death, and there had always been something precarious about the way Elsa chose to live, as though she courted danger, needed it, breathed it in like oxygen.

He raised his glass to her memory, the nearest he would get to an expression of regret. He was sorry, of course, that she was gone – he'd grown used to her company even if he hadn't always liked her – but he couldn't quite bring himself to grieve. That emotion was reserved for the woman and child he had lost.

What he was left with now was a dilemma. Did he reveal to the necessary authorities that Elsa had been an informer? There was a possibility, albeit a slim one, that this was the reason she'd been murdered. From what he'd gathered, however, her killing seemed more likely to be the result of a moment of panic, a desperate lashing-out by a burglar who'd been caught in the act.

He knew that the flat would be dusted for fingerprints. If he admitted to having been there in the past, his own prints would be taken as a means of elimination. But it was where they would find them that worried him – not just in the living room, but in the bedroom too. And that could cause major problems. Paying a snout was one thing; having a sexual relationship with them quite another, especially when money was changing hands. Although it would be impossible to prove that he was guilty of anything more than an error of judgement, it could be enough to cast a shadow over his career. With the Ghost Squad about to be disbanded, he might easily find himself sidelined and consigned to some dusty basement for the next five years.

His other option was to say nothing, to pretend he'd never known her and hope that Judith kept her mouth shut. But would she? It was possible she'd already told the police that she'd met him, and not just at the café but at Elsa's flat too. He wondered how likely that was, bearing in mind that she had found the body and was probably still in a state of shock. Well, there was only way to find out. He would have to talk to her as soon as he could.

Saul had been in touch with a constable he knew at Cowan Road and had managed, with some subtle questioning, to discover that Judith was staying at a boarding house on Silverstone Road. Unless the crime was solved quickly, officers would be bringing her into the station in the morning to try and pick her brains. That was the point where they would start to ask about Elsa's friends and acquaintances. He would need to get to her first and be armed with a persuasive argument as to why she should help him.

The ideal scenario would be one where he could out Elsa as an informer to his colleagues but avoid the tricky matter of their relationship. He didn't have to worry about the neighbours on Barley Road. Usually, he'd arrived and left after dark, and even on those few occasions he hadn't, he'd made sure that his hat had been pulled down over his face. Also, he suspected he hadn't been the only male visitor to Elsa's flat.

He stared up at the ceiling, thinking of the approach he would take with Judith. He had the impression that she was, fundamentally, an honest person and wouldn't take kindly to being asked to lie to the police. Except it wouldn't be a lie so much as an omission. He checked his watch. It was only ten past three. He had a few hours yet to construct a convincing story.

32

There was a light, tentative knock on Judith's door at half past seven, as though whoever it was didn't want to wake her if she was still sleeping. She got up from where she'd been sitting by the window, walked across the room, and opened the door to Mrs Gillan. The landlady gave her an apologetic smile.

'I'm sorry to disturb you, love, but there's a policeman downstairs, name of Detective Sergeant Hannah. Shall I tell him to come back later?'

'No, it's all right, thanks. I'll be down in five minutes.'

Judith retreated into the room, relieved to hear that Saul was here. She felt the need to be with someone who had known Elsa and cared about her. He would have some news, perhaps, about the investigation. She quickly ran a comb through her hair and frowned at her reflection in the mirror. Her face was pale and tight: the legacy of a sleepless night. Every time she'd closed her eyes, all she had seen was Elsa's body.

With her clothes still at the flat, she'd had no choice but to wear the green dress again. She made a half-hearted attempt to smooth out the creases with the palms of her hands – it was hardly a priority at a time like this – and then slipped on her jacket. She hurried down the stairs and found Saul waiting in the hall.

'I'm sorry to call by so early,' he said.

'No, it's fine. I'm glad you have. Do you have any news? Do the police know who did it yet?'

Saul shook his head. 'No, but it's early days. They'll catch him, I'm sure. How are you? It's a stupid question, but it's hard to know what to say in circumstances like these.'

'How are *you?*' she asked, aware that his friendship with Elsa was of far longer standing than her own. 'You knew her much better than me.'

'It's been a shock,' he said, glancing away from her. His face was grey, unshaven, and a faint whiff of whisky drifted off his breath. 'Now I just want to get on with catching the bastard who did it. Look, can we go somewhere and talk? I know a place we can get breakfast.'

Judith wasn't sure if she was capable of eating, but she nodded anyway. She wanted to be doing something, anything, rather than sitting around feeling helpless. 'All right.'

'I've got the car outside.'

As Saul drove through the East End, he drummed out a beat on the steering wheel. He seemed jumpy and anxious, but that was hardly surprising given what had happened. 'Is it comfortable where you're staying?' he asked. 'We can find you somewhere else if you like.'

'No, it's . . . it's as good a place as any.' Beyond the fact that it was clean and tidy, Judith hadn't taken much notice of the room she'd been allocated. Mrs Gillan had provided her with towels and soap and a toothbrush. The elderly but still sprightly landlady had been kind and considerate without being intrusive. 'It'll do for now.'

Saul wound through the back streets of Bethnal Green until

they came to a café called Leo's. There was a row of black taxis parked outside and he pulled in behind them. 'You can always tell a good caff by the number of cabbies who eat there. Mind, there aren't many other places round here open on a Sunday.'

They went inside – it was warm and smoky and noisy – and sat down at a table in a corner. A waitress came over to take their order. 'Just tea, thank you,' Judith said.

Saul frowned. 'Have some toast, at least. You need food. You have to eat.'

Judith was instantly reminded of Elsa saying much the same thing when she'd gone into Connolly's after coming face to face with Ivor Doyle. The memory, sharp and poignant, filled her with an overwhelming sense of sadness. 'Toast, then,' she agreed, not wanting to get into a debate about it.

Saul ordered Spam fritters and eggs for himself. When the waitress had left, he sat back, took out a cigarette, lit it and sat forward again. 'I need to ask you something. When you talked to the police last night, did you mention me?'

'You? No. Why would I?'

He looked relieved. 'Good, that's good. No, I just thought you might have told them that I'd been at Elsa's flat.'

Judith stared at him. 'Why? Shouldn't you have been?'

'It's complicated. Look, I've got a favour to ask.'

She waited, but he didn't elaborate. 'A favour?' she prompted.

Saul glanced around the café, making sure no one was ear-wigging, before he continued. 'I don't know if you realise this – I don't suppose you do – but Elsa was a police informant. She was *my* informant.'

'What?'

'It wasn't big stuff, just what she picked up from working at the caff: who was selling what, who was talking to who, who was flashing the cash, that kind of thing. She wasn't fond of villains. I think she viewed it as doing her bit for law and order.'

Judith, surprised by this revelation, thought about it some more. 'God, you don't think that was why she was killed?'

'It's possible. Anyway, I have to let the investigators know in case there is a connection.'

'And that's a problem?'

'Not in itself. The problem arises from my relationship with Elsa. She was my informant but she was also . . . well, *more* than that, if you get my drift.'

'Oh,' Judith said. 'I didn't . . . You mean . . . ?'

'It wasn't serious, but it was still something.'

'You don't have to tell them, do you?'

'That's where the favour comes in. You see, if I reveal that Elsa was my informant and that I used to see her at the flat, they'll need to take my fingerprints for elimination purposes. And . . . ' He paused, gave a wry smile. 'Well, they won't just find those prints in the living room.'

Judith hadn't guessed that anything was going on between them, but then she'd only seen them together once. 'Does it matter? Is it against the rules?'

'It's a grey area, but that's not what I'm worried about. If I come clean about me and Elsa, they won't let me anywhere near the case. I'll even be a suspect for a while – a complete waste of time that could be better spent. I won't have access to any information, any progress, any clues to who might have killed her. I'll be kept at a distance and I don't want that. I have to know what's going on. If this does turn out to be more complicated – and I think it might – I need to be involved. It's the last thing I can do for her. Do you understand?'

'So you want me to lie?'

'To twist the truth a little. What difference does it make? All you have to do is forget you saw me at the flat.'

Judith wasn't sure how self-serving his request was. Was he just trying to keep out of trouble, or did he genuinely want to find Elsa's murderer? A bit of both, she suspected. But at least she knew he wasn't in the frame. He couldn't be. He'd been with her when Elsa was killed. Well, she didn't know *exactly* what time Elsa had died, but she couldn't see how Saul could have ransacked the flat, committed murder, driven from Kellston to Soho and then calmly gone for cocktails at the Montevideo. She glanced at him. No, she didn't think he was capable. It would take a psychopath to do something like that.

'What about last night?' she enquired. 'Do I tell them I went for a drink with you?'

He shrugged. 'Why not? If they ask. You could say we met in Connolly's last week, that Elsa introduced us.' He stubbed out his cigarette and slid the metal ashtray to the end of the table. 'I presume you won't be telling them about Ivor Doyle.'

Judith frowned. 'Why would I? He hasn't got anything to do with this.'

'They may ask why you came to London.'

'Do you think?'

'It's all routine stuff, background, filling in the detail. They'll want to know how you came to be staying with Elsa, that kind of thing. It's nothing to worry about. Just keep it simple and tell them you're here looking for work.'

Already Judith was starting to dread the forthcoming interview. On top of having to relive the horror of what she'd witnessed, she now had the additional stress of what she *wasn't* allowed to say. She had no desire, however, to reveal the details of her sham marriage to the police: that was a can of worms she preferred to keep firmly closed.

'If it helps,' Saul continued, 'I think you're right to keep Doyle out of it. It's only going to muddy the waters. I won't say anything about him. You have my word.'

Judith had the uncomfortable feeling that she was being manipulated, that a quid pro quo was being deftly put in place – his silence for hers. She didn't like it, but she couldn't see what choice she had. If the police got wind of Doyle's duplicity, she'd lose all control of the situation. Not that she had much anyway, but she wanted to be free to deal with the betrayal in her own way.

Her delay in responding must have unnerved him, because eventually Saul added, 'Yes, there's no need to mention Doyle. I reckon it's for the best. And I doubt Mr Tombs would be too happy about you dragging his favourite locksmith into a murder inquiry, especially at the moment.'

Judith stared at him. There was, she thought, an implied threat in the comment, as though he was now trying to scare her into keeping his secret. Had she been feeling less fragile, she might have challenged him, but she wasn't in the mood for confrontation. 'What do you mean, *especially at the moment?*'

Saul shrugged again, glancing across the room as though he might have said too much. 'Oh, he's always up to something. You can count on it. This moment, any moment. And if there's one thing he doesn't want, it's the law sniffing round.'

The food arrived, and Judith dropped the subject. She didn't forget it, though. Saul knew more than he was saying. If Tombs was planning something big, Ivor Doyle would be involved too. She stored the knowledge away, a nugget of information that could be useful in the future.

Saul tucked into his Spam and eggs while Judith sipped her tea. Just the sight of his plate was enough to make her stomach queasy. How could anyone eat at a time like this? She wondered if he'd had any feelings at all for Elsa. It was hard to tell. He was a closed-in sort of man, not the type to wear his heart on his sleeve.

He looked up and said, 'You should try and eat some of that toast. You could be down the station for a while.'

'How long?'

'They'll be busy. They might keep you waiting.'

Judith drank some more tea. 'Why was the flat ransacked like that? Was it just money they were looking for?'

'That's the big question. I mean, why would anyone think that Elsa had any? She was only a waitress. She didn't earn much.'

'So maybe they were after something else.'

'Like what?'

Judith saw a sly gleam in his eye, and knew that he was probing. 'I haven't got a clue. I really haven't.'

Saul speared a piece of fritter with his fork, raised it partway to his mouth and paused. 'Didn't she say something to you about going away?'

'To Morocco.'

'Are you sure she was serious? She often talked about getting out of London, but she never did anything about it.'

'She'd started packing, so ... yes, I'm pretty sure she was serious.'

'I wonder where she was getting the cash for a move like that.'

Judith shook her head. 'She didn't say.' It seemed odd that Elsa hadn't mentioned her plans to Saul. Would she ever have told him, or would she just have disappeared into the blue one day? 'I'm surprised she didn't talk to you about it.'

He gave a low, mirthless laugh. 'Don't be. She only ever told me what she wanted me to know.'

'How long had she lived in Kellston?'

'I'm not sure; a few years at least.'

Judith wished she'd been more curious, asked more questions, but she'd been too wrapped up in her own unfolding drama. 'If it wasn't money, what else could they have been looking for?'

'I've no idea, but whatever it was, Elsa wasn't going to give it up without a fight.'

'And we don't even know if they found it or not.'

'No.' Saul buttered some toast, added jam and slid the plate across the table. 'Here, have a few mouthfuls at least. You'll feel better for it.'

Judith felt like a five year old being coaxed to eat. She nibbled on a corner and her stomach heaved. She put down the toast and pushed the plate away. 'I can't stop thinking about it, what they did to her. Every time I close my eyes . . . Does it ever go away, that picture in your head?'

'It fades, in time.'

Judith wondered how many horrors he'd experienced, both in his job and during the war. She found him a difficult man to like, an even harder one to trust, but it wasn't as if she was swimming in friends and allies in London. He was all she'd got and he was better than nothing. 'I'll keep quiet about seeing you at the flat.'

'Thank you.'

'But I need something in return.' She was hardly in a position to try and make deals, but she suspected that his secret was more damaging than hers. 'I want to know what's happening with Elsa's case. They'll tell you, won't they? You're one of them. And you knew her better than anyone.'

'You don't want to get involved in this.'

'I'm already involved. I found her.'

A sigh slid from Saul's lips. 'You know what I'd do in your position?'

'Go home?' she suggested.

'Yes. Once the police have taken a statement, I'd run for the hills, get as far away from this godforsaken place as possible.'

'I'm not going to do that. Not yet. I have to know who killed Elsa.'

Saul put his elbows on the table and gave her a long look. 'You may live to regret it.'

'That's my choice. So, do we have a deal?'

33

While Judith was being interviewed, Saul talked to his colleagues and tried to learn as much as he could about the events of the previous evening. Opinion was divided as to whether it was a burglary gone wrong or deliberate murder made to look like a burglary. Saul was still on the fence. Although Elsa's history of informing could easily have provided a motive for a vengeful criminal, he knew she'd always been careful. And he'd been careful too, never mentioning her name to anyone until today.

Her handbag, containing her purse, was missing, but that didn't mean much. It could have been taken to put the police off the scent. And the fact that she'd been planning on going away pointed towards her being up to something. But what? They were all still in the dark.

He flicked through the scene-of-crime photographs, pausing when he came to the ones of Elsa lying on the floor. The post-mortem was being carried out this morning, but it didn't take an expert to work out how she'd died. A blow to the head had caved in the side of her skull. Her attacker had used a blunt instrument, a hammer perhaps, but the weapon hadn't been found yet.

When it came to next of kin, the police had drawn a blank. To date, no relatives had been traced. Saul wasn't able to help them out. It occurred to him how little he had actually known about Elsa, but he couldn't say for sure whether that was down to her being secretive or his general lack of interest. He had never asked about her past, just as she had never asked about his. They'd demanded nothing from each other, given nothing, taken nothing. He supposed she would leave a void in his life, but he would fill it in the usual way, with whisky and cigarettes, with other women and self-loathing.

Whilst various theories about Elsa's murder were being passed to and fro, Saul had half his mind on Judith. Was she sticking to her side of the deal? She struck him as the type who wouldn't easily bow to pressure, but the strain of the last twelve hours must have been immense. All it would take was one careless slip of the tongue. Hopefully, they wouldn't be too hard her. She wasn't, so far as he could tell, a suspect, but they would still push for any information she could provide them with.

Judith, he knew, had a false impression of Elsa, but it wasn't one he was about to correct. She had mistaken Elsa's hospitality for kindness, whereas he was sure Elsa had just been looking for an angle, a way to take advantage. It might be wrong to speak ill of the dead, but the only person Elsa had ever looked out for was number one. Had she found her angle with Ivor Doyle, approached him, asked for money to keep quiet about his marriage to Judith? And would that be reason enough for Doyle to kill her? He didn't think so. Murdering Elsa wouldn't stop the truth coming out. He'd need to kill Judith too – and anyone else she might have told about her lost husband's miraculous resurrection.

Saul asked if he could use the phone, and put in a call to

Scotland Yard to see if he had any messages. There was a dedicated phone line for the Ghost Squad, manned by two trustworthy officers on shifts. Apart from tracking him down at his regular haunts, this was the only way his narks could make contact. He was told he had one message, from Margaret, requesting a meet at the usual place this morning at nine. He glanced up at the clock – it was ten past already – uttered some hasty thanks, put down the phone, made his excuses to his colleagues, grabbed his jacket and headed for the street.

He drove quickly, hoping she'd still be waiting. 'Margaret' was the pseudonym Maud Bishop used; she was, understandably, paranoid about anyone on the other end of a phone line knowing her true identity. Could this be about Elsa? He knew the two women had worked together at Connolly's, and she must have heard about the murder by now.

It was fortunate it was a Sunday and the roads were quiet. He was at the meeting place in under three minutes, his eyes scanning the wasteland as he parked up. No sign of her, but she could be sitting on the other side of one of the walls, keeping her head down in case anyone she knew passed by. On the other hand, she could have given up on him and gone home.

He strode towards the remains of the houses, his shoes crunching on the debris. The closer he got, the more convinced he became that she wasn't here. Damn it! If only he'd made that phone call ten minutes earlier. But no sooner had the curse escaped his lips than Maud appeared, rising from the ruins like a victim of the Blitz – wide-eyed, ashen-faced, shaking with shock. She stumbled towards him, her skinny arms wrapped around her chest.

'I thought you wasn't coming.'

'Sorry, I only just got your call. I've been—'

'Have you got him yet? Have you got the bastard that killed Elsa?'

Saul shook his head. 'Have you heard something?'

Maud gave him a quick, scared glance before her gaze slid away from him. 'I don't know if it's important. It's just . . . ' She hesitated, clearly wanting to talk but afraid of doing so. While she grappled with these contradictions, she raised a hand to her mouth and chewed on her nails.

Saul remained patient, or at least gave a passable impression of being so. He resisted the urge to push, suspecting it would be counterproductive at this point.

Eventually Maud blurted it out. 'She said she had money coming in. A "legacy", that's how she put it, from an aunt who'd died.'

'Did she say what this aunt was called?'

'No, but she lived on the Isle of Man . . . or was it the Isle of Wight? I can't rightly remember. I think it was Man. Do you reckon that's what they were after? Do you think they killed her for the money?'

Saul knew that the Cowan Street officers had been through all the paperwork at Elsa's flat and found nothing relating to a legacy. There would have been solicitor's letters, information about the inheritance. Of course, she could have been carrying it around in the missing handbag, but he didn't think this was likely. 'She ever mention this aunt to you before?'

Maud shook her head.

'Did she say how much?'

'No.'

'Was she talking about it to everyone, or just you?'

'No, we was in the kitchen, just the two of us. And she was speaking quiet like. I don't reckon anyone could have overheard.'

'And she definitely said the money was coming in rather than that she'd already got it?'

'In a week or two, that's what she said.'

Which rather scuppered the theory of someone trying to rob

her, Saul thought. Unless the killer had got the wrong end of the stick and thought she'd already received the money. 'Did you believe her, about the inheritance?'

Maud, startled by the question, said defensively, 'Why wouldn't I?'

Saul sensed she had more to tell, that she was holding out on him. He had a nose for half a story and suspected this wasn't even half. Although Maud was always nervous when they met, today she was like a cat on hot bricks, unable to stay still, shifting from one foot to the other, the fear rising off her like vapour. 'If there's anything else you can remember . . . It's important. If we're going to catch whoever did this, I need to know everything.'

Maud launched another assault on her fingernails, while her eyes darted around.

'Maud?'

Finally she spat it out. 'I think she knew something about Lennie Hull's murder. I don't know, I'm not sure, but she said something odd, said that if anyone came in asking questions, I was to tell her about it.'

Saul felt that familiar tingle that came when he was onto something big. 'Lennie Hull? Are you sure?'

'I ain't deaf. I know what I heard.'

'You think the money she was getting was connected to that?'

'How would I know? I don't know nothin' about what happened to Lennie. I don't, I swear I don't.'

But there was something about the way she said it, the frightened insistence, that made Saul think otherwise. Maybe Elsa had told Maud more than she was letting on. 'Why would she wait so long if she did have information?'

But Maud just lifted and dropped her bony shoulders. 'It was on her mind, that's what she said. She'd been thinking about it.'

'Perhaps she approached the killer, tried to get money out of him for keeping quiet about what she knew . . . or thought she knew. That's possible, isn't it?'

Maud gave a visible shudder. 'She wouldn't do nothin' stupid like that.'

'She'd be too scared, right?'

'Elsa weren't scared of a soul and that's the truth of it.'

It *was* true, Saul thought, and perhaps that had been her undoing. If she had been attempting to blackmail Lennie Hull's killer, she'd clearly underestimated him. 'Did she say anything else?'

'That she had a bad feeling about it, that's what she said.'

'Why should she?'

'How do I know, Mr Hannah? But she were right, weren't she? That bad feeling of hers was because . . . ' Maud stopped and quickly crossed herself. 'It's like she knew, like she sensed somethin' bad was coming her way.'

Saul left a respectful silence before asking, 'Did she tell you she was planning on leaving Kellston?'

'No, she wasn't going nowhere, not that I knew of.' Maud frowned. 'What makes you think that?'

'Something someone said. They could have been wrong.'

'She wouldn't have gone without telling me.'

'You were close, then? You were good friends?'

Maud hesitated, as if weighing up the answer in her head. 'I wouldn't say close exactly, but I saw her most days. She could be . . . I don't know, sharp, I suppose, but she was the sort who'd be there if you ever needed her.'

'Did she have any family, parents, siblings, cousins?'

'She never spoke about any.'

'Boyfriends?'

'She never said.'

That was a relief to Saul. Even though he hadn't exactly been a boyfriend and had been reasonably sure Elsa wouldn't have mentioned him, it was reassuring to have it confirmed. 'If this is connected to Lennie Hull's murder—'

'It can't be,' Maud said too quickly. 'Can it? I mean, she couldn't have ...' Her voice went up in pitch. 'What if Pat finds out?'

'Finds out what?'

'He might think Elsa said something to me, that I know something.'

'And do you?'

'No, I told you. I don't know nothin'. I don't!' She edged away from him as though he was about to try and arrest her. 'I've got to go. I've got to get back.'

She turned and began to walk towards the road, her head down, her stride long and purposeful. He could have run after her, but he didn't. There was no point. She'd talk when she was ready and not before. It was frustrating to have a lead dangled in front of you and then yanked away, but the meeting hadn't been a complete waste of time. He was pretty sure now that Elsa had been playing games with the devil – and the devil had won.

34

By the time Judith emerged from the interview room, she was experiencing the kind of exhaustion that comes from trying too hard not to say the wrong thing whilst simultaneously attempting to come across as being completely honest and trustworthy. Had she spotted a hint of scepticism in the eyes of the officers? It might just have been her guilty conscience. She had not exactly lied to them, but she hadn't been entirely straight either.

Saul was waiting for her in the foyer. 'All right?' he asked.

She nodded. 'I will be once I get out of here.'

'They've finished with your suitcase. I've put it in the car.'

'Thanks,' she said, glad that she'd finally be able to change out of the creased dress and put on something else. 'Is there any news? Have they made any progress? They won't tell me.'

'There's not much to tell at the moment. I don't suppose Elsa ever mentioned Lennie Hull to you?'

Judith walked through the door he was holding open for her. 'No, never.' She briefly lifted her face to the sun before turning to look at him. 'Why would she?'

'No reason. I just wondered.'

'Of course there's a reason. You wouldn't have asked otherwise.'

He made a dismissive flapping gesture with his hand. 'It's probably nothing. Someone told me that she was talking about his murder yesterday, that she had it on her mind. I thought she might have said something to you.'

'No, not a word. But I didn't see her for long. I went back to get changed in the afternoon. She said she was staying in, that she was tired after work, and that was about it.'

'Did she seem jumpy, nervous about anything?'

Judith sighed as she got into the car. 'No, she was fine, she seemed fine, the same as always. I've already been through all this with your colleagues.'

'I know, I'm sorry. You must be sick of questions by now.'

'Why would she be talking about Lennie Hull? That all happened years ago.'

'Five,' he said. 'And yes, why would she?'

'Do you think Elsa was killed because she knew something about his murder?'

'I reckon there's a chance. Someone I was talking to . . . they said Elsa had mentioned it recently.'

Judith now found herself with something else to worry about. As they set off along Cowan Road, she remembered what Saul had told her last night. 'You said if you had a shortlist for Hull's murder that Ivor Doyle would be on it.'

'And he is.'

The question stuck in her throat but she had to ask it. 'You don't . . . you don't think he had something to do with what happened to Elsa?'

'It's a leap, but it's not impossible.'

Judith felt her insides clench. 'He *couldn't*,' she said. 'He couldn't do that.' And yet she didn't really know what he was capable of. If he had killed once, he could have done it again.

But to murder a woman in cold blood was very different to exacting vengeance on the man who'd damaged Nell so badly. 'You really think Elsa knew something?'

'Knew something, saw something, heard something. But whatever it was could have been enough for the killer to want to silence her.'

'Who told you that Elsa was talking about Hull?'

'A reliable source,' he replied.

'You're not going to tell me.'

'I can't. But I believe them, and you should too.'

'Have you told anyone else about this?'

Saul nodded. 'Only the inquiry team. I couldn't keep quiet about it, just in case it is important.'

'So why didn't you mention it before I went for the interview? I've just sat there for over an hour, deliberately avoiding Ivor Doyle's name, and now you're saying they could start investigating him. I'm presuming he's on their shortlist as well. What happens when they find out we were married? It's going to look pretty suspicious.'

'I didn't mention it because I didn't know. I only found out twenty minutes ago. And look, so far as they're concerned, you're a widow, Dan Jonson's widow. There's no reason for them ever to make the connection to Ivor Doyle. You're not going to tell them, I'm not, and Ivor Doyle sure as hell isn't, so you don't have anything to worry about.'

Judith wished she had his confidence, but she didn't. The truth had a habit of rising to the surface when you least wanted it to.

'It's only one strand of the inquiry,' he continued, 'and a minor one at the moment. It could just be a coincidence that Elsa was talking about Hull. It doesn't have to mean anything.'

'You don't believe that.'

Saul was silent as they drove down the high street and turned into Silverstone Road. He pulled up outside the boarding house and switched off the engine. 'I had a look at the scene-of-crime photos while you were being interviewed. It doesn't seem like a normal burglary to me. The way the flat was turned over makes me think they were looking for something specific.'

'Like what?'

'Like something that could put the finger on Lennie Hull's killer.'

'Why would she wait five years to do that?'

'Who knows? The workings of Elsa's mind were always a mystery to me. Maybe she was just biding her time, keeping it in reserve for a rainy day.'

'And do you think they found it, whatever they were looking for?'

'Your guess is as good as mine.' He got out of the car, walked round to open her door and then took her suitcase out of the boot. 'You sure you're all right here? I could take you somewhere away from Kellston if you'd prefer.'

'No, it's fine.'

'Not the best view in the world,' he said, gazing down the road towards the high walls of the asylum.

Judith automatically thought of Nell and wondered what it had been like for her in that place. And she thought of Ivor Doyle walking down this road, maybe even stepping on this very piece of pavement, when he went to visit her. Were people even allowed to visit? She didn't know. All she did know was that the walls had a bad aura, as though whatever lay beyond was dark and cruel and sinister. She shivered and quickly averted her eyes.

'What happens next?' she asked as they went up the drive to the boarding house.

'If you've got any sense, you'll get on the first train home.'

'And if I haven't?'

234

'Just stay away from Ivor Doyle. Keep your distance until this is sorted out.'

They came to a halt at the front door. Judith took the suitcase and thanked him for the lift. 'You'll let me know if you hear anything?'

'I'll stay in touch.'

She went inside. As she passed the lounge, she sensed a certain frisson in the air. Some of the residents put down their papers and magazines and turned their heads to look at her. By now word must have got around that she was the one who'd found the murdered girl. Her sudden appearance had ruffled the usual Sunday lethargy, arousing morbid curiosity and fuelling speculation.

She hurried up the stairs to her room, went inside, dumped the suitcase on the bed and sat down beside it. What now? Stay away from Ivor Doyle was what Saul had advised, but she couldn't do that. If she wanted to find out why Elsa had died, she had to follow the clues – and the only ones she had led straight to him.

35

Alf Tombs leaned against the bridge, watching the goods train as it pulled out of Kellston station. There was a loud screech, then a hiss, like an angry dragon rising from its lair. The steam rose in plumes, thick and grey, and dark smuts drifted in the air. He swept his hair clean with the palm of his hand. In the distance, church bells pealed, calling the good and the faithful to worship. As he was neither, he remained where he was, waiting for Doyle.

Renee had been up at the crack of dawn, when she'd gone off to Mass. She had been hoping, perhaps, to atone for his many and various sins – or at least not get the blame for them. Today the churches would do brisk business. A murder always reminded people of their own mortality. They would gather to talk in hushed voices, to gossip, to revel in the horror and give thanks that they hadn't been the victim. *There but for the grace of God . . .*

He checked his watch again: almost eleven. The streets around the station were Sunday quiet, not even a stray kid in sight. With a killer on the loose, mothers were keeping their children on a tight leash. An overreaction, but an understandable one. Barley

Road, the scene of the crime, would still be crawling with filth, and word would be going down the line to all the local spies and informers to come forward with any information they might have. The usual suspects would be pulled in for questioning, grilled and then released.

It was bad timing so far as Alf was concerned. With the Heathrow job on the horizon, he didn't need Old Bill poking their noses where they weren't wanted. One weak link, one loose mouth was all it took to turn a successful job into a disaster. Fortunately, he had his own spies, including a handful at Cowan Road. Every man, as they said, had his price.

Another five minutes passed before Doyle turned up. He strolled onto the bridge, the sleeves of his white shirt rolled up, his jacket flung over his shoulder. He looked like a man without a care in the world, but then appearances could be deceiving.

'Morning, Alf. Trouble, I take it?'

Alf nodded. 'We may have a problem. You hear about the waitress that was topped last night?'

Doyle shook his head. 'What waitress?'

'Her name was Elsa Keep. She worked at the caff, Connolly's. Dark-haired girl. You knew her?'

'It doesn't ring any bells. I haven't been in Connolly's for a while.'

'Someone broke into her flat on Barley Road. She ended up in the morgue.'

'And that's a problem for us because?'

Alf scrutinised Doyle's face, but could see nothing more than mild curiosity. 'I got a call this morning. Seems the law think there could have been a connection with Lennie Hull's killing. Some nark shooting their mouth off.'

Now, suddenly, Doyle was paying attention. 'What?'

'It's just a whisper, could be nothing.'

'What's this girl got to do with Lennie?'

237

'Your guess is as good as mine. Could she have found out about Nell?'

Doyle scowled and shook his head. 'How could she? No one knows about that but us.'

'So we thought. You haven't heard anything then, over the past week or so?'

'No, shit, of course not. You think I wouldn't have told you?' Doyle gazed down at the tracks for a few seconds before raising his head again. 'Look, they're probably just whistling in the wind. A rumour or the likes. You know how it is round here.'

'Maybe, but I think you need to have a chat with that friend of yours. Judith Jonson was the one who found the body.'

'Judith? For fuck's sake. Are you sure?'

'She's been down Cowan Road this morning. Turns out she was staying with the girl. You'd better find out what she knows – and what she's told the law. You need to be prepared if they come knocking at the door.'

'They won't. Why would they?' But Doyle sounded worried. 'Just because Hull's name has come up doesn't mean anything. Half the East End wanted that bastard dead. And there's nothing that leads back to Nell.'

'I hope you're right. Anyway, have a word with your lady friend, see what she says.'

'I don't know where she is.'

'Silverstone Road, number forty-two. It's a boarding house.'

Alf noticed Doyle flinch as he mentioned Silverstone Road. From what he'd heard, Nell's time at the asylum had been bad, a nightmare of the worst order. 'Yeah, is that a coincidence or is she trying to wind you up? What is it with this Judith? Strikes me she's out to cause trouble, mate.'

'I'll sort it.'

'You sure there's nothing I should know?'

'Like what?'

'Like who the hell she is, and why she seems to be right in the middle of this Elsa Keep business.'

'She's just a girl from years ago, that's all.'

Alf wished he knew more about the redhead, but Doyle was staying tight-lipped. He didn't like being in the dark, on the back foot, not when it came to the serious stuff. It made him uneasy. Something smelled bad, and he always trusted his nose. 'Tell me what she says.'

'I doubt she knows anything. She's only been in London five minutes.'

'Long enough to get herself involved. If she's bearing a grudge, you'll have to watch your back. And Nell's too.'

Doyle didn't disagree with the comment about the grudge. Instead his mouth twisted a little. 'She can't know,' he insisted, as though repeating it enough would eventually make it true. 'What's the deal with this Elsa Keep? What do you know about *her*?'

'Only what I've told you. You don't find it odd that this is all happening at the same time as your lady friend appears on the scene?'

'She's not my lady friend. You make it sound like . . . ' Doyle shook his head. 'For God's sake, this hasn't got anything to do with her. It can't have.'

'Let's hope you're right.'

'Just because she's been staying with this Elsa, just because she found the body . . . it doesn't mean she knows anything about Hull.'

Alf was listening carefully and thought he caught something overly defensive in the other man's voice. Why was he trying to protect the Jonson broad? 'Maybe you don't know her as well as you think you do.'

'I'll talk to her. I'll go and see her now.'

'Watch what you say.'

*

Alf watched Ivor Doyle walk back across the bridge. He kept his eyes on him until he disappeared from view. He sensed a change, something he couldn't quite put his finger on. It was to do with honesty, he thought, or lack of it. He lit a fag and pondered on the situation.

He'd always had a soft spot for Nell, ever since she'd started working at the club. He could still remember the day she'd turned up for her audition: just another dumb blonde with big ambitions, or so he'd thought until she stood behind the microphone, opened her mouth and started to sing. That was when he'd known she was something special. Her voice hadn't been the biggest or even the best, but it had possessed a kind of purity that made you stop and listen.

Nell's career had been stopped in its tracks, and now the past was snapping at her heels. Lennie Hull had ruined her life, her future – or maybe Doyle had. Doyle was the one who'd dragged her into his mess and left her high and dry when it all went wrong. If she'd never met him, she would have been the better for it.

He thought about Judith Jonson. Where had she come from? Why was she refusing to leave Kellston? What was her connection with Elsa Keep? If the redhead was a threat, if she knew too much, then she'd have to be sorted. What if Elsa had told Judith what she thought she knew about Lennie Hull's murder? Nell was at risk here, in danger if the truth came out. She needed protecting, but could Alf trust Doyle to do it? Maybe his loyalties were divided, Alf didn't believe Ivor's protests about not caring for Judith. Maybe he didn't have the heart to do what was necessary, to scare Judith from looking into the deaths of Elsa Keep and Lennie Hull. If that was the case, then there was only one solution: Alf would have to get rid of Judith Jonson himself.

36

Having managed to acquire some writing paper and envelopes from Mrs Gillan, Judith spent the next hour composing a couple of letters, one to Charlotte and one to Annie. Even at this point, when the most terrible things had happened, she was still unable to tell the whole truth. She informed them both that she was in London, and mentioned Elsa's death, but decided it was better, safer, that neither of them knew about Ivor Doyle. Now that she had lied to the police, there was no going back. She had to stick to her story and hope her duplicity never came to light.

Although she wanted to go home, *longed* for it, she couldn't forget about Elsa. She had to find out why she'd been killed and who had done it. In her head she went over and over the conversations they'd had, looking for clues, trying to read between the lines, but nothing more than pure bewilderment came from these attempts to ferret out the truth. If Elsa had inadvertently given her a clue, she had no idea of what it had been.

At midday, she went downstairs with the letters. She darted past the lounge before she could become the focus of attention again, and hurried out of the front door. Here she took a right and headed for the high street, where she remembered seeing a pillar box.

Once the letters had been dispatched, she wondered what to do next. She couldn't stop brooding on Elsa's murder – it was still too fresh, too raw – and if such horrors couldn't be expelled from her mind, she preferred to endure them in the fresh air rather than the confines of the boarding house. She would go for a walk, she decided, and try to get her thoughts in order.

Without any clear idea of where she was going, Judith set off towards the south side of Kellston, a part she hadn't explored before. The day was hot, the sun shining brightly. With little traffic on the roads and few people about, everything seemed oddly quiet. She walked slowly, only taking in her surroundings in a vague sort of fashion, and had covered less than a hundred yards when she heard footsteps. Glancing over her shoulder, her heart leaped into her mouth when she saw Ivor Doyle right behind her.

'What are you doing here?' she asked, flustered.

He drew alongside and gave a casual nod as though there was nothing out of the ordinary in him showing up like this. 'I heard what happened. Are you all right? I've been worried about you.'

'Why's that?' she snapped. 'I'm not your concern any more.' As soon as the words were out of her mouth, she regretted them. If she wanted the truth, if she wanted to find out if he'd had any part in the killing, she had to be less confrontational. Despite her suspicions, she didn't feel afraid of him. Wary, yes, but not fearful. A part of her still couldn't believe he was capable of murder, and she wasn't sure if this made her an optimist or an idiot. 'Sorry,' she said quickly. 'It's all been such a nightmare.'

'Don't apologise. I get it. It's a godawful thing to have to go through.'

'How did you know? I mean, who told you I found her?'

'Oh, this place is full of gossips. I heard your name mentioned

242

and figured there couldn't be that many Judith Jonsons in Kellston.'

'I suppose not.'

'Are you on your way somewhere, or . . . ?'

'No, I just came out for a walk.'

'Do you mind if I come along? I could do with stretching my legs.'

Judith gave a light shrug, feigning indifference. 'If you like.' She was under no illusion that he was here out of concern for her well-being, but was prepared to play along in the hope that he'd inadvertently reveal more than he meant to.

'So,' he said as they set off down the road again, 'do the law have any idea who did it yet?'

'If they do, they haven't told me. But then I don't suppose they would.'

'You've got an idea of what they're thinking, though.'

'Thinking?' she echoed.

'Whether it was just a burglary that she walked in on, or . . . ' He gazed off into the middle distance. 'Or if it was deliberate.'

'Who'd want to kill Elsa?'

'I've no idea. Were you close friends, the two of you?'

Judith gave him a sidelong glance, deciding to keep her cards close to her chest. 'Close enough.'

'How did you meet?'

'What does that matter?'

'It doesn't. I'm just curious.'

But Judith didn't elaborate. Instead she asked, 'Did you know her?'

'No.'

'By sight, though. You must have seen her in Connolly's.'

'I haven't been in Connolly's for years. I don't spend much time in Kellston these days.'

'Long enough for you to hear my name mentioned.'

He smiled briefly, raised a hand in a kind of acknowledgement and then let it fall back down to his side. 'I was passing through. I had to see someone.'

Judith wondered if he knew about Elsa being an informant. 'What else did you hear?'

'Nothing,' he said. 'Nothing much. Well, there's a whisper it could have been something to do with the killing of Lennie Hull, but that doesn't make any sense. Did she ever mention him to you?'

'That's the man you had the trouble with, isn't it?' Judith said, playing for time while she wondered how he knew about the Hull connection. If Saul was to be believed, it had only come to light this morning, so either Doyle's contacts penetrated deep into the police ranks or he was more involved than he was letting on.

'The same,' he said.

'No, Elsa never talked about him.'

'Are you sure?'

'I think I'd remember.'

They walked on in silence for a while. An old grey brick wall, too tall to see over, flanked the pavement to their left, and this eventually gave way to a pair of wrought-iron gates, one of which was open. Judith stopped to gaze along the path. A graveyard stretched out before her, still and quiet and enticingly peaceful. 'Let's go in here.'

Doyle drew back, pulling a face. 'What do you want to go in there for?'

There was something about his reluctance, an unwillingness she didn't understand, that made her more determined. 'Why not? It looks nice. It's better than walking along the road.'

'There's nothing nice about graveyards.'

'I've always found them quite restful.'

'They're full of dead people.'

'Well, the dead can't hurt you.'

Doyle's mouth twisted. 'I wouldn't be so sure about that.'

Judith stared at him for a moment, wondering what he meant. She could have asked him to explain, but she didn't want to give the impression that she was even moderately interested in what he felt or why. Instead, ignoring his obvious dislike of the place, she strode forward through the gate and started along the main path. She was in no doubt that he'd follow, and she was right. Putting aside his reservations, he soon caught up and fell into step beside her.

'You don't have to come with me,' she said.

'It's too lonely here. It's not safe to walk on your own.'

As if he was doing her favour, or maybe just trying to scare her. Refusing to be manipulated, she gave a snort. 'Oh, I'm sure I'll be perfectly all right.'

'That's what this lot thought,' he said, gazing around at the graves, 'and look what happened to them.'

Judith suppressed a smile, clamping her lips together. She'd almost forgotten about that dry sense of humour. *Keep your guard up*, she told herself. *Don't relax, not for a minute.* He wasn't with her because he wanted to be. He was after something and she had to stay alert if she was going to find out what it was.

They came to a tall weeping willow, its branches cascading down like a waterfall. It was here that a narrow path veered off to the left, leading to a wilder, less manicured part of the cemetery. She decided to take this route, partly because it looked more interesting and partly because she suspected he wouldn't want her to. And she was right about the latter.

'We should stick to the main path,' he said.

Judith ignored him. Knowing he was already ill at ease, it gave her a small advantage, she thought, to take him in a direction he wasn't comfortable with. The Victorian cemetery was full of towering plinths, grand monuments and mausoleums, with smaller graves scattered in between. As they proceeded along the path, the grass either side became longer, laced with ivy and wild flowers. It had a sad kind of beauty, a haunting quality.

She stopped occasionally to read an inscription, a lament to a lost mother or father or child. He hovered by her shoulder like an impatient man in a queue, shuffling his feet and sighing.

'Have you thought any more about going home?' he asked.

Judith rolled her eyes. 'It's not a good time.'

'I'd have thought it was the ideal time.'

'The police might want to talk to me again.'

'Why should they? You've told them everything you can, haven't you?'

He was fishing again, trying to get inside her head. She decided to throw him a bone. 'If it helps put your mind at rest, I haven't told them about us.'

'I wasn't worried. I never worry about things I can't do anything about. But thank you anyway.'

'I didn't do it for you.'

He left a short pause before he said, 'I know you think I'm just trying to get rid of you, but Kellston really isn't a safe place right now. If Pat Hull gets to hear the rumours about Elsa knowing something about his brother's murder, he's going to come looking for answers. And seeing as Elsa isn't around . . . '

Judith frowned. 'What are you saying exactly?'

'You're Elsa's friend, you were staying with her, you found her body and you've been talking to the law. Where do you reckon will be his first port of call?'

Judith suspected he was using scare tactics again, or at least she hoped so. She didn't fancy being on the receiving end of an interrogation by Pat Hull, especially if he was anything like Lennie. Home was growing more appealing by the minute, but she refused to give in to the easy option: to take to her heels and run away. For Elsa's sake, she was going to stay no matter what the consequences. 'If he comes to talk to me, I'll tell him exactly what I told the police.'

'Good luck with that. Pat isn't what you'd call a reasonable man. If he thinks you're holding out on him ...'

'Then we'll just have to hope he doesn't,' she said, with more bravado than she felt.

But Doyle hadn't finished yet. 'Pat's got the same vicious streak as his brother. And he hasn't got any qualms when it comes to women; from what I've heard, he takes pleasure in hurting them. The man's an out-and-out bastard, a sadist. You don't want to get on the wrong side of him.'

Judith wondered what the odds were of Pat Hull remaining in ignorance, and wasn't optimistic. If the news had reached Doyle this quickly, it was only a matter of time before it reached Hull too. The thought didn't do much for her peace of mind.

'Do *you* know who killed Lennie?' she asked.

He was, perhaps, prepared for the question, for his face remained impassive. 'Me? I've no idea. I've already told you: I wasn't in London when it happened.'

'But you heard rumours?'

'Have you?' he asked, batting the question back.

'No,' she lied, recalling Saul's shortlist and the position Ivor Doyle held on it. 'No, nothing.'

He gave her a querying look, as if he didn't quite believe her. 'Elsa must have heard them, though.'

'If she did, she didn't tell me.'

They wandered on along the path. The sun beat down, creating shadows all around. A light breeze rustled through the trees and bushes. Suddenly, from behind, a crow cawed loudly, making Judith jump. Then, beating its wings, it took off from the ground and rose high up into the sky. A chill ran through her. There were superstitions about crows, about them being omens of evil. In an attempt to disguise her agitation, she followed its trajectory, raising her face and shielding her eyes against the glare.

It occurred to her, somewhat belatedly, that roaming through the most deserted part of the graveyard with a possible murderer probably wasn't the smartest move in the world. His show of reluctance to come this way could have been a ploy, knowing she would do the very opposite of what he wanted. What if he was just waiting for the right moment, for the opportunity to put his hands around her throat and squeeze the very life out of her? No one would hear anything. No one even knew she was here. As creeping panic spread inside her, she tried her best to hide it. She turned and said through dry lips, 'We'd better be getting back.'

The path was only wide enough for them to go in single file, and so, as she walked ahead, she had to endure the thought that he was right behind her, waiting to pounce. Her senses seemed heightened as she listened to his every step. She felt the warmth of the sun on her arms, saw the ground ahead with peculiar clarity – the earth, the tiny stones, the straggle of weeds – and discerned a bitterness in her mouth, something that might have been the taste of fear.

She heard him light a cigarette and was glad of it. People didn't smoke when they were just about to strangle someone, did they? You needed both hands free to commit an act like that. Unless he had a knife. Her back arched a little as if anticipating the cold metal of the blade. Then, unable to bear the tension, she glanced back over her shoulder.

'What's wrong?' he asked.

'Nothing.'

'You look like you just saw a ghost.'

She shook her head as though she didn't understand. 'Do I?'

'Still, you're in the right place for it. More ghosts here than you can shake a stick at.'

Judith forced a smile and walked on. It wasn't until they

reached the main thoroughfare that she finally relaxed. She could see other people now: an elderly lady carrying a posy, a couple with a pram, a middle-aged woman clearing dead flowers from a grave. Her pulse began to slow, her heart to take on a more regular rhythm. It was time, she decided, to do some probing of her own. 'Elsa's flat was ransacked. They turned it upside down. What do you think they were looking for?'

He didn't answer straight away. There was a short hesitation, which he tried to cover by taking a drag on his cigarette. 'Money, jewellery, the usual stuff, I suppose.'

'If it was just a burglary. But what if it wasn't? What if the rumours are right?'

'Then your guess is as good as mine.'

'What could she have had that her killer would have wanted so much?'

'I've no idea.'

As they approached the gates, they passed a young woman, attractive and smartly dressed, perhaps on her way home from church. Judith noticed how her gaze brazenly focused on Doyle, weighing him up, taking him in, her eyes resting for too long on his face. She felt a knee-jerk spurt of irritation, almost proprietorial in nature. The girl didn't know they weren't a couple, and clearly didn't care one way or the other. Judith, of course, shouldn't have cared either, but it was the rudeness she objected to – or at least that was what she told herself.

Doyle threw his cigarette butt on the ground and asked, 'Did Elsa have a gun?'

Judith was still quietly seething over the girl, and it took a moment for his question to register. When it did, she was both surprised and puzzled. 'Why on earth would she have a gun?'

'People do,' he said. 'To protect themselves.'

From what? she almost asked, but the answer to that was self-evident. 'No, I never saw a gun.'

'I was just wondering if she seemed worried or anxious about anything. Did she give that impression?'

'No. not at all.' In fact, Elsa had seemed the very opposite, glad to be leaving, looking forward to a new life in Morocco. Judith didn't share this information with Doyle. She wanted to press him further on the issue of the gun – why he'd asked, what had put it in his head – but didn't want to come across as being too suspicious.

'Maybe it *was* just a burglary,' he said.

'Except the flat wasn't broken into. The lock wasn't forced or anything. She either let them in or went out for a while and left the door open.'

'Would she be likely to do that?'

'I don't know. I wouldn't have thought so.'

'Well then,' he said.

They were quiet again until they reached the street. As they walked towards Silverstone Road, Doyle kept glancing back, his head quickly twisting like a nervous twitch he couldn't control.

'Why do you keep doing that?'

'I thought I saw someone.'

'Who?'

'No one. It's nothing.'

Judith stopped and stared back the way they'd come. The street was empty. Had there really been someone there or was he just trying to put the wind up her? It was another of his games, perhaps, designed to put her on edge. And if it was, it was working. When they began to walk again, she had that prickle on the back of her neck, the feeling they were being watched. Real or imaginary? She couldn't tell.

Doyle stuck by her side until they reached the boarding house. 'Think about what I said. Kellston's not a safe place to be at the moment.'

'Thank you for your concern,' she said drily.

'I mean it. You know where I am if you need me.'

'Why would I need you?'

Oddly, the retort seemed to wound him. 'Of course, why would you? I can't expect . . . ' He gave her a long, almost wistful look. 'Take care of yourself, Judith.'

She followed his departure, standing at the foot of the drive with his words echoing in her ears. Once upon a time she had known the tall, blond man strolling away from her, had believed she understood him, but now she had no idea who he was or what made him tick. He was not a friend, that was for sure, but was he the enemy? She still hadn't figured out the answer to that.

37

Jimmy Taylor was in a cold sweat. He'd had a bad night's sleep, his head full of horrors, his ears alert to the sound of cars stopping in the street. He'd been waiting for the knock on the door, for the law to come and arrest him. If one of the neighbours had seen him at the flat, they wouldn't be slow to point the finger. *That Taylor boy was hanging round*, they'd say. Maybe he'd even been spotted following the waitress across the green. That wouldn't be good. They'd have him right in the frame, no doubt about it.

Daylight hadn't brought much reprieve. Over breakfast, the murder was all his mum could go on about. *It's a terrible thing. Who'd do something like that to the poor girl?* He could have told her there was nothing 'poor' about Elsa Keep – she'd been a nasty, sarcastic bitch – but had wisely kept his opinions to himself. So far as he was concerned, the mouthy cow had got what was coming to her.

'Why aren't you eating?' his mum had said. 'Those eggs don't grow on trees.'

But Jimmy couldn't eat, not when he had the worry of a noose being placed around his neck. He was sure the redhead, that Judith Jonson, had clocked him in the crowd, but so what? That didn't mean anything. Half the neighbourhood had gathered by then, full of ghoulish curiosity. He had as much right as anyone else to stand and gawp.

He put down his pint and wiped his forehead with the back of his hand. It was warm in the Fox, crowded, and a thin sheen of perspiration had gathered under his hairline. He wished he hadn't come now. All anyone was talking about was the murder. The women were the worst, acting all shocked and upset but actually enjoying every minute of it, going over and over what had happened while they revelled in the gory details. He wanted to yell at them to shut the fuck up, to find something else to bloody talk about, but knew better than to draw attention to himself.

Three girls were standing right behind him – he was perched on a stool at the bar – and their shrill voices put his teeth on edge. He didn't turn to look at them but stared into the mirror instead. They were ordinary, plain, nothing to write home about. Factory girls, he reckoned. The leader, tall and mousy-haired, was wearing bright red lipstick. She was holding forth about the killing, repeating all the rumour and gossip and embellishing it.

'I heard she were strangled with her own stockings and raped. Someone she knew, they reckon, a boyfriend or the like. It makes your blood run cold, don't it? In her own home and all. He could be local, couldn't he? He could be anyone.'

There were things Jimmy could have told them, things that would have made their toes curl. He had been up close to death and seen what it looked like. He'd smelled it, touched it, breathed it in. Elsa Keep was departed, gone forever, and she'd never walk these streets again. They'd have her body at the morgue, laid out, still and cold, or maybe some bloke in a white coat was cutting her up right at this moment, slicing through her flesh, making notes on the obvious – that someone had caved in her skull. Did they work on a Sunday, these men who took bodies apart? Perhaps they did when it was a murder case.

The cops were going from door to door, looking for clues, for leads, for anything that would give them the answers they wanted. Jimmy's hand reached for the pint again, his fingers tightening around the glass. Maybe he should have stayed away from the pub today just in case he jogged someone's memory. He hunched his shoulders, trying to make himself smaller, and scowled into his beer. None of it was his fault. He hadn't known what was going to happen. It wasn't fair that *he* should be made to suffer in this way. If he could turn back time, he would, but the deed was done. The dead couldn't rise again.

The crowd pressed in, hot-breathed, menacing, a great stifling weight of lies and suspicion. He imagined that people were already whispering about him, their eyes drilling into the back of his head. *We always knew he was a wrong 'un.*

38

Maud stood at the sink and stared out of the kitchen window at the scrappy back yard. Her red hands were poised half in and half out of the water while she listened to Mick moving around upstairs. It was five o'clock in the afternoon and he'd only just come home. She wouldn't ask where he'd been – she *never* asked – but she could tell from his thumping footsteps that his mood wasn't a good one. Her pulse quickened. She could feel her heart starting to hammer while she waited for him to come back down.

The kids were in the front parlour, listening to the radio. Hopefully they'd stay there, stay quiet and keep out of their father's way. When he was in one of his black tempers, there was no saying what he might do. Or rather there was plenty of saying, and all of it was bad. He had no regard for anyone, including his own flesh and blood. He was scum, the pits, the lowest of the low, and the drink only made everything worse.

Maud had been dreading this moment all day, ever since she'd found out about the murder of Elsa Keep. She was regretting going to see Saul now. Had she told him too much? She'd have been better off staying out of it, but it was too late for regrets. It was the shock that had sent her flying through the front door to the phone box on the corner. She should have stopped and thought. If Mick ever found out . . .

It was over five minutes now since he'd stomped into the kitchen, stinking of booze, throwing her a dirty look before he went upstairs to do whatever he was doing. Getting his gun, perhaps. It wouldn't be the first time he'd pushed the cold, hard barrel of the revolver into her throat because she'd done something to displease him. Or even if she hadn't.

Stay calm, she told herself. Don't say anything to provoke him. It was only a couple of weeks until the Heathrow job. All she had to do was keep him sweet until then. But keeping Mick happy was harder than pushing a camel through the eye of a needle. He could pick a fight in an empty room, and this one wasn't empty.

When she heard the tramp of his boots on the stairs, she stood back from the sink, wiped her hands on a cloth, took a few deep breaths and prepared herself for the worst. He swaggered in with his hands in his pockets, reintroducing that stink of beer and sweat and tobacco. His gaze took in the room, flicking left and right in a vague, unfocused way before finally settling on her.

'What's wrong with you?'

'Nothin',' she said. 'There's nothin' wrong.'

'You got something to tell me?'

Maud shook her head. 'You want a brew? I was just putting the kettle on.'

'If I want a fuckin' brew, I'll ask for one.' He sat down at the table, fumbled for a cigarette and lit it. 'You ain't answered the question, love. You got something to tell me?'

Maud's eyes widened. She probed at the empty space in her mouth where he'd knocked out two teeth last week. The gum was still sore and swollen. She knew that anything she said would be the wrong thing, and so she just shook her head again.

'What's the matter, cat got your tongue?'

'What could *I* have to say?'

Mick drew on his fag and glared at her. 'What about that waitress who got topped last night? Ain't you got nothin' to say about that?'

Maud felt the dread gathering inside her. 'Elsa Keep, you mean?'

'How many dead waitresses do you know?'

'Yes, I heard about it. Her at number four told me. She were passing by this morning, going down the alley and she . . . Yes, that was terrible. Poor girl. A burglary, that's what they're saying.' Maud's hands had started to shake. In order to disguise it, she went to put the kettle on, but immediately changed her mind. Mick and boiling water weren't a good combination. 'I . . . I didn't know her that well. Elsa, I mean.'

'You worked with the woman, didn't you?'

'Well, yes, sometimes, but I was in the kitchen and—'

'So you must have known her well enough. You bitches always talk to each other. Bleedin' gossips, the whole damn lot of you. Couldn't keep your gobs shut to save your lives.'

'Elsa wasn't the chatty kind.'

'Sure she was. You all are. Pat's heard a whisper that she knew something about Lennie, about who did for him. You ever hear her talk about that?'

'No,' Maud said smartly. 'Never, not a word. How would she know anything?'

'That's what I'm fuckin' asking you.'

'No,' she repeated. 'And even if she did, she wouldn't say nothin' to me, would she? She'd know I'd come straight home and tell you. I wouldn't keep quiet, would I? I *wouldn't*.'

For a moment she thought she'd got away with it as his booze-fuelled brain worked through the logic of her argument. He had to come to the conclusion, surely, that her fear

257

of him outweighed anything else. But then a cruel smile slid onto his lips.

'You're a fuckin' liar, Maud. You think I can't tell when you're talking shit?'

'I'm not, I swear. Come on, Mick, I'd never keep somethin' like that to myself, not in a hundred years. I'd never do that. I'd never—'

He moved so quickly, she didn't have time to react. Suddenly he was off the chair and lunging at her. He grabbed hold of her throat with his left hand, forced her back and pushed his face into hers. She felt the cold hardness of the sink against her spine. She smelled his stale, beery breath and saw the mad look in his eyes.

'You know more than you're telling, you lying cow! Come on, spit it out!'

And Maud knew that unless she came up with something fast, words wouldn't be the only thing she was spitting out. 'You should ask the girl, the redhead, the one who found her. Those two were thick as thieves.'

'Who the fuck are you talking about?'

Maud's voice was growing hoarse as his fingers tightened round her throat, squeezing her windpipe. She spoke as quickly as she could while she still could. 'I don't know her name. She was staying with Elsa, though. I saw them in the caff together. She turned up last week, and then all this . . . *She's* the one you need to ask.'

Mick's eyes flashed with suspicion. Saliva had gathered at the corners of his mouth, pale and glistening. He already had her pinned, but he pressed his body harder against hers. Then he lifted the cigarette and wafted it close to her face. 'Her name. What's her fuckin' name?'

Maud flinched, feeling the heat. She tried to dredge up what Betty Wharton had told her this morning, but she'd been so

258

shaken by the news of the murder, she hadn't taken much else in. 'I don't know. I don't know.' Suddenly something came back to her, a fragment of information, which she flung out in desperation. 'She's at the Gillan place on Silverstone. You can find her there.'

Mick moved slightly, removing the pressure on her throat. Then, just as she released a thin, premature breath of relief, he placed the tip of the cigarette against her ear lobe. She yelped in pain, her head jerking back, her hand rising to try and cover her ear. She could smell the stink of the flesh, feel the agony of the burn. He slapped her hand away, grabbed her by the shoulders and hurled her across the kitchen. She hit the wall with a dull thump and slithered to the ground.

He stood over her, shaking his head. 'Why do you make me do this, Maud? If you just told the fuckin' truth in the first place.'

Maud didn't move other than to gently cup her ear. A soft groan escaped from her lips. She made no attempt to stand up, knowing this would only make matters worse. She gritted her teeth against the pain, waiting for the next onslaught, for the boot in the guts or the ribs, and was surprised when it didn't come. Instead he gave her one last sneering glance before leaving by the back door and slamming it behind him.

Maud didn't immediately get up. She rocked back and forth, wishing she was dead. No, wishing *he* was dead. And he'd be as good as when they put him behind bars for the Heathrow job. She thought about the girl she'd just thrown to the wolves, but she didn't feel any remorse. Why should she be sorry? Pat Hull would have found out about her anyway. It was every man for himself in this world.

39

At half past five, Judith had forced herself to go downstairs to the dining room, hunger finally getting the better of her reluctance to face the other guests. There had been six of them in all, four elderly ladies and a couple of middle-aged men. The former had shared one large table, while the latter had sat at a smaller one. A place had been set for her with the female contingent, and there had been polite smiles, introductions – she could only recall a couple of the names now – followed by a rather stilted conversation, most of it about the weather.

Her fellow guests had possessed that typical British reticence when it came to finding out what they wanted to know. Politeness forbade them from asking any straight questions, although clearly Elsa Keep's murder was the only thing on their minds. They had shot Judith quick, furtive glances, perhaps hoping that she would be the one to raise the subject, but she had disappointed. She'd had no desire to talk about the killing or her discovery of the body.

The conversation, such as it was, had been interspersed with long silences. There had been some chat between the men about a local cricket match, but even that had fizzled out after a couple of minutes. All that had been left was the scrape of knives against plates and the weight of words unsaid. The atmosphere, bordering on the oppressive, had added to the gloom of her mood.

After the meal, coffee had been served in the lounge, but Judith had made her excuses, gone upstairs to get a jacket and escaped outside to catch the last of the evening sun. She felt as though she hadn't had any time yet to even begin to come to terms with Elsa's death. First there had been the police, then Saul, then the police again and finally Doyle: everybody wanting answers from her, answers that she didn't have.

She walked at a brisk pace up the high street, trying to make sense of it all. But, of course, there was no sense to murder, to that sudden and irrevocable action. In truth, she had hardly known Elsa – their friendship had been a brief one – but that didn't stop the swell of emotion inside her. Now that the initial shock was wearing off, other feelings were taking its place. She sighed into the warm evening air. Elsa had been there when she needed someone, and for that she would always be thankful.

She came to the green, stopped and then made her way over to the bench. She sat down and looked towards Connolly's. It was closed, although she wasn't sure if that was because it was a Sunday or out of respect for Elsa. She closed her eyes, fighting back the tears. There had been too much loss in her life recently, and her sense of bereavement over Elsa was all jumbled up with the loss of Dan.

As she opened her eyes again, she became aware of a man crossing the road towards the green. Judith had no idea where he'd come from – she'd been too preoccupied to pay much attention to anyone else – but something about him made her nervous. This nervousness grew into a more defined anxiety as he came closer. He was in his forties, tall and broad with a jowly, unshaven face. And it wasn't just his appearance that put her on edge – it was the fact that he seemed to be heading straight in her direction.

By the time she realised she was right, it was too late to do anything about it. The man was looming over her, massive and menacing.

'You're Elsa Keep's friend, right?'

'Er, yes, I knew her,' Judith replied hesitantly.

'Yeah. Sorry for your loss,' he said, his voice devoid of any sincerity. 'Don't mind if I sit down, do you?'

Judith, sensing that any rebuttal of this suggestion would be futile, merely shrugged. 'Do I know you?'

'The name's Pat Hull,' he said. 'You may have heard of me. Or my brother, at least. Lennie. Ring any bells, love?'

Judith shrank back as he sat down next to her. Her mouth had gone dry. She thought about standing up, trying to walk away, but that probably wasn't the best of ideas. Ivor Doyle had warned her, but she hadn't listened. And now she was face to face with a monster who, if Doyle was to be believed, took the utmost pleasure in hurting women. How did she answer the question? Deny any knowledge of his brother? No, that wouldn't be sensible.

'Yes,' she eventually managed to say. Then, deciding that attack was the best form of defence, she quickly added, 'Look, I don't know what you think I know, but it really isn't anything. I barely knew Elsa. We only met recently. She never even mentioned your brother to me. I understand there's a rumour that there could be a connection between the deaths, but as far as I can see, there isn't any evidence to back that up.'

'No evidence, huh?' His voice sounded harsh and mocking. 'You sure about that?'

Judith, feigning ignorance, assumed a puzzled expression. 'None that I know of.'

'So why does the law think otherwise? Don't you forget I have eyes and ears everywhere, darlin'.'

'I wasn't aware they did.'

Pat Hull's mouth twisted into a sneer. 'You may think you're clever, sweetheart, but you're not. What's your fuckin' game? What's in it for you?'

'I don't have a clue what you're talking about.'

He grabbed hold of her left wrist, his fingers pressing into the flesh. 'Don't mess with me,' he hissed into her face. 'You and that Elsa bitch were up to something and I want to know what it was.'

Judith tried to wrench her arm away, but to no effect. 'Let go of me!'

'I'll let go when you tell me what's going on. What did that tart know that got her killed?'

'Nothing. I've already said. I barely knew her. Why would she tell me anything?'

'Because you were in it together, the two of you.'

Judith gave up the struggle to free her wrist, aware that she was only causing herself additional pain. 'In what? For God's sake, this is crazy. There was nothing going on. *Nothing*. It's all just rumour and gossip and rubbish. How many times do I have to tell you?'

'Until I start believing you.'

'Elsa's dead. She was a decent person, kind. She'd never have done anything bad.'

'Keep talking. Maybe you'll eventually say something that interests me.'

Judith quickly glanced around, but the green was empty. She saw a couple of lads, teenagers, on the high street and thought about yelling for help. But what if they didn't come? They might just think it was some kind of domestic. And by then she'd have antagonised Hull even more. 'I can't tell you what I don't know.'

At last he let go of her and rose to his feet. Then he leaned over, placing his hands against the back of the bench, either side of her shoulders. 'If I find out you've been lying, I'll smash that pretty face of yours into a thousand pieces. You understand, love?'

'I'm not lying,' Judith said, as calmly as anyone could when a six-foot-something brute was threatening to disfigure them. 'I swear I'm not.'

He hovered there for a few more seconds of intimidation before standing upright again. 'I'll find out, you see. I always do. No one fucks around with Pat Hull and gets away with it.'

There didn't seem to be much Judith could say to that, and so she kept quiet.

'You understand?'

She nodded. 'Yes, I understand.'

Hull gave her a long, nasty look before turning away and walking off the way he'd come. She kept her eyes on him as he recrossed the road. Her pulse was racing, her heart hammering out a frantic beat. She rubbed at her wrist, knowing there'd be bruising there soon. Any sensible woman, she thought, would go straight to Cowan Road police station and report him.

She was on the point of doing exactly that when caution kicked in. What if the police began to wonder if there was any truth in Hull's suspicions? They might go digging into her past, looking for the real reason she'd come to London. At the moment, she was only a witness, a victim even, but that could rapidly change. If they uncovered her connection to Doyle, they might start to view her in a different way.

After further thought, she decided it was too risky. Although she resented letting Hull get away with his filthy threats, the alternative would be much worse. Smarter to keep her head down and hope for the best – the best being that Hull didn't find out the truth about Elsa being an informant, about Saul Hannah, about Doyle, about everything. Because if he did, he'd be back, and she'd have more to worry about than a few bruises on her wrist.

40

Nell McAllister usually avoided mirrors. What she saw reflected back was a constant reminder of what Lennie Hull had done to her. She'd been pretty once, able to turn any man's head, but those days were long gone. Now the only reason anyone looked at her was out of curiosity, disgust or pity. Make-up could only go so far to disguise the scars on her face, and nothing could hide the odd, ugly angle of her jaw. But mirrors couldn't be avoided at the Montevideo; the walls were covered with them, wide and gilt-framed, glittering in the dim light.

She went to the bar and ordered a pink gin. 'Is Alf around?'

'Could be,' the barman replied evasively.

'Would you tell him Nell's here?'

'He expecting you?'

'He'll see me,' she said.

The young man mixed the drink and put it on the counter. As Nell paid, she noticed how his gaze slid away from her. She could say she was used to it by now, but that wouldn't be entirely true. Every embarrassed look, every glance of disgust left another small scar to add to the collection.

While she waited, she sipped the pink gin. The place was almost empty, in part because it was early, only six thirty, but mainly because it was a Monday. The club had always been quiet on Mondays. How long since she had last been here? Four years? Five? She couldn't remember exactly. The ECT treatment had messed with her head. Some memories were thin and wispy, so distant she could barely grasp them, whilst others were so brightly vivid it could all have happened yesterday.

Nothing much had changed here, though. The same tables, the same blue plush seats. Only the people were different. Once the barman would have leaned over the counter and flirted with her, but now he was glad of an excuse to scuttle along the bar and pick up the phone. Her eyes strayed towards the small stage where she'd once performed. The songs were still in her mind, melodies that haunted her. She never sang out loud now, not even on her own; the music had left her lips for good.

She was halfway through her second gin before Alf emerged from the door at the back. She watched him walk across the floor, a prepared smile fixed on his face. She had liked Alf once, although not as much as he'd liked her. Now she wasn't so sure what she felt. Grateful, of course, for the help he'd given her after the Lennie business, but wary too. It was never a good thing to be beholden to someone like Alf Tombs.

'Nell,' he said, leaning down to kiss her cheek. 'To what do we owe the pleasure?'

'Oh, I was just passing and thought I'd drop in to see the old place.'

Alf went along with the answer even though he knew it was a lie. 'Well, you're more than welcome. We don't see enough of you these days. I'm always telling Ivor that.' He nodded towards the barman, who immediately delivered two fresh drinks, another gin for her and a whisky for Tombs.

266

She shouldn't really be drinking – she wasn't supposed to with the pills she took – but she needed some Dutch courage. 'You got a ciggie?' she asked.

Alf lit one for her and passed it over. 'Everything all right, Nell?'

'Sure. Why shouldn't it be?'

'No reason. But if there is anything on your mind, I'm here. You know that, don't you? We're old friends, you and me. We've been around the block together, and the rest. There's nothing I won't help you with – if I can. Is everything all right with Ivor?'

Nell shrugged, trying to think of the right way to approach the subject. Trouble was, thinking wasn't exactly her forte these days; things got all tangled up in her head, like snakes in a basket. In the end, she decided just to come out with it. 'What do you know about Judith Jonson?'

Alf's eyebrows shifted up.

'That's not an answer,' she said.

He hesitated, maybe considered spinning her a line – men made a habit of covering for each other – but then decided against it. 'Not much. She's from up north by all accounts. I believe she was staying with that girl who got murdered – Elsa Keep. What's Ivor told you?'

'As little as he can get away with.' Nell drained her second gin and started on the third. 'Someone he used to know, an old friend. That's what he *says*. She came to the house to see him, just turned up on the doorstep. I suppose I always knew she would one day.'

Alf inclined his head, curious. 'Why? What's so special about Judith Jonson?'

'Hasn't he told you?'

'Ivor keeps things to himself. You know what he's like.'

'Yes, I know what he's like.' Nell tapped her cigarette against the edge of the fancy glass ashtray. She left a short, dramatic pause – she had not forgotten all her show-business techniques – and then announced calmly, 'Judith is Ivor's wife.'

Alf laughed as though she was joking, but his face quickly straightened again. 'No way. He's married to her? The redhead?'

'You've met her, then?'

'No, I've heard about her, but we've never met. What? His wife? She can't be. Are you sure?'

Nell reached into her bag, took out a folded sheet of paper and handed it to him. 'Here, it's a copy of the marriage certificate. I found it in his things.'

He scanned the page and looked up at her. 'But this says Dan Jonson, not Ivor Doyle.'

'That was the name he was using when he left London. He got fake ID papers so Lennie couldn't track him down.'

'That didn't work out so well. But then if you rip off the likes of Lennie Hull, what do you expect?'

'It was Lennie who was doing the ripping off. He owed Ivor. Ivor only took what was rightly his.'

Alf handed back the certificate. 'How long have you known about this?'

'A while. A year or two.'

'So why haven't you talked to him about it?'

'It was in the past. Sometimes it's better to let sleeping dogs lie.'

'And now the dog's woken up. What are you going to do?'

Nell turned back to her drink, seeking answers in her glass. 'What I want to know is what *he's* going to do.'

'You're going to have to ask him that.'

Except Nell didn't want to have that conversation. Ivor had already lied to her about who the girl was, the stranger who'd shown up at Ironmonger Row. *An old friend*. Well, she was more than that, much more. *Judith*. She submerged the name in pink gin and frowned. Had he loved the girl he'd married during the war? She supposed he must have, for a while at least. Nell knew that Ivor didn't love her now, not in the way he once had. Her feelings were different too, but she still needed him. He was her rock, her anchor. Without him, she'd be lost.

'If it helps, I get the impression he wants her to leave,' Alf said.

'But she hasn't left.'

'Not yet.'

'Maybe she wants him back. Do you think that's it? Is that why she's come here?'

Alf gave her a wry smile. 'I never presume to know what goes on in a woman's mind.'

He leaned against the bar, looking thoughtful. 'What I don't get is what her connection is to Elsa Keep. Do you have any idea?'

'Should I care?'

Alf's lips pressed together as though he didn't want to say.

'Alf?'

He pulled a face. 'Maybe. I'm not sure. Has Ivor not said anything?'

'If he had, I wouldn't be asking.'

But still Alf didn't enlighten her. 'It's probably nothing.'

'It's obviously something.' She touched him lightly on the arm. 'Come on. Don't hold out on me.'

'It's just a rumour, probably bullshit.'

'So, tell me the bullshit.'

Alf looked at her, glanced away, looked back. 'There's a rumour doing the rounds that Elsa knew something about Lennie's Hull murder.'

Nell felt a trickle of ice run down her spine. 'What does "something" mean?'

'That she knew who killed him. But that can't be true, can it? I mean, there's only three of us know what happened – you, me and Ivor. I've not said a word, and I'm presuming you haven't either. So unless Ivor told Judith Jonson . . . but I can't see why he'd do that.'

'You . . . you think she may have told Elsa Keep?'

Alf made a *who knows* kind of gesture with his hands.

Nell trusted Ivor with her life – he had saved her, got her out of that hellhole of an asylum – but it wasn't beyond the bounds of possibility that he'd told his wife things he shouldn't. And it was perfectly possible too that Judith had passed this information to the Keep woman. But that meant . . . A series of disjointed thoughts jockeyed for position in her head. 'It can't have been why she was murdered, though.' She stared at Alf. 'If we're the only ones who know . . . '

'Don't look at me,' Alf said, raising his hands again, this time palms out. 'I only just found out about it. I'd never even heard of Elsa Keep until yesterday.'

'Ivor wouldn't have done anything like that,' she said softly.

'No,' Alf agreed, 'unless . . . '

That cold feeling was settling into her bones. 'Unless what?'

'Maybe he thought it was the only way to protect you. I'm not claiming he did, but everyone has their breaking point. He's not been himself recently, not since that girl showed up.'

'I'd know if he'd done anything like that. I would. He couldn't hide it, could he?'

'No, of course he couldn't. Not from you. Anyway, he was with you on Saturday evening, wasn't he?'

'Saturday?' Nell repeated. 'I . . . I'm not sure.'

'It's only two days ago. You must be able to remember.'

Nell did remember, but she didn't want to say. She'd presumed Ivor had been with Alf, but that obviously wasn't the case. When had he come home? It had been late, after midnight. She stubbed out the cigarette in the ashtray, using more force than was strictly necessary. 'Yes, yes of course. He was with me.'

Alf smiled indulgently. 'Good,' he said, patting her on the

270

shoulder. 'Nothing to worry about then.' But his eyes told a different story. His eyes said he didn't believe her.

Nell was starting to wish she hadn't come here. She didn't want to listen to these things, didn't want to hear them. She wanted to put her hands over her ears and pretend that everything was fine. Why *had* she come? Because she'd needed someone to talk to and Alf was the only person who could really understand.

'He'll stick by you,' Alf said. 'I'm sure he will. This thing with the redhead, it'll pass.'

'His *wife*,' she reminded him.

'If he'd wanted to be with her, he would be. He chose you, Nell. That tells you all you need to know.'

Nell's thoughts were jumping around like they were electrified. Every time her mind settled on one thing, it got jolted off to another. She couldn't concentrate, couldn't pin anything down. 'Would Ivor really have told Judith? And how did she know Elsa Keep? I don't understand what this Elsa's got to do with it all. I keep going over that night I followed Lennie . . .'

'You don't want to dwell on that.'

'Ivor couldn't have killed that Elsa woman.'

Alf put a finger to his lips. 'Keep your voice down, Nell, unless you want the whole club to hear.'

'Where is she? Judith. Where's she living now?'

Alf shook his head. 'I've no idea.'

'Yes you do. Of course you do. Why won't you tell me? I've a right to know.' Her voice was rising again, the pitch growing keener. 'I suppose he's with her, isn't he? That's where he is now.'

'You need to calm down.'

'I am calm. I'm perfectly calm.' She gave a brittle laugh, took a step back and almost lost her balance.

Alf grabbed her arm to steady her. 'You should go home.'

'I haven't finished my drink.'

'So finish it,' he said, 'and then I'll get you a cab.'

'Why won't you help me?' Now her tone was plaintive, pleading. 'Why won't you?'

'I've always helped you, Nell. Whenever I can.'

And then she felt bad, because it was true. He was the person she'd run to after that awful night, when Lennie's blood had been all over her, when she hadn't known what to do, when everything had been falling apart. 'I'm sorry,' she said, pawing clumsily at his arm. 'You're right. I'm sorry. I'm sorry.'

'Come on, let's go.'

She allowed him to manoeuvre her through the club, one hand firmly on her elbow. Outside, the cool evening air cut through the haze in her brain. She had a sudden vivid memory of stumbling through the dimly lit streets of Kellston, of banging on his door, of moving from the darkness into the light of the hallway.

There had been a bath run, clothes destroyed, a doctor called. The man, small and plump, had been one of Alf's tame doctors, paid to keep his mouth shut. Not that he'd known the truth anyway. She'd heard Alf explaining about how she'd been taken ill at the Fox – one of her 'episodes', as he'd described it – and no mention, of course, had been made of Lennie Hull's dead body sprawled out in the alley. Had the doctor ever put two and two together?

She was still pondering on this when Alf managed to hail a cab. He opened the door, bundled her into the back and thrust a note at the driver while giving her address. Nell opened the window, leaned forward and stared out at him. 'Just tell me where she is, Alf. *Please*. That's all I want to know.'

He hesitated, seemed about to turn away but then stopped. 'The Gillan place,' he eventually said. 'Silverstone Road.'

Nell flinched. Of all the boarding houses Judith could have chosen, why that one? The house was only a hundred yards from the asylum. It was as if the woman was goading her, taunting her, reminding her of the horrors of the past.

'Stay away from her, Nell. Don't do anything stupid.'

Nell nodded and sat back. But she knew that some things couldn't be ignored. They had to be faced square on. She'd had enough of avoiding the truth, of putting her head in the sand. It was time to face the enemy.

41

Alf Tombs waited in the street until the cab disappeared from view. Why had he told her where Judith Jonson was? It had been a spur-of-the-moment decision, but he didn't regret it.

If Ivor had been straight with him, open, he'd have kept his mouth shut, but right now he didn't feel he owed the bloke any loyalty – he reserved that for people he trusted. Ivor had fallen short in this department: too many secrets, too much information withheld. And Doyle's inability to clear up his own mess and send Judith Jonson packing was dragging him – Alf Tombs – down too. The longer that bitch was swanning around Kellston, asking questions and reminding everyone about Elsa Keep, the longer it would take for the police to move on. And having the law sniffing around was never good for business.

There was something about the triangle of Judith, Elsa and Ivor that made him uneasy. He suspected Judith knew about Lennie Hull's death and Nell's part in it all. That wasn't good for Nell. If the law got wind of it, she'd be facing a murder charge. He suspected she'd crumble under close questioning, break down and confess. From there it was a short walk to the hangman's noose.

Back in his office, he unlocked the top drawer of his desk and took out the Heathrow plans. He went over the schedule, the route, the timings, but his mind wasn't really on it. His thoughts kept shifting back five years to that night when Nell had turned up on his doorstep, wild-eyed and gibbering, her clothes covered in blood. He had made an urgent call to Doc Welby, stoked up the fire and poured a glass of brandy down her throat.

'You don't understand,' she'd repeated over and over. 'Alf, you don't know, you don't know what I've done.'

But he'd understood perfectly. He'd seen Nell watching Lennie Hull in the Fox, her eyes fixed on him, her body rigid. Had anyone else noticed? The pub had been busy, crowded, so hopefully not. Hull had had a skinful and was none too steady on his feet as he left. She had gone straight after him, sidling round the customers, but Alf hadn't thought anything of it.

'I didn't mean to, I didn't. I was just—'

'Don't talk. You'll be safe here. You don't have to say another word.'

But then she'd started to rock and wail, a high keening noise that made him wince.

Renee had woken up and come out of the bedroom to see what all the fuss was about. 'What's going on?'

'It's only Nell McAllister. She had an accident but she'll be all right. It's nothing to worry about. I'll deal with it. Go back to bed.'

Renee, after a brief hesitation, had done as she was told.

He'd given Nell a dressing gown, run a bath, told her to get out of her clothes. He'd got rid of the bloodstained evidence as quickly as he could, and then as soon as the doctor arrived he'd made sure he shot her full of sedatives before she could say anything to incriminate herself. Welby hadn't asked for an explanation – that was what he was paid for – but Alf made out that she was simply in the throes of another of her 'episodes'. It wasn't the first time Welby had treated her for hysteria and it wouldn't be the last. The two of them had put her to bed in the spare room, where she could sleep it off.

Alf scratched his chin and stared down at the Heathrow plans. Then he pushed them to one side and poured himself a Scotch. That missing gun had always bothered him. At the time he'd considered going out to look for it, but decided it was just too risky. The body might have been found already, and even if it hadn't, he didn't want to be seen in the vicinity of the corpse.

Nell had gone downhill after Lennie's murder, eventually ending up in the Silverstone asylum. He didn't know if she had ever confessed to the doctors or psychiatrists, but if she had, they would probably have taken it with a pinch of salt. In their eyes she was just another crazy girl from the wrong side of the tracks. And they'd have probably frazzled her brain for good with their ECT and their drugs if Ivor hadn't got her out of there.

It had been a stroke of luck him turning up in Kellston like that. Ivor had needed money to get Nell private treatment, and Alf had needed someone with Ivor's skills to gain easy access to post offices and warehouses. It had been a good partnership, a profitable one, but you needed trust in this game.

He put his feet up on the desk and drank his Scotch. He was back to the same question he'd started with. Had he done the right thing? He still wasn't sure. This whole business with Nell and Judith Jonson could blow up in his face.

42

By the time Wednesday came around, Judith had packed her suitcase twice before changing her mind and unpacking again. The encounter with Pat Hull had shaken her and made her think seriously about going home. She had got off lightly, all things considered, but might not be so lucky on the next occasion. However, the idea of running away didn't sit comfortably with her. No one had been arrested yet for Elsa's murder, and she was determined to stick it out until the killer was caught.

It was a good feeling, a liberating one, to be on the bus heading for the West End. She'd spent most of the last few days inside, only occasionally venturing out when she could no longer bear the sight of the four walls of her room with their pink blowsy roses. Even then, she hadn't gone further than the local shops, always looking over her shoulder in case Hull put in another appearance.

Saul had called this morning – there was a phone in Mrs Gillan's quarters – and asked if she'd like to meet up at one o'clock. She hadn't hesitated. There was only so much hiding you could do before you began to go crazy, and she figured – so long as she wasn't followed – that she'd be relatively safe away from Kellston.

She was sitting on the lower deck and had spent the first ten minutes scrutinising the other passengers and watching the road behind in case someone was on her tail. Paranoia was becoming a constant companion. Now, however, she was starting to relax and enjoy the sensation of being out in the world again. She gazed out of the window at the busy streets, the shops and all the people dashing about. London was a hurrying kind of place, with everyone seemingly in a rush to get somewhere else.

It was a quarter to one when she got off the bus in Oxford Street and joined the throng. She walked up towards Charlotte Street, the name inevitably reminding her of her friend back in Westport. Charlotte would be home from her honeymoon and settling into married life. It felt like a long time since she had last seen her. The letters to her friends would have arrived in Westport by now; so much had happened, tumultuous things, and she'd barely begun to explain them all.

The Fitzroy Tavern, on the corner of Charlotte Street and Windmill Street, was easy to find. She must have passed the pub last time she'd been here, when she and Saul Hannah had gone to the Montevideo, but she didn't recall noticing it. She went through the door to the large L-shaped saloon, where she immediately saw him. The place was busy, doing a brisk lunch-time trade, but he had managed to bag a table near the entrance.

'Let me get you a drink,' he said, rising from his seat.

She asked for a lemonade – it was too early for anything stronger, and anyway, with the threat of Hull still looming, she wanted to keep her wits about her – and sat down while he went to the bar. While she waited, she examined her surroundings. The walls were decorated with First and Second World War memorabilia: regimental insignia, helmets, flags and propaganda posters. Above the counter was a clock, its case made from half a beer barrel. It had stopped with its hands at eleven o'clock. At the far end of the room a coin-operated pianola played tunes that mingled with the roar of conversation and the tinging of the cash register.

Saul returned with the drinks – a lemonade for her, a pint for himself – and placed them on the table. She waited until he'd sat down before she asked, 'Is there any news? Have you heard anything?'

He shook his head. 'Nothing. No useful fingerprints – he must have been wearing gloves – and no sign of the murder weapon.'

Judith's face twisted in disappointment. 'It's been four days. Don't you have any clues?'

'They've pulled in all the local thieves but none of them seem likely candidates. Which just leaves what we've already talked about – someone bearing a grudge, maybe someone she informed on, or someone connected to Lennie Hull's murder.'

This reminded Judith of her altercation with Lennie's brother. 'Pat Hull isn't happy. He pounced on me on Sunday, wanting to know what Elsa was up to. He seems to think I was in on it too, whatever "it" was.'

Saul looked concerned. 'Are you all right? He didn't hurt you, did he?'

'Nothing too serious,' she said, extending her arm to show him her wrist with its mushroom-coloured bruises. 'I told him I didn't know anything, that I'd barely known Elsa, but I'm not sure he believed me.'

'Christ, what a bastard. Did you report him?'

'I considered it.' She gave a shrug. 'But then I thought it was only going to muddy the waters.'

'Muddy waters are better than a hospital bed.'

'Well, it didn't come to that.'

'Not this time,' he said ominously.

Judith brushed aside the comment, not wanting to dwell on

what Hull might do next. 'What I don't understand is where it came from. How did he find out about the link to Lennie's death? You were only told on Sunday morning.'

'From Cowan Road,' he said. 'Some stations are as leaky as a dripping tap.'

'You mean a police officer told him? Why would they do that?'

Saul smiled grimly. 'Everyone has a price, as they say.'

Judith was shocked. Although she'd read the occasional story in the papers about crooked officers, she'd always thought it was a case of a few bad apples. She was relieved now that she'd kept her mouth shut about her connection to Ivor Doyle. If the police were leaking information to Hull, this particular gem would have made him even more suspicious. 'What about your contacts? Anything new?'

'Silent as the night.'

'Because they don't know anything, or because they're not prepared to tell you?'

'Your guess is as good as mine.'

Judith sipped her lemonade. 'I saw someone else on Sunday – Ivor Doyle.'

'I thought you were going to stay away from him.'

'I was. I *am*. But he just showed up out of the blue. Actually, he said something odd. He asked whether Elsa had a gun. Why would he do that?'

'Didn't you ask him?'

Judith frowned. 'Of course I did, but he wasn't what you'd call forthcoming. He just muttered something about people keeping guns to defend themselves. But why should a waitress need a gun? And Elsa didn't strike me as being scared of anyone.'

'Perhaps that was her mistake.' Saul communed with his pint for a while, downing a quarter of it in one long draught. Then he put the glass down on the table. 'The gun that was used to kill Lennie was never found.'

'What are you saying, that Elsie may have ... No, I can't believe that. *You* can't believe it. Why would she have killed him?'

'That's not what I meant. You'd have to have a death wish to hang on to a murder weapon you'd used yourself. But maybe she got hold of it somehow, or was pretending she had.'

'Calling someone's bluff? Blackmailing them?'

'It's not impossible. She said she had money coming in, but where was it coming from? Perhaps that's why the place was turned upside down. The killer was looking for the gun.'

'Money?' she asked. 'What money?'

'A small legacy, apparently. It's what she told someone.'

'And it wasn't true?'

'We can't find any evidence of it.'

Judith pondered this for a moment. 'And we don't know if they found the gun – or even if there was anything to find. God, why would she do something so stupid? If they've already killed once ... I mean, that's not just playing with fire, it's putting yourself directly in the firing line.'

'That was Elsa,' he said. 'She liked playing dangerous games.'

'Why do you think that was?'

Saul shrugged, gave a half-smile. 'You'd have to ask a psychiatrist that. Some people found it hard to adjust after the war. They lived in a state of heightened anxiety for such a long time, and then everything goes back to normal and it all seems ... kind of grey, perhaps. Lacking something.'

'Do you feel like that?'

'No,' he said. 'I'm just glad the damn thing's over.' He took another gulp of his pint and added thoughtfully, 'Maybe it had nothing to do with the war. Maybe that was just Elsa's personality. You don't owe her anything, you know.'

'It's not to do with that,' she said. 'Well, partly perhaps, but ... I liked her. I want to find out what happened, and why.'

281

'Even if it leads back to Ivor Doyle?'

'Do you think it will?'

'He seems to have an unhealthy interest in Elsa's death. He came to find you, and asked about the gun. I'd say there was something going on, wouldn't you?'

Judith gave a sigh. 'I wish I could say no.'

'It could all get pretty complicated.'

'It's already complicated.'

Saul nodded. 'Perhaps you should move out of Kellston, get somewhere else to stay. I can help you find another boarding house if you like.'

'I'll think about it.'

'Will you?'

'Of course,' she lied. She had no intention of leaving Kellston right now. Even with the threat of Pat Hull, she knew she had to stick it out, that this was where the answers lay. And if Doyle didn't know where she was, how would he find her again? She had no doubt that he hadn't finished with her yet. And perhaps she hadn't finished with him either.

'Let me know what you decide.'

'I will. And you'll keep me updated on any progress with the case?'

'Naturally,' he said. 'We should get together soon. How does Saturday sound? About seven? We could meet here again, maybe go on and get a bite to eat.'

Judith hesitated, unsure as to whether he was suggesting more than an exchange of information, and if so how she felt about it. 'Saturday?' she asked, playing for time.

'If you're not busy. I always work better on a full stomach.'

She smiled vaguely. Perhaps she was overthinking the situation, and as the only alternative on offer was a long, lonely evening at the boarding house, she decided she might as well take him up on the offer. 'All right, then. Seven o'clock.'

282

'Good.'

Judith couldn't tell from his expression whether he was pleased or indifferent. Although her feelings towards him had softened, she still wasn't sure if she entirely trusted him – or even liked him, come to that. Still, so long as there weren't any embarrassing misunderstandings . . .

Saul gestured towards a man who was sitting at the bar chatting to the landlord. 'Do you know who that is?'

Judith shook her head. 'Should I?'

'That's Albert Pierrepoint, the hangman.'

She stared over, intrigued. He seemed an ordinary sort of man, in his mid forties, short and plump-cheeked, dressed in a dark blue suit and a brown trilby. Although he wasn't the only hangman, he was the only one she'd heard of. It was Pierrepoint who dispatched many of those found guilty of murder, and who'd been sent to Nuremburg to execute more than two hundred German war criminals. 'You wouldn't think it to look at him, would you?'

'They say he's the best, that he takes the time and trouble to make sure it's quick.'

'I wonder how he can bear it, to be that close to death so often.'

'They say his father was a hangman too, and his uncle.'

As Judith continued to study him, she had one of those uneasy feelings, like someone had just walked over her grave. When Elsa's killer was found, they would be hanged too. And what if Ivor Doyle was the guilty one? The thought of it made her stomach clench. She loathed him, despised him, but she still couldn't bear the thought of him dangling from the end of a rope. A pulse began to throb in her temples. Her hands were clammy. Like the crow in the graveyard, the presence of Pierrepoint felt like another bad omen.

43

By Thursday afternoon, the weather had changed again, the blue skies turning grey, a thin drizzle smattering the pavements. Judith had a restless feeling, a need to be doing something, but all she had managed so far was a trip to the chemist to buy talc and toothpaste. Now, reluctant to return to the boarding house, she sauntered up the high street searching for distraction.

The shops had little to offer, but she gazed into their windows anyway. She also kept her eyes peeled for Pat Hull. She was safe enough, she reckoned, if she stuck to public spaces and stayed around other people. When she reached the green, she looked over at the bench and scowled, as if the wooden seat held some responsibility for all the bad things that had happened there.

She switched her gaze to Connolly's, and at that very moment, the door opened and a woman walked out. Judith studied her for a moment: she was skinny and hollow-faced, and was wearing a brown raincoat and a headscarf. Was that Maud? Elsa had mentioned her, the work colleague who was more often than not on the receiving end of her husband's fists. And Judith thought, although she couldn't be sure, that she had seen her before at the café.

On impulse, she crossed the road, dodging the traffic, and hurried to catch up with the woman. As she drew alongside, she smiled and said, 'It's Maud, isn't it? I'm Elsa's friend, Judith.'

Maud gave a tiny jump, startled by the approach. Neither confirming nor denying her name, she continued to walk while she stared back at Judith with eyes full of suspicion. 'What do you want?'

Despite the hostile response, Judith wasn't deterred. 'It's awful what's happened, isn't it? Poor Elsa. Who'd do such a thing? I still can't believe it. And no one's even been arrested yet.'

Maud shot her a quick, anxious glance, and increased her pace as though she might be able to shake her off.

Judith persisted. 'They seem to be interested in some money she was supposed to be getting. Did she mention that to you? Did she say anything?'

'I don't know nothin' about no money.'

'Maybe that was why they broke in, to try and steal it. Or perhaps they were after something else. Do you have any idea of what that might be?'

'How would I know?'

Judith was having to take long strides to keep up. 'Because you worked together. You must have chatted. I'm just looking for some clues. The police don't seem to be getting very far. Did Elsa seem worried about anything, about any*one*, to you?'

'No.'

'Are you sure?'

'We never had much time for chat. It's busy in the caff.'

'Some time, though.' Judith didn't understand why the woman was being so defensive. 'What about Lennie Hull? Did she ever mention him?'

Maud stopped suddenly and turned to face her. Her voice was

fierce and her eyes full of fear. 'I don't know nothin', all right? Just leave me alone.'

With that, she hurried off and Judith didn't attempt to follow her. Had she hit a nerve there? It certainly felt like it. Or maybe it was just the shock of the murder. People reacted to death in different ways. But no, she was pretty sure it was the mention of Lennie's name that had really spooked Maud.

She stood for a while, not sure what to do next. It was only when she realised she was blocking everyone's path that she finally set off again. She recrossed the street and skirted round the green, taking the longer but less lonely route to Barley Road. With no clear idea as to why exactly she was going there – and dreading the thought of it – she walked slowly, dragging her feet like a reluctant child. A vague plan was forming in the back of her mind, but it was so wrong, so stupid, she didn't dare acknowledge it.

As she approached the house, she could see the bright police tape still stretched across the top of the steps where the metal stairway led down to the basement. There was, however, no sign of any officers or any official cars. She presumed they'd have finished their work by now, although they didn't seem to have accomplished much.

The closer she got, the more nervous she became. Did she really have the courage to do this? She fingered the key in her pocket, the key to Elsa's flat. No one had asked for it back, and until a few minutes ago she'd forgotten all about it. There was nothing to stop her from going inside and searching for the gun – well, nothing apart from her own disinclination to step over that threshold again. The gun might not even exist, or could have already been removed by Elsa's killer. And then, of course, there was the worry of being discovered.

As regarded the latter, she concocted a story, should she need it, about having left something behind – an item of clothing perhaps – to explain her presence in the flat. It wouldn't go down well, but she'd just have to act innocent and pretend she didn't know that access was still prohibited.

The other problem was the neighbours. What if they rang the police and reported her? She glanced at the windows of the flats above, but they were covered by net curtains. It was impossible to tell if anyone was watching or not. The trick, she supposed, was to try and not look furtive, which wasn't easy when what you were doing was utterly furtive.

With this in mind, and after a quick look round, she strode forward as though she had every right to be there. She ducked under the tape, jogged down the steps and unlocked the door before she could have a change of heart. Once inside, she stopped and listened for any indication that someone might have seen her – the sound of another door opening, or footsteps on the pavement – but there was only silence. She doubted if anyone had a phone in their home round here, and so any call would have to be made from a phone box.

Once she was sure that no one was going to challenge her, she relaxed a little. But as she moved forward into the living room, she instantly tensed again as her eyes took in the disarray. She thought of what had happened here, the horror, and felt her mouth go dry. Deep breaths: one, two, three. She couldn't afford to lose her nerve. Now that she was here, she had to make the most of whatever time she had.

But where to start? It wasn't a big flat, and there weren't many places to hide something as bulky as a gun. The police, she presumed, hadn't conducted any kind of search, being unaware of what Elsa might have been involved in. They had left their mark, though, with a fine layer of fingerprint dust over every available surface. Her own prints had been taken down at the station, a procedure that had made her feel curiously guilty, even though she had not done anything wrong.

She knew it was pointless checking the more obvious places – the killer had already done that – and so she stood in the middle of the chaos and slowly did a three-hundred-and-sixty-degree turn. Her gaze roamed over every corner of the room as she tried to think of where *she'd* hide something. She looked up, looked down. She even studied the edges of the carpet, but could see no spot where it might have been pulled up from the floor.

The cupboards over the sink had been emptied of pots and pans and plates. The table had been turned over. Even the chairs had been taken apart, their stuffing pulled out and the cushions ripped open. She could still smell the whisky from where the bottle had smashed on the floor.

Once the possibilities of the living room had been exhausted, she moved on to the main bedroom, but it was the same story here. All the obvious places, the wardrobe, the drawers, had been thoroughly ransacked. She poked around, but with no success. It felt strange, uncomfortable to be going through Elsa's stuff, and more than once she was tempted to give up and leave. But she'd come this far – she might as well see it through.

In the bathroom, the cabinet had been emptied and the lid dragged off the cistern and dropped on the floor. She reached in behind the toilet and felt between the pipes. She looked under the bath and the sink. She checked the lino for signs of disturbance. Nothing, nothing, nothing.

The final room was the spare where she'd been sleeping. She didn't even want to go inside. Standing by the door, she stared at the spot where Elsa's body had been lying. There were bloodstains on the carpet, dark red, almost brown, gruesome. It made her feel sick just to look at them. The room was too small, too sparsely furnished to hide anything in, and anyway Elsa would hardly have taken the risk of the gun being accidentally discovered.

Judith retreated to the living room, disappointed that her

search had been a failure. What had she been thinking? That she could just waltz in here and find the weapon that been used to murder Lennie Hull all those years ago? The chances had been one in a million. And that was if there even was a gun. Perhaps she and Saul had been barking up the wrong tree entirely.

She went over to the window and glanced up at the street. Still empty so far as she could see. Well, she was wasting her time. She should quit while she was still ahead – ahead being the fact that she hadn't, as yet, been caught in the act.

But still she lingered.

The gun had to possess some link to the killer – why else would they be so desperate to get it back? Fingerprints, probably, along with other stuff. She'd read somewhere that an expert could match a bullet to the gun it had been fired from. The police, she presumed, still had the bullet that had ended Hull's life.

Her gaze fell on the Gauguin print, the picture of the three women that would forever remind her of Elsa. It was lying on the floor, half out of its frame, torn apart like Elsa's life had been. She knew that she should leave it where it was, but still she crouched down and picked it up. It must have meant something for Elsa to have had it on the wall, to have looked at it every day.

'I'm sorry,' she murmured, although she wasn't sure what she was apologising for. Maybe just her incompetence in achieving anything useful. She gazed at the picture and wondered what the three women had been thinking about as Gauguin had painted them. Perhaps nothing more profound than what they were having for lunch that day.

As she held it up, examining the detail, she noticed a narrow piece of tape, no more than an inch or two, on the inner edge of the broken frame. It was perhaps a repair from a previous break, and yet there didn't seem to be any evidence of earlier damage. She touched the spot and was sure she could feel something underneath. Her heart began beating faster. Carefully she picked at the tape with her fingernail until she had managed to free a corner and could peel it back.

Her eyes lit up. What she had discovered was a small silver-coloured key. She lifted it away from the frame and turned it over in her fingers. There was a number engraved on it: 22. But what did it mean? The key was too small to fit a front door, but it could be for a box or a safe, maybe even a shed or garage. She knew it was important – the fact Elsa had hidden it was testimony to that – but without knowing what lock it belonged to she only had one half of the puzzle.

She quickly checked the rest of the frame, making sure she hadn't missed anything else. Excitement and frustration made her fingers clumsy. She searched every edge, every corner, but there was nothing more. Sitting back on her haunches, she wondered what to do next. Take it to the police? That was what she *should* do, but caution whispered in her ear. She couldn't trust them. If past experience was anything to go by, the news would rapidly get back to Pat Hull, and she could do without another of his angry confrontations. Also, the police would probably be less than pleased that she'd let herself into the flat in the first place.

She tapped the key against her teeth, trying to think. Well, the first thing she should do was get the hell out of there. She jumped up, shoved the key in her pocket and hurried over to the front door. She opened it carefully, only a crack, listened and then peered up towards the street. When she was sure there was no one in the vicinity, she slipped out, closing the door softly behind her.

She paused again before climbing the steps, her ears tuned to the slightest sound, and only when she was certain it was safe did she make her way up. Her eyes darted left and right as she ducked under the tape, praying she wouldn't be seen. Her pulse was racing, her breathing shallow. As she walked along the street, she kept expecting someone to shout or come running after her. The urge to look over her shoulder was almost overwhelming, but she managed to resist until she'd covered fifty yards.

Even then, she didn't immediately relax. This time she chose the shorter route across the green, wanting to get back to the boarding house as fast as possible. What she was carrying was precious – her hand closed around the key – and probably a major clue as to who had killed Elsa and why. She needed somewhere safe, away from prying eyes, where she could sit down and try to work out where she went from here.

Of course, Ivor Doyle would probably be able to tell her in a second what kind of key it was and what it was likely to fit, but he was the last person she was going to ask. Maybe she would show it to Saul instead and get his thoughts on the matter. Anyway, she didn't have to make a decision right now.

Her nerves remained on edge as she hurried across the green and on into the high street. She passed Connolly's without a second glance – all thoughts of Maud were long gone – and was oblivious to the shop windows and their displays. Even the rain barely registered as it drizzled onto her hair and shoulders. She waited at the junction for the lights to change, bouncing impatiently on her heels.

It was only as she turned into Silverstone Road that it occurred to her that the key could belong to a locker, like those left-luggage ones at the bigger railway stations. But which station would Elsa have chosen? Liverpool Street, Euston and King's Cross were the closest, but she might have gone for somewhere less obvious. There was Victoria, Waterloo, Paddington and probably others too. Except wouldn't the key have some kind of markings on it to identify where it came from? Unless it had come with a tag that Elsa had removed.

Judith was still weighing up this possibility – and wondering how long it would take her to visit all the various stations – as she walked through the front door of the boarding house. It was quiet inside, as hushed as a church. She had made it across the hall and onto the first step of the stairs when Mrs Gillan appeared from the back of the house.

'Ah, here you are. You've got a visitor. I put them in the lounge.'

'A visitor?' Judith's first thought – and it wasn't a good one – was that Pat Hull had come for her. She gripped the banister. 'Who is it? I wasn't expecting anyone.'

'She didn't say, but I believe her name's Nell, Nell McAllister.'

Judith's mouth dropped open.

44

It took Judith a moment to recover from the shock. Nell McAllister here, only yards away, the woman Dan Jonson had left her for. She could feel the blood draining from her face. Why had she come? What did she want? She hoped the woman wasn't going to shout and cry and create a scene. There had been enough drama over the last couple of weeks to last her a lifetime.

Mrs Gillan must have noticed her expression. 'If you don't want to see her, I can tell her you're unwell.'

This, Judith thought, wouldn't exactly be a lie – she *did* feel sick – but there were some things that couldn't be put off. If she didn't see Nell today, she would have to see her tomorrow, and then she would have it hanging over her all night. It was better, she decided, to get it over and done with.

'No, no, it's quite all right. Thank you. It was just a . . . a surprise, that's all.'

Mrs Gillan nodded, hesitated as if she might be about to say something else but then retreated to her quarters.

Judith took a few more seconds to steady her nerves before pushing back her shoulders, bracing herself and advancing into what she suspected could be a war zone. God, she hoped not, or she might end up getting thrown out of this boarding house too. The way her luck was going, she'd soon be blacklisted in every establishment in Kellston.

She paused at the door to the lounge and looked in. It was empty apart from a woman who was sitting in the corner, hunched over and biting her nails. Nell suddenly turned her head and looked straight at her. Judith's first impression was that she must once have been pretty – maybe even beautiful – for beneath the scarring and the odd alignment of her jaw, there were still traces of a fine bone structure. Her hair was blonde, waved, and her eyes were very blue, the colour of the eyes in china dolls.

Judith crossed the room with trepidation. She had no idea how a person was supposed to act in these circumstances. The rules of etiquette had not yet been written for situations like these. She could hardly smile, but she didn't want to scowl either. It wasn't the woman's fault that Ivor Doyle was a liar and a cheat, and yet it was hard not to think of her as being the enemy.

In the event, Nell McAllister seemed even more nervous than Judith was. Jumping to her feet, she gave her a trembling smile.

'I'm so sorry to just come by like this – it must seem odd to you – but I thought . . . I thought we should meet.'

Judith gestured for her to sit down and took the chair opposite. There was an awkward pause while both women settled into their seats. When Nell didn't say anything more, Judith felt obliged to fill the silence.

'So, he told you about me?'

Nell's mouth twisted and she shook her head. 'Who, Ivor? No, he didn't tell me anything, not a word. But I've known for a while that he was married to someone called Judith – I found the certificate, you see – and so when you turned up at the house and I heard him say your name ... well, it wasn't too hard to work out.'

'I don't understand. Have you never talked to him about our marriage?'

Nell gave a slight shrug. 'What's the point? He'd have told me if he'd wanted to. It's in the past. It doesn't matter.' Then her body seemed to stiffen and her tone suddenly rose in pitch, becoming almost accusing. 'It *is* in the past, isn't it?'

'Oh, I think we can safely say that.'

'So what are you doing here? What do you want?'

What Judith wanted was the truth, the truth about everything, but she knew she wouldn't get it from Nell. She could see the fear in her eyes, and felt some sympathy. It was hard not to. The woman was brittle and anxious, damaged in more ways than the physical. While she tried to think of a suitable answer, she watched Nell's hands twist around each other. 'Loose ends, that's all.'

'I always knew you'd turn up one day.'

There wasn't much Judith could say to this, and so she asked instead, 'How did you know where to find me?'

Nell's mouth opened, but then, as if she'd had second thoughts, quickly closed again. Her eyes slid over the room before returning to Judith. 'I don't remember,' she said, unconvincingly. 'Someone told me.'

'Someone?'

Nell ignored the question. 'Ivor doesn't know I'm here. You won't tell him, will you?'

'I shouldn't think I'll be seeing him again.' This wasn't exactly the truth, but it seemed the wisest reply in the circumstances. She had the feeling Doyle hadn't finished with her yet, that he'd be back at some point to talk more about Elsa.

'He hasn't done anything wrong.'

Judith could have disputed this; abandoning your wife and

letting her think you were dead seemed pretty wrong to her, but Nell was in the dark about all that. 'Did I say he had?'

'It's what you *think*, though, isn't it?'

'I don't understand.'

Nell lifted a hand to her mouth and started chewing on her fingernails again. She cast quick, nervous glances in Judith's direction. 'I suppose he's told you all about me.'

Judith was about to deny this, but then thought better of it. 'A bit.'

'He's always tried to do the right thing. It hasn't been easy for him. He's only ever ... but sometimes it just all goes wrong, doesn't it? You don't mean for it to, but it does. Like it gets out of control and suddenly instead of getting better, everything gets worse.'

'Like with Elsa Keep?'

'What?'

'Elsa Keep,' Judith repeated, trying her best to maintain a calm and level tone. 'She's the girl who was murdered last Saturday.'

'Your friend, you mean?'

Judith nodded. 'Ivor's mentioned her to you, then?'

'It's been on the news. Everyone's heard about it.'

'But not about the two of us being friends.'

Nell considered this for a moment and then said, 'It seems nice here. Do you have a pleasant room?'

At first Judith thought she was making a clumsy attempt to change the subject, but as she looked more closely, she saw that Nell's eyes, currently roaming around the lounge, had an odd, glazed expression. 'It's fine, the room's fine. We were talking about Elsa.'

'Ivor didn't have anything to do with that.'

'I never said he had.'

'Just because he ...' Nell stopped and frowned, glaring at

Judith as though she'd been trying to trap her. 'What do you want from him, from us?'

'Nothing. Why should I want anything?'

'Because you're here. You must want something.'

Judith shrugged. 'You're the one who's come to see me. What do *you* want?'

This turning of the tables seemed to confuse Nell. She attacked her fingernails for a few seconds, uncrossed her legs and crossed them again. Everything about her was jumpy and agitated. She couldn't sit still, couldn't look Judith in the eye. As if an army of ants was climbing over her, she scratched the back of her head, her neck, a knee, an elbow. Eventually, a long, soft sigh escaped from her lips. 'You know about Lennie Hull.'

It was a statement, not a question. Judith wasn't exactly sure what she meant – what Lennie had done to Nell? What Ivor had done to Lennie? – but sensing she might learn more from keeping quiet, she simply nodded.

'You told Elsa Keep. Ivor told you and you told Elsa.'

Judith put her hand in her pocket, felt for the key and was reassured to feel the cool, hard metal between her fingers. She decided to be blunt. 'Is that why Elsa had to be killed? Did she know too much?'

Nell seemed more anxious than shocked at the implied accusation. The tip of her tongue slid across her upper lip. 'Ivor was with me on Saturday.'

'Of course he was.'

'He didn't go out. He was home all night.'

'There's nothing to worry about, then.'

Nell gave a thin smile. 'Is it money? Is that what you want?'

Judith wondered if this amounted to an admission of guilt – Ivor's guilt, at least. 'All I want is Elsa's killer found.' And yet she wondered if this was really the case. If Ivor Doyle was exposed as the murderer, he'd be charged, tried and hanged. She remembered Pierrepoint sitting at the bar in the Fitzroy Tavern, and a shiver ran through her.

Nell's gaze made another circuit of the room. She spoke without looking directly at Judith. 'Lennie shouldn't have done what he did to me.'

'No.'

'He was evil, and that's the beginning and end of it.'

Judith tried not to stare at the scars on the woman's face, at the damage that could never be undone. Instead, she studied her clothes, old and stained, a blue dress and grey cardigan, a pair of shoes with worn-down heels. As if she'd dressed in a hurry, not bothering to look in the mirror. There was chipped polish on her fingernails, and only a section of her hair had been brushed. An odd smell drifted off her, something slightly musty.

'He deserved it,' Nell continued, her voice high and sharp. 'If anyone deserved to die, it was him. After what he did to me . . . He was always up here, in my head.' She made a fleeting gesture with her hand. 'As if he hadn't finished with me yet, as if he wanted to hurt me some more. It wouldn't go away: every day, every night. I had to try and stop that, didn't I? I had to do something. But I didn't mean to . . . not really . . . I only wanted to scare him, to make him feel like I'd felt, but then . . .'

Judith nodded, the hairs on her arms standing on end. Was Nell really saying what she thought she was? Was she actually confessing? In order to avoid any doubt, she phrased her words carefully. 'There are people who think Ivor did it.'

Nell gave an odd little laugh. 'Ivor? He wasn't even here. How could he?'

Judith found herself both confused and bewildered. How were you supposed to react to someone admitting to murder? And was it even true? The damage to Nell wasn't just physical; it was in her mind too. Perhaps she was delusional, acting out some fantasy. Or maybe she loved Ivor enough to try and cover for him, to shift the blame onto herself. 'So, what about Elsa?'

'What about her?' As if everything was perfectly normal, as if the awful words about Lennie had never been spoken, Nell smiled.

'I suppose Ivor was scared that she'd tell the police.'

'Ivor isn't scared of anything.' Nell paused, stared at Judith and said defiantly, 'He was with me all night. He didn't go anywhere.'

Judith was about to press her on this when the door to the lounge opened and one of the elderly ladies came in carrying a ball of wool and some knitting needles. Muriel, that was her name. She smiled at them both and settled herself into an armchair by the unlit fire. Judith silently cursed. There was no way the conversation could be resumed now that they had company, not unless they were going to conduct it in a whisper.

Nell clearly thought the same. 'Oh, is that the time?' she said, glancing at the clock on the mantelpiece and rising to her feet. 'I really have to go.'

'I'll see you out.'

'There's no need,' Nell said. 'Really there isn't. Goodbye.'

And before Judith could even consider following her, she had rushed across the room and out into the hall. There was the tap of her heels on the wooden floor, closely followed by the sound of the front door being opened and closed. She was gone.

Judith sat back, stunned by what had happened. She wished Nell hadn't told her what she had; she felt overwhelmed by it, burdened. What was she supposed to do now? She closed her eyes, clenched her hands in her lap. The only noise in the lounge was the soft, rhythmic clacking of Muriel's knitting needles. It stirred a memory in her, a school history lesson about the French Revolution where old women had sat near the guillotine and knitted between executions.

45

Saul Hannah was making the most of his liberty. By the end of September, when the Ghost Squad was disbanded, he would no longer have the same freedom to roam. He'd have to account for his movements, work as part of a team, answer to a boss. His hours would be shorter, but that was nothing to look forward to. His work was his life and everything revolved around it.

For now, however, the streets of Mayfair and Soho were still his territory, and he prowled from pub to pub looking for familiar faces. There was always more of a buzz around Soho on a Friday. By the evening, the whole place would be heaving. Payday meant customers with money to spend, welcome news for the hookers, the bookies' runners, the drinking and gambling clubs, not to mention the dips who preyed on the drunk and the careless.

He wasn't searching for anyone in particular, just putting himself out there in case someone felt like talking. A word here, a word there could eventually add up to something useful. There was still no news on Elsa's killer. It was almost a week now, and the trail, if there had ever been one, was rapidly growing cold.

He wondered how Judith would cope if Ivor Doyle was eventually revealed as the murderer. She might despise her husband for what he'd done to her, but it was a thin line between love and hate. Could it have been him? It had certainly been peculiar him asking if Elsa had possessed a gun. Or maybe he'd been doing someone else's dirty work – Tombs's, for example.

There was a rumour doing the rounds that Alf Tombs was planning something big. He'd been seen with Geordie Mack, and that only meant one thing – guns. Saul had inadvertently dropped a hint about it when he'd taken Judith to Leo's, something along the lines of Tombs not being too happy about his locksmith being dragged into a murder inquiry, *especially at the moment*. She'd picked up on it, of course, but he'd managed to gloss over the error. He didn't think she'd say anything to Doyle, but you never knew with women. He frowned, annoyed at himself. It was unusual for him to make careless mistakes like that.

He walked into the Bell and ordered a pint. It worried him that Judith Jonson was getting in over her head. That business with Pat Hull could be just the tip of the iceberg – if Hull thought she knew more than she did, he'd be back. And what if she'd been seen with Doyle? That wouldn't go down well. Hull might start thinking she was in league with him, trying to conceal the identity of Lennie's killer. Tombs and Hull had been at loggerheads for years, an ongoing battle that could easily explode into all-out warfare.

But she wasn't his responsibility. The choices she was making were hers, and if she was stubborn enough to stick by them, there was nothing he could do except watch her back, although he couldn't do that twenty-four hours a day. And that was something else that bothered him – the fact that he *wanted* to. Somehow that woman had got under his skin and he couldn't stop thinking about her.

Monaghan arrived at the same time as his pint. He sidled up to Saul, leaned an elbow on the bar and glanced furtively round the pub.

'I've checked,' Saul said. 'There's no one here.'

'No harm in checking again.'

'You want a drink?'

Monaghan always wanted a drink. 'That's very courteous of you, Mr Hannah. I'll take a Scotch.'

Saul beckoned the barman over and put the order in. Then he turned back to his companion, nodding as he examined his face. 'You're looking slightly better, Roy, if you don't mind me saying.'

'Some wounds never heal,' Monaghan replied mournfully. He briefly stroked the scar on his bony face, wincing at the memory of the beating. 'Ten years of my life I gave to that man, and what thanks do I get for it?'

Saul grinned, thinking that he sounded like a wife who'd been cheated on and dumped. 'That's the trouble with villains, Roy. You just can't trust them.'

'There ain't no loyalty no more, that's the problem.'

'You nicked off him, for God's sake. What did you expect him to do, give you a medal?'

Monaghan attacked his Scotch with gusto, emptying half the glass in a single gulp. 'A misunderstanding, that's all it were. If Alf had given me five minutes to explain . . .'

'I don't reckon any amount of explaining was going to get you out of that one. Anyway, delightful as it is to see you again, I'm presuming there's a reason?'

Monaghan gave another shifty look round the pub. 'I heard a whisper Alf's out to get Pat Hull.'

Saul snorted. 'Tell me something I don't know. Those two have been at each other's throats for years.'

'No, this is serious.'

'It's always serious. What makes this any different?'

'Shooters,' Monaghan said softly. 'They've both been tooling up.'

Saul lifted an eyebrow. He already knew why Hull needed guns, and it was nothing to do with Tombs. 'Well, with a bit of luck, they'll shoot each other and make everyone happy. You heard anything about the Elsa Keep murder?'

'The waitress?'

'Yes, the waitress.'

'Nah.'

'Nothing at all?'

'I've just said, ain't I?' Monaghan downed the last half of his Scotch, put the glass down on the bar and stared at it with a desperate kind of longing. Knowing that he wouldn't get another unless he came up with something interesting, he trawled his brain for further information. 'Maybe there is something, now I come to think of it. That blonde you were asking me about, Nell McAllister, Doyle's girl. She was in the Montevideo the other night – Wednesday, I think I was.'

'Fascinating,' Saul said.

'She don't go out much, ain't been there for a while. Turned up to have a chat with Alf.' Monaghan paused to gaze at the empty glass again. 'She weren't too happy, by all accounts. That Elsa might have been mentioned, something to do with her and Doyle.'

Saul's ears pricked up. 'Might have or definitely was?'

'I can only tell you what the geezer told me. He's the barman there. Reckoned Nell was in a state, though, been on the hard stuff and more besides. Not all there, if you get my meaning.'

'Doyle wasn't with her?'

'Nah, just her and Alf. It got a bit heated and he put her in a cab.'

'They rowed?'

Monaghan shrugged his skinny shoulders. 'You know what

women are like when they've had one too many. Everything's a bleedin' drama.'

Saul wasn't sure what to make of it all. Lots of people must be talking about Elsa's murder – that was hardly odd or unusual – but when you put Tombs and Nell together ... Alarm bells went off in his head. It could be something and nothing, but then again ...

Alf Tombs paced from one side of the room to the other, pausing every time he reached the window to gaze down into the street. His little office in Soho was a bolthole the law didn't know about, a good place to store incriminating paperwork and everything else he preferred to keep private. Here, with only his own thoughts for company, he could make plans, plot the future and reminisce about the past.

Diagonally opposite was the Colony Room Club, a drinking establishment for artists, musicians, writers and the like, and a venue with a reputation for behaviour as questionable as its bilious green walls. It occupied a small room on the first floor, reached by a flight of stinking steps, the memory of which still made his nose wrinkle. He had only been there once, and once had been enough.

Alf was a live-and-let-live kind of person and didn't much care what other people got up to behind closed doors. Although the experience had been interesting, he had found the atmosphere toxic: too many egos colliding and clashing, too much rowing and bitching and general nastiness. He preferred to drink in more civilised surroundings, and in the company of those he understood.

As he looked through the window, he noticed Francis Bacon strolling down the street. Although the bloke was feted as a genius, Alf didn't get it. He couldn't see how that stuff was art, more like an angry explosion of paint on canvas. He continued to watch until the artist had passed through the door to the club – if past history was anything to go by, it would be a long while before he emerged again – and then resumed his pacing of the office.

Alf had a lot on his mind. He was concerned about Heathrow and considering a change of plan. Maybe it would be better to let Hull go ahead with the heist and intercept him on his way back. That way they would get all the reward with none of the risk. This, he knew, would be the sensible option, but the temptation to get in there first still pulled at him. It would be payback for the New Bond Street job he'd lost out on, and would send a message to Hull that he couldn't be messed with. Reputation was everything in this game.

He'd seen nothing more of Nell since she'd turned up at the Montevideo, and little of Doyle either. Something was brewing, though. He could feel it in his bones. Could he trust Doyle on the Heathrow job? Although it pained him to admit it, he wasn't sure he could. Since Judith Jonson had come on the scene, everything had changed. She had stirred up matters that should have been laid to rest years ago. She was causing trouble, big trouble, and he'd had enough of it. It was time, he decided, to give the girl a taste of her own medicine.

He sat down at his desk, flipped through the phone directory, found the number he was looking for and dialled. It took five rings before it was answered.

'Jimmy,' he said. 'How are you doing? It's Alf, Alf Tombs. I was hoping you could do me a favour.'

Jimmy Taylor listened, nodded and swiftly wrote down the name and number he was given, then said goodbye and replaced the receiver. He couldn't deny that he'd almost shit himself when he'd heard Judith Jonson's name mentioned. His heart had started racing, thumping in his chest, and his hands had gone clammy. There was no way Tombs could know what had happened at Elsa Keep's, and yet the fear of exposure was always with him.

'Who was that?' his dad asked.

'No one,' Jimmy said. 'Just someone asking about opening hours.'

It was another twenty minutes before he was able to nip out. He didn't want to use the phone at the shop just in case it could be traced. Truth be told, he'd have rather not got involved – he had enough to worry about at the moment – but no one refused Alf Tombs a favour.

He stepped inside the phone box by the bus stop and pulled some change from his pocket. It was a woman who answered.

'Good afternoon, *Kellston Gazette*.'

Jimmy asked for Donald Smart, and the woman asked who was calling. Unprepared for this, he hesitated, racking his brains for a fake name. A white bakery van went by on the street, the company name emblazoned in blue across the side: Malcolm Goodrich & Sons. 'Er . . . Goodrich,' he said, 'Jack Goodrich.'

While he waited for the woman to put him through, he watched the people going in and out of the station and tapped his free hand impatiently against his thigh. Eventually, Smart came on the line.

'Mr Goodrich? Hello, how can I help?'

Jimmy spoke quickly, wanting to get it over and done with. 'It's about the Elsa Keep murder. I may have some information for you. Well, not about the murder so much as the girl who found the body. Judith Jonson, right?'

'I believe so.'

'I don't know if you've been told, only she's a tom . . . a prostitute.'

'You sure about that?'

'She got thrown out of a local B and B for it. Sycamore

306

House, it's called, on Station Road. You can check if you like. Mrs Jolly, that's the landlady's name. Could be Elsa Keep was on the game too. Might be important, don't you think?'

'Are the police aware of this, Mr Goodrich?'

'How would I know? I ain't told them, if that's what you mean.'

'And are you aware of Judith Jonson's whereabouts now?'

'Nah, mate, ain't got a clue. Dare say she's still around, though. Shouldn't be too hard to find.' And then, before Smart could ask him any more questions, Jimmy hung up. He took his change, had a quick look round and exited the phone box.

Maud Bishop had got used to the trains, so much so that she barely noticed now when they went past. Even the shuddering of the house had become normal, a brief stirring of bricks and mortar, a trembling in the foundations. It was only the smuts that bothered her, the dirt that billowed out and rained down on her washing. As she unpegged the sheets, she thought about the place she'd move to, somewhere far away from the railway, somewhere clean and fresh and quiet.

She hadn't spoken to Mick since yesterday morning. He'd been out till the early hours, rolling in bladdered at about four o'clock, and was still sleeping it off. Thankfully, he'd been too pissed to wake her up and force himself on her. Small mercies, she thought, but she wasn't out of the woods yet. When he woke with a hangover, he'd be looking for someone to blame.

She tentatively touched the lobe of her ear, where the fag burn still throbbed and stung. *Bastard*. Her life would be so much better without him – no more pain, no more fear, no more stepping on eggshells in case she did or said something to offend him. All within her grasp so long as she played it smart.

Until this moment, Maud hadn't made up her mind as to whether she'd tell Mick about Judith trying to talk to her. She was tempted to keep quiet, but wondered if anyone had spotted them from the caff. That place was always full of Mick's cronies. What if one of them tipped him off about the redhead approaching her? It seemed unlikely, but no risk – no matter how small – was worth taking.

Yes, as soon as he got up, she'd speak to him, tell him the woman had been asking about Elsa. That way he couldn't catch her out. And with a bit of luck, it would send him straight out of the door again to pass the news on to Pat Hull.

46

For Judith, Friday had been another of those fruitless days. She had caught the bus to Euston to check out the left-luggage lockers, but the key – although it seemed to be about the right size – hadn't fitted into number 22. It had been a tricky, furtive business, hanging round until there weren't any porters in sight. With no good explanation as to why she was trying to get into a locker she hadn't rented out, extra caution had been called for.

When Euston had proved a washout, she'd moved on to King's Cross and St Pancras, but it had been the same story there. Feeling downhearted – her detecting skills clearly left a lot to be desired – she'd stopped for a late lunch. A sandwich and a pot of tea at the Lyons' Corner House in Piccadilly had provided sustenance while she perused her *A–Z* and wondered whether it was worth travelling across town to any of the other stations.

She had tried to put herself in Elsa's head. Where would she go? Judith had been thinking bus routes, the cheaper option, but maybe Elsa had taken a train, in which case Liverpool Street would be a likely candidate. After lunch, she had caught the Tube, fought her way through the crowds and been disappointed yet again.

After that, she'd decided to call it a day and catch the train back to Kellston. By then, the Friday-evening rush had already begun and the journey was a cramped and uncomfortable one. Now, as she walked up the steps to the forecourt, it was a relief to be smelling what passed for fresh air in London.

Judith took a few deep breaths – petrol and exhaust fumes – on leaving the station and started walking towards the boarding house. She found herself thinking about Nell and what might have been a confession to Lennie Hull's murder. And if she had killed Lennie, couldn't she have murdered Elsa too? Or had Ivor Doyle decided to do that job for her? She was so distracted by these possibilities that she didn't, at first, even notice the middle-aged man who had fallen into step beside her as she turned the corner onto Silverstone Road.

'Judith Jonson?'

She jumped a little, startled. 'Who are you?'

'The name's Donald Smart. I'm a reporter with the *Kellston Gazette*. I was hoping we could have a chat about Elsa Keep.'

'No,' she said. 'We couldn't. I've got nothing to say.'

'I realise this must be an upsetting time – you were friends, weren't you? – only I really think—'

'Well, if you know it's an upsetting time, what are you doing here?'

Smart gave an ingratiating smile. 'My apologies, I don't mean to intrude, but there's been a development. It could be nothing, but I thought I'd better check with you first.'

'What sort of development? What do you mean?'

'Perhaps we could go somewhere more private and talk.'

Judith stopped walking and stared at him. 'No, I'm not going anywhere. Just tell me what's happened.'

Smart was in his fifties, with thin, greying hair and a weaselly

310

face. He had a cunning air about him, something sly. 'Are you sure?'

'Please, just tell me.'

Even though Silverstone Road was quiet, with only a few people going by, he made a show of looking around and then lowered his voice. 'Very well. We've received information suggesting that you and Elsa Keep may have been involved in prostitution.'

The words hit Judith like a thump to the guts. Ivor *bloody* Doyle was her first thought. He was at it again, trying to blacken her name and drive her out of London. 'That's ridiculous! Do I *look* like a prostitute?'

'Well, they come in all shapes and sizes, love, but I'm only repeating what I've been told. I'm not saying I believe it, but we need to check these things out.'

'Well, now you've checked it. Someone's just trying to cause trouble.'

'And why would they do that?'

'How would I know? The world's full of crazy people. I'm not a prostitute and nor was Elsa. Do you have any idea how insulting that is? It's just ridiculous. Who even told you that? Who told you I was—' She stopped, realising she was doing exactly what he wanted – getting flustered and saying more than she should.

'I can't reveal my sources, I'm afraid.'

'No, I'm sure you can't. But you're happy to repeat their vile slurs. If you print them in that paper of yours, I'll sue.'

'Look, we're both on the same side here. We both want to find the animal who killed Elsa Keep, don't we? See him punished for what he did? Maybe we just got off on the wrong foot. Why don't we go and get a cup of tea, start again?'

Judith gave a snort. 'Did you speak to them face to face, or was it just a phone call?'

Smart made a vague gesture with his hands.

'I thought as much. What kind of information is that, from someone who hides behind a phone? It's pathetic. And just out of interest, how did you even know who I was?'

'I didn't. A chap in the office gave me a description. He was covering the story when it broke, saw you leave the flat with the cops. I've just been waiting for a redhead to walk down the street.'

Judith nodded, hoping he'd had a long wait. It would serve him right. 'I've got nothing more to say. Please leave me alone.'

'We can work together,' he persisted. 'Come on, Judith. For *her* sake. A good story might jog someone's memory, move the investigation on a bit. You want that, don't you?'

In order to make her point, Judith began walking again. All he was doing was digging for dirt; he didn't give a damn about Elsa or how she'd died. She was starting to wonder if anyone did. The police didn't seem to be making much progress, and with every day that passed, the chances of finding Elsa's killer receded.

Smart stuck to her side. He produced a small white business card and held it out. 'If you change your mind,' he said.

She took the card in the hope that it would get rid of him. 'Goodbye, Mr Smart.'

Finally he got the message. Judith hurried on down the road, her shoulders tight with anger. Some of that rage was directed towards Smart, but most at Ivor Doyle. It was only as she neared the boarding house that it occurred to her that Mrs Jolly might have been the culprit this time, passing on her gossip to the local paper. But Doyle was still to blame; he was the one who'd started it, who'd planted the seed in the first place.

She was so distracted, she didn't notice the dark car parked up a few yards from Mrs Gillan's. Her eyes were focused somewhere in the middle distance, her thoughts a long way from her surroundings. She'd walked straight past it when she heard her name being called.

'Hey, Judith!'

Turning her head, she saw Pat Hull getting out of the car with a fat grin on his face. Her anger was instantly replaced by fear. Adrenalin pumped through her body. Should she make a dash for it? The boarding house wasn't far away, and if she . . . Those few seconds of indecision cost her dear. By the time she'd decided to run, Hull was already in front of her, blocking her path and grabbing hold of her arm.

'Not thinking of leaving us, are you, darlin'? Only that ain't too polite. I might start thinking you ain't pleased to see me.'

'Get off! Let go of me!' Judith struggled to free herself, but to no avail. His hard, thick fingers were squeezed around her fore-arm as tight as a vice. She glanced frantically up and down the road – empty – and then towards the boarding house, hoping someone might spot what was going on, but the window was unoccupied.

'Don't even think about screaming,' he said. 'I'll punch you so bloody hard you won't remember your own name.'

And Judith thought he would too. It wasn't an idle threat. She could see it in his eyes, the lust to hurt. Any excuse would do. 'What do you want? I've told you everything I know.'

'Then maybe you need your memory jogging. You and me are going to go for a little drive so you can think about it.'

The car had its engine running. There was a thickset man behind the wheel, smoking a cigarette and watching the pro-ceedings as though they were some kind of entertainment. Now she was wishing she hadn't been so short with Donald Smart. If she'd just kept chatting to him until they'd reached the safety of the boarding house . . . 'I'm not going anywhere.'

Hull pushed his face into hers, breathing out a mixture of tobacco and alcohol fumes. 'Don't make this more difficult than it needs to be, love. Just get in the car before I break your fuckin' arm.'

He propelled her towards the vehicle, holding her with one hand while he opened the back door with the other. 'Get in!'

But Judith knew that if she did that, there was every chance she'd be spending the next two weeks in hospital. And that was if she was lucky. If she wasn't, Mr Smart could be filling the pages of the *Gazette* with yet another murder story. No, she'd rather take the chance of a broken arm than of ending up in a ditch somewhere. With all this running through her mind, she kicked out hard with her heel, trying to catch him on the shin.

Hull moved his leg out of the way, giving a derisive laugh. 'You'll have to do better than that, darlin'.' He slammed her hard against the car and she felt the breath rush out of her lungs. 'Don't fuckin' mess with me, you hear?'

He had hold of her neck and was pushing her head down, trying to force her into the back seat. There was nothing she could do. He was too strong, too powerful. Then, just when she thought everything was hopeless, a voice came from behind her. She'd have known that voice anywhere. 'Let her go, Hull, or I'll blow your bloody brains out.'

Instantly, she felt Hull release his grip. Ivor Doyle was standing feet away and he was holding a gun. She lurched away from the car, rubbing at her arm as the two men squared up to each other.

'Stay out of this, Doyle. It's none of your business.'

'It's my business if I say it is.'

'That bitch knows something about Lennie.'

'Judith,' Doyle said, keeping his eyes on Hull, 'you know anything about Lennie?'

'No,' she said.

'There, you've got your answer. I'd jump in that car if I was

314

you, while you've still got the chance. I get twitchy when I get impatient. Be a shame to make a mess of this nice clean pavement.'

Hull glared at him. 'You haven't heard the last of this.'

'Stay away from her,' Doyle said. 'You understand?'

Hull gave a sneer, got into the car and slammed the door. The motor roared off leaving a trail of exhaust fumes in its wake.

Doyle slid the gun into his pocket. 'You all right?'

She nodded, still in shock, still shaking. She supposed she should thank him for saving her skin, but instead she asked, 'What are you doing here?'

'Just waiting in line. You're kind of popular today. So, what's Hull's beef with you?'

'You heard him. He thinks I know something about his brother's murder.'

'And do you?'

'Do *you*?' she batted back.

'No.'

Judith didn't believe him. She had every reason not to. 'Do you always carry a gun around?'

Doyle patted his pocket. 'Only when I think I'm going to need it. Who was the other guy, the grey-haired bloke?'

'A reporter from the *Gazette*.' Recalling what the man had said to her, she scowled. 'Was that anything to do with you?'

'What do you mean?'

'Were you the one who called him?'

'Why would I do that?'

Judith knew he wouldn't confess even if it had been down to him. She wrapped her arms around her chest and took a step back. Her legs suddenly felt wobbly, like they were about to give way. Her head was starting to swim. She sat down on the low front garden wall of the nearest house, leaned forward and closed her eyes.

Doyle sat down beside her. 'Just breathe,' he said. 'It's the shock. Hull has that effect on people.'

Judith breathed deeply, in and out, in and out. Gradually, the dizziness cleared and she was able to sit up straight again. 'You never told me what you're doing here. I mean, what you *want*.'

'I thought we should talk.'

'What about?' she asked.

'Nell was here, wasn't she? She came to see you.'

'What makes you think that?'

'You're not a good liar, Judith. You never were.'

'I'll take that as a compliment.'

Doyle looked at her, shook his head and glanced up at the sky. 'It's going to rain. Let's find somewhere we can talk.'

'Not the boarding house,' she said. 'It's not private there.'

'There's a caff near the station. It shouldn't be too busy. Can you stand up?'

He rose to his feet and held out his hand, which she ignored. Slowly she pulled herself upright. What had just happened didn't feel real, more like a scary gangster film she'd been watching at the cinema. These things didn't happen in real life. Except they did, and they had. In the films, the good guy always won, but what if there weren't any good guys? What if everyone was bad? A feeling of hopelessness, of helplessness, was seeping down her spine.

47

The café was small and quiet, with only a few customers. Doyle ordered a couple of teas at the counter, and then chose a table at the back away from everyone else, where they both sat down. The rain, which had only been a drizzle on the walk to Station Road, began to come down harder, lashing against the windows and obscuring their view of the outside world.

Judith placed her elbows on the red checked cloth and looked at Doyle. 'I suppose you're going to say I told you so.'

'Why make a bad day worse?'

'I don't even understand why Hull thinks I know any more than the last time he asked me.'

'Something's rattled his cage. Maybe it's the people you've been talking to.'

She wondered if he meant Nell, but Hull couldn't have been aware of that unless he'd been watching the boarding house. 'Like who?'

'You'd know better than me.'

'There was that woman who worked with Elsa at Connolly's. Maud?'

Doyle gave a short, mirthless laugh. 'Maud Bishop?'

'I don't know her surname. She didn't want to talk about Elsa, though. Couldn't get rid of me quickly enough.'

'There's your answer,' he said. 'The bloke who was driving Hull around today, that was Mick Bishop. He's Maud's husband. She must have told him that you're still asking questions.'

Judith rolled her eyes. 'God, I wish I'd known that. I wouldn't have gone near her.'

'She's probably had a pile of grief from Mick already. If Elsa did know something about Lennie's murder, Hull may have wondered if Maud did too.'

'Wouldn't she have told Mick if she did?'

'Depends where her loyalties lay. She may have preferred to keep her head down and stay out of it.'

'She was certainly jumpy, scared even.'

A girl came with the teas and put them down on the table. They waited until she'd gone before resuming the conversation.

'Were they close, Maud and Elsa?'

'I've no idea,' Judith said.

'Elsa might have spoken to her about what she knew, or thought she knew.'

'She might.'

Doyle piled several sugars into his cup and gave the tea a stir. Judith's gaze flicked from his hand to his face. Had *he* killed Elsa? She had no way of telling. Back in the days when she'd known him inside out – or thought she had – she'd have been certain as to whether he was lying or not. But now she couldn't be sure one way or the other. He had just saved her from a beating, but that didn't mean she could trust him.

'What are you thinking?' he asked.

She shrugged. 'It's all such a mess, isn't it?'

'Yes, it's a mess all right.' He drank some tea, looked at her over the rim of the cup. 'We need to talk about Nell.'

'Do we?'

'Look, I know you've seen her and I'm pretty sure I can guess what she said. But what you have to remember is that she isn't well. She gets ideas in her head, delusions, fantasies, whatever you want to call them, and thinks they're true. They seem real to her, you see, like they've actually happened.'

Judith watched him closely while she asked, 'Like shooting Lennie Hull, for instance?'

Doyle didn't flinch or show any sign of surprise. 'She wanted him dead, course she did after what he did to her, but she isn't capable of murder.'

Judith supposed it was admirable that he was trying to protect the woman he loved – an unwanted flicker of envy rose in her breast – but that didn't mean she had to believe him. 'Anyone can be pushed over the edge.'

'Not Nell.' He took out a cigarette, played with it for a while, finally put it in his mouth and lit it. 'Are you going to tell the law?'

Judith was tempted to keep him on tenterhooks, but couldn't quite bring herself to do it. The desire for vengeance still raged inside her, but she wanted *him* to pay for what he'd done, not Nell McAllister. 'Tell them what?'

He looked at her for what seemed a long time, and then slowly smiled. 'So you believe me?'

'I didn't say that. To be honest, I don't care who killed Lennie Hull. Maybe Nell did, maybe she didn't. It doesn't matter to me. I'm only concerned with who killed Elsa.'

'And you think it could have been me?'

She met his gaze, unflinching. 'I can't dismiss the possibility.'

Doyle smiled again. 'Doesn't that kind of put you in the firing line? I mean, if I killed Elsa to stop her talking about Nell, then why wouldn't I kill you too? In fact, why didn't I let Hull do the job for me just now?'

'I don't know the answer to that. Maybe you didn't want to give him the pleasure. Maybe you had an attack of conscience.'

'Oh, I think we've already established that the one thing I *don't* have is a conscience.'

Judith pulled a face. She sipped her tea and watched the rain. A few minutes passed and neither of them spoke. Eventually she asked, 'Just out of curiosity, why didn't you take Nell with you when you went up north all those years ago?'

'It wasn't my choice.'

She waited, but he said nothing more. 'Not your choice?' she prompted.

Doyle gave a sigh. 'It's a long story.'

Judith looked out at the rain and then back at him. 'Well, I don't know about you, but I'm not in any hurry to leave.'

He still seemed reluctant to speak, his mouth tensing into a straight line. He shifted in his chair, and his eyes darted around the café, settling on nothing. Then, just when she thought he wasn't going to tell, he sighed again and started. 'You already know some of it, the stuff about Lennie. We had a falling-out and I took some furs that I reckoned were owed to me. He found out sooner than expected, before we'd had a chance to clear out. I'd gone to get petrol, and when I got back, a bloke I was pals with came out of his house and tipped me off that Hull was waiting. He reckoned Nell had got away – he'd seen one of the goons drive after her, but when the car came back she wasn't in it – so that was one less thing to worry about.'

Doyle pulled on his cigarette and scowled. 'I kept my head down until it got dark and then went over to Amy's flat. She was Nell's best friend and I figured that was where she'd be hiding out. Amy told me that she was in hospital, that she'd hurt her ankle but it was nothing too serious. She said I should get out of London and fast – that was what Nell wanted – and that Nell would join me when her ankle was fixed.'

He sipped his tea, put the mug down, shook his head. 'I shouldn't have taken her word for it, but I did. I should have asked more questions, pressed her more. But Nell didn't want me to find out what Lennie had done. She was scared I'd go after him, that it would all end badly one way or another. And I don't think she wanted me to see the state she was in.'

'Did she tell the police?'

'How could she? If she did, she'd have had to explain about the furs, about the theft, and then she'd have been in even more trouble. Anyway, she wasn't going to stand up and give evidence against Lennie Hull. He'd have made sure she was dead before it ever came to trial.'

'So you left without her.'

'I thought it would only be a week or two before she joined me. I found somewhere to stay, got a job and then wrote to her at Amy's address. It was a while before I heard back. She said that she'd changed her mind, decided she couldn't leave London, that she was sorry, et cetera.'

'And you didn't suspect anything?'

Doyle stubbed out the cigarette and immediately lit another. 'Too much hurt pride to read between the lines. I just thought she'd dumped me. It was only later that I found out she didn't want me to stay with her out of pity or guilt. The doctors had patched her up as best they could, but their best – as you've seen – was far from perfect.'

Judith wondered what she'd have done in Nell's position. Could she have let him go? It would have been heartbreaking, but then so would the alternative: to never be sure if he'd stayed out of love or obligation. 'How did you find out?'

'When I was shipped back after Anzio, I bumped into Amy's brother, Dennis, in the hospital. He told me what had really happened, said Nell was in a bad way, that she'd lost her mind and they'd put her in Silverstone asylum. I only

321

meant to go and see if I could help. It was my fault, you see, my responsibility.'

And what about me? Judith wanted to say, *Wasn't I your responsibility too?* But she held her tongue, knowing how bitter it would sound. She wouldn't give him the satisfaction of hearing how much he'd hurt her.

'When I saw that place ... Christ, it's a hellhole. I knew I had to get her out of there. She was in a terrible state and there was no one looking out for her, not really. Amy did what she could, but ... Anyway, private hospitals cost money, which is why I went to Alf Tombs. I needed ready cash, and quick. I never meant to stay, but somehow the longer it went on, the more difficult it was to leave. She needed me and I owed her.'

'You could have told me,' Judith said. 'Did you think I wouldn't understand?'

'That I was robbing post offices in order to fund Nell's care? Not really. I wasn't the man you married any more. I was living outside the law, and that wasn't what you'd signed up to.'

'For better or for worse,' she said. 'Isn't that how it goes?'

'They're just words.'

'Words that are supposed to mean something. You could have got the money some other way.'

'Like what?'

'You had cash sitting in our bank account.'

'A drop in the ocean. Do you have any idea how much these fancy hospitals cost? It's like feeding a bottomless pit. And there was no saying whether Nell was going to get better; the best we could hope for was that she wouldn't get worse.'

'So you decided the best way forward was to stay dead, to disappear for ever. Just leave me with the memories and let me go on grieving for the husband I'd lost.'

'I never decided anything. I wish it hadn't been like that. I wish ... ' He looked at her sadly. 'Time went by, the war ended . . . You already thought I was dead, and it seemed easier to leave things that way. I suppose I took the coward's way out.'

'There's no suppose about it.'

Doyle acknowledged her retort with a shrug.

'You must love her,' Judith said, even though the words caused her pain.

The statement hung in the warm, smoky air of the café. 'She's Nell,' he replied eventually. 'She needs me.'

Judith knew instinctively that his life wasn't a happy one. It was, in many ways, as blighted as Nell's and her own. She supposed she should be pleased about this, but suddenly all she felt was overwhelmingly tired. Exhaustion washed through her body and she just wanted to lie down, close her eyes and succumb to the blankness of sleep. She pushed back her chair. 'I have to go.'

'It's still raining,' he said, 'and you haven't finished your tea. Why don't you wait a while?'

Almost as if he wanted her to stay. But she couldn't bear to be in the same room with him any longer. Wearily she got to her feet. 'It's only round the corner.'

'I'll walk with you.'

She quickly gestured for him to sit back down. 'There's no need.'

'Hull might be hanging around.'

'He's gone,' she said, with more confidence than she felt. 'Please, I'll be fine.' She looked down at him, trying to fix his face in her mind. This would be the last time she saw him. Nothing good could come from her staying in Kellston; it was time to put the past behind her and move on. 'I'm going home tomorrow. I'm going back to Westport.'

'What about Elsa Keep?'

'I'll leave it to the police.'

He nodded, staring at her intently. 'Take care of yourself, Judith. And I'm sorry. I really am.'

She turned to go, but then stopped, remembering something Saul Hannah had mentioned.

'Dan,' she said, the name slipping automatically from her lips. 'Whatever Tombs has got planned, keep well away from it.'

'What?'

'I don't know any more than that. It's just something I heard. If you want to help Nell, you need to stay out of jail.'

She left the café without waiting for him to respond and with no idea if he'd take any notice. Well, it was up to him, but at least her conscience was clear. She stepped out onto the street and lifted her face to the sky. After a while, she couldn't tell the difference between the rain and her tears.

48

The next morning, Judith packed her case again, convinced that this time she would not be changing her mind. With luck, the police would do their job properly and find Elsa's killer. She hoped it wasn't Ivor Doyle, but if it was, she wanted to be as far away as possible. In her head, she went over his story, wishing he had made different choices and taken different paths. She couldn't blame him for wanting to help Nell, but the price paid had been a high one.

She took a leisurely breakfast in the quiet dining room, perusing the train timetable while she ate and searching for trains leaving Euston at around eleven o'clock. Now that she had made the decision to go, what she felt most of all was relief. No more looking over her shoulder, no more fear, no more waking in the middle of the night with that knot of dread in her stomach.

There were a few things to do before she left, including paying the bill at the boarding house, a phone call to Cowan Road to let them know she was leaving London – she hoped they wouldn't object – and one to Saul cancelling their arrangement for tonight. She felt a small twinge of regret about the latter.

He was an interesting if complicated man, burdened as he was by the horrors of the past. Had circumstances been different, something might have developed between them. In another time, another life . . .

She was just finishing her cup of tea when the doorbell rang. Everyone looked at everyone else, but no one moved to answer it. Eventually Mrs Gillan's footsteps were heard out in the hall. There was a murmur of voices, the sound of the door being closed, and then Mrs Gillan came into the dining room.

'There's a visitor for you, Mrs Jonson. I've put them in the lounge.'

Judith instantly stiffened. What if Pat Hull had come back? Or Nell? Maybe even Ivor Doyle. She had no desire to see any of them again. What she wanted to do was hide under the table and hope whoever it was would go away. But, of course, she couldn't. 'Thank you,' she said, rising from her chair with affected calm.

She walked slowly to the lounge, trying to put off the moment for as long as possible. Nerves fluttered in her chest. If she hadn't been so tired yesterday, she would have left then. Oh, how she wished she had, but it was too late for regrets. She paused out-side the lounge, took a few deep breaths and with reluctance pushed open the door.

A woman rose from a chair by the unlit fire. Her presence was so unexpected, it took Judith a few seconds to register who it actually was. When she did, her face lit up with surprise and amazement.

'Annie! What are you doing here?'

'Well, that's a fine way to greet an old friend!'

'Oh, I didn't mean that. I'm *so* glad to see you, I really am.'

The two women hugged and kissed, talked over each over, laughed and eventually sat down.

'I got your letter,' Annie said. 'I was worried about you. We both were. Charlotte wanted to come too, but George has some important dinner he has to go to, so of course the poor girl has to go with him . . . ' She raised her eyebrows. 'But she sends her love, and she hopes to see you soon. Are you all right, though? Of course you're not. It's all been so dreadful, hasn't it? I can't believe what's happened.' She paused to take a breath. 'Now, you have to tell me everything.'

'I'm not sure what else there is,' Judith said. 'I think I put it all in the letter. They still haven't caught the man who did it.'

'What about what wasn't in the letter?'

'What do you mean?'

'Dan,' Annie said. 'That's why you came back to London, isn't it?'

Judith could have lied to her – or tried – but she had neither the strength nor the inclination to keep up the pretence. The hesitation told her friend all she needed to know.

Annie's hand rose to her mouth, stifling a tiny scream. 'My God, you've found him, haven't you? You have.'

It took Judith a while to struggle through the story, partly because it was hard to talk about and partly because of Annie's constant interruptions. With so much to tell – and so many detours – a good half-hour had passed before she reached the end. By now, Annie looked stunned, her eyes wide with shock.

'How could he? What's wrong with the bastard? How could he do that to you?'

But Judith didn't have any answers for her.

'What kind of person lets you think they're dead, for God's sake!'

Annie's words jogged her memory, reminding her of Elsa, who had said much the same thing. 'If I report him for deserting, he could end up in prison, and then who'd take care of Nell?'

'She's not your problem.'

'But it doesn't achieve anything, not really.'

'It puts him where he belongs: behind bars.' Annie's eyes skimmed the room as if to make sure they were still alone. She kept her voice almost to a whisper. 'Do you think she did kill that Lennie bloke?'

'I don't know. I'm not even sure if I *want* to know. To be honest, I've had enough. I just want to go home. In fact, I'm already packed. If you'd got here an hour later, you'd have missed me.'

'Just my luck,' Annie said. 'The first time I've been to London and it's going to be the fastest visit in history.'

Judith saw the disappointment on her face and felt bad about it. Her friend had come all the way from Westport and now she was going to have to turn around and go straight back. 'Well, I don't *have* to go today. We could stay for the weekend if you want.'

'I couldn't ask you to do that. Not after everything you've been through. You just want to get home. I understand. It's all right. I don't mind, I really don't.'

'Come on,' Judith said, standing up. 'Let's go and see if Mrs Gillan has any spare rooms.'

Ten minutes later, Annie was installed across the landing from Judith. The plan for the day was to do some sightseeing and visit the West End shops. In the evening, they could meet Saul in the pub as arranged. Judith wasn't quite sure how Saul would feel about this, but he could always clear off if he wasn't happy. She doubted he'd have anything of importance to tell her, and there was nothing she wanted to tell him either.

Annie knocked on the door and came in just as Judith was putting on her coat. It was grey outside and it looked like more rain was on its way. As she slipped a hand into her pocket, her fingers touched the tiny key she had found. Pulling it out, she held it up for Annie to see.

'Look, this is the key that was hidden in the painting at Elsa's.'

Annie took it from her and turned it over in her palm. 'It's like the keys to the lockers we have at work.'

Judith stared at her. She hadn't even thought of that. 'I don't know if they have them at Connolly's. It's only a café.'

'People nick stuff from anywhere. There's probably a room where the waitresses can leave their coats and bags. If it gets busy, anyone can slip in and help themselves.'

Judith, who had spent so much of yesterday travelling from station to station, gave a sigh. 'But it's got the number 22 on it. They wouldn't have that many lockers, would they?'

'They could have got them second-hand, just bought whatever was in the shop.'

'Surely the police will have checked at Elsa's work? I mean, they were looking for paperwork for this legacy she was supposed to be receiving. Wouldn't they have searched her locker if there was one?'

'Searched *her* locker, perhaps, but what if this isn't for hers? Maybe there are spares. She could have taken the key for one that isn't used.' Annie's eyes gleamed. 'Why don't we go and try it out? We can sneak into the staffroom and take a look.'

'Are you joking? What if we get caught? We'll be charged with theft or attempted theft or whatever they feel like charging us with. I've seen enough of that police station already. I don't want to spend the rest of the weekend there too.'

'Oh, it won't come to that. All we have to do is nip in and see if there are any lockers and what numbers are on them. It'll only take thirty seconds.'

'And if there is a number 22?'

'Then you'll know there's something important in it. Elsa wouldn't have gone to the bother of hiding they key otherwise. You can decide what you want to do next. You don't have to open the locker. You can give the key to the police or to that Saul, or chuck it in the river. It's up to you.'

Judith thought about it. On the one hand, she knew that if she didn't go to Connolly's she would always be wondering what if, but on the other, she was almost scared of what she might find there. If Annie was right, there would be some tough decisions to make.

'So?' Annie said. 'Yes or no? Time to make your mind up.'

Judith finally gave in to temptation. She took the key off Annie and put it back in her pocket. 'If this all goes wrong, I'm going to blame you.'

Annie grinned. 'Perhaps we can share a prison cell. I've always wondered what it's like in those places.'

49

Judith and Annie peered through the glass door of Connolly's. It was getting on for ten, and the café was about three quarters full, the customers mainly women in groups of three or four with shopping bags at their feet. A waitress – not Maud – scurried between the tables, taking orders. The two friends glanced at each other, nodded and went inside.

Judith tried not to think too much about Elsa as they made their way to the rear of the café. Here, to the left of the counter, was a door marked 'Staff Only'. They found an empty table as near as possible to this, sat down and surveyed their surroundings. Now that they were here, Judith's confidence in the plan, not that great to start with, was rapidly receding.

'It's too busy,' she muttered.

Annie shook her head. 'The busier the better. No one's going to notice.'

Nerves fluttered in Judith's chest. She glanced around, trying to look casual. Was anyone paying them attention? She placed her elbows on the tabletop, moved them off, put them back again. It was only half a dozen steps to the staffroom, but it looked like a mile.

The waitress, middle-aged and harassed, came over to take their order. Annie asked for a pot of tea for two.

'Anything else?'

'No thanks.'

When she'd gone, Annie said, 'I'll do it if you like. I'll go in. I don't mind.'

But Judith shook her head. She didn't want Annie getting into trouble. This was something she had to do herself. 'What if there's someone in there?' she hissed.

'Then just say sorry, you were looking for the ladies'. Say you haven't got your glasses or something.'

Five minutes later, the waitress returned with a tray and the bill. Annie gave the teapot a stir, put milk into the cups and poured the tea. 'Don't worry, nothing terrible is going to happen.'

Judith, who seemed to have been head to head with trouble for the past couple of weeks, wasn't so sure. She looked over at the man behind the counter. John Connolly, she thought his name was. 'What about him?'

'I've been watching. He's in and out to the kitchen. We'll just have to time it properly.'

Judith sorted out the bill, putting the money in a saucer. She could barely drink the tea. Every sip took her closer to the moment when she'd walk over to that door and open it. She could still change her mind. It wasn't too late. Except she knew she wouldn't. Having come this far, she might as well see it through.

A group of women at the table next to them finished their drinks and went to pay at the counter. While they crowded round the till, keeping John Connolly occupied, Judith had a quick glance round to see where the waitress was. The woman was across the other side of the café with her back to them, chatting to an elderly gent.

'Now,' Annie urged. 'And don't walk too fast.'

Judith got to her feet. 'Wish me luck.'

'You don't need it, love. You'll be fine. Just look confident, like you're supposed to be going in there.'

Judith straightened her spine, pushed back her shoulders and made a beeline for the door. With every step she took, she kept expecting to be challenged; for a voice – John Connolly's, the waitress's – to ask her where she thought she was going. Her heart was beating hard, her pulse racing. As she pushed open the door, she prayed there wouldn't be anyone inside.

God, on this occasion, was kind to her. The staffroom was empty. It was a smallish room, with a table and four chairs in the middle. And behind the table, against the far wall, was a bank of six tall lockers with their numbers emblazoned across the front: 20, 21, 22, 23, 24 and 25. Judith sucked in a breath. Annie had been right. Still she waited for a moment, her back to the door, until she was sure that no one was going to follow her in.

When a few seconds had passed, she grabbed the key from her pocket and dashed across the room. The key slid smoothly into the lock of 22, giving a tiny click as it turned. Quickly she pulled the locker door open, bracing herself for whatever she might find.

Her gaze scanned the space inside, top to bottom, and disappointment swelled in her. Nothing. Dammit! She stood on her toes and checked the high shelf. This time she was rewarded. Right at the back, pushed against the rear panel, was something dark. Her heart skipped a beat.

She reached in and grabbed the object. It was heavy, and swathed in a piece of grey rag. She held it in her left hand and unwrapped it with her right, and her eyes widened as she realised what it was. A gun, a goddam gun. It was black, and smattered with brown stains. Rust, or blood? Lennie Hull's blood, perhaps. The horror of it made her recoil, and she almost dropped the weapon on the ground. She felt sick, light-headed, as if she might be about to faint.

Pull yourself together.

Being careful not to touch it, she quickly wrapped up the gun again and slipped it into her bag. She was just in time. At that very moment, the door opened and Maud Bishop walked in. On seeing Judith, she gave a start, shock instantly registering on her face. Her voice was sharp and accusatory.

'What are you doing? You're not allowed in here.'

Judith felt her mind go blank. She had a couple of seconds of blind panic before the answer came to her. She forced a smile. 'Oh, there you are. I've been looking everywhere for you. I just wanted to say sorry, you know, if I upset you trying to talk about Elsa the other day. It was insensitive of me. I just ... er ... I just wanted to apologise before I left. I'm going home soon, you see.'

Maud didn't look convinced by this explanation. Her gaze took in the room and settled on the open door of the locker. She frowned as she stared at it, then opened her mouth, but before she had the chance to say anything more, Annie barrelled through the door.

Judith took the opportunity to shore up her story. 'Look, I found her,' she said to Annie. 'Here she is. This is Maud, Elsa's friend.'

'Hello,' Annie said, all sweetness and light. 'I'm *so* sorry about your loss. It must have been a terrible shock.'

Maud's gaze jumped between the two of them and then returned to the locker. 'You've taken something,' she said, glaring at Judith. 'You're a bloody thief. I'm going to get John.'

As she turned, Annie blocked her path. 'I don't think that's a good idea.'

Maud tried to push her out of the way and a brief, ungainly struggle followed.

Judith was starting to panic. She had to do something radical before the police were called. Trying to explain why she had a gun in her bag – probably a murder weapon – wasn't going to be the most comfortable of conversations. She said, loud enough to be heard above the fracas, 'You know about Lennie Hull, don't you?'

It was a shot in the dark, but as though she'd been slapped in the face, Maud stopped dead. There was a short pause before she turned her head to look at Judith. 'I don't know what you're talking about.'

'Yes you do. There's no point in pretending. Elsa told me everything.'

The colour drained from Maud's sallow cheeks. 'I don't know nothin',' she said, but the fight had gone out of her and the denial was soft and whiny, as though she didn't have much confidence in it.

Judith saw her weakness and pounced. 'I don't suppose Pat Hull will be too happy if he finds out you've known all along who killed Lennie. Or your husband. He works for Pat, doesn't he?'

Maud swallowed hard, her Adam's apple bobbing in her throat. 'What do you want?'

Judith assumed a more conciliatory tone. 'I'm not here to cause trouble, not for Nell, not for anyone. I promise. We'll just walk out of here and pretend this never happened. You won't ever see us again.'

'You've got the gun, haven't you?'

Judith resisted the urge to glance down towards her bag. She could feel Annie's eyes on her but didn't meet her gaze. 'I'm not going to the police if that's what you're worried about. Or Pat,' she added, sensing that this might be a greater concern.

335

Maud lurched a few steps towards the table, slumped down into a chair and covered her face with her hands. 'She said she'd got rid of it. She *swore.*'

'Elsa didn't always tell the truth.'

'She said—'

But Judith never got the chance to hear the rest of what Elsa had said, because at that very moment the door swung open and John Connolly strode in. He stopped, stared at the three women and frowned.

'What's going on here? Maud?'

Maud uncovered her face and looked up, but seemed incapable of offering an explanation.

Judith stepped in to try and save the situation. 'We're friends of Elsa's. We just came to ... you know, to offer our condolences. After what happened. It's all been such a shock, so ...'

'Terrible,' Annie chipped in, taking a handkerchief from her pocket and dabbing at her eyes in an overly dramatic way. 'Poor Elsa.'

John Connolly shifted from one foot to the other, clearly uncomfortable at this display of female emotion. 'Oh, right. Yes, it's an awful business. Very sad. We're all very ... Yes, indeed. Terrible.'

'We should be going,' Judith said. 'I know you have work to do. We don't want to disturb you any longer.'

Maud stood up, using the edge of the table to steady herself. She glanced again towards the lockers, her brow furrowed, her mouth partly open. There was a terrible moment when Judith thought she was about to point the finger. Annie was already edging towards the door.

'Well, we'll be off,' Judith said to Maud. 'Don't worry. I'll take care of everything.' She nodded towards Connolly, trying to resist the urge to exit at speed.

As they walked out of the staffroom, no one spoke. Judith

336

held her breath as she negotiated the narrow aisles of the café, barely able to believe they'd got away with it. But had they? Maud could already be making accusations, John Connolly heading for the phone. The gun felt like a dead weight in her bag.

Even when they were outside, when she had released her breath into the damp summer's air, Judith still didn't feel safe. She wanted to run, to sprint away like a frightened thief. Her scared eyes scanned the street for Pat Hull. Her ears were pricked for the siren of a police car.

'Well, that didn't go too badly,' Annie said.

'Apart from the heart attack I'm currently having.'

'You were brilliant. It was a gun, then, was it?'

Judith nodded, her eyes still searching, her heart beating wildly.

'God, what are you going to do with it?'

Judith had no idea. All she knew was that she had to get away from Kellston. A black cab went past on the other side of the high street and she lifted a hand to hail it. The driver did a U-turn and pulled up beside them.

'Oxford Street, please,' Judith said as they climbed into the back.

50

Maud slumped back down after the two women had left, her legs too weak to hold her. Her head was swimming and she had palpitations in her chest. She could have stopped them, or at least tried harder, and now it was too late. The redhead had walked off with the gun, and God alone knew what was going to happen next. Tears of anger and frustration rose to her eyes and she wiped them away with the back of her hand.

'You take a minute, Maud. I mean, take as long as you need.'

'Ta, Mr Connolly,' she gulped.

After her boss had withdrawn, she couldn't stop staring at the open locker. The key had been missing for ages, taken by mistake – or so everyone had thought – by Pauline Baynes when she'd left to get married. Ever since then, no one had been able to use number 22. The perfect hiding place: in clear sight but somehow invisible. The law, although they'd searched Elsa's locker, hadn't even thought to look through the others. Why would they?

Now everything was under threat, all Maud's plans for the future. Mick would knock her into the middle of next Sunday if any of this came out. It would be just her luck to end up in the bleedin' morgue at the very time there was actually some hope of escape. Sod's law. A small whimper escaped from the back of her throat.

She tried to recall exactly what the redhead had said: something about not causing any trouble. But of course she'd say that; the thieving bitch was hardly going to say any different. If it had just been the redhead, she might have stood a chance, but she'd been outnumbered, two to one. By the time John Connolly had arrived, the stakes had been too high to start throwing accusations around.

Maud stood up with care, pausing for a moment to test her legs before walking over to the locker. For a while she stared at the emptiness inside, and then she slowly closed the door. 'God help us,' she muttered under her breath. 'God help *me*.' There was nothing she could do now but hope and pray.

She headed back towards the kitchen, where a pile of dirty dishes would be waiting. As she passed through the café, she cursed her own stupidity. She should have guessed that Elsa wouldn't get rid of the revolver. That girl – God rest her dark, lying soul – couldn't be trusted further than you could throw her. Regrets were pointless, useless, but she couldn't keep them at bay; she would always rue the day she had handed over that gun.

Jimmy Taylor couldn't help himself. He had to keep going back to make sure the hammer hadn't been found yet. Time and again he crossed the green, pausing to examine the ground under the bushes, the place where he had made a shallow trench with his hands. He would wake up in a cold sweat at night, imagining a dog had dug up the hammer, or that an eagle-eyed copper had noticed some disturbance. It was in those dark, scary moments that he vowed to hide it somewhere safer, but then when he returned to the spot in daylight, he always changed his mind. The fear of being caught in the act outweighed the fear of discovery.

He had wiped the hammer clean with the handkerchief in his pocket – but was it clean enough? It had been done quickly, frantically, and maybe he had missed a print or two. This fear was with him constantly. He had become sullen and irritable, prone to snapping at everyone.

'Cheer up, son. It might never happen,' his dad kept saying.

But it had already bloody happened. How was he supposed to carry on as normal when his life was hanging in the balance? He had thought of going to Alf Tombs, spilling his guts, telling him everything, but was afraid the confidence might not be kept. And once the truth was out, it was out; there was no taking it back. It was partly Tombs's fault that he'd ended up in this situation in the first place. If he hadn't asked him to find out where the redhead was living, he'd never have approached Elsa Keep.

Jimmy had started to drink more, finding escape in oblivion. Drowning his sorrows – wasn't that what they called it? Although they weren't sorrows exactly, more regrets. If only he hadn't followed Elsa, if only he hadn't gone back to the flat . . . But he couldn't turn back time no matter how much he wanted to. Her dead face haunted him, her glassy eyes angry and accusing.

Nell had an odd fizzing sensation in her head, like a lit fuse burning down. Sometimes, once things started, they couldn't be stopped. She ran a fingertip along the window ledge, leaving a thin stripe in the dust. Ivor was on edge too – did he know she'd been to see his wife? – and the pair of them were tiptoeing round each other like wary cats.

Judith. Nell could remember the lounge with its dark furniture and cold fireplace, could remember Judith's red hair, but couldn't quite recall the details of the conversation. Elsa Keep, the murdered woman, had come into it somewhere. Alf had talked about her too. *Judith.* The name hung on her lips. What did the woman want? Not Ivor, or so she said. *Had* she actually said that? There was a reason for her being here, there had to be, but no one seemed to know exactly what it was.

Nell moved away from the window and went over to the bed, where she had laid out four dresses on the coverlet. Today was Alf's birthday, and tonight they would be expected to attend a gathering at the Montevideo. She didn't want to go, and neither did Ivor – social occasions were a strain for both of them – but their absence would be noted. Which dress to wear? She touched each in turn, indifferent to their charms. She had to choose, but the effort was too much. Later. She would do it later.

She took one of Ivor's suits out of the wardrobe and laid it down beside the dresses. She felt faintly puzzled by it, the same way she felt when she looked at Ivor himself. He'd been a different man since coming back from the war, still kind, but distant. What she saw in his eyes was pity and guilt. But it was not his fault. How many times had she told him? It was Lennie Hull who'd done the damage, venting his anger on her. It was Lennie, and Lennie alone, who bore the responsibility.

Nell flinched. Usually the pills helped to blank out the worst horrors of the past, but she had stopped taking them a couple of days ago. They made the bad thoughts go away but left her listless and vague, as if her head was stuffed with cotton wool. She needed to think clearly at the moment. Things were changing, shifting, tilting. History was rising up in waves, scenes rolling through her mind, so clear it could all have happened yesterday. That song was in her head again: 'Don't know why there's no sun up in the sky ... Stormy weather ...'

She squeezed her eyes shut, saw again the soft mink coat and the girl who had held it up before draping it around her shoulders. She wanted to pull the young girl close, to stroke her hair, to tell her everything would be all right, but it was too late: she was broken, damaged beyond repair, not just on the outside but on the inside too. She was clinging on by her fingertips, too afraid to let go.

Peace was all she wanted, an escape from the guilt and the pain. She wanted to lie down and drift away, but she couldn't take that final step. It was not death she feared but what came after. What she had done was a mortal sin and she'd be punished for it. God would not forgive her, and she could not forgive herself.

51

It should have been a thrill walking through Selfridges, viewing the colourful displays and the vast array of clothes and cosmetics, but the experience was tainted by the presence of the gun. While Annie rushed from counter to counter, eyes like saucers, all Judith could think about was the fact that she had a murder weapon in her bag. It was surreal, crazy. She had to get rid of it, but how? The temptation was to chuck it in the Thames and hope it sank to the bottom, never to be found again, but there were no guarantees. Stuff probably found its way to the riverbanks every day, or was dredged up by the barges. Could fingerprints survive water? She had no idea.

Annie was examining the silk scarves now, her fingers running over the material, her mouth turning down at the corners as she checked out the prices. She glanced over at Judith. 'Which one, the blue or the red?'

'They're both nice. The red, maybe. I don't know. The blue?'

Annie frowned at her. 'Stop worrying. It'll be fine.'

'I'm not worried.'

'So why are you clutching that handbag like your life depends on it? Come on, let's go and get some food. I'm starving.'

Judith loosened her hold on the bag, but not by much. 'Aren't you going to buy one?'

'Oh, I can't decide. I'll think about it over lunch.'

They walked to the Lyons' Corner House, the only place Judith was familiar with, bought soup and sandwiches and settled into a booth. The place was crowded and noisy, filled with shop girls and shoppers. The smell of damp coats, perfume and cigarettes hung in the air. Snippets of talk drifted over as they ate: *He said . . . She said . . . So I told him I wasn't born yesterday . . .*

Judith kept the handbag between her left hip and the wall, terrified of it getting stolen. She took a spoonful of soup, glanced down at the bag, took another spoonful. What if the damn gun went off? With no idea as to whether it was safe or not, she eased herself along the seat a little.

Annie watched from across the table. 'Why don't you just put it in the bin?'

'I can't.'

'You can, you just won't.'

'I don't know what to do for the best. I don't even know what the *best* is.'

'Nell's not your responsibility,' Annie said. 'And if she did . . . well, you know . . . do what you think she did, then it should be the police who deal with it.'

'Even if it means . . . ' Judith lowered her voice. 'It's going to have her prints on it. And they'll probably be able to tell if it was the gun that killed Lennie Hull. They will, won't they?'

'And what if it was *him*? What if it was Dan?'

Judith sighed into her soup. 'I need more time to think.'

The afternoon was spent sightseeing: Buckingham Palace, the Mall, the Houses of Parliament, and finally Westminster

Abbey. The latter had been lucky to survive the Blitz. In May 1941, a cluster of firebombs had landed on the roof, one burning through the lead and getting lodged in a beam. As they wandered around, Judith raised her gaze to the altar. Although she had never been especially religious, divine intervention felt like her only hope. A sign would have been useful, an indication of what to do about the gun, but God seemed uninterested in her dilemma.

It was getting on for five by the time they left the Abbey. Although it was too early for the meeting with Saul, they began to meander back towards Soho. Annie, enthralled by everything, was in her element. She loved the crowds, the shops, the hustle and bustle of London. Linking arms with Judith, she dragged her along on a wave of enthusiasm, stopping every few yards to stare at this or that with wide, excited eyes.

Judith, who knew Soho moderately well by now, was able to guide them through the busy streets, past the theatres and cinemas, the bars and restaurants and sleazy clubs. Although Saturday night hadn't properly begun, the area was already teeming, the air buzzing, the atmosphere rich in anticipation.

'Watch your bag,' she advised, clutching her own even tighter. 'This place is full of pickpockets.'

They were halfway along Beak Street when Judith noticed a coffee bar called Carlo's. For some reason it rang a bell, although she couldn't remember exactly why. They had gone a few feet past when a voice rang out behind them.

'Red! Hey, Red!'

Instantly it came back to her, and as she turned, she saw the Yank hurrying towards them with a wide grin on his face. *Oh, no.*

'How are you doing, babe?' he asked as he drew alongside.

'Quite well, thank you,' she said coolly, not wanting to encourage him.

'Great to see you again. Small world, huh? You ever find your guy?'

Judith nodded, edging away as she did so. 'I did.' He was one of those people it was hard to get rid of, and she didn't want to encourage him. Annie, however, had other ideas.

'You going to introduce us, then?'

Judith, left with no other alternative, said quickly, 'Annie, this is Pete. Pete, Annie.'

'Good to meet you, Annie.' He put out his hand and shook hers vigorously. 'Now you two ladies are going to join me for a coffee, yeah? I'm not going to take no for an answer. I'm a lonely Yank in London without a soul to talk to.'

Judith sorely doubted this – the man must spend at least half the day trying to pick up random women – but before she could decline the invitation, Annie jumped in.

'Well, we can't have that. We're not in a hurry; we've got nowhere to be until seven.'

Judith shot her a glance, but Annie ignored it.

Pete slid in between the two of them, took an elbow in each hand and propelled them back towards Carlo's. 'That's settled, then. Coffee all round.'

'Where are you from?' Annie asked. 'New York?'

'Hell, no. I'm a Texas boy, born and bred.'

The café was warm and smoky, with bright lemon-coloured walls. There was music playing – something jazzy – which battled to be heard above the noisy chatter and the screeching hiss of the coffee machine. They squeezed through the crowd until they found an empty table at the back. Pete went off to the counter, and Judith looked at Annie, raising her eyebrows.

Annie laughed. 'He's all right. Why not? It's just a bit of fun.'

Judith sat back in her chair and eased off her shoes, glad to be sitting down at least. She wasn't sure if she could remember what fun was. The last few weeks had been relentlessly dark and miserable. Glancing around, she saw that the clientele was mainly young, under thirty, a mix of men and women, casually dressed.

'I wish we had somewhere like this in Westport,' Annie said, peering around the other customers to try and catch a glimpse of Pete. And then, as if the mention of Westport had reminded her, she dug into her handbag and said, 'Oh, I almost forgot. There was a letter for you. I think it's your reference from Gillespie and Tate.'

Judith took it from her and put it into her own bag, taking care not to disturb the gun. 'Thanks. I'm going to have to look for a job when I get back.'

'You could always get one in London. I bet there's tons of jobs going here, good ones, too.'

'I've had enough of London, thank you very much.'

Annie pulled a face. 'Sorry, of course you have. Listen to me going on. What an idiot! Are you all right? We can go if you'd rather. We don't have to stay.'

'No, it's fine. I'm sure he's harmless enough, and I'm glad of the sit-down. You can do the talking, though, seeing as you accepted the invite.'

In the event, there was no problem when it came to conversation. Pete was a prize talker, as was Annie, and between them there wasn't so much as an awkward pause. Judith left them to get on with it. She welcomed the thinking time, the opportunity to weigh up the options when it came to the gun. Was she going to give it to Saul or not? What she didn't want was to end up taking it back to Westport with her.

By the time they came to leave, only one thing had been decided for sure – Pete was coming with them to the Fitzroy Tavern.

'Well, I don't want to be a wallflower,' Annie said as though Judith and Saul were an item. 'You don't mind, do you?'

Judith didn't mind. She wasn't sure how Saul would feel about it, though.

52

What Saul Hannah felt when Judith arrived at the Fitzroy with two companions in tow was a stab of disappointment. He'd been hoping, although he'd barely admitted this to himself, to spend the evening alone with her. Perhaps some sign of dismay showed on his face, because she apologised and gave a hurried explanation as to how Annie had turned up out of the blue this morning. Pete was, she said, a friend of Annie's.

'Don't I know you from somewhere?' Pete asked as the introductions were made. 'I'm sure I've seen you around.'

Saul shrugged. 'I don't think so.'

'Yeah, you look real familiar.'

Drinks were bought and small talk made. Saul thought Judith was nervous, on edge, but perhaps she'd just had a tough week. Annie, on the other hand, seemed completely relaxed. He could feel her eyes on him from time to time, as though she was weighing him up. She was the friendly sort, flirtatious, and most of her attention was focused on the American. Pete was one of those loud, brash Yanks who might have been a deserter – there were swarms of them still in London – or maybe just a GI who hadn't returned home. He claimed to be a mechanic, but the pristine state of his fingernails somewhat belied the story.

Judith leaned in towards him and asked softly, 'Have you heard anything? Is there any news about Elsa?'

Saul shook his head. 'You?'

He thought she hesitated a touch too long. 'No, nothing.'

'And Hull's left you alone?'

Again that pause. 'He turned up at the boarding house – well, outside it – but Doyle was there, so—'

'Doyle was there? What did he want?'

Judith gave a wry smile. 'What he always wants,' she said. 'To get rid of me.'

But there was more to it, he thought, something she wasn't telling him. This made him curious. He watched her hands fiddle with her handbag, putting it on her lap, on the table and then back on her lap again. She looked tired and distracted.

'And that's all?' he asked.

'That's enough, isn't it?'

'I suppose it is.'

Annie wanted to go dancing, and Saul quickly suggested the Montevideo. 'We can eat there, too. It's only down the road. Five minutes away.' He had a particular reason for wanting to be there. It was Alf Tombs's birthday and he'd heard there was going to be a gathering at the club. Checking out who was and wasn't in the gangster's inner circle at the moment could be useful.

'Is it nice there?' Annie asked.

'As nice as anywhere else.'

Judith shot him a look, but didn't raise any objections. Ten minutes later, they were on their way.

53

The Montevideo was much busier than the last time they'd been here, with most of the tables taken and the dance floor rapidly filling up. Judith hadn't really wanted to come, but hadn't wanted to disappoint Annie either. Out of all the possible clubs in the area – and she imagined there were plenty – she wondered why Saul had chosen this one.

She scanned the room as they sat down, but there was no sign of the gangster. Or maybe it wasn't Tombs she was really searching for. Every time her gaze caught a flash of blond hair, her heart skipped a beat. She had no desire to see Doyle, didn't even want to think about him, and yet her eyes still sought him out.

Wine was ordered – two bottles of white – and they ate a light meal with it, meat in a sauce which the menu claimed was chicken but which didn't taste like it. Judith, wanting to keep a clear head, went easy on the alcohol. After the meal was finished, Pete and Annie took to the dance floor, giving her a chance to talk to Saul. She wanted to tell him about the gun, wanted to hand it over, to be rid of it, but something held her back: perhaps it was simply the consequences.

He lit a cigarette and looked at her. 'What's on your mind?'

'Nothing. Everything. I'm not sure.'

'Sounds confusing.'

'Elsa, I suppose,' she said. 'I didn't really know her, did I?'

'No one knew Elsa. If you're looking for answers as to why she did what she did – whatever that might have been – you're not going to get them.'

'What if they never find out who killed her?'

Saul rubbed at his face. 'Someone, somewhere knows who did. Eventually they'll talk.'

Judith, aware that the information she was withholding could be crucial, was on the verge of coming clean when she glanced across the room and saw Alf Tombs taking a seat at the centre table. He had a middle-aged woman with him, wearing a black dress and pearls. His wife, perhaps. But it was neither of these two who made the breath catch in the back of her throat. Directly behind them was another couple: Ivor Doyle and Nell.

She turned to Saul accusingly. 'Did you know they were going to be here?'

'No, of course not. How could I?'

She frowned, not entirely believing him. But she had a bigger problem to deal with. Quickly she looked over at the dance floor. Fortunately Annie only had eyes for Pete at the moment, her arms draped around his neck, completely oblivious to the rest of the world. But how long was that going to last? There was no saying what she might do when she spotted the man who had once been Dan Jonson: scream, shout, make a scene. Annie could be a loose cannon, especially when she had a few drinks inside her.

Judith was still pondering on the horror of this as she looked back at the centre table. More people had joined Tombs, and there were now twelve in all. Enough for a jury, she thought irrelevantly. Doyle must have felt her gaze on him, because he suddenly shifted his gaze, his eyes meeting hers. She could have sworn he flinched.

Her first instinct was to get up and leave, but that was easier said than done. She could hardly abandon Annie, and other than dragging her off the dance floor, she couldn't see what else to do. There was also a part of her that didn't want Doyle to think he had the power to drive her away. She had as much right to be here as he did.

'Ignore him,' Saul said.

She wished she could. She gulped down some wine, revising her earlier decision to go easy. Now wasn't the time for sobriety. She needed some Dutch courage.

A smile played around Saul's lips. 'Just let them get on with it. I suspect this might be the last party Tombs will be enjoying for a while.'

Judith wondered if Doyle had taken heed of her warning. 'What makes you so sure?'

'Just a hunch,' he said smugly.

She watched the table whilst pretending not to, casting fleeting glances that took in Ivor Doyle, Nell and Tombs. There was something strained, she thought, in the way they were behaving towards each other. Or perhaps she was just transferring her own awkwardness onto them.

Nell seemed jittery, unable to keep still. Everything about her was fretful, tense, strung out. Her smile was false and her laughter too high. About ten minutes after she'd arrived, she got up again and left, presumably heading for the ladies'. On impulse, Judith decided to follow her.

'Excuse me,' she said, rising to her feet. 'I just need to ... I won't be long.'

The toilets were outside the main room, off the foyer. Judith wasn't sure why she wanted to talk to Nell again: maybe simply to get things straight in her head, to be certain she was making the right decision. Once she handed over the gun to her, there could be no going back. She was almost there when she felt a restraining hand on her shoulder and spun round to see Doyle.

'What are you doing?' he asked.

'What do you think?' she said, glancing towards the ladies'.

His eyes darkened. 'Why can't you leave her alone? You said you were going home, for Christ's sake.'

'And I am – when I'm ready.'

'Don't do this, Judith. You hate me. I understand that. You've got every reason. But please don't take it out on Nell.'

In that moment, Judith almost changed her mind about what she was going to do. Anger and resentment flared back into life. She wondered how it was that this man she had once loved so much knew so little about her. Her voice, when she spoke, was tight and brittle. 'Is that really what you think of me? Is it?'

It was then that something suddenly altered. His mouth turned down, his shoulders slumped, and all she could see in his eyes was despair and defeat. 'Fine. Go ahead. Do whatever you want.'

Judith looked away, unable to hold his gaze. There was a time when all she'd desired was to see him as broken as her, to have power over him, to know that she could bring his world crashing down around his ears. She only had to hand over that gun to the police and . . . But she knew she couldn't do it. 'Swear to me you didn't kill Elsa.'

'Of course I didn't. I never even knew the woman.'

'Swear to me.'

'All right,' he said. 'I swear. Happy now?'

Judith wrinkled her nose, happiness being about as far away from her at the moment as Morocco. She wanted to believe him, *had* to believe him if she was going to go ahead.

'We need to talk. Is there somewhere private we can go?'

Doyle shook his head. 'What is there left to say? I can't apologise anymore.'

'It's important. It affects Nell.'

He shrugged, looked across the foyer and settled on a dimly lit corner away from the ladies' and shielded by a pillar. There was a plush blue sofa here, although Judith wasn't sure why. Perhaps it was for people waiting for taxis. Or for those too drunk to make it out of the door. She sat down with her bag on her knee.

Doyle sat down too, keeping as much distance as the sofa allowed. 'So?'

'I found something,' she said, 'something that Elsa had hidden. I think it might be . . . ' She quickly peered around the pillar, making sure no one was watching them. 'It was in her locker at work.'

'What was in her locker?'

Judith took the cloth-wrapped bundle out of her bag and handed it to him. 'It's a gun,' she said softly.

'What?'

'Take a look if you don't believe me.'

Doyle raised his eyebrows, carefully unfolding the grey cloth with what could only be described as scepticism. But his expression instantly changed. 'Shit,' he murmured. Quickly he covered up the gun again and put it in his pocket. 'Let's get out of here.'

Before Judith could respond one way or another, he was on his feet and striding out of the club. She followed in his wake, walking as fast as she could in her heels, struggling to catch up. By the time she got outside, he was already sitting in a car parked ten yards up the street. The engine was running as she opened the passenger door and climbed in.

'Where are we going?'

'Not far.'

He was true to his word, only travelling a short distance

before pulling onto the forecourt of a shop that was closed for the night. He stopped under the 'Customers Only' sign, flicked on the overhead light, took the cloth package out of his pocket, unwrapped it and stared down at the gun.

'Is that it?' she asked. 'Is that what Nell used to kill Lennie Hull?'

Doyle didn't answer. He slid open the gun, removed the clip, peered at it and frowned. 'Is this how you found it?'

'Yes. Why? What's wrong?'

'It's fully loaded. All seven bullets.'

Judith looked at him. 'What are you saying, that it's not the right gun?'

'No, it's the right one. A Beretta 1934,' he said. 'It used to be mine. I had to leave it behind when I went up north.' Although he'd finally come clean about Nell's guilt, he looked completely baffled. 'It couldn't have been reloaded. Why would it have been?'

'It wouldn't. Not if Elsa was using it as blackmail. She'd want it to be exactly as it was.'

'Exactly. Except Elsa wasn't blackmailing Nell. Or me. So unless . . . '

Judith waited, but he didn't go on. Instead he quickly reinserted the clip into the Beretta, cleaned the gun thoroughly, wrapped it in the cloth again and put it back in his pocket. By the time he'd completed this procedure, her train of thought had finally caught up with his.

'Nell didn't kill Lennie Hull, and Elsa knew who the real killer was.'

'And she must have approached them. Big mistake.'

Judith couldn't argue with that, but something still puzzled her. 'So why does Nell say she did it?'

'Because she genuinely believes she did. She was there and she wanted to scare Hull. She was waving the gun around and it went off by mistake. At least that's what she's always thought. When someone else shot him, she must have gone into shock. She chucked the Beretta and ran. And ever since then, she's been convinced that—'

'But she would have seen if someone else was there.'

But Doyle, even if he knew the answer, wasn't sharing it with her. He put the car into gear and drove back towards the club.

54

Judith wasn't sure how long they'd been away, maybe ten or fifteen minutes. When she sat down beside Saul, he gave her a quizzical look.

'Everything all right?'

'Yes, sorry, I was feeling a bit ... I just stepped outside for some air.'

Doyle was already seated at the centre table. Had anyone noticed they'd both been missing at the same time? She didn't know and didn't really care. There were too many other things on her mind. Once she'd handed over the gun, she'd thought that would be the end of it – Nell wouldn't need to worry about a murder charge – but it seemed she'd just opened another can of worms. Still, that was none of her business. She had done what she felt to be right, and whatever happened next was beyond her control.

She drank some wine and looked towards the dance floor, hoping to catch Annie's eye. Now that she'd got rid of the Beretta, she just wanted to go home. Well, not home exactly, but back to the boarding house. She was done with the night, done with socialising, with Doyle, Saul and just about everything. A line had been drawn and it was time to leave.

Getting Annie's attention, however, proved easier said than done. She and Pete were smooching to a slow tune being played by the band. Judith tried for a while, with no success, then sat back and sighed.

'So,' Saul said, 'what did Doyle want?'

'Doyle?'

'He followed you out. I'm presuming he had something to say.'

Judith could have denied it, almost did, but decided it was just as easy to tell a partial truth. 'Oh, nothing much. He thought I'd come here to cause trouble. I soon put him straight.'

Saul nodded. 'Right. It's not down to you, then?'

'What isn't?'

He inclined his head in the general direction of the centre table. 'Our friends appear to be in a less than convivial mood. Not much party spirit, unless I'm mistaken.'

Judith looked over. He was right. It was clear that some kind of argument was in progress between Doyle and Tombs. Words were being exchanged, voices raised. Doyle's face was tight and furious. As she watched, the row quickly escalated, the two men getting to their feet. The woman in black made a vain attempt to calm Tombs down, taking hold of his arm, but he brushed her aside.

Judith couldn't have said who threw the first punch, but there was a flurry of blows as Doyle and Tombs went head to head. Suddenly the music stopped and the dance floor cleared. People moved out of the way, not wanting to be part of the collateral damage. As the scrap continued, tables were overturned, sending bottles and glasses smashing to the floor.

'Now that's what I call a waste of good champagne,' Saul said.

Judith stared at him. 'Shouldn't you do something?'

'What would you suggest?'

As Judith stood up, she noticed Nell standing to one side, her face oddly blank. Her hands were clasped in front of her, a demure pose more suited to church than a club in Soho. If she was taking in what was happening, she was showing no sign of it. Judith quickly switched her attention back to the fight.

The two men were hearing nothing, seeing nothing but each other. They were locked in combat, beyond words, beyond anything but the furious moment. Punches turned into a kind of grappling, and eventually they both ended up rolling on the ground. First Tombs was on top, and then Doyle. It was impossible to tell who was getting the better of it.

Doyle was the younger man, stronger, but Tombs had experience and guile. By now, both their faces were bloodied, their energy starting to wane. And then, just when Judith thought it couldn't get any worse, it did. The Beretta dropped out of Doyle's pocket and landed on the carpet. Both men saw and reached for it simultaneously, a mad grasping, a stretching out of hands. A shot rang out. A woman screamed. And then there was an odd, eerie silence.

Only at this point did Saul finally leap out of his chair.

The next few seconds felt like an eternity. As Saul rushed across the room, Judith found herself praying. *Please God, don't let him be dead. Don't let him be dead.* This was all her fault. She was to blame. If she hadn't handed over the gun . . .

She followed Saul, barely breathing as he helped to pull the two men apart. There was blood on both of them, too much blood. But it was Tombs and Tombs alone who eventually staggered to his feet. Doyle lay supine, his body limp, his head twisted to one side.

55

Judith felt pain rip through her. She had gone full circle, she thought, from believing her husband to have been killed in the war, to finding out he was still alive, to now seeing him shot right in front of her. She swayed on her feet as noise and activity erupted through the silence. Suddenly everyone, everyone but Ivor Doyle, was moving.

'Don't just stand there,' Saul shouted at the barman. 'Call a bloody ambulance.'

Annie appeared by Judith's side, grabbing hold of her arm. 'Come away,' she said, trying to shield her from the horror.

But Judith resisted, continuing to stare down, watching as Saul did his best to staunch the blood. So there was a chance? A glimmer of hope flickered inside her. Ivor was still breathing. She could see it now, the shallow rise and fall of his chest. The past flashed through her mind, everything from the day they'd first met to the events of recent weeks. There had been a time when she'd wanted revenge, *yearned* for it, but now all she wanted was for him to live.

By the time the ambulance arrived, the club was almost empty.

Most of the customers had made themselves scarce, probably because they preferred to avoid any contact with the law and had no desire to give evidence against a gangland boss. As Ivor was stretchered out of the room, Judith glanced around for Nell, but there was no sign of her. Alf Tombs was leaning against the bar, bloodied and dishevelled, drinking what looked like a brandy.

Saul came over to her and said quickly, 'You should get out of here. The police are on their way. Go out the back.' He pointed towards a door at the rear of the room. 'I'll let you know how things go.'

'Won't they want to talk to us?'

'Yes,' he said, 'but you don't want to talk to them. They might have some awkward questions, don't you think?'

It was then that she realised he either knew or had guessed about the origin of the gun. She hesitated, but Annie yanked at her arm.

'Come on, let's go.'

This time Judith allowed herself to be dragged away. It would mean trouble for Annie too if the truth came out about the Beretta. It was probably an offence to flee the scene of a crime, but it was an even bigger one to have contributed to it.

As they ran through the back corridor, all Judith could think about was whether Ivor Doyle would survive. At this very moment he was on his way to hospital, maybe bleeding to death. How had it come to this? She still had no idea what the two men had been fighting about, but figured it had to be something to do with the gun.

Eventually they came to a door that led them out to the side of the building. They fled up a narrow path back onto Charlotte Street and joined the throng. By now, news had travelled about the shooting and a curious crowd had gathered outside the club. They squeezed past just as a couple of squad cars were pulling up at the front door.

Annie released an audible sigh of relief.

'Where's Pete?' Judith asked, suddenly noticing his absence.

'Oh, he cleared off a while ago. He wanted me to go with him, but . . . I don't think he's too keen on the police. That Saul seems all right, though. You don't think he'll say anything about us being there, do you?'

Judith shook her head. 'No, he won't say anything.' She suspected Saul's motives in telling them to go hadn't been entirely altruistic. With her as a common factor, he wouldn't want his colleagues making any awkward connections between the murder of Elsa Keep and the shooting of Ivor Doyle. He had as much to lose as she did if the truth came out.

They were halfway along Goodge Street before Judith saw a black cab and hailed it. She gave the Silverstone Road address and got in the back with Annie. She wished she could go to the hospital, but that was Nell's place, not hers. It was awful not knowing, a stone of dread that lay in the pit of her stomach.

They were quiet for most of the journey, neither of them wanting to discuss the events of the night within hearing of the driver. As they travelled through the streets of London, Annie reached out her hand and took Judith's.

'Try not to worry,' she said. 'It'll be all right.'

Judith wasn't so sure. It had been a long time since anything was right.

56

Nell had a curious feeling of lightness as she walked beside the river. The burden of the past five years had been lifted from her shoulders. She was free of guilt, of regret, of everything that had dragged her down. For the first time since that fateful night, old tunes sprang to her lips and she sang softly as she gazed across the inky water. People called it Father Thames, sometimes Mother; she preferred the latter – it seemed more welcoming somehow, more loving.

In the dark, she didn't need to worry about the looks from passers-by. Her face was no different to theirs in the shadows. Voices floated in the night air, snatches of conversations, a few random words sprinkled here and there. They drifted through her, round her, a gentle lapping like the sound of the water against stone.

How odd, she thought, that Ivor's wife had been the one to find the gun and hand it over. The girl with the red hair. When Ivor had returned to the table, he'd had that look on his face: hard and soft at the same time. He hadn't been happy since he'd come back to London. A part of him had been broken.

She would often catch him staring into the middle distance with something or someone on his mind. But that hadn't been what she was thinking about. Yes, when Ivor had come back to the table . . .

'I've got the gun,' he'd said quietly. 'Judith found it. You didn't fire the damn thing. You didn't shoot Lennie Hull.'

She hadn't seen how that was possible. She'd been there with the black gun in her hand. She'd heard the explosion of sound, seen part of Lennie's head blown into the street, on to her clothes, across her face. She had tasted his blood in her mouth.

'It was someone else,' Ivor had said. 'There was someone else there too.'

But Alf, who was sitting beside him, had shaken his head. 'You're wrong. You must be. Perhaps it's not the right shooter.'

'You think I don't know my own gun when I see it?' Ivor staring at him like he was turning something over in his mind. 'I'm telling you, Nell's innocent.'

'If you say so.'

'Why were you so interested in Elsa Keep?'

'What?'

'You heard me. Elsa Keep. What was it about her murder that bothered you so much?'

'You know what. There were rumours about Hull. I was just looking out for Nell.'

'Are you sure about that?'

Alf curling his lip. 'And what's that supposed to mean? You should be grateful. I put myself on the line for that girl. If it wasn't for me—'

'The only person you ever look out for is yourself.'

'I was here for her when no one else was.'

'If that's what you like to call it.'

Both of them talking like she wasn't there, like she was invisible. The other guests exchanging nervous glances. But

364

she trusted Ivor, knew he wouldn't lie to her. If he said she hadn't fired the gun, she hadn't. She didn't really understand what he was getting at with Alf, but it didn't matter. Nothing mattered now.

She had left when the fight started. That was what men did to settle things – tried to hurt each other. As if there hadn't been enough hurt already. She had wanted to be alone, to breathe in the night air, to sing and celebrate her redemption. God wouldn't turn her away now. She was saved. The angels would open up the gates and she would step inside. The only thing left to do was to clean her body and cleanse her soul . . . She looked down at Mother Thames and smiled.

57

Judith was picking at her breakfast, grateful that Annie was present to make small talk with the other residents. They had waited up until the early hours, but Saul hadn't come. Whether that was a good sign or a bad one was impossible to judge. She had slept badly, waking too often to stare into the darkness. If she had given the gun to Saul instead, or even thrown it away, everything would have worked out differently. What ifs revolved in her head, different decisions, different outcomes. She knew it was pointless – what was done was done – but guilt continued to haunt her.

Breakfast was almost over by the time Judith saw the car draw up by the kerb. Quickly she rose to her feet, excused herself and hurried outside. She was on the street, waiting, even before Saul had climbed out of the driver's seat. She tried to read his face as he walked towards her. He looked tired, crumpled, as though he'd had even less sleep than she had.

'Is it bad news?'

'Doyle's out of danger,' he said. 'He got lucky. He'll be back on his feet in a few weeks.'

Judith almost wept. 'Thank God!'

'Yes, another inch to the left and he'd have been pushing up daisies. You must be relieved.'

She nodded, unsure as to whether he was referring to Ivor Doyle still being alive or her part in providing the weapon that had almost killed him. Maybe both. 'Can we walk?' she asked, wanting to escape the curious eyes in the dining room.

'Of course.'

It was a bright day, the sun already beginning to warm the air, the sky blue and cloudless. Judith waited until they were a few yards down the road before she asked, 'What's happening with Tombs?'

'He's been charged. Naturally, he's claiming it was an accident and that the gun wasn't his. He won't come clean about what the fight was over either. "Something and nothing", he says, but no one believes that. We haven't been able to talk to Doyle yet.'

'It all goes back to Lennie Hull, doesn't it?'

'You tell me,' he said.

But Judith had no intention of telling him anything. She had made enough mistakes already without adding to them. Saul, even if he had proved trustworthy, was still on the side of the law. 'What about Nell? What does she have to say about it all?'

Saul left a long pause before answering. 'I'm afraid I have some bad news on that front.'

Judith stopped walking, looked at him and frowned. 'What do you mean?'

'There was an accident, or ... No one's entirely sure. Unfortunately, she was pulled from the river late last night.'

For a few seconds Judith was speechless, rocked by the information. 'You're saying she's ... what? I don't understand. You're saying she's *dead*?'

Saul nodded.

'My God, does he know? Does Ivor know?'

'Not yet.'

Judith felt overwhelmed. 'It must have been an accident. I mean, why would she . . . ' She couldn't figure out why someone who'd just been told – and she presumed Ivor *had* told her – that she hadn't committed the crime she thought she had would deliberately throw herself into the Thames. 'No, it can't have been on purpose.'

'Did you see her leave the club last night?'

'I didn't notice. She was there when the fight started, and then . . . I'm pretty sure she was gone before Ivor was shot.'

'Yes, that's what I thought too.'

Judith began walking again. It was a way of avoiding Saul's eyes, of not having to look at him while she tried to absorb the reality of Nell's death. 'She knew about me, but she also knew I wasn't a threat. I didn't want Ivor back; I didn't want anything to do with him.' Her voice, sounding overly defensive, went up in pitch. 'But what if it *was* my fault? What if she saw me there last night and—'

Saul cut her off before she could continue. 'You can't think like that. The girl wasn't well, hadn't been for a long time. If you want someone to blame, look no further than Lennie Hull. If anyone pushed her to the edge, it was him.'

'So you do think it was suicide?'

'I don't know, and nor do you. Perhaps no one ever will. There was a lot of booze around. She'd been drinking, too much probably. She could have just lost her footing and stumbled or slipped.'

Judith shivered. She felt an icy coldness in her bones as though her own body was sliding under the waters of the Thames. When she had handed over the gun, she had done it with the best of intentions, but now it felt like she had made a terrible mistake. 'What do you think the fight was about?'

'Doyle probably figured something out.'

'About Lennie Hull's murder?'

'What makes you say that?'

'Because everything seems to lead back to that man. Do you think Tombs had something to do with it?'

Saul lit a cigarette and took a couple of puffs before replying. 'Thinking it and proving it are two entirely different things. He's had five years to cover his tracks.'

'And Elsa? Did he kill her too?'

'If he did one, then he probably did the other.'

Judith hadn't noticed where they were going, but now she realised they had retraced the route she had taken with Ivor Doyle. She stopped by the wrought-iron gates and gazed into the graveyard. If it was true about Tombs, then he really was the devil. Perhaps it was time to stop hiding the truth. 'Nell came to see me,' she said. 'She more or less confessed to shooting Lennie Hull. I think she genuinely believed she'd done it.'

'And then you gave Doyle the gun.'

'How did you know that?'

'I didn't, not for sure.'

Judith gave a grim smile. Her gaze slid over the grass and the tombstones, her mind more preoccupied by the dead than the living. 'I found it in a locker at Connolly's. When Doyle looked at it, he realised it hadn't been fired.' She paused and then asked, 'Will you tell the police?'

'I *am* the police.'

'You know what I mean, the *others*.'

'That might not help Doyle much. For one, it would prove the gun was in his possession, and for two, if he thought Tombs was guilty of Hull's murder but had let Nell go on thinking it was her, it would give him a motive to try and blow the bastard's brains out.' Saul pulled on his cigarette. 'No, we're better off keeping quiet and I'm pretty sure Doyle will see it that way

369

too. Tombs will serve some time at least. It might not be perfect justice, but it's better than nothing.'

'And Elsa? What about justice for *her*?'

'I won't give up. I'll keep on digging. If he did do it, I'll get the evidence one day. Don't worry: he'll pay one way or another.'

'So what now?' she asked, at a loss as to what to do next.

'It's over. You should go home.'

It wasn't the first time she'd heard those words, but it was the first time she had agreed with them. Judith looked across the graveyard and thought about other people's lives, their secrets, hopes and fears – all turned to dust eventually. She thought of Charlotte and Annie, of the sea and the smell of salt in the air. 'Yes,' she said. 'It's time to go home.'

Epilogue

September 1950

Judith leaned against the rail of the ferry, watching the land recede. No one could say she hadn't given it a try. She had spent the past year in Westport, trying to rebuild her life: new flat, new job, realistic expectations. But she hadn't been able to settle. Something had changed, a shift she couldn't fully explain. The town felt too small, too claustrophobic, as though it was slowly suffocating her.

Annie and Charlotte had come to see her off at the station. The image was still in her head: the two of them standing on the platform, waving to her. She would miss them, but it wouldn't be for ever. One day, she would probably come back. Westport was still home, after all. It just wasn't the right place for her at the moment.

She switched her attention to the grey water below. Inevitably, she thought of Nell, wondering what had been in her mind when she'd stood on the bank of the Thames that night. There was a connection between them – they had loved the same man – but the past had unravelled them both. And what of Ivor Doyle? She briefly closed her eyes.

A gull wheeled overhead, its white wings catching the sun. She was not sure what she expected from this new adventure: maybe only a chance to spread her own wings and have some new experiences before it was too late. She had never been abroad in her life, and although Amsterdam wasn't a million miles away, it felt like she was embarking on a great journey. Nerves fluttered in her stomach, but she had no regrets. Sometimes you just had to jump and hope for the best.

Maud Bishop had covered her face with her hands when the judge passed a twelve-year sentence on her husband, not in horror as some people might have presumed, but in order to hide her delight and relief. She was *free*. Within a matter of weeks, with the help of Saul Hannah, she had received the insurance money – her reward for secretly grassing up six armed robbers – and fled London with her kids.

Edinburgh was the destination she had chosen at random from the board at the train station. She had intended to move on, to find somewhere less busy to live, one of the surrounding towns perhaps, but had quickly seen the advantages of staying. There was work here and there was anonymity. In a city this size, no one would find them.

Maud often thought about that night six years ago when she'd gone out looking for Mick. Three days he'd been missing. The cupboards were bare and the kids hadn't eaten. She had traipsed from pub to pub, all his regular haunts, until, disappointed, she had given up the search and headed back towards home.

It was as she'd turned a corner near the station that she'd seen the two of them rowing in the street, Lennie Hull and the fair-haired girl. Nell, that was her name. Nell had been waving a gun in his face while Lennie laughed and sneered at her. As Maud had stopped to consider what to do next – she didn't want to get involved – the other man had appeared from the shadows.

Even in the dim light she'd known who it was. Everyone knew Alf Tombs. At first she had thought he was going to intervene, but that hadn't been his intention at all. It had been over in a moment, a single well-aimed shot that had almost blown Hull's head off.

Tombs had buggered off as quickly and silently as he'd arrived, but the girl hadn't moved. Like she was in shock, paralysed. Eventually, she had thrown the gun into the gutter and started to run. Maud had waited a while before emerging from the shadows. She remembered the sudden stillness in the air, the aftermath of death. Why had she picked up the gun? To this day she wasn't sure. To try and protect the girl, perhaps. But the girl hadn't shot Lennie, so that didn't make much sense.

It was then that she'd panicked. People must have heard the shot. What if they came and found her there? She had shoved the gun in her bag and hurried away. That had been her first mistake; her second had been to tell Elsa about it. And that wouldn't have happened either if she hadn't run slap bang into her just outside the Fox. Maud, stunned and scared, had garbled out the story.

'Give the gun to me,' Elsa had said. 'I'll get rid of it.'

And Maud hadn't thought twice about doing just that. Grateful, that was what she'd been. The gun linked her, as a witness at least, to Hull's murder, and she had no desire to stand up in court and give evidence against Tombs. Truth was, she was glad Lennie was dead. The man had always been a nasty bastard.

She should have known better than to have trusted Elsa, but it was too late for regrets. What was done was done. The girl had chanced her arm, probably tried to blackmail Tombs, and come off the worse for it. Maud could have told Saul, told him everything, but she had not cared enough for Elsa to jeopardise her own plans.

As she pushed the pram along Princes Street, she had high

hopes for her baby daughter. Rosie would not grow up with fear and loathing, a victim of her father's fists. She would have love and safety and opportunities. As would all her other kids. A Scottish accent was, she decided, a small price to pay for a better future.

Even after a year, Jimmy Taylor hadn't stopped thinking about the hammer. He still returned to the green at regular intervals, dreading the thought that the council might decide to do some landscaping, or that the bush would die and be dug up. He would stare at the dull brown dirt while he smoked a cigarette and rue the day he had ever crossed paths with Elsa Keep.

He replayed that night in his head over and over again. He had only gone to the flat on a whim, not even intending to ring the bell. Just to look. Just to see who was coming and going. But when he'd got there and peered over the railing, he'd seen that a light was on and the door ajar. He'd waited for a while, but no one had appeared.

Curiosity had eventually got the better of him. He'd looked around, made sure the coast was clear and then gone quietly down the metal steps. He'd pushed the door open a bit wider and said, 'Hello?'

Nothing.

'Hello?' A bit louder this time, but still she hadn't responded.

It was only as he'd crossed the threshold that he'd seen the state of the place. Someone must have broken in. If he'd been smart, he'd have turned tail that very second and got the hell out of there, but he wasn't and he hadn't. Instead he'd carried on, sidestepping the debris, until he'd noticed the hammer lying on the floor. The head was stained red and he'd already picked it up before realising that was the wrong thing to do. Blood, was it? Shit. He'd sucked in a breath through his teeth, and immediately let the hammer fall to the ground again.

To this day he didn't know what had possessed him to go into the small room. He could smell death, perhaps, or sense it, the hairs on the back of his neck standing on end. The sight of her body had simultaneously repulsed and fascinated him: those open, glassy eyes, the stillness, the waxy colour of her skin.

And then the adrenalin had kicked in. Get the fuck out of the place! He'd been almost at the front door when he'd remembered the hammer, the weapon with his fingerprints all over it. Going back, picking it up, making a split-second decision as to whether to take it with him or try and clean off the prints right there. His heart beating so hard it could have burst right out of his chest.

It had taken every last inch of restraint for him not to sprint up the steps. Instead he had gone up carefully, his ears tuned to the slightest sound, hoping no one was watching from a window as he made his way to the green, ill-lit and empty. He could have taken the hammer home, but hadn't dared. What if someone had seen him? What if the law came knocking at the door? To be caught in possession would be a death warrant.

It had not occurred to him to use the hammer to dig the hole. Instead he had crouched down and dug the soil out with his bare hands, scrabbling in the shadows, praying that no one would cross the green. Using his jacket, he had cleaned the hammer as best he could and then placed it in its shallow grave.

Jimmy still hoped they'd catch the killer – not for Elsa's sake but for his own. He was sick of waking with cold sweats in the middle of the night, sick of being forever on edge. How could he rest easy while evidence that could convict him lay just below the surface? But he remained too scared to dig it up, too afraid of the consequences if he was caught in the act. Even dead, Elsa Keep was trouble. Some women were like that.

*

375

Alf Tombs knew he had got off lightly, all things considered. Yes, he was banged up for a few years, but it was nothing he couldn't handle. Had the truth come out, he'd have been looking at a visit from Pierrepoint, and a rope around his neck. Doyle could have pointed the finger, but he wouldn't have been able to prove anything, not when it came to Lennie Hull *or* Elsa Keep. If his old friend had come clean about the gun being his, he would have ended up in the dock too.

He had no regrets. Lennie Hull had got what was coming, and so had Elsa. She'd brought it on herself, trying to blackmail him like that. As if he was going to let a broad like her, a *nobody*, hold him to ransom. She hadn't understood what she was getting into. She'd underestimated him, and that had been a big mistake.

It had bothered him for a while, the hammer disappearing like that. He'd been wearing gloves, so no fingerprints, and had left the weapon on the living room floor. Where had it gone? It was a mystery. He could have just shot the blackmailing bitch, but he'd needed it to look like a burglary gone wrong.

It was unfortunate about Nell, but not his fault. And all right, he could have told her at the time that she hadn't shot Lennie, but that would have been tricky without implicating himself. Anyway, she should have been grateful that he'd done the job for her. It was the case, however, that Nell's guilt had come in handy later on when Doyle had come back to London, a bit of leverage when it came to persuading him to open all those post office doors.

To this day, he wasn't sure how Doyle had discovered the truth. It had come as a surprise, an unwelcome one, when he'd produced the gun Nell had been waving around the night Lennie had gone to meet his maker. Alf knew he should have reacted differently. Perhaps Doyle had always suspected something was off, always had a niggling doubt in the back of his mind.

Still, it hadn't worked out so badly in the end. Being banged up had meant an end to his plans for the Heathrow job. All that planning, all those hours of hard work, blown out of the water in a matter of minutes. He'd cursed Doyle at the time, but not for long. Pat Hull and his gang had turned up at the airport to find a bloody reception committee waiting for them. Someone must have tipped off the filth. You had to laugh! Maybe there was a God after all.

Alf gazed around at the four bare walls of his cell and grinned. There was no denying that people sometimes got away with murder.

Already Saul Hannah looked back with nostalgia on the Ghost Squad, at a time when he roamed freely and never had to sit behind a desk. Now his days were more regimented, his work closely supervised. It didn't suit him, working as part of a team. He was often bored, and frequently irritable. His colleagues, decent men most of them, didn't know what to make of him. His superiors looked on him with suspicion.

He continued to try and cultivate his snouts, usually when he was off duty. Soho was still his hunting ground, the place where the lowlifes and the disenfranchised gathered in numbers to mingle with their own, or just to drown their sorrows. Nothing ever really changed. Tombs was banged up, Pat Hull too, but already others had slipped into the vacated spaces. The criminal world abhorred a vacuum.

He often thought about Tombs and Doyle and the damaged girl who'd been pulled from the river. Sometimes when he saw a redhead in the street, he'd do a double-take, thinking it might be Judith Jonson. Where was she now? He might have taken a chance if he'd been braver, but the past continued to haunt him. He could not forget what he had lost, and nor could she.

Saul had not forgotten about Elsa Keep either. When Tombs got out of jail, he'd be waiting. What went around came around; no one could escape justice for ever.

As the waves rose and fell, Judith kept her gaze fixed firmly on the horizon. She could not have said whether the anxiety she was feeling was down to the heaving of the boat or to what lay ahead. What did she know of Amsterdam? Art and canals and bicycles. She breathed deeply, drawing in the salty air.

Her fingers curled around the envelope in her pocket. She had read the letter a hundred times, thrown it away and retrieved it from the bin. Now it was covered in tea stains. She had read the lines and between the lines, made up her mind and changed it again. Doubt was her constant companion.

When the ferry docked, she picked up her suitcase and joined the queue to disembark. Every step took her closer. As she passed through Customs, her eyes were already searching for the fair-haired man, for the face she would know anywhere. This time it would be on her terms. No long-term plans or promises. There was no going back, but maybe, just maybe, there was a new way forward.